This Book

Family Lies

Tamara Merrill

TABLE OF CONTENTS

The City Chronicle
November 7, 1936
Tattletales by Sharon Chatsworth

Rumor has it that there is trouble in paradise. A little bird whispered to me at lunch today that at least one of the fabulous Augustus marriages seems to be headed for divorce. The Mister, in this case, has been seen on the town once too often with a certain very clever lady.

Chapter 1

Walter Augustus, founder of the complex Augustus Industries manufacturing empire, gazed steadily at his grandson from under his bushy eyebrows. He cleared his throat and removed his gold rimmed glasses. Slowly and deliberately he polished his already spotless lenses. John Augustus shifted on the hard leather chair. He hated it when his grandfather cleaned his glasses in that meticulous manner. It could only mean trouble.

In fact, John admitted to himself, being called into the old man's office at four o'clock on a Friday afternoon meant trouble. Walter cleared his throat and moved the pen and ink well a fraction of an inch. He swung his swivel chair away from the large leather topped desk and looked out the window at the city spread beneath his twelfth floor office.

"Well, John." He swung back to face his grandson. Carefully he replaced his glasses. "What do you have to say for yourself?"

"Say, Grandfather? Say about what?" John wiped his damp palms on his gray flannel trousers and avoided looking at Walter.

"John, I will not tolerate caginess. You know full well what I'm talking about. I want an explanation of your behavior." Calmly, Walter removed his glasses and placed them in the center of his desk pad. He folded his hands and waited.

John squirmed. He felt like a small boy caught talking in church. He wanted to protest his innocence and demand his right to privacy. The conflicting emotions chased across his handsome face.

Walter waited. He loved this grandson, perhaps more than any other of his grandchildren, certainly as much as he'd loved the boy's father. "Tell me, John. Tell me about this fancy woman. Is it true?" John's blue eyes flashed and Walter smiled slightly. "Come on, boy, speak up. We haven't got all day."

"I'm not a boy." Anger tinged his voice. "What's going on in my private life is not your business."

Walter noted that he'd not denied the existence of another woman. Sadly he shook his head, "You're wrong, John. When your actions reflect on our family name or on the company, it is indeed my business. You've been most indiscreet and I cannot allow your behavior to continue."

"Allow!" John leaped to his feet. "What do you mean allow? You don't have the right to tell me what to do. I'm not a child. I won't listen to this." He stomped to the door and flung it open.

"John." Walter's voice was quiet but the chill in it stopped John in his tracks. "If you are a man, come back here, sit down and act like one."

John turned and glared at his grandfather. The hostile words died on his tongue. There was no vexation in the old man's eyes, only a deep sadness. John's own anger drained away and he carefully closed the heavy oak door and moved wearily to the dark leather sofa. "She's not a fancy woman, Grandfather. She may not be my wife, but I love her." John slumped forward, head in his hands.

Walter touched his shoulder. "It's wrong, John. I understand your feeling. I know you think you love this woman and perhaps you do, but it's wrong. Unless you are prepared to give up your birthright, you'll have to give her up."

John stumbled to his feet and crossed to the window where he stood staring at the darkening city. Walter watched him. He looks like his father, Walter thought, the same slim, straight long-limbed body, the dark thick hair and the startling blue eyes. But Michael always had a sullen, pouty expression, a belief that the world owed him everything. John has none of that. He's a warm, caring man, a good man. Walter nodded to himself. I've got to make him understand that this woman is a mistake. He waited patiently until John squared his shoulders and turned away from the window. "Sit down and we'll talk. Do you want a drink? It's nigh on to closing and I'm ready for a bit of something."

"I guess I could use a drink."

Walter went to the fine mahogany bookcases that lined two walls of his office. "Scotch?" he asked opening the cupboard that housed the bar. John nodded. Walter poured ancient scotch over ice. He moved slowly keeping his back turned to allow John time to compose himself. Taking the drinks, Walter returned to the high backed leather chair that he'd sat in for so many hours over the last fifty years, pondering problems and making the decisions that had created the huge success of his family and of his company. He gestured, indicating the wing chair opposite him. "Sit, John." He raised his glass. "To the future. May everything continue." He drank deeply and sighed. "Now then, let's begin at the beginning."

"I'm not sure which beginning you mean. How did you come to know about Valerie?"

"I've known for some time, John. You've been seen by most everyone in the city and, of course, they've been unable to keep such gossip to themselves. However, I was willing to let you enjoy yourself until lunch today."

"Why today? I didn't even see Valerie today."

"Sylvia came to see me." Walter watched closely and saw surprise drain the color from John's face.

"Sylvia? Why would my wife come to see you here?" John paused. Emotion rushed across his face as he realized the impact of Walter's statement. "Oh God, she knows, doesn't she?"

"Yes, she knows. And more important, she wants a divorce."

"A divorce! That's perfect." John's face lit up and he grinned at Walter, his fear replaced by relief.

"Perfect, John? How can you call the breakup of your marriage, due to your own stupidity, perfect?"

"But it is perfect. I want to be with Valerie, not with Sylvia. You just told me Sylvia doesn't want to be with me. A divorce will make everyone happy."

"There will not be a divorce." Walter's tone was firm and final.

"What do you mean? Of course, there will be a divorce. We both want one. Syl and I have been unhappy for several years."

"No, John. There will not be a divorce. Not in this family."

"Family? The family has nothing to do with a divorce. It's between the two of us." John's voice rose in anger.

"The family has everything to do with your life, your marriage, your career, the bread you eat and the wine you drink." Walter spoke carefully and distinctly making sure that John understood each and every word. "We are a great and influential family. You will not disgrace us or yourself by divorcing your wife and marrying a hussy."

"Grandfather," John's voice shook with ill-concealed emotion. "Don't speak of Valerie that way. I won't listen to this. I can't." John shook his head and struck the arm of his chair with his clenched fist. "I'm a man, not a little boy. I need to do what I feel is right for myself."

"True, John. You're certainly old enough and I hope wise enough to make your own decisions." Walter paused. He rubbed the bridge of his nose, considering his next words carefully. "I want to help you. I'd like to keep you from harm. I suppose that I've been too blunt, so allow me to start again."

Walter pushed himself up from his chair and moved to the window. Gazing out at the setting sun, his shoulders slumped slightly, his body seemed smaller. John was reminded that his Grandfather was growing old. At this moment he looked every one of his seventy nine years. A minute passed, perhaps two. Then Walter straightened his back and turned. Once again, he looked strong and indefatigable. Only the deep sadness in his eyes betrayed his inner tension. "John," he said. "I do indeed understand how you feel. I am aware of the troubles you have had in your marriage and most likely will continue to have. I do not begrudge you love, no matter where or with whom you find it.

But scandal has never touched this family's name, and it must not do so now."

"Grandfather, divorce is not a scandal. Not when the two people involved are in agreement. Sylvia and I don't love each other. We'll both be more happy apart than we've been these last five years."

"John, even if I agreed with your reasoning, which you know I don't, there could be no divorce. Stop and consider the implications of a divorce between yourself and Sylvia, not the emotional but the practical problems it would cause."

John rose and paced the floor. His normally calm and controlled movements were shattered. He pulled at his hair and fussed first with the drape and then the books on the shelves.

Walter waited calmly, sure in the knowledge that this young man would do the right and reasonable thing, the sensible thing.

"I understand, Grandfather. It's the business isn't it? You need a grandchild, a child born of myself and Sylvia, a child who will assure the merger of Augustus Industries and Alexander Shipbuilding. The bottom line is money." John shuddered and slumped into his chair. He hid his face and drew in several deep breaths.

"Money is not a dirty word, John. You can treat it with contempt because you have never known life without it, but stop and consider for a moment what your life would be without the Augustus name and fortune."

"Would that I could walk away from all of this," John gestured grandly. "But you're right. It is too pleasant an existence to give up easily."

"Staying with Sylvia doesn't mean you must live a drab and unhappy life. Pour another drink. I've something to tell you."

John left the offices of Augustus Industries and hurried out into the early winter twilight. His head was bent, his face troubled. The doorman received no reply to his pleasant comment on the weather, and no thank you for the cab he summoned. John noticed nothing. He considered the events of the last hour. He longed to go to the warmth of Valerie's love, and he knew that he must not. He needed time to adjust to his grandfather's demands and amazing revelations. John halted the cab on 54th street and stepped out. He gave the driver a bill much too large to pay for his short ride and hurried across the street and into the park.

The park was John's refuge. It always had been. When he was very young, his nurse had brought him here every afternoon. As a school boy, he played ball with his friends, climbed the trees and hid from the duties in his life. As a man, he walked the familiar paths whenever he needed to be alone. It was a good park. The trees grew tall and dense. The grass was fragrant with wild flowers. Even now, covered with the thin first snow of winter, it was a friendly place, a soothing place.

John's thoughts tore at his heart. He was John Augustus, heir to one fourth of the great Augustus fortune, favorite of the Gods, husband to Sylvia Alexander Augustus, beautiful socialite and only heir to the Alexander Shipbuilding millions. Theirs had been a wedding made in heaven. All the papers said as much. It had been the social event of the season, a blessed event. If that were so, where had they gone wrong? Why was the marriage no longer anything but an empty shell? Was he at fault? Was Sylvia? She was always so busy with their social life, still anxious to please her father. But John knew he was the one who turned to someone else. He had broken the vows, not Sylvia. No matter how unhappy they might be together, Sylvia would never take a lover. Or would she? No. He would have heard. Grandfather was right about that. People did love to talk. And now she knew about Valerie. Somehow he'd have to soothe his wife's feelings, make her believe in his love again, trust him again and agree to make this marriage last. Because, Walter was right, they needed to have a child. He would have to do and say whatever was necessary to assure the birth of that child.

Having made his decision, John squared his shoulders and crossed the park to his house. As he approached the tall brownstone, the butler swung the door open. The warm glow of lights spilled out into the darkening winter twilight. "Good Evening, Sir."

"Good Evening, Duncan." John handed his hat and coat to the butler and stepped to the carved oak hall tree. He glanced at himself in the mirror and picked up his mail from the silver Tiffany tray. He leafed through it without seeing the envelopes or addresses, his mind still occupied. How should he talk to Sylvia? What tack should he take? "Is Mrs. Augustus in?"

"Yes, Sir, she's in the drawing room with Mr. Samuel and his wife. I believe they are waiting for you." The hint of reproof in Duncan's voice was lost on John.

"Sam and Helen? What are they doing here?"

"It's Friday night, sir. They were expected for dinner."

"Oh, damn. I'd totally forgotten. Is Sylvia angry?" John turned back to the mirror. As he smoothed his hair, he caught Duncan's disapproving look. John grinned ruefully, Sylvia's English gentleman will never accept my American casualness, he thought. He patted the lion that graced the base of the hall tree. That lion had been his friend and talisman as long as he could remember. Tonight he'd need all the luck he could muster from any source. John straightened. His face took on the determined look that caused people to remark on his resemblance to his grandfather. Then, with a visible effort, he forced himself to relax and crossed the parquet floor of the spacious entry.

Duncan pulled the high, heavy doors open and John entered the drawing room feeling, he thought, much the way the condemned man must feel on his way to the firing squad. Mentally he shook himself. Sylvia turned. Her golden hair gleamed copper in the firelight. The apricot tone of her gown accented the rust velvet sofa on which she sat, one arm flung gracefully across the back cushions, the other hand holding a half full cocktail glass. "Hello, John." Her cultured voice dripped with icicles.

"Hello, Darling." John crossed the large room with its elegant furnishings and Chinese accessories and bent to kiss his beautiful wife. He noticed the skillful way Sylvia avoided his lips. The caress glanced off her hair. He chose to ignore the rebuff and extended his hand to Sam. "Good Evening, Sam. Sorry I'm late. Got caught up in a discussion with Grandfather, and the time seemed to fly by. You're looking beautiful as usual, Helen." He kissed his cousin's wife. "Do I have time for a cocktail or have I delayed dinner long enough?"

Sylvia rose from the sofa. "I think we'd best go in to dinner. The Beef Wellington is bound to be dry and tough by now. Come, Sam."

Sam responded instantly to the tension in Sylvia's voice. Setting his glass on the wide oak mantel, against which he'd been lounging, he crossed the room and extended his arm to escort Sylvia to dinner.

The Beef Wellington was not dry, however, as perfect as the food was the two couples were unable to relax. At last dinner dragged to a close and the women excused themselves. Sam lit a cigar and stretched his long legs out as he relaxed in the Chippendale chair. "Well, Cuz, what's going on?" He inhaled deeply and blew smoke toward the ceiling in thoughtful rings. "I read Chatsworth's column this morning, so I know the cat's out of the bag. If you need someone to talk to, I'm available and better than most. At least I'm your friend first and a member of the "fabulous Augustus clan" second."

"There's really nothing to talk about, Sam. I've made my decisions, and I intend to clean up this mess as quickly as possible. I'd appreciate it if you'd squelch any rumors you hear around town and start a few that allude to bliss in paradise instead of trouble."

"All right, that's exactly what I'll do. But if you need a friend, call on me." Sam watched John and noted the weariness in his eyes. They'd grown up together, side by side in matching brownstones, until they'd gone off to separate colleges, John to Harvard and Sam to Stanford.

In California, Sam had learned a more relaxed lifestyle than that of his childhood. He married Helen, a wine country heiress and brought her back to grace his home and life. Attributing it to her country childhood, they'd chosen to escape from the city and had purchased a sprawling Tudor style house at the lake. There they had, in rapid succession, produced four charming, sun-drenched children.

John had followed in the footsteps of his father and his grandfather. Harvard had been his goal from birth and there he excelled, not only in the classroom but on the playing field. He did all that was expected of him and more. He graduated first in his class and immediately entered the Augustus Industries complex where he showed his good business judgment and used his ability to manage people in the promotion of the family business. His choice of Sylvia and their decision to make their home in one of the family brownstones on the park had met with approval. Never once in his thirty two years had John stepped out of bounds.

Sam shook his head in wonder over his cousin's control. They may have been raised as brothers, but there was a world of difference in their attitudes. "You know, Cuz, I think you look a bit pinched. Why don't we move into your den and have a game of billiards before we join our ladies?"

"You're right, Sam. I do need a respite before I face Sylvia."

The den was John's room. In it, he was at ease. The furnishings fit his six foot, two inch frame, the chairs and sofa large enough to stretch out. The accessories were minimal, many books and a few good wood carvings of the old west. Sylvia's passion for "anything Chinese" had not touched this room. John dropped onto the sofa and propped his feet on the coffee table. "Sit, Sam."

Sam slumped into the new leather leisure chair. He wriggled down and sighed. "This thing is so comfortable. I've got to convince Helen to get one although," he grinned, "I'd probably have to fight the whole family to get to sit in it."

"Sam..." John started and paused. Sam looked up expectantly. "Walter called me into his office this afternoon to discuss the Chatsworth column, but more important, his belief that political tension throughout the world will drag all nations into another World War. He doesn't think that the Augustus complex is ready to produce on the scale that will be needed when the armed forces start ordering uniforms, blankets, bandages and all the other supplies we're capable of providing. I'd like to hear your opinion, not only your opinion as our legal advisor, but your gut reactions."

"Actually, John, I've given this a lot of thought. During the last fifteen years the business and therefore the Augustus family have absorbed huge losses. We've kept people working when the work just hasn't been there for them to do. It's been our policy to take care of our own. While I admire Grandfather for his stand and I'm proud of the good that his policy has created, it's also created a severe cash shortage. The company has almost no reserve, certainly not enough for a rapid expansion program. It would be necessary to borrow against the contracts when and if we sign them."

"He's looking at expansion now. He doesn't intend to wait until war is declared."

"And does he have a plan for producing the capital?"

"Of course," John smiled. "He wants to merge with Alexander Shipbuilding."

"Damn," Sam swore softly, aware at once more of the turmoil John was experiencing.

"Damn is right," John agreed. "It was all made very clear to me this afternoon in Grandfather's indomitable way. My duty is most apparent."

The City Chronicle
December 17, 1936
Tattletales by Sharon Chatsworth

A very reliable source told me today that a repentant gentleman has purchased a most magnificent jewel to brighten his lady's Christmas. It seems that the trouble we reported earlier this winter turned out to be only snow flurries, not a blizzard. This reporter wishes all the holiday best to the whole fabulous "A" clan.

Chapter 2

The deep white calm of winter covered the city in a cozy blanket. Here and there lights flashed on as the sun sank into the river. John left his office in the Augustus building and stepped into the cold evening. He flipped up the fur collar of his camel hair topcoat to protect his bare head from the frigid wind. "I suppose Sylvia's right. I really should learn to wear a hat." He spoke aloud unaware of the doorman's puzzled glance.

The doorman watched him walk down the street, "There goes an unhappy man," he said to his dog. The dog barked and wagged his tail pleased at the attention.

It was true that John was not a happy man. The past month had caused him to examine his life and his desires as he learned the high price of compromise. It seemed impossible that so much could change in so short a time. Only a month ago, he thought, I was ready to ask Sylvia for a divorce, marry Val and live happily ever after. And here I am carrying jewels home to a woman I can barely stand in the hope that she will bear my child. Where is the sense in that? But sense or no sense, it's what I've determined to do, and do it I will.

The Augustus home was aglow with Christmas lights and the spirit of the season. In each window hung a wreath of greens tied with a large red bow. On the front door, boxwood and a pineapple symbolized the Southern hospitality Sylvia was known for. The house was waiting shining in the way a house does when it has been spruced up and is ready for the guests to arrive at the gala. Tonight, John and Sylvia were giving the first party of the Christmas season and everyone would be there.

Inside, the air was filled with the ripe odors of delicious baking. The buffet was ready in the dining room. The table had been laid with the finest pure white linen and draped with red ribbon and cedar garland. The holiday effect had been heightened by the many candles, of different shapes and sizes all red and all set in crystal, which nestled in the cedar.

From the kitchen came the brisk voice of the cook giving orders to the extra help. John glanced in at the open kitchen door and withdrew quickly. It was clearly much too busy in there to even attempt a peek at the food. He fingered the jewelry box in his pocket. A month of careful courting had not returned Sylvia to his bed, but perhaps the size of the emerald he'd purchased would.

Slowly, he climbed the graceful curve of the stairway. The rail had been wrapped in cedar and more red ribbon. The fragrance of Christmas lifted John's mood. He rapped on Sylvia's door.

"Yes."

John opened the door and entered. Sylvia turned quickly to see who dared intrude on her privacy. The green velvet gown she wore swung slowly and settled into soft folds. The high waist emphasized her full breasts and slender neck. She stood still for a startled moment, silver backed hairbrush extended, her blond hair falling in waves and curly wisps. John approached her. Time slowed and for a moment seemed to stop.

"You look so beautiful tonight, darling." He cupped her chin and tipped her face. With his fingertips he traced her lips slowly, lightly and then kissed her softly. "I love you, Sylvia."

Sylvia's eyes darkened. She raised her hand and stroked his cheek. "Do you, John?" She turned back to the mirror and began to twist her hair up into an intricate knot. "Do you, John," she repeated, "or is this some kind of game?" Her green eyes seemed to flash with a shimmer as cold as the emerald in John's pocket.

"Forgive me, Syl. I know I've given you a bad time this last year. I don't really know why I needed to have that silly fling. I've told you before, she meant nothing to me. It was only a foolish defiance of Grandfather's rules. Just a way to prove that I was a man."

"You've never needed to prove your manhood to me." Sylvia watched John in the mirror, carefully scrutinizing his face.

John knew this was his chance to convince her. Inside, he flinched, his stomach clenched like a fist.

"Not to you, Darling." He chose his words carefully, hating himself but needing to use everything he knew about Sylvia to convince her of his desire to make their marriage a success. "To Grandfather. I'm so tired of the way he thinks he can control all our lives, especially mine. I know it was a dumb, foolish thing to do. But I did learn how much I love you. I want to share my life with you. I want your love again. I know I'll have to earn it back, but I'm willing to do whatever is necessary. Please, Syl. Please give me another chance. Can't we try to make this marriage work?"

"John, I want to believe you." Sylvia laid her brush on the dressing table and moved to him. John took her hands in his and drew her toward himself. "During this past month, I've watched you very closely and I do see a change in you. I'm not sure what caused the change or why it occurred after you had that long talk with Sam on the Friday that awful Chatsworth woman mentioned your affair, but I feel that you are sorry and that you'll not stray again."

John didn't protest that he'd never actually had an affair instead he said soberly, "I have changed, Syl. I only want to be your husband and to make a good life for us. Look, I bought you a present today." He reached into his pocket and withdrew the small pale blue velvet box. "The moment I saw this, I thought of you. It reminded me of your beautiful eyes."

Sylvia took the box and opened it. The large square cut emerald pendant flashed as it caught the light. She gasped. "It's gorgeous. I love it." Carefully she lifted the gold chain and traced the diamonds encircling the stone with the tip of her finger. "Oh, John, it's the most beautiful thing I've ever owned. Help me put it on."

She raised the necklace to her throat and John closed the clasp. They stood reflected in the mirror, the perfect couple. Sylvia shifted in his arms and wrapped him in an embrace. She pulled his face down to her lips. "Thank you, dear. I believe what you say. I know you love me."

John returned her kiss, first gently, then more demandingly. As they kissed, he watched in the mirror. There's no going back now, he thought. Good bye, Val. Sylvia pulled away and smoothed her gown.

"I think this will work after all, John." She gave a little nod as if agreeing with herself. She patted his arm. "Our guests will be arriving in less than an hour, and you haven't even changed. Go on now, get ready for the party. I'll see you downstairs." She shooed him from the room.

In his dressing room, John scarcely noticed the clothing laid ready for him. He sank into a chair. Oh, God, he thought. How can I go through with this farce? I can't stand that woman. I don't want her to be the mother of my children. I want a warm loving woman. I want to be with Valerie. I want her to be the mother of my child. He rose from the chair and stripped for the shower. Damn! He slammed his hand against the wall. The shock of the contact made him aware of his futile thoughts. "John," he spoke aloud, addressing his image, "you've agreed to go through with this, and an Augustus never goes back on his word. Now get with it, boy." He stepped into the shower.

But the hot water couldn't keep his thoughts away from Valerie. He remembered the night they met. Sylvia was in Charleston, visiting her father and he'd gone alone to a party. The evening was exactly like a hundred others until he went into the library to enjoy a smoke and found a small creature curled up fast asleep in a large chair. At first he'd thought it was a child but as he watched the sleeping girl he realized it was a beautiful young woman. Funny but he'd felt no embarrassment at all. It had seemed right to be there even before she'd opened her eyes and said, "Hello. Have I been sleeping long?"

Those first days had passed in a delightful romantic swirl, lunches, dinners, phone calls and trips to all the tourist places in the city. Valerie had known from the beginning that he was married and there had never been a need to lie. The night Sylvia was due back from her trip John declared his love for Valerie. She sealed his lips with her finger and whispered, "I love you, too. Please don't say anything you'll be sorry for. Don't make any promises."

John lathered his body and remembered the touch of Valerie's perfect body in his arms, the warmth of her soft, fragrant skin, the excitement of her kisses. He groaned. He'd promised himself that he'd never see Val again. He'd not only have a child with Sylvia he'd make his marriage work. But, damn it, he missed Valerie. He missed being in love with her. Stepping from the shower he forced himself to get his thoughts under control. This night would be a real test of his acting ability. He'd do all that was necessary to seduce his wife. He would not think of the brief time he'd had with Valerie nor of the happiness her love had brought to him. Tonight he had a job to do.

The party glittered and glowed. The women were beautiful, the men handsome. The music supplied by the Pete Dawson band was just loud enough and very danceable. And dance with Sylvia, John did, every chance he got. He asked her to dance. He cut in when she danced with others. It was apparent to everyone gathered in the Augustus house that John Augustus was in love with his wife, everyone except Sam and Walter. They sat in the conservatory among Sylvia's prized orchids and talked.

"Sam?" Walter's voice was deep and somber. "Are you paying attention to the trouble this world is in? I'm afraid it won't be long now before the world will be at war. The United States, also. Our economy demands it."

"Surely, Grandfather, we won't go to war for purely economic reasons!"

"Oh, they'll make it sound patriotic, but the underlying factor of war is always economic. And I'm proud to say that Augustus Industries will rise to the challenge. We'll be right there doing our patriotic part."

"And making a profit," the cynicism in Sam's voice rang harsh and bitter.

"There's nothing wrong with an honest profit." Walter nodded. "We'll make a profit and help the free world survive at the same time."

"The free world may survive, but will John?" Sam watched the pain cross Walter's weathered face. "I know what's going on," Sam continued. "I know that he's agreed to do whatever is necessary to bring about the merger with Alexander Shipbuilding. He's willing to deny himself happiness for this family. How did you manage to talk him into it, Grandfather?"

Walter stood up and moved away from Sam. Absentmindedly he stroked the leaves on a tall rubber tree. "John's a good man. He simply chose to do the right thing."

"Right thing," Sam asked. "How can you say he's doing the right thing? Unless my eyes deceive me, he's going to succeed in his pursuit of Sylvia and will soon bring an unwanted child into a loveless marriage. How can you say he's doing the right thing?" Sam's temper rose rapidly and he strove to contain his fury knowing if there were a way to reason with Walter, it would never be found in anger. "What in the world did you say to convince him? What method of coercion did you use?"

Walter turned and looked at Sam. His steel gray eyes flashed and for a moment Sam felt he'd pushed too hard. Walter turned back to the tree. He reached out and touched the trunk. He seemed to be using the tree for support. "I didn't need to threaten him. I told him the truth about his father and explained his obligations to the Augustus name. He understands the importance of family loyalty; that in the end that loyalty is all there is."

Sam studied Walter, there was something about the old man, a lack of confidence or perhaps a sadness that he'd never noted before. Walter spoke again and his voice seemed to come from far away, as if he spoke only to himself. "Fifty years ago, I was a lot like John. Edith and I had been married almost eight years. Your father was five and Mary Elizabeth, three. We had planned to have a large family, but the doctors felt it was best that Edith bear no more children. She was a good wife, Sam, a good woman."

He lowered himself slowly unto a wicker lounge. The wicker creaked under his weight. "I would say we had a good marriage. We didn't talk much but we respected one another. But a man needs more than a stable marriage he needs to give love and to feel loved."

"After Mary Elizabeth was born, that part of our marriage ended. Edith seemed to transfer all her affection to the children. We owned the dry goods stores then, just those first three stores, but our life was good. We always had plenty. My father had seen to that, and the stores were growing and prospering. On the outside, it looked like a fine life. Everything a man could want." Walter stopped. His eyes clouded as he stared at a memory.

Sam stayed silent, knowing his grandfather was ready to tell him the reasons behind John's decisions.

"I wasn't content," Walter picked up his story. "I had all the yearnings of a young man and nowhere to expend them so I turned to the business. I devoted all my energy to it. For a while, life was very exciting. I kept terribly busy."

"But work alone doesn't fulfill a young man. I fell in love. Who she was is of no consequence to you. She was a beautiful lady, a warm loving woman. She gave me her love and caring without reservation. It was an experience unlike any I had known with Edith. Of course, we couldn't marry but we were content in our love. When she became pregnant I was thrilled beyond words. I wanted nothing more than to share the miracle of a child with my love." Walter dashed away tears, impatiently, with the back of his knotted hand. "She died when the baby was born."

The tears began to flow freely down his weathered cheeks. "I promised her I'd raise our son, and I did. The night of his birth I brought him to my home and gave him into Edith's care. Edith never asked who his mother was or how he came to be in my possession, but I'm sure she knew, not all the details but she knew. That child was John's father, Michael."

Sam sat in stunned silence. This was a family secret he'd never heard, never so much as a whisper, from anyone. His concern for his grandfather's obvious pain was shadowed by his amazement that this stern patriarch could have committed these acts. Walter shook his head ruefully, "Shocked, Sam? It all happened a long time ago but now that I've started the story I'd like to tell you the rest. If I'm not mistaken, you'll need the facts. Go in and get me a drink, please, and then we'll finish."

Sam fetched the drink for Walter and one for himself. He avoided the other party goers and returned to the conservatory where Walter was again in full control of his emotions.

Walter began at once, "I'm sure you've heard stories about your Uncle Michael."

Sam nodded. "Father talked about him often."

"Often, but seldom or never with pleasure, I'm sure. Those two never got along, and I can take the responsibility for that. I spoiled Michael unmercifully. He was my favorite, and deny it as much as I did; I always gave him his way and anything he wanted. That was a mistake, one I've paid for time and time again. Even while I was spoiling him, I knew I was making a mistake but I couldn't seem to help myself. I gave him all the love I'd wanted to give his mother."

"When he grew to manhood, he still believed he could always have his own way, that I would protect him from the results of his careless, self-centered ways. Edith tried to reason with me many times, but when it came to Michael I refused to see. I built Augustus Industries for him for the other two children, too, of course. But it was always Michael that I dreamed of taking into partnership."

"He was a handsome man. Many women were seduced by him and a woman was his downfall. I sent him to Europe to oversee an expansion program, and while he was in France he had an affair with a young girl. She became pregnant." Walter stopped and drew in a deep breath. Visions of the past clamored for his attention. Keeping his voice emotionless he quickly recited the remaining facts. "When he refused to marry the girl, her brother shot and killed him. Minette fled to America and to me. I arranged to allow her to stay. We gave out the story that Michael had married her secretly and then died in a tragic accident. Edith knew the truth, of course, but no one else has ever known. Walter fixed Sam in his stern gaze, "I'm telling you now because John will need your help. I've told him about his father's birth, and he knows the story of the tragic accident, but I haven't told him about his own birth and I don't intend to. You're a wise young man, Sam. There is streak of kindness in you that is a rare thing in this world. I know I can count on you to never mention this conversation to anyone. Minette is a good woman. She has been a magnificent mother to John, and neither of them should suffer from her youthful mistake."

Sam clasped Walter's hand. "You can rely on me, Grandfather."

"I know that, Sam, now we'd best go back to the party before someone sends out a search party."

The two men returned to the laughter and festivities. Walter flirted with the women in his courtly manner and Sam danced with the wives of his friends and acquaintances, but neither man was fully aware of the party. They both watched as John courted his wife, Walter approving of every move and Sam with a feeling of deep despair.

John escorted Sylvia into the dining room and whispered as he filled her plate, "When can we throw these people out? I want to be alone with my wife."

"Oh, John," Sylvia giggled. "Don't be so impatient. We have all night." She leaned against him lightly and caressed his arm. "It won't be long. People will begin to leave in an hour or so."

John brushed his lips across her hair, "You look very beautiful, Syl."

"And you look very handsome, Darling. If you're done with that plate, I think you should dance with the senior Mrs. Logan. I've promised this dance to Sam."

Sylvia moved onto the dance floor with Sam and John stood watching silently for a moment. To the casual observer he appeared to be enjoying the sight of his wife dancing with his cousin, his best friend. But sadness darkened his eyes and was not relieved as he turned to Mrs. Logan, smiled the "Augustus Grin" and asked her to dance. The memory of Valerie swaying in his arms as they danced to the music of Harry James filled his mind. Could it have been only six weeks ago, he asked himself. It seemed like forever.

At last the band shifted to slow romantic numbers and the couples began to drift away with shouts of Merry Christmas and gracious thank yous. Sam and Helen were the last to leave. At the door, Sam clasped John's arms and gave them a squeeze. "Take care, Cuz," he said and quickly moved out into the cold night.

Sylvia closed the door and gave John a quizzical look, "What was that all about?"

"You know Sam," John shrugged. "He always gets sentimental at Christmas. Come on, love. Let's go upstairs." He extended his hand and together they climbed the curving stairway. Sylvia led him to the room she'd claimed as hers alone and without hesitation John followed her inside.

This room made him nervous. The lush red silk brocade and richly patterned carpet set a tone that he found oppressive. Tonight he tried not to notice the surroundings. He struggled to keep his mind on the job he was about to complete.

Carefully John drew Sylvia into his arms and pulled the hairpins from her hair. The golden curls fell about her smooth white shoulders; he brushed them aside and bent to press his lips against the hollow of her throat. Unbidden, the memory of Val's soft scent rose in his mind. He forced it away. Sylvia's arms were around him now and he knew he must respond. Slowly, he unfastened her gown and pushed it down her arms. Sylvia let it drop to the floor. Gracefully she stepped out of the crumbled velvet.

Clad only in scanty silk undergarments, she was a beautiful sight, one that would gladden the heart of any man. John felt no response in his loins. He groaned.

Sylvia unbuttoned his shirt and rubbed her palm across the hairs of his chest, "Come, darling. It's time for bed." She kissed him ardently. John returned the kiss, aware of how strange her lips felt beneath his own. He thought of the joy of kissing Valerie. He remembered the excitement of her mouth. The memory stirred deep in his body. He felt himself respond. He kissed Sylvia again and again, thinking of Valerie, blotting out the reality of who he held in his arms. Sylvia's hands roamed over him stroking, caressing and removing his clothes. Still touching him, she moved backwards to the bed and drew him down and John thrust himself deep into his wife.

The City Chronicle
July 4, 1937
Tattletales by Sharon Chatsworth

Congratulations to John and Sylvia Augustus on the birth of their son. This new Yankee Doodle Dandy, weighed in at 8 pounds 6 ounces this morning at 4:12. Both mother and child are reported doing well. He will be christened Michael John in honor of his paternal grandfather, who met with such a tragic young death in Europe. This reporter wishes the best of luck to the three of you.

Chapter 3

John paced the corridor of Mercy Hospital. To the nurses, he appeared to be another nervous father, but John was deep in thought. He alternated between furious all-consuming anger and amazement at his own gullibility. This time Sylvia had really done it. Should he confront her with his knowledge? John wondered. Surely, she didn't believe he wouldn't guess the truth.

"You can go in now, Mr. Augustus." The starched voice of a nurse interrupted his thoughts.

John halted in his pacing. He looked at the door to Sylvia's hospital room. Damn! he thought. I don't want to talk to that bitch. Turning on his heel, he strode rapidly down the hall and, without waiting for the elevator, plunged down the stairs.

The nurses at the station gazed after him in surprise. "What's wrong with him?"

"Who knows? New fathers are a strange lot. Better tell his wife she won't be having a visitor after all. Make it sound like he stepped out to buy flowers or something."

John raced down the stairs and across the reception lobby, oblivious to the turned heads and open mouthed stares of the people he passed. He crashed open the doors, into the warm July morning, and almost knocked Sam off his feet. "Hey, Cuz. What's the rush?" Sam held John's arm. "Baby here yet? How's Sylvia?"

"The baby's here. Sylvia's fine, I'm sure." The sarcasm in John's answer caused Sam to take a good look at him.

"Wow! You look like hell. Helen said you'd need moral support, but I think you need more than that. Let's get a drink." Sam asked no questions. He guided John to the car and deposited him in the passenger seat. Climbing behind the wheel he commented. "I don't suppose you know where to get a drink at six AM?"

John shook his head mutely.

Sam drove into the downtown area, watching for an open bar. From time to time, he glanced at John aware of the intense emotions chasing across his face but he stayed quiet allowing John time to gain control.

"I don't need a drink," John finally said. "I need coffee and breakfast. It's been quite a night. Stop up there at "Sarah's Place.""

Sam pulled into the parking lot, and the two men entered the nearly deserted diner. They slid into the wooden booth and accepted coffee from the waitress.

"This place hasn't changed a bit in the last twenty years." Sam said looking at the scarred tables and checked curtains. "Still serves the best food in the city, too. I'd rather have breakfast here than in any one of those fancy places with the big prices."

"The baby's not mine, Sam." John dropped the words quietly without looking up.

Slowly, Sam set his coffee cup on the table. He drew in a deep breath. "Are you sure?"

"Yes."

They sat in silence, staring into their coffee. The silence seemed to stretch forever.

"Absolutely sure?"

"Absolutely," John answered. "The baby weighed in at eight pounds six ounces. Even I know that a seven and a half month baby isn't likely to be that big."

"Maybe not likely, but isn't it possible?"

"Sam, stop looking for an excuse. Sylvia and I went to bed together exactly three times before she told me she was pregnant. Before that, we hadn't even slept in the same room for months. I should have known she was up to something. Sylvia has never forgiven anyone for anything in her entire life, but she always knows exactly how to use people."

John drained his cup and paused while the waitress refilled it. "I hate to admit that I was stupid enough to believe that her attitude toward life with me could change so radically in the space of a day. Damn it, Sam, I could kill that bitch." He slammed his cup on the table. The waitress looked in their direction.

"John." Sam kept his voice calm, almost a monotone. He avoided looking at John and fiddled instead with the silverware. "Your intentions weren't exactly honorable, either."

"I haven't seen Val since last November. I haven't even talked to her, though God knows I wanted to a million times. I've played this thing as straight as an arrow."

"I know that. I meant your reasons for the reconciliation weren't love and happily-ever-after."

"Maybe not, but I honestly have tried during the last seven months."

Sam looked at his cousin. Torment had left deep lines etched beside his mouth. His blue eyes were dull and glazed with unhappiness. His boyish warmth was stilled. "When was the last time you laughed, John?"

"Laughed?" John was puzzled. "What have I had to laugh about?"

"I didn't mean that literally. I just wondered if anything in your life is giving you happiness these days? You've changed."

"Of course, I've changed. Everything's changed." John ran his hand through his hair and rubbed his eyes. "I'm tired, Sam. Tired of this whole silly charade, tired of being an almighty Augustus but mostly I'm tired of living with that woman."

"Now wait just a minute. You've had a long night filled with a lot of emotion and a mighty rough surprise. Don't make any rash decisions."

"Heavens, no," John sneered. "I mustn't make rash decisions. I must, at all costs, consider the Augustus name. Hell, Sam. I'm married to a whore and now I'm saddled with God knows whose little bastard , and if I don't give it my father's name and raise it as an Augustus, the world will think I'm the bad guy. Where's the sense in this?"

"I don't suppose there is much sense to it. Not any more sense then there was in your agreeing to a reconciliation in order to force the merger Grandfather wanted."

"Damn Grandfather. And damn the merger."

The waitress chose that moment to bring their breakfast. They ate the simple, hot food in silence and then signaled for more coffee.

"You're right, Sam. I made my bed and I'd best lie in it. I must have heard Grandma say those words a million times to my mother, but this is the first time they've held such meaning for me. I did agree to this thing, and I'll carry it through. But I'll be damned if I'll let Sylvia think she's gotten away with making a cuckold of me." He crumpled his napkin and tossed it on the table. "Let's get to the office."

"Aren't you going back to the hospital?"

"No. Sylvia will just have to play queen without her prince consort today."

The City Chronicle
September 15, 1937
Tattletales by Sharon Chatsworth

Sound the trumpet. Beat the drums. Today a new
and awesome dynasty of wealth has been achieved.
To the surprise of almost no one, a merger between
Alexander Shipbuilding and Augustus Industries
was revealed today. The families merged several
years ago when John Augustus married Sylvia
Alexander. The recent birth of their son Michael
seems to have been the binding factor for the
business merger.

Chapter 4

John stood at one side of the drawing room and
watched his guests. The entire city had turned out
to pay homage to his son. Not my son, John
thought, Sylvia's son.

During the christening ceremony he'd almost
blurted out the truth. When the Reverend Smithson
asked, "What name do you give this child?" John
flinched and bit his tongue to avoid saying, "Any
name but mine." The pause had been much too
long and Sylvia glared at him furiously. Not that
John cared. Sylvia's opinion was of no interest to
him.

He wondered if anyone else had noticed. Sam
knew and perhaps Walter had guessed, but the rest
of the world accepted young Michael as an

Augustus. I'd better learn to accept him, too, John mused. Either accept him or get out.

"What in the world are you brooding about, John?" The rich southern voice of his father-in-law jerked John's mind back to the christening party. "Oh, just thinking, Alex."

"You certainly aren't very cheerful. Is there something troubling you?" Alex's genuine liking for John sounded in his voice. "This should be a proud day for you. You've a fine son and the merger of our companies is a very important occurrence."

"The merger is exciting, Alex." John plucked a glass of champagne from a waiter's tray and raised it toward Alex. "To AmCo."

Alex tilted his glass in reply. "I like that name. Amalgamated Manufacturing. It has a strong enduring sound." He drank deeply and raised his glass again. "To your son."

"To your grandson," John replied and sipped his champagne.

The choice of words surprised Alex and a shudder of foreboding ran up his spine. But John grinned and the feeling was lost in the general noise of the party.

"I'd better circulate," John said. "We'll have plenty of time to talk this evening."

John moved away and spoke to each of his guests. He performed his duties as the genial host, accepting congratulations both for the merger and on the birth of the child. At last he found himself next to Sam. "Hell," he said leaning wearily against the fine carved paneling. "I never dreamed this would be so hard."

"What?" Sam asked.

"This charade, the constant pretending that I'm happy and thrilled and content. That everything is just fine and dandy." He clenched his fist and pounded it lightly into the palm of his other hand. "I don't think I can keep this up, Sam. I really don't think I can."

"Is Sylvia giving you a bad time?"

"No. Not a bad time. We've had it out and she's quite content to remain my wife in name only. In fact I'm sure she prefers it this way." John fell silent and Sam stood waiting for him to go on. "It's the fact that I hate her. And as if that isn't enough, I hate the baby."

"The baby?" Sam frowned. "The baby isn't responsible for being born."

"I know that. I know it logically but emotionally, that's a whole different game." John rubbed his hand across his eyes. "When I look at that child, my stomach turns. I want to know who his father is. I don't want him to have my name. I can't bring myself to touch him. I refuse to call him my son."

"John..." Sam started.

"It can't go on this way," John interrupted. "I can't live like this, and I know it isn't fair to subject the child to my hate. I'm going to ask Grandfather to let me go to Europe."

"Now?" Sam raised his eyebrows.

"Yes, now, the sooner the better." John pushed himself away from the wall and straightened his shoulders. "We'll need someone in Europe to smooth the merger between the foreign offices and it'll allow enough time to pass so the Sylvia and I can decently separate and divorce."

"I see your point, Cuz." Sam smiled sadly. "Okay. If that's what you honestly think is best, I'll throw any influence I have in your direction."

"Thanks, Sam." John clasped his arm. "I knew I could count on your support."

As John moved through his guests, he found himself weighing conversations, analyzing every word to discover if each person knew or suspected about Sylvia's son. I'm jealous, he realized, surprised by the emotion. I don't love her, and I haven't for a long time, but I'm jealous.

"You okay, John?" Alex was at his side again.

"I'm fine," John answered. "I was just thinking that I'd like our guests to leave."

"Walter's already decided the party should end. He went into the library a few minutes ago and suggested that you, Sam and I join him there as soon as we can." Alex looked over the group, still chatting and laughing. "I'll give Sylvia the word, and we'll clear them out."

"What word is that? I've never known Syl to leave a party early."

I'll tell her I want the party to end and she should plead fatigue and go upstairs. After all she is a new mother."

John stood amazed as he watched Alex stride across the room and bend solicitously over Sylvia.

Sylvia rose and turned toward the gathered guests.

"I hate to be tiresome," she said with a pretty little smile, "but I'm a bit tired and I'd like to lie down. Thank you all for coming this afternoon."

Immediately, there was a flurry of goodbyes. Within minutes, the house was empty of guests. John was dumfounded. He turned to Sylvia, a caustic remark on the tip of his tongue. But the picture she made in her soft blue jersey gown, holding the baby tenderly in her arms, lifted his disgust at her submissive behavior and he made no comment. I don't suppose she's having an easy time with this charade either, he thought.

"Well now, that's done," Alex boomed. "Let's move into the library and get down to business."

John and Sam started to the door with Alex, and Sylvia handed the baby to the nursemaid. "I'll be right in, Father," she said. "I just want to freshen up a bit."

"There's no need, Sylvia. Why don't you go up and rest until dinner," Alex smiled at his daughter.

"But, Father," she protested. "I'm interested in the merger. I want to know what changes are being made."

"Sylvia, a woman's place is not at a business conference." Alex frowned. "Don't worry, your husband will tell you everything you need to know later." He patted her arm lightly. "Run along now, we've got work to do."

Sylvia turned to John, but something in his stance told her he wasn't going to help in an appeal. With anger strengthening her spine, she spun around and swept out of the room and up the stairway. Alex chuckled, "She looks just like her mother when she gets her dander up."

John murmured to Sam, "Did you see that?"

"I saw it, but I'm not sure I believe it." He laughed. "Wish I had that kind of control with Helen or even with my children."

They entered the library. Walter looked up from the ledger open on his desk. He waved them toward chairs. "Did you clear them out?"

"Everyone's gone, Grandfather." Sam was unable to suppress the laughter in his throat, "Even Sylvia and the baby."

"Where'd Sylvia go?"

"I sent her to rest. A woman doesn't need to know the inner workings of a business," Alex replied serenely.

"Alex, your southern attitudes amaze me." Walter chuckled. "Do you mean to tell me that Sylvia didn't even put up an argument over being barred from our talk?"

"Not even a murmur, Grandfather." Sam was still grinning. "She was as demure as a doe."

"Don't let her acquiescence fool you," Alex defended his daughter. "She's a strong-minded young woman and when she gives in to my wishes that easily, I know there's something on her mind. She's got a real interest in this merger and I doubt that she'll be willing to be left out of our discussion. I was simply buying time so I could discuss a more private matter."

"What's that?" Sam was intrigued.

"I think, as Walter does, that the free world will be at war before many more months have passed." Alex turned to Walter, who nodded his agreement. "Walter has the two of you as his major heirs. I have Sylvia. Ordinarily, I would feel no concern. But with the world poised on the brink of trouble, I want to know that both Sylvia and her child are fully protected, no matter what may befall her marriage, her husband, or me."

"Alex," Walter's surprise stressed his voice. "You know how I feel about Sylvia. When she married John, she became a part of our family."

"I know that's how you feel now. And I know you would always be fair. But you and I are old men, Walter. Today's world is very different from our familiar safe one. When divorce," John glanced up startled, but Alex continued without glancing his way, "breaks up a family. Strange events may take place. I want my little girl and her child safe and well cared for. I like you, John." He looked directly into John's wary eyes. "I don't want to hurt you, but I feel it is essential that we speak frankly."

John exchanged a look with Sam, afraid of what was coming. "Of course, Alex," he said. "Say whatever's on your mind."

"Sylvia is a headstrong woman. She lacks patience and understanding." Alex waved away Walter's protest. "After her mother left us, I spoiled her shamefully. And I'm afraid, John, that you are the one who will suffer for my folly. She has no sense of loyalty. I know that and I accept it. After all, I taught her to be self-centered. But in a marriage," he shrugged. "Perhaps you've already had a taste of what I'm talking about."

"Alex," John said, "I'm confused. What are you trying to say?"

"Simply, John, that I doubt that Sylvia will remain true to her marriage vows if the two of you are separated for any period of time."

John and Sam exchanged amazed glances. Walter looked shocked. "How can you say such a thing about your own daughter?" he managed to ask.

"I can say it because I'm a realist. I love Sylvia more than life itself, but I know her faults. If John goes to war or if he causes her disappointment, she'll rebel," Alex answered sadly. "She's just too much like her mother to do otherwise."

John felt he had to say something to defend his marriage but his mind was boggled with the insight of Alex's words. It was as if Alex had been a party to the events of the last eighteen months.

Watching John, Sam came to his rescue. "What do you have in mind, Alex?" he asked.

"I want you to rewrite my will, Sam."

"Shouldn't this be a private matter between the two of us?"

"Perhaps, but I want both Walter and John to be aware of certain provisions. I want Sylvia's inheritance to consist of my one half of the AmCo stock. And I want the inheritance to be contingent on her remaining married to John."

"Alex, you can't do that. It's not fair to Sylvia," Sam protested, glancing at John.

"Fair or not, I want it done," Alex said firmly. "If she should decide on a divorce she will not inherit. I want no money from AmCo to go to Sylvia or to her support unless she and John stay married until Michael and any other children they may have reach majority."

No one spoke. Silently, the Augustus men looked at each other and then, embarrassed by such an edict shifted their gaze to inanimate objects. John felt the shackles that bound him to Sylvia grow tighter and for a moment he was afraid to allow himself to even consider the meaning of Alex's words.

Finally, Walter rose from his chair and paced slowly back and forth. "Are you sure, Alex? Have you considered this carefully?"

"Walter, I know in my heart that I'm doing the right thing. Sylvia needs a steadying influence, and I know that money is the strongest, most constant influence available."

"Sam," he continued, "We can work out the details tomorrow, but I want this taken care of immediately."

"Alex, I'm not sure..." Sam started when a light knock sounded at the door.

"Yes?" Walter questioned.

The door swung inward, and Sylvia swept into the room. Her face glowed as she smiled her brightest, most appealing smile. "Michael's tucked in for the night, and I'm freshened up. Now I want to hear the plans you're making for our exciting new company."

"Ring for some coffee, daughter, and we'll let you stay." Alex patted a place next to him on the sofa, "as I was saying, gentlemen." He turned back and pretended to resume a conversation. "With the world in the mess it's in and with the changes that are taking place, I think we're in for some very exciting times. I'd like to see AmCo grow and change as quickly as possible."

Sam, the first to recover, picked up the thread. "I've done the research and completed the survey we talked about. The results are exactly as you predicted, Walter. Of the twenty thousand passengers crossing the Atlantic yearly, we calculate that at least one-fifth would go by air if there were such a service available."

"It sounds as if the development of a transatlantic air service will make more sense than building another grand ocean liner," John said, excitement brightening his eyes.

"We'll have to contend with the British, you know," Alex cautioned.

"They're usually a reasonable lot," Walter interjected. "They're as interested in a pound as we are in a dollar. If we approach them correctly I'm sure we can reach an agreement."

"AmCo is going to need a representative in Europe both for this and to smooth the legalities of our foreign offices merging." Alex spoke thoughtfully, "I've considered each of my top men here in the states and abroad and, frankly, I'm not entirely satisfied that anyone is right for the job. Do you have anyone from Augustus Industries in mind?"

John's heart began to beat faster, he counseled himself to be patient, not to over sell his own candidacy.

"I think whoever goes should be a major stockholder. That would show the most strength." Walter spoke slowly, choosing each word carefully as he thought aloud. "It needs to be one of the four of us. No one else will be as sympathetic to the development of AmCo. Family would be best."

Alex nodded. Sylvia kissed his cheek, "Family is always best," she said.

"Agreed, but I'm too busy with the legal aspects of this merger to be running off to Europe, no matter how important the trip may be," Sam stated firmly.

"And I'm too old," Walter said with a touch of sadness. "As much as I hate to admit it, I know it's true. That leaves either Alex or John. How about it?"

"Sounds like the kind of challenge I'd enjoy." John's voice was full of enthusiasm.

"That settles it then. I'd much rather be here in the states." Alex sounded relieved.

"What about me?" Sylvia asked. "I'd love to live in Europe."

John concealed his contempt behind a cold smile, "The baby's much too young to travel, Syl. I'm sure you'll manage to stay busy here in the states no matter how long I'm gone."

The City Chronicle
November 3, 1938
Tattletales by Sharon Chatsworth

Today, John Augustus is expected home. His family will welcome him back to their bosom after long and eventful months spent abroad. The past year has marked many changes in our world. One of the most exciting of these changes is the creation of direct air transportation for passengers between the United States and Europe. This service can be attributed to the diligent work and diplomacy of our own native son, John Augustus. Congratulations to you and to AmCo, Inc. Thank you for making world travel a "quicker" pleasure.

Chapter 5

John stood at the embarkation gate and waited to board his flight back to the states. It was difficult to believe that a year had flown by so quickly. Despite the raising threats of war, the mobilization of the German military, the resignation of the Czech government and Chamberlain's willingness to appease Hitler, living and working in Europe had a soothing effect on him. For days at a time, he'd been able to forget the baby. Even when talking to Walter or Alex, he'd managed to keep all conversations on business. There had been casual references to Michael a time or two but these he'd been able to ignore. Now, he'd be faced with the physical fact of the child. Even though he was still many hours from home, he could feel the knot of apprehension growing in his stomach.

"You may board now, Mr. Augustus."

His feet moved automatically, carrying his lean body on board and to his seat. Oblivious to the other passengers, he looked out the window, watching as the plane began to roll slowly down the rough runway. He felt a touch on his arm as the plane's speed increased. He glanced down and saw a gnarled hand, the knotted fingers heavy with rings of gold and diamonds.

"Don't worry, young man," a melodious voice assured him. "These contraptions always get off the ground and back down again quite safely. I really don't understand how they manage, but they do."

John turned to his seat companion ready to protest his lack of fear, and found himself gazing into the deepest, darkest violet eyes he had ever encountered. For a moment he felt himself sinking into those eyes. Then he found his voice. "Thank you, Madam. I appreciate your kind concern."

"How lovely, an American." The rich voice held a hint of laughter. "All my favorite men are American. Are you going home?"

John felt himself drawn to this delightful stranger. Only minutes before he'd been sunk in depression. Now he felt renewed, even eager to greet a new experience.

"I am going home and I'm delighted to have such a charming traveling companion." John grinned and the lady smiled in return as she extended her hand.

"I'm Lillian Rathborne."

"John Augustus." He kissed her hand and grinned again.

"How unAmerican." This time she grinned, "But how utterly charming."

"Mrs. Rathborne, I'm honored to make your acquaintance."

"Please call me Lily. I'm old enough to be forgiven the informality and young enough to delight in an attractive man all to myself on this long flight."

"Lily, then," John agreed. "Where are you headed?"

"New York."

"For the holidays?" John sat watching her face, fascinated by her wide, mobile mouth and flashing eyes. he felt as if he knew this woman.

"For the holidays perhaps," Lily paused thoughtfully. "But mostly, I'm on a search for a lost treasure."

"Treasure?"

"Yes, a very personal treasure that has been misplaced much too long."

The plane lifted slowly and then soared skyward. John took a deep breath. He always felt a personal responsibility to the passengers on any flight connected with AmCo Airways and was able to relax now that a smooth, on time take off had been accomplished.

"Are you comfortable, Mr. Augustus? Can I get you anything?"

"I'm fine, Janice." John hardly glanced at the lovely attendant hovering by his seat, "How about you, Lily? Need a pillow or anything?"

"No thank you, Miss." Lily turned slightly to face John. Her unusual eyes twinkled. "John Augustus, I should have recognized your name. You certainly aren't frightened by the concept of flight, are you?"

"No, I wasn't concerned about the flight."

"Well, if it's not the flight, it's most likely none of my business," Lily said firmly. "So we'll talk of other things."

John nodded. He dreaded the reunion he would have to face and he didn't want to think about the problems it would cause. He smiled at Lily, "Tell me about your treasure hunt. I love a mystery."

"And I love to talk about myself and my family."

Lily settled herself deeper into her seat and drew a deep breath. "If I were younger, I suppose I'd find it bad form to talk to a stranger but perhaps not. It has always been my experience that traveling together seems to breed an instant intimacy. Don't you agree?"

John nodded, fascinated by this unusual woman, a woman so different from the women in his family, yet with a familiar quality about her. "Are you English, Lily?' he asked.

"No, I am French. But I've spent so many years in England that my accent has all but disappeared."

"You married an Englishman?"

"Yes, my second husband. I was widowed more than thirty years ago in France. When I fell in love again, I was fortunate enough to fall in love with an Englishman."

"I take it you love England and her people."

"Love?" Lily considered her next words carefully. "I'm not sure love is the right word. I find their ability to live well and happily while controlling their emotions to be of great comfort. It's a quality the French lack."

John regarded Lilly thoughtfully. "It's certainly true that giving in to your emotions can cause many terrible things to happen in one's life."

"Not only terrible things, young man, also some very good things," Lily said sternly. "When one is my age, one is ready for peace. But at your age, the fulfillment of your dreams should be your primary concern."

John felt his eyes fill with tears. He gazed out at the clouds for a moment while he regained his composure. This woman had a strange effect on him. He sighed, "I seem to have lost sight of my dreams, Lily."

"Then find them again and pursue them." Lily spoke impatiently. "Don't waste your life on doing your duty," she shook her gray head empathically. "Take the advice of an old woman, John. Live each day fully and to its utmost. Be true to yourself, because in the end there is no one else. Sacrifices are not appreciated if, in fact, they are even noticed."

"That sounds good, Lily, but what about family? I have a duty, a responsibility to them."

"Pshaw," Lily snorted. "Duty has been the downfall of many a good man. Face life squarely. Don't be afraid to demand the things you desire."

For long minutes the two sat in silence, each immersed in his own thoughts. John's mind churned through the maze of contradictions. He knew he was headed home to a loveless marriage, to a child he couldn't claim as his own, to a wife he despised. Yet he'd been telling himself that he was willing to fulfill his duty to the family until now, as he listened to this woman, he realized how cheated he felt. He wanted out of the situation. Yet he didn't think he had the courage to do anything about it.

He decided to change the subject, turning to Lily, he said, "About your treasure hunt, what is it you are searching for?"

But there was no answer. Lily Rathborne had drifted off to sleep. John returned to the contemplation of his own problems. Gradually the hum of the engines relaxed him and he too slept.

Hours later as the sound of the engines changed, as the plane began it decent for the landing in Bermuda, John stirred and came awake. He gazed again at the composed face of his seat companion. Why did she seem so familiar? Perhaps he'd seen her in a crowd? No, he thought, it's more than that. I feel as if I've always known this lady. Lily opened her eyes and smiled. Something about the mouth, John decided. It's the mouth that reminds me of someone.

They disembarked into the warm Bermuda sunshine and John gallantly offered his arm to Lily. "Come with me, my dear," he said in his most flirtatious manner. "Let me buy you a fabulous dinner at an exciting club I know."

"Why, sir," Lily spoke archly, responding to his game. "I'm not certain I can trust you."

"Trust me! Of course you can trust me, I intend to ply you with the finest food and wine this lovely island has to offer and when you are sufficiently relaxed I intend to discover all the hidden secrets of your life."

"A woman my age certainly can't refuse an offer like that."

Lily hooked her hand through his arm and they grinned at each as they set off in a horse drawn cab. The large Negro driver was delighted at their happiness and gaily pointed out the sights as he kept the horse trotting at a brisk pace through the narrow twisting lanes.

The tropical sun sparkled on the white terraced rooftops and pastel colored houses. Here and there they caught brief views of the pink tinted beach and azure sea. Laughing they pulled up in front of the dignified Bermuda Club. A doorman wearing a dove gray top hat and tails handed them down and bowed them through the tall louvered doors.

In the cool green oasis created by lush green ferns and a bubbling fountain they ate the spicy Creole cuisine, sipped their wine and gossiped as if they were old friends. The time slipped past. All too quickly, the waiter stopped at the table to remind them that it was time to leave if they were to catch the continuing flight.

After settling into their seats, John took Lily's hand, "I didn't succeed in finding out your secrets after all, but I did have time to make a new friend. It's a real pleasure traveling with you, Lily."

"And with you John, if I could choose another grandson, I would certainly choose you."

The flight attendant arrived with pillows and blankets. For a few minutes they were busy loosening clothing and getting comfortable for the long flight into New York. Then they had time to sip at glasses of wine and resume their conversation. "It won't be long before you will be able to fly direct from Europe to America. I'll miss this stopover in Bermuda," John said.

Lily nodded and smiled gently. "Progress is an amazing force. Why, when I was your age, I never would have dreamed of going to America, and certainly not of flying anywhere. Yet here we are as calm as you please floating through the night headed for the future."

"To the future," John raised his glass in a salute to Lily's words. To the future, he thought. What kind of future am I headed toward? In only a few hours I'll have to face the family.

Lily saw the pain and sadness settle over his handsome face. How regrettable that thoughts of the future can make such a fortunate young man so sad, she mused and turned her face toward the window.

Lost in their private thoughts, John and Lily drifted to sleep. John's head came to rest on Lily's shoulder and she stirred in her sleep, adjusting to accommodate the weight without waking.

The plane touched down in Miami and was refueled. Passengers deplaned and others came aboard. Neither John nor Lily chose to leave the plane. They stirred and talked only briefly and as soon as the plane was aloft again they slept.

Finally the rising sun caused the sky to brighten. The passengers stirred and stretched. An attendant collected the pillows and served strong, hot coffee. Lily and John freshened themselves and prepared for the landing. "I feel a bit unreal," Lily commented. "It seems impossible that we have arrived on this foreign shore while I slept."

"Air travel is certainly making the world a smaller place." John watched the approaching land. He felt his dread of the meeting he was facing grow and deliberately pushed it aside. "Have you visited America before?" he asked.

"Only in my heart," Lily smiled sadly. "My daughter came here many years ago and I've often dreamed of seeing her again."

"Is she meeting the plane?"

"No."

The abrupt answer surprised John and he sipped at his coffee wondering if he should pursue the question. He remembered Lily's words about hunting for a lost treasure and decided it would be wiser to change the subject. He liked this elderly gentlewoman and didn't want to upset her. "Tell me about your treasure hunt," he said. "What are you looking for?"

Now it was Lily's turn to sip slowly and stall a moment while she found the right words. "It's not a what," she said at last, "but a who."

"A who? You mean a person?" John's curiosity mounted.

"Yes, a person, a very dear person whom I haven't seen in more than thirty years."

"Thirty years," John echoed. "That's a long time all right."

"Perhaps too long, but I sincerely hope not."

John clasped the frail hand with its' many rings. "It won't be too long, Lily. I know whom ever you seek will be glad to see you. I've only known you a very short while but I know you are a special lady."

"Thank you, John. They say time heals all wrongs. I pray that is so."

"Could I help you? Do you have an address?" John struggled to control his inquisitiveness, intrigued but not wanting to pry into a private matter.

"Not only do I not have an address, my dear, I don't have a name."

"No name!" This time his astonishment couldn't be contained and the exclamation burst from his lips. Other passengers turned to look. He lowered his voice and repeated, "No name, Lily. How do you expect to find someone with no name in a city the size of New York?"

"Worse than that, I'm not sure my treasure is in New York. I may have to search all of America."

John stared at Lily, her self-assurance left him speechless. The plane began the final descent. Lily calmly smoothed her hair, tucking the pins, that held it in its' intricate knot, in more tightly. "Surely," John managed to ask, "you must have a clue, a partial name, or something. Some idea of where this person may be living."

"No clues. But a great deal of faith." She patted his hand. "I believe, John. I truly believe that my search will be rewarded. Love is a powerful force. And I have love."

The plane bumped to a stop. John pulled a business card from his lapel pocket. He handed it to Lily. "Take this. I want you to call me any time if I can help in any way. Promise me you will."

Fatigue from the long trip had caused smudges beneath Lily's beautiful eyes but they sparkled as she smiled at him. "I promise." Carefully she tucked the card in her leather handbag. "You've been most kind, John. I'll look forward to seeing you again."

Departing the plane, Lily pulled her soft fur coat tightly around her erect body to keep out the sharp wind that whistled around corners and tossed rubbish into the crisp air. With John's light touch on her elbow she slowly and elegantly descended the airliner's stairs. On the tarmac an AmCo car and driver waited for him. He started to offer Lily a ride to her hotel but a group of reporters, swarmed toward him and she was swept away into the customs building with the other passengers.

John caught her eye and raised his hand in a gesture of farewell. He thought he saw her wink but he couldn't be sure. He turned to the reporters and patiently began answering their questions about his flight and the political tensions in Europe.

"So what da yah think, Mr. Augustus?" asked a brash young reporter, his hat pushed far back on his head. "Will there be a war in Europe?"

"I'm not a politician," John replied carefully, "But I'd say that it appears likely. The situation is certainly tense." He smiled at the reporters. "That's enough for tonight. I haven't been home in nearly a year and I think it's time I get going."

"Sure thing, Mr. Augustus." The young reporter grinned at him. "I bet you're anxious to see your beautiful wife and that son of yours. Welcome home."

John shook a few extended hands and moved toward the limousine. He answered their jibes and well wishes but his eyes were distant, his thoughts caught by the reporters words. Son of mine? I have no son. The driver opened the door and John smiled automatically as he slid into the warm interior.

"Home," John muttered. "What home?"

"Did you say something, Sir?" the driver asked, instantly alert.

"Home," John repeated. "Just home."

"Of course, Sir."

Expertly the driver swung the car around on the tarmac, drove through the wide gates and entered the stream of traffic. John leaned back against the smooth leather and closed his eyes. A tumble of confused thoughts and feelings assailed him. He dreaded the meeting with Sylvia. He had no idea what he'd say to her and as for the boy; he could get along just fine if he never had to see him at all. He shook his head to clear it, ran his fingers through his thick hair and straightened his shoulders; this was no time for self-pity.

Too soon, they glided to a stop in front of the tall brownstone. The driver sprang out and opened the door. John looked across the street at the park. He turned as if to go to its' comforting shadows. "Aren't you going in, Sir?"

"Yes." John turned back. "Yes, of course, I'm going in."

He mounted the stone stairs and reached for the brass door pull. The high door swung open and Sam's cheerful face beamed at him. "Welcome Home, Cuz." Sam wrapped his arms around John in a bear hug. "I thought you might have trouble walking in here alone," he whispered. "Come on in. The whole family's here to greet you."

Sam kept his arm draped casually over John's shoulders and drew him forward across the wide entry and into the sitting room. The whole family had indeed gathered. The room shone with the warm light of the fire. Candles glowed and were reflected in the polished table tops. Minette held him close for a long minute and whispered her greeting to her son, "Accueillez à la maison, mon fils précieux."

John smiled at the words, the same phase she'd used to greet him every day of his childhood on his return from school. He kept her close as he greeted Sam's parents, Uncle Peter and Aunt Ruth. His Aunt Mary Elizabeth swept forward in her regal manner and dutifully he kissed her soft cheek. Helen jumped up to greet him, her hug as warm as Sam's. He was comforted, welcomed back to the bosom of his family.

"Darling!" Sylvia's shrill, brittle voice caught his attention.

He watched as she moved dramatically across the room, each step bringing them closer to the moment he'd dreaded for weeks. "Hello, Syl," he said, his words as cool and clear as ice water. "You're looking very well."

She hesitated only an instant, took the final steps and placed her arms around his unresponsive body.

Standing on tiptoe she kissed his lips and threw back her head in a happy gesture. "It's good to see you, Darling." Stepping back, she smiled mockingly.

To the onlookers John knew that her motions would appear normal but he could see her cold angry eyes. Deliberately, he turned away. "Excuse me, Sylvia. I'd like to greet my grandfather."

Walter sat in a throne-like carved Chinese chair that had been drawn close to the blazing fire. How old he looks, John thought as he crossed the room.

Walter smiled and the tired lines were erased from around his eyes. "Hello, John." He held out his hand and John clasped it.

"Hello, Grandfather. How are you?"

"I'm fine. Just fine and even better now that you're back home again."

John placed his free hand over his grandfather's and squeezed gently, surprised by the emotion he felt at the old man's greeting.

Walter nodded, his eyes lit by his assurance that all was right with his world. "Yes indeed, it's good to have you back. Pull a chair over here and sit. I want to hear all about Europe and what's really going on over there. I'm sure we haven't been hearing the whole story from our politicians. Is there going to be a war?"

"War!" Sylvia interrupted and gave a pretty little shudder. "Grandfather, don't let's talk about gloomy subjects. John's only been home a minute. I'm sure he wants to see his son and catch up on all the family news."

John glared at Sylvia, his face a frozen mask. She drew back and caught her breath; a flicker of fear twisted her mouth. Very carefully and deliberately, his voice pitched so low that no else in the room, but Walter, could hear, he snarled, "Don't play games with me. I have no son. Remember?"

Stunned by the anger, Walter rose and placed his hand on John's shoulder. John shrugged and Walter's hand fell away. "I'll speak with you later, Grandfather."

Walter and Sylvia watched him walk away, his back straight and unyielding. They could hear him as he joined the gathered family his voice was happy and calm as if the last words had never been spoken in that cold dead manner. "I'm sorry, Sylvia." Walter sank back into his chair.

"Are you?" she asked, a bright mocking lilt in her voice. She looked at the old man and allowed a threatening note to creep into her voice, "You may not be sorry yet, Walter, but you will be. I'm tired of you mucking about with my life." Sylvia tossed her head; the fire picked out the gleaming highlights in her hair and caused the silk threads of her gown to glitter. Casually she swept across the room and joined the crowd around her husband.

Walter stayed by the fire. He watched his family. They were all so familiar to him. He felt that he knew the weaknesses and the strengths of each. Sam hovered close to John keeping the group busy with small talk and heading off another clash between John and Sylvia. Always the peacemaker, Sam's ability to avoid conflict had proven to be a real asset during this past year. He'd guided the merger between the two companies with a sure steady skill that had resulted in a strong company. One that was ready to meet the challenges of the changing world. The company was ready but was the family. Had he made a mistake by urging John not to dissolve his marriage?

Hours later John sat alone in his study; the family gone, the house quiet. Nothing left but his own confusion. He poured himself a brandy from the cut crystal decanter. Anger smoldered in him, a physical presence that caused his stomach to twist and churn. "Damn!" he swore and downed the brandy with a single gulp.

"What a waste of good French brandy," Sylvia's mocking voice broke his solitude.

"What are you doing here?" John demanded.

"I live here. Remember?"

"I remember all right. I remember everything."

"Not everything, Darling." Sylvia glided to the bar and filled a snifter for herself. She tilted the glass toward the light. "Remember when you used to tell me that my hair was the same color as brandy in candlelight?" Gracefully, she spun in a slow circle. "Remember when you thought I was the most beautiful woman in the world? Remember when..."

"That's enough." John filled his own glass again and took a sip. "What's your point, Syl?"

"Point? What do you suppose the point is husband of mine?"

"I'm not sure. I came back tonight expecting things to be the same as they were when I left for Europe and instead I find you pretending that we are the perfect couple. You have the whole family assembled to greet me as if it were the most natural thing in the world."

"It is the most natural thing. Nothing has changed. We have an agreement and we have no choice but to abide by that agreement." She raised her glass and sipped. "Remember that agreement, John? My point is that agreement. We are bound together, 'til death do us part. Bound by the golden cord of money and money binds much tighter and more securely than any other cord."

John acknowledged her statements with a glance but didn't answer.

"Not only money, John. Bound also by my son, Michael. He's your son, too, in the eyes of the world. He bears your name."

"My name but not my blood!"

"I doubt that you could prove that statement." She placed her drink on the bar and sat on the high stool. The silk of her stockings whispered as she crossed her legs. Her skirt slipped up exposing her thigh. She's a bitch, John thought, but a damn beautiful one. He moved away and sat in his lounge chair.

Sylvia smiled, amused at his discomfort.

"What is it you want, Syl?"

"The question isn't what I want. The question is, are you going to act like my husband, like Michael's father, or are you going to behave the way you did this evening? Do you intend to keep your part of the agreement?"

"I'm here, aren't I?"

"Being here isn't enough. In fact, it is the least important part. What happens inside this house, when no one is with us, matters not at all compared to the face we present to the world."

John was irked by her cool, aloof manner. He knew she was making sense but it was hard to admit that she might be right. He took the time to finish his drink as he considered the alternatives.

Sylvia waited, confident in her power to get what she wanted. Finally she reached for the silver cigarette box and fit one into her ivory holder. The flick of the lighter brought John's attention back to her. "When did you take up smoking?" He asked.

Sylvia merely looked at him and slowly exhaled. The pause lengthened and at last she replied, enigmatically, "I've taken up a lot of things you know nothing about, John. That's exactly why we must talk now, tonight. I have to know what you intend to do. How you intend to keep your agreement."

"It sounds as if you know what you want, Syl. Why don't we start there," John moved to the bar and poured a fresh drink. He raised the decanter to Sylvia in a silent question. At her nod, he refilled her glass and then stood behind the bar waiting.

Sylvia shifted, uncomfortable under his steady gaze. She took a deep breath and, without looking at him, began. "My father is very ill. I've spent the last few weeks in Charleston and I'm going back next Tuesday." Her eyes filled with tears. "He's dying, John."

Instantly sympathetic, John covered her trembling hand with his. "Syl, I'd no idea. No one told me. Are you sure?"

"The doctors say it's just a matter of time." She drew in a shaky breath, bravely holding her tears in check. "He loves his grandson and he thinks we have a good strong marriage. I don't want him to be troubled by the truth."

John patted her smooth, slender, hand his fingers touched the gold band he had placed there. "Of course, I'll help keep our problems away from, Alex. I know how much you love your father and how much this must hurt. Tell me what I can do."

"Come home with me."

John withdrew his hand. He busied himself drawing circles of moisture on the mahogany bar. Sylvia twisted her rings round and round and waited for his answer. He wanted to say no. The mere thought of going to his wife's childhood home sent a chill down his spine. In the best years of their marriage he'd been uncomfortable in the large, stately house surrounded by the visible signs of the extravagant love Alex poured over his only child.

John raised his head and was caught by the helpless anguish in Sylvia's eyes. Only a beast could refuse her request.

"All right, I'll go."

Air rushed out of Sylvia and he realized she'd been holding her breath.

"Thank you," she said simply and hung her head.

"I think I'll finish this and then go up to bed." John swirled the amber liquid in his glass.

"Shouldn't we talk about things?"

"I'm sure we should but let's not. I've had a very long day and you have enough on your mind.

Sylvia slid off the stool. Her perfume drifted to him stirring his senses. He was aware of the way the golden silk clung to her full breasts and accentuated her slender waist. Heat rose in his body. She touched his arm. It was as if an electric shock flew up his arm to his heart. He pulled back, abruptly. Sylvia dropped her hand. "I suppose you're right," she said. "There's nothing that can't keep until tomorrow."

John followed the movement of her hips as she walked to the door. He remembered the fervor of their early marriage. "Sylvia?"

"Yes?" She turned; her hand on the brass doorknob.

Disturbed by the intensity of his reaction to her touch, John hesitated unsure of his response. He struggled to regain his composure and managed to say, "Nothing. Just good night."

"Good night, John. I'm glad you're home."

The door closed gently and John was left with the faint scent of her heady perfume. He caught a glimpse of himself in the mirror and raised his glass in an ironic salute. "Here's to love and marriage," he said. Drained the glass and went upstairs to his solitary bed.

John rose early, ate his breakfast alone and asked that the car be brought around for his trip to the office. He accepted his hat from the butler and stepped out into the bright sunny morning. The crisp sunshine lifted his mood. He smiled and squared his shoulders. "Duncan, send the car around to the other side of the park. I'll walk through and meet it there." He started out but turned back, "Here," he said, and handed the surprised butler his hat. "I won't be needing this."
John strode across the street and entered the park with a jaunty gate. He inhaled the crisp fresh air. The ground was covered with red and gold leaves and John smiled to himself remembering the games he and Sam had played, rolling and scuffling their way through the park to school. A scruffy dog ran across the path trailing a leash and closely followed by a small boy. John laughed aloud and paused to watch the chase. The dog hesitated for just an instant but it was enough for his master to capture him and then the two fell together onto a pile of leaves. The boy's laughter joined with the dog's loud barks. John shook his head ruefully and smiled at their pleasure. Despite everything, it felt good to be home.
He quickened his step and continued across the park, anxious to reach the office and catch up on the doings at the home office.

Walter stood as John entered the large corner office. "John. We didn't expect to see you this morning. Don't you want to spend some time at home with your wife and son?"

John managed to keep his face expressionless. "They aren't up yet, Grandfather." He turned to Sam. "Pour me some of that coffee, Cuz. And then let's get down to business. I've a million things to tell you about Europe and I want to know everything that has happened here."

The morning passed quickly as John talked of the tension in Europe and of his belief that war would spread rapidly, when it came. Walter and Sam questioned him closely and expressed their own concerns and conclusions. The merger of the two companies had been accomplished smoothly and the new AmCo Corporation was ready to produce on a scale that could meet any wartime demands. Not only had they established the transoceanic air service for passengers, the factories were ready and able to produce war planes, guns, ammunition and even uniforms and bandages.

Walter sighed and removed his glasses. He polished them carefully. John smiled at the familiar gesture. "What's the matter, Grandpa?" he asked, unaware of his use of the childhood name.

"Nothing's really wrong." Walter settled the wire frames over his ears. "I'm sorry to see the world gearing up for a war. I know that may be hard to believe the way I pushed this past year in order to get everything ready but I am sorry." He stood and pointed to the framed pictures on his office wall. "See those photographs? Many of the men there never came home from the last war. They were my friends and the sons of my friends, brave men who fought for their country and for what they believed in. They were strong and honest and some of them were very young, but they died. This time it'll be your friends who fight and your friends who die. History repeats itself but the world never learns."

The silence stretched as each man thought about the implication of Walter's words. It was true. War would mean not only increased profits but death and destruction a grim reality that the three men found difficult to dwell on.

"Enough," Walter started for the door. "Let's go to lunch and then John had better get home to his wife."

John and Sam swung into step behind Walter and followed him from the office and across the spacious reception area. John greeted people and shook hands as he acknowledged their welcome. "It feels good to be back in the home office," he admitted as they entered the elevator and began the descent to the street. Walter clapped him on the back and grinned.

Lunch ended all too soon for John. He tried to think of reasons why he should return to the office but Walter brushed each one aside and insisted that he spend the rest of the day with Sylvia. "I'm going to Charleston with her next week," John protested. "I need to get caught up on the details of our operation here so that I can be of use."

"You've worked hard enough for ten men this past year," Walter declared. "I want you to take the time to get to know your son, have a little honeymoon with your wife. It's time to straighten out your differences." John bristled at the insinuation but Walter hurried on. "She needs to have your support if Alex dies she'll need your strength."

Sam watched John. His eyes conveyed his appreciation of the spot John was in. He raised an eyebrow as if to say, "What can I do?"

John clenched his jaw, his eyes narrowed slightly, but he managed to bite back his anger. "Right, Walter," he said crisply. "I'd better get home and see what's happening."

Returning to the house, John was relieved to find it empty of all but Duncan and Mrs. Peters, the housekeeper. Duncan supplied him with the information that Sylvia had gone out to lunch with a friend and that the child had been taken to the park by his nurse for his afternoon outing. John thanked him and went at once to his study.

The familiar room closed around him creating a haven. He sat in the lounge chair resting his head against the high back. His eyes closed. Immediately scenes of the past began to play through his mind. Memories of Valerie and the love they'd shared were mixed with memories of Sylvia. He thought of Lily and saw again her warm smile and lovely eyes. The remembrance of that pleasant interlude erased his discomfort and he drifted peacefully his body truly relaxed for the first time since he'd reached this house.

"Hello, John." Sylvia's strident voice broke into his dreams and jerked him awake. He sat up quickly, confused by the surroundings and by the tone of Sylvia's greeting. "Were you taking a nap, Darling?" she asked making a mockery of the endearment.

"I guess I was," he answered, unsure of the reason behind what appeared to be an attack. "I think I must be confused by the time change." He stretched and ran a hand over his hair as if to straighten it. "Did you enjoy your lunch?"

"No, Darling, I did not enjoy my lunch." This time the sarcasm fairly dripped from the words. "It is very hard to explain to the world that my husband, who has been home less than 24 hours, prefers the office to the company of his wife and son."

John watched Sylvia carefully. He was caught completely off guard by her attack and couldn't think of a response. She crossed the room swiftly the slim skirt of her gray wool suit flared slightly at the knee and created a fashionable silhouette over her shapely legs. "I wonder how much that suit cost." John thought. He smiled slightly at the irrelevance of his thinking. Sylvia turned and caught the smile still on his lips.

"Don't laugh at me, John." Anger sparked her eyes and the green lights flashed across the room. "It may not matter to you, but I'll not have my friends laughing at me and feeling sorry for me."

"I'm sure no one is laughing at you," John said calmly.

"That's a fat lot you know!" Sylvia stamped her foot. John laughed aloud. "Stop it! Stop it right now!"

Annoyance smoldered in his eyes, "You stop it, Syl. You're acting like a child. Why don't you sit down and tell me what's the matter now."

"Matter! You know perfectly well what's the matter. Everyone in the city is talking about us and I won't have it. I won't."

This time John controlled his smile. He realized what a spoiled child she was. A petulant pout shaped her lips and tears trembled in her eyes. "How did I ever choose this spoiled brat to be my wife," he asked himself. "Don't exaggerate, Syl. Everyone in the city is not talking about us. Everyone doesn't know or care about our lives."

"Everyone who counts does and is!"

"Who did you have lunch with?" John asked attempting to get to the truth of Sylvia's complaint.

"I lunched with a friend." She wrung her hands nervously and paced the floor.

"I know that, Syl," John said patiently. "Duncan told me, but what friend? Why are you so concerned about what people might say?""

"I must be more upset by Daddy's illness then I realized." Sylvia's tone changed completely as she smiled as him flirtatiously. She crossed the room swiftly, kissing his cheek as she passed his chair. "I'm just going to run upstairs and change. Pour me a glass of wine would you, Darling. I'll be right back."

The door closed behind her retreating back with a solid click and John stared at it bemused by Sylvia's rapid change. I wonder what she's trying to hide now, he wondered. There was a light tap at the door and Duncan entered with wine and two glasses.

"Mrs. Augustus said you'd want this, sir."

"Put it over there." John waved toward a table. "I'd rather have a cup of good strong American coffee."

"Certainly, sir. Right away." Duncan almost clicked his heels together as he responded to the suggestion. "Will you want anything else?"

"Not now, thank you." John stood up and stretched. It felt good to work the kinks out of his body. The nap had refreshed him, but he wasn't ready for a sparring match with Sylvia, at least not until he was sure what the fight was really about. He went into the bath and slashed water on his face and combed his hair and returned to the study as Duncan entered with the coffee.

"That smells great. Just set it here, please."

"Certainly, sir," Duncan arranged the silver pot and the porcelain cups. He poured a cup and looked at John. "I'm sorry, sir. I don't remember how you like your coffee."

"No reason why you should, Duncan. I drink it black." John accepted the cup from the butler. He examined the delicate design that circled the rim. "Are these new cups?" he asked. "I don't remember having any that were such delicate Chinese porcelain."

"Yes, sir. They only arrived last week. Mrs. Augustus had them made special in Kowloon."

Duncan's animation over the china surprised John, and to encourage him he asked, "Did we buy an entire service?"

"Of course, service for sixteen, the serving pieces and embroidered cloths and napkins. It really makes a lovely table, sir. We used it just the other night when Mr. Phillips dined and he was quite pleased with the table."

"Mr. Phillips? I don't believe I know a Mr. Phillips."

"That will be all, Duncan." Sylvia interrupted. Duncan composed his face into its' accustomed somber lines and the animation drained away.

"Yes, madam." He started for the door.

"Just a moment, Duncan" John's voice, though quiet, had an ominous quality. "Who is this Mr. Phillips?"

Duncan turned and faced John. Not a muscle in his face betrayed emotion, but John noticed his fist clench and flex, a slight wariness crept into his eyes. He answered his voice a careful monotone, "Mr. Mark Phillips, sir."

"Thank you, Duncan. You may go." John waited for Sylvia to say something, but she allowed the heavy silence to linger as she poured herself a glass of wine and settled into a chair. John sipped at his coffee. Still Sylvia didn't speak although John could feel the nervous energy she was putting forth. He decided to wait her out, knowing full well that silence was something Sylvia couldn't stand. He crossed to the window and drew the drape aside. The same small boy he'd seen this morning was just crossing the street into the park with his dog. Twilight hung in the branches of the trees and a thin winter moon appeared as the light faded. It's so peaceful, John thought, so restful and calm. Behind him Sylvia stirred and he allowed the drape to drop.

"I suppose you want to know who Mark Phillips is." She swallowed hard, lifted her chin, and boldly met his gaze.

He shrugged. "I don't suppose I really want to know, but I suppose I must. Who is he?"

"Mark Phillips is a friend of mine." Nervously, she tossed her hair back in a gesture of defiance.

"I gathered as much," John said patiently. "If he weren't your friend, I'm sure he wouldn't have been invited to dinner."

"I have to have friends, John."

"Certainly, we all need friends."

"Don't patronize me." Sylvia's voice flared with anger. "You've been gone almost a year." She strode across the room to fill her glass from the decanter of wine. He watched as tilted the glass and took a long drink.

"You've learned to drink a lot, Syl."

"Don't try to change the subject either."

"I wasn't trying to change anything. I was just making a remark."

"You've got some nerve criticizing anything I do. I'm not the one that went to Europe for an entire year and didn't write even one letter home to his wife. I'm not the one that finally arrives home and doesn't even look at his son. Oh no, I'm not that one." She spate out the words contemptuously. "I'm the one who has to put on a brave front for the friends and relatives, the one who has to pretend that letters came every week and that you asked after your son and wanted to see pictures and hear stories about his growth. I'm the one that had to pretend to know what job you were doing and how it was going." Sylvia paused in her tirade and drained the glass with a second gulp. "I'm the one who stays at home and pretends everything is just fine."

"No one asked you to pretend anything. You choose to act that part."

"Choose? How can you say such a thing?" Sylvia slammed her glass on the table then quickly picked it up and with trembling hands filled it again.

"Sylvia," John explained his voice heavy with irony, "I wanted us to give our marriage a real try. I did everything I could think of to make you happy during your pregnancy but when you gave birth to another man's child that was just too much."

"Stop sounding like a martyr. You aren't exactly blameless you know."

"True." John finished his coffee and continued. "I'm as guilty as you are but for very different acts."

"Different!" Sylvia sputtered indignantly. "Adultery is adultery. Just because you didn't get pregnant doesn't make your affair all right."

"What makes you so sure I committed adultery?"

"Don't make me laugh. Everyone in the city knows that you were running around every night with that slut Valerie Hawkins."

John's fists clenched. The color drained from his face. He glared at his wife. Sylvia saw the hate in his eyes and drew back. Slowly, he forced his fists to uncurl. He paced the floor as he talked, "Valerie is a dear friend of mine, a very dear friend. I wanted very much to share her life and her bed but she wouldn't hear of it. She has standards that you have never thought of. I'm going to tell you this now and this will be the only time we will ever talk about it. Do you understand?"

Mutely, Sylvia nodded. She'd pushed him too far and she knew she wasn't going to like what he had to say. "I do not love you, Sylvia. Perhaps I never did." He shook his head sadly. "God knows, I lusted after you. You are a beautiful woman but I do not love you. I do not trust you and I do not want to share my life with you. I have agreed to remain your husband and I won't break that promise." His icy gaze swept over Sylvia. The contempt he felt was apparent in his voice and in his eyes. "I'll be your husband in the eyes of the world but not within this house. Do you understand?"

She sat, considering her answer, twisting her wedding band around and around on her slender finger. Her green eyes coolly assessed his anger.

"I mean it, Sylvia, we'll settle the rules of this game here and now and then we'll abide by them. If I'm to act as your husband, you will act as my wife."

"I am your wife," she protested.

"Stop it," he slammed his hand against the bar. She jumped. "Just this once, Syl, we are going to talk to each other without lies and without pretending. You are not my wife in any way but name and your child is not my son." John watched her face. "Do you understand?"

"I'm sure I understand. You're angry and probably a little jealous." Sylvia smiled a sweet, seductive smile. She smoothed her skirt and allowed her hand to slide slowly over her silk clad leg. "You needn't be. Mark Phillips is a friend nothing more. Just a friend."

"Syl," John sat down, weary from the emotion. "I don't care who or what Mark Phillips is or was," he said carefully. "We are talking about how we will live this lie of a marriage we have agreed to. I am not jealous. I just don't give a damn. The time for caring is over." He leaned forward and poured himself another cup of coffee. "However, if you are having an affair with him you are not to entertain him or any other lover in this house."

Across the room he could feel Sylvia's tension. He tried to relax as he looked at her beautiful face. His words had caused her to pale, the bright green eyes darted away from his and suddenly seemed more vulnerable then he'd ever seen her look. He steeled his heart and asked again, "Now do you understand?"

"I understand," her voice was pitched so low that the words barely reached his ear.

"Good." John examined the cup he held in his hand as he considered what his next words should be. He knew that she was feeling hurt and frightened. For a second he thought of trying to soften his harsh words but he knew that would do no good. He'd meant what he said. He didn't love her, didn't want to share her life. "We need to talk this out, Syl. Somehow we have to have a working marriage that will fool your father when we go to Charleston, one that will keep the gossip in this city from reaching Walter's ears."

"Why?" Her quiet question shocked John, didn't she understand anything.

"Oh God," he swore.

"Why, John?" Sylvia sat up straighter and set her glass on the table next to the coffee tray. "We stayed married long enough for the two companies to merge, to give my child a name. You did what you needed to do for your grandfather and I did what I needed for the child. Why stay married for even a moment longer?" Excitement caused her words to tumble over one another, "You don't love me and I don't love you. Why not a divorce?"

"We can't divorce, Syl," resignation colored John's voice.

"Can't, John? Of course, we can. Maybe not in this state but one of us could go somewhere else and file. I wouldn't contest and you surely wouldn't. We don't want to be married."

"I need a drink after all. May I fill your glass?"

"Sure," she grinned as she handed him the glass. "We'll drink to our freedom, to our new lives, to our happy future living apart."

John filled the glasses, a straight shot of whiskey for himself, wine for Sylvia. His hand shook and a few drops spilled on the smooth bar top. He wiped them dry, taking the minute to compose himself, then, downing a gulp of the fiery liquid, he faced Sylvia. "If only it were that simple, Syl." He studies the amber liquid in his glass, unable to decide how to tell her what he knew he must say.

"Oh, John," Sylvia's laugh bubbled out. "I'd almost forgotten what a spoil sport you can be. Of course, it's that simple. Why the Horton's were divorced while you were gone and it didn't even cause a ripple. She went to Nevada or Mexico or some such place. I don't remember where, but I'm sure any attorney could tell us what to do." She sprang to her feet. "I'll call Sam right now. He'll know."

"Sit down." The command stopped her. She turned and seeing the frozen expression on his face dropped back into her chair. "I said it's not that simple for us." He strode across the room and stood over her. Anger twisted his features and he appeared to be much older than his years. "You don't have to like what I have to say, Syl, but you have to listen."

He waited for her nod of agreement and then sat down carefully, drew in a deep breath and began. "Do you remember a night, just before I went to Europe, when your father was here for some event?"

"Naturally, that was Michael's christening." Hurt at his forgetfulness put a petulant note in her voice.

"That's right it was." John continued, ignoring her tone. "Alex sent you upstairs with the baby so that he could talk to Walter, Sam and me without you hearing."

Wariness caused Sylvia's eyes to darken. She sat so still in the chair that she scarcely seemed to breathe. "Syl, I'm sorry but your father wants us to stay married."

"Well, my goodness. Of course he does, John." Relief lighted her face as the fear of the unknown drained away.

"It's more than that, Syl. He's changed his will and you can't inherit unless we are married." The words dropped into the room like rocks into a pool of still water. John could see the ripple of disbelief wash over Sylvia. Using both hands she pushed herself up and out of her chair. Silently she poured a glass of wine and lifted her glass toward John in a mock toast.

"Exactly," she spit out the words, "what are you talking about?

"My understanding is that if we divorce the money will be frozen in a trust fund until your child reaches his majority."

"Frozen?"

"Yes. You would be unable to touch anything. It would simply be held and then turned over to your son when he reached whatever age Alex stated in the will."

"But that's not fair," Sylvia protested. "Why would Daddy do a thing like that?"

"I suppose he wants you to be happy and taken care of, that he wants us to stay married." John shook his head. "I don't really know. Why would he do it?"

"It's because of Mama isn't it?"

"What do you mean? How can it have anything to do with your mother?"

"It's our family secret, John. I don't think anyone in Charleston knows the real story about my mother." Tears trembled in her eyes. "I only discovered it by reading some old papers I found in his desk one time."

"She died when you were very young, what does that have to do with this?" John's voice showed his puzzlement.

"She didn't die." The tears spilled over and rolled silently down her cheeks. "She ran off with another man and broke my Daddy's heart." She groped for a handkerchief and John obliged with the one in his breast pocket. "Daddy loved her so much. He found her and the man but all he wanted was for her to be happy so he settled a great deal of money on her. She wasted it all on that man and then he gave her more and she wasted it on another. Over and over, the same thing happened."

Now John understood the strange provisions Alex had insisted upon. He couldn't count the number of times he'd heard Alex mention how much Sylvia reminded him of his wife, how much she looked and acted like her.

Sylvia mopped her eyes. "He loved her so much, so much more then he loves me." Self-pity colored her words.

"Stop that, Syl. You know that he loves you more than life itself. Why, he's always given you everything you ever wanted and more besides."

"That's true." Sylvia smiled slightly as she pushed her tears away and regained her self-confidence.

John watched the transformation of tearful little girl into poised young woman with a slightly cynical half smile. What an actress she is, he thought. I wonder if I've ever really known this woman.

"We're just over reacting, darling. We'll go down to Charleston together and I'll talk to Daddy and tell him that I need this divorce to be happy. Pour me one more glass of wine." She extended her arm gracefully and smiled flirtatiously. "This time we really will drink to our happiness." She saw John's frown and laughed at him. "Don't be an old fuddy-duddy. Everything will be fine. You'll see, my Daddy will give me what I want."

John woke to a pale gray morning. The flowered chintz curtains billowed slightly as the icy wind tried to come through the window he'd opened a crack before going to bed. He grinned at the bright colors, ruffles and flowers that surrounded him. It was an attractive room but certainly not one in which he could be comfortable. He stretched and stuck one foot out of the covers. "Brrr" he shivered and leaped up, pulling on his robe and slamming the window shut.

The radiators rattled and he knew the room would be warm by the time he finished his shower. He whistled, tunelessly, as he showered and shaved, his mood lighter than it had been in a year, certain that Syl was right about being able to convince her father. A child cried in the hallway and a strange woman's voice tried to hush him. John's mood darkened. He addressed himself in the mirror. "It's time for you to meet that kid and face the fact that at least for a few more days it is necessary to act as his father."

He saluted his image and left the room, but once he was out in the hall he hesitated as he realized that he had no idea where to find the child and his nurse. It didn't seem possible that they'd be with Sylvia this early, more likely the nursery. He approached the door and halted, unsure if he should knock or enter. Finally he raised his hand, abruptly the door swung open.

"Oh!"

John grinned at the startled girl. "I didn't mean to frighten you, Miss." He continued to smile as his swift appraising glance took in the trim blue uniform, the starched white apron tied around a tiny waist and the wide blue eyes beneath an untidy mass of bright carrot colored hair. "I'm Mr. Augustus." He extended his hand.

She grasped the offered hand and half shook it as she bobbed in an almost curtsey. "It's me who should be apologizing, Sir. I've a bad habit of not watching where my feet are a goin'. You've come to meet the babe, I'm sure. Do be comin' in." She pushed the door open wide and beckoned. "He's a delightful lad. Good as gold and twice as handsome."

John stepped into the bright nursery and there in the middle of a braided rug sat the child. Not the child, he reminded himself. Michael. Cautiously, he approached the rug and knelt. He gazed at the boy and, silently, the boy looked back. In those long moments they took measure of one another and came to an understanding.

"Hello, Michael." John said softly. Still wide eyed and quiet the boy picked up a bright red block and held it out to John. John accepted, "Thank you," he said. The boy smiled and John smiled in return.

"He likes you, sir." The girl's voice interrupted his survey. He glanced up.

"What did you say your name was?"

"I imagine I forgot to say, what with the surprise of seeing you in the hall and all I'm Annie, sir. Annie Bowen."

"Well, Annie. It's been a pleasure to meet you." John stood and the child's clear gaze followed him. "It's obvious you're doing a fine job with Michael. He seems to be a healthy boy." John brushed at his trouser legs and turned toward the door.

"Would you like to hold him, sir?" John hesitated. "He's not a crier and it seems to me he knows you." Annie attempted to reassure him having misunderstood his hesitation.

"No." The brusqueness of his tone caused her to glance at him in surprise. "Not this time, Annie," he said softening his voice. "Perhaps, next time."

John hurried away, overcome by an intense stomach wrenching wave of emotion. He clenched his shaking hands and forced away the image of the child's trusting gaze. He hurried toward the dining room struggling to gain control of himself.

The coffee he ordered arrived so quickly he knew that Mrs. Peters must have been ready and waiting for his arrival. He thanked her for the thoughtfulness, appreciating the differences between hotel living and being back in his own house. Then he asked, "Has Mrs. Augustus had been down yet?"

"No, sir." answered Mrs. Peters. "She usually has coffee in her room. Would you like your breakfast served now?" John nodded, picking up the paper and opening it. Mrs. Peters remained standing. John looked up.

"Excuse me, Mr. Augustus, but I don't know what you'd like for breakfast."

John sighed. "No, I suppose you don't. I'll have two eggs over easy, bacon very crisp, toast dark, I prefer whole wheat. No jam. If you serve sausage I like that almost burned. Never any cream or sugar in my coffee. Sometimes I like an English muffin instead of toast. Anything else?"

"No, sir. Thank you, sir. I'll have it ready in a few minutes." She paused, her embarrassment flushing her cheeks. "Do you want it served here or in the breakfast room?"

"Breakfast room!" John thundered. "What breakfast room? I grew up in this house and we never had a breakfast room."

"Now, John." Sylvia swept into the room in a long blue, silk morning robe. "We'll eat in the breakfast room, Mrs. Peters." She patted John's arm. "I had the small sun porch off the atrium converted to a breakfast room, Darling. Don't you remember, I wrote you all about it?"

Mrs. Peter escaped the room and John shook off Sylvia's hand. "I don't remember, because you never wrote to me about any such thing. In fact you never wrote to me at all."

"Well then, we're even aren't we, John? You never wrote to me either." She smiled sweetly. "Let's not start the day with a fight."

"This is my home, Sylvia. It has been my home since the day I was born and before that it was my family's home for twenty years. I'm not a stranger here and I won't be treated as one." He glared at her and demanded, "What else have you changed?"

"Not much of anything." Sylvia avoided his eyes and poured a cup of coffee. "A little redecorating, the breakfast room, a bathroom for the nursery, some new appliances in the kitchen."

He struggled to regain a semblance of composure, "Sorry, Syl." "That sounds reasonable enough. It's just that I'm so disoriented, this place doesn't feel like home to me."

"You've been gone a long time, John."

"Just a year."

"True, but some years are longer than others."

John's anger drained away, diluted by her philosophical comment. "You're right. Some years are very, very long." A twist of pain caused his eyes to darken as he thought of Valerie. He brushed it away. "Come on, show me this breakfast room. We'll eat and then I'll call Sam and see if he can tell us what to do about a divorce."

John carried a final cup of coffee with him to the phone in the study. He pushed the door shut for privacy and waited for the operator to connect him to his cousin's house. After several rings the phone was answered by a giggling child. "Good morning."

John felt his face break into a smile at the giggle. "This is your Uncle John. May I speak to your Daddy, please?"

"Are you the one that just flew in a big aeroplane all the way across the ocean?" The child demanded.

"Yes, I am." John answered, amused by the wonder in the child's question.

"Did you look out the window? Could you see the water? How high did you fly? Does it bump when you come down?" The excited questions tumbled out.

John laughed. "Yes, I looked out the window and I could see the water and sometimes a ship. I'm not sure how high we flew but I'll check and let you know, and yes, it bumps a little bit when you come down."

He paused and could hear Helen asking, "Who are you talking with?"

"It's my Uncle John."

"Give me the phone, Chris." And then Helen's laughing voice was directed to him. "Good Morning, John."

"Hi Helen, I take it Christopher has become enamored with the idea of flight."

"Obsessed is more the word. All we hear from him is talk of flying."

"I admit I find it a fascinating subject myself. I'll take him out to the airport with me one day and give him the nickel tour. Okay?"

"He'd love that, John. Did you want to talk to Sam?"

"Yes, if he's available."

"For you? Of course, he is. Hang on a minute and I'll track him down."

John waited again and the faint voices of his cousin's family floated through the wires and reached his ears. He thought longingly of how grand it must be to have a warm, loving wife and family.

"Hi, Cuz. What's happening?"

"Morning, Sam. I need to discuss business with you for a minute."

"Sure. Let me clear a couple of these kids out of here." He made shooing sounds. "Okay, what's on your mind?"

John plunged in, "Syl, and I had a long talk last night. We both want a divorce." Silence answered him. "I agreed to have a child and stay married so that we could achieve the merger. That's done. The child will always bear my name but we want to put an end to this farce."

"John," Sam's somber tone frightened John, "I'm not surprised and I certainly understand but it's not that simple."

"I knew you'd say that. But it is simple. We've talked it over, neither one of us will contest. You must know how to handle the mechanics."

"Sure, I know how to do the paperwork but I think we'd better talk. How about if I come into the city today?"

"Sam, I don't want you to give up your weekend for this."

"Chris wants me to take him in to the museum anyway. I'll drop him there and he can look around for an hour, or so, on his own."

"Are you sure?"

"Natch, I'll be there in about an hour. Okay?"

They rang off. John pondered Sam's words. Something had disquieted him, not the words, perhaps the tone. He went to tell Sylvia that Sam was coming.

John and Sam settled in the study and waited for Duncan to serve coffee and depart. When Duncan was finished Sam's sobered and he started, "Divorce? Are you sure, John?"

"We're sure, very sure. Neither one of us is happy. You know that." He looked at Sam, hoping for a sign of reassurance.

"I know that you're caught in a rather unpleasant experience, Cuz, but I don't think divorce is going to be your answer."

"It's the only answer," John declared, emphatically.

"The one thing every attorney knows is that there is never only one answer." Sam sipped at his coffee and hesitated before asking, "The biggest question that comes to mind is, what about the boy?"

"He's Sylvia's son, not mine."

"Don't be so stubborn." Sam paced the floor in his best courtroom manner. "He bears your name. To the world, and to the courts, he is your son. Like it or not you have agreed to that condition. It's not Michael's fault and he should not suffer due to the peculiarities of birth."

"You sound like a minister," John protested.

"Perhaps, I do see Michael's future and the protection of that future as a moral issue." Sam continued to pace. "He is an Augustus and will need to be raised as such. He will attend the schools, meet the right people and will, one day inherit at least part of the business. You can't deny him those rights."

John waved aside the lecture. "I'm sure he could do those things even if his parents are divorced."

"He might. Then again, a divorce is an awkward thing. One of you will have to be declared at fault."

"Not if we went somewhere else to obtain the divorce."

"That's not true, John. In this state, divorce of a resident is not recognized if it is granted in another state or country."

"One of us can establish residency somewhere else."

Sam continued in his most reasonable way, "Certainly that is a legal possibility, which brings us back to the moral issue. In this city, everyone would know and everyone would talk about the divorce. You would create huge problems for Michael to surmount in the future."

"Huge," John conceded, "but certainly not insurmountable."

"I won't argue with you, Cuz. I'm here to point out the issues and then I want you and Sylvia to talk things over and make your own decisions." He finished his coffee and carefully set the cup on the saucer. "The next issue is money. You are a very wealthy man. I'm sure you'd find it possible to support Sylvia in the style she likes."

"I hadn't thought about that," he hesitated. "Sure, I'd support her until she remarries."

"She might not ever remarry."

"Don't be silly. You know she would."

"I don't know any such thing and neither do you." Sam refilled his coffee and allowed John to think over his statement. "In the eyes of the law, you would be responsible for the welfare of Michael and Sylvia, especially since Alex won't leave anything to Sylvia in the event of this divorce."

John waved that aside. "We're going down to Charleston next week. I've told Syl about Alex's ideas and she's certain she can change his mind."

"I can't disclose the full will to you, John, but since Alex talked to you openly, in my presence, I feel free to tell you that Sylvia receives even less then you think she will if this marriage fails and you should know that a divorce will affect the corporation, too." He began to pace the floor again. "It's a very uncomfortable situation, Cuz. I want you to be happy and I know that you think happiness isn't possible as long as you are married to Sylvia, but life is a strange river full of twists and turns. Think long and hard before you make this move." He looked John squarely in the eye. "Go to Charleston. Talk to your father-in-law. Consider divorce from every angle and then when you come back we'll talk again."

"I won't change my mind, Sam, and neither will Syl. I'll talk to Alex and I'll consider everything carefully but this time I'm going to do what's right for me not just what's right for the mighty Augustus Empire."

"Fair enough, Cuz." Sam ignored the cynicism and held out his hand. "Let's shake on it and then I'd better go gather my son from the museum before he talks them out of a dinosaur."

John extended his hand. "So, Chris is interested in more than just airplanes."

"Christopher is interested in everything," Sam said proudly. "He has what is best described as an inquiring mind. I find it impossible to stay one jump ahead of him. Thank goodness he's old enough now to use the library. I was running out of answers."

They walked to the door and Sam stepped out into the cold wintry air. "Feels like snow." He looked up at the sky and then back at John. "You'll miss a lot of good times if you give up your son, John." He raised his hand in farewell and turned to his car. John closed the door and leaned against it. He felt the impact of Sam's words. Every man wants a son, a son to teach and to raise in his own image. But, he told himself, a son of his own not some other man's son. He pushed away from the door and went to tell Sylvia about his conversation with Sam.

The City Chronicle
November 9, 1938
Tattletales by Sharon Chatsworth

Mr. John Augustus and his wife Sylvia headed south today for a few days of vacation in her hometown, Charleston, South Carolina Mrs. A. wore a stunning traveling costume, consisting of a royal blue suit cut in the distinctive, trim lines of a Dior original. Thrown casually across her shoulders was a white fox stole, a gift from her traveling hubby perhaps?

Chapter 6

Sylvia lay in her made up berth and idly watched the lights of a town flash past. She paid no attention to the rhythmic clack of the train on the track as she prepared the arguments she would use with her father. For as long as she could remember she'd been able to convince Alex to let her do or buy anything she wanted. And, always, she'd planned her attack carefully before approaching him. Sylvia knew that more than anything in the world Alex wanted her to be happy and that knowledge was her most powerful weapon.

This time getting her own way might take some real manipulating but she felt confident that she could win. She considered her wardrobe and decided to wear a full skirted, white wool dress with just a simple string of pearls. For a second she wished she hadn't bobbed her hair, but since she couldn't change the cut she would just brush it out as full as possible and wear only a touch of makeup. Looking a bit pale would help promote the image of unhappy young maiden. Satisfied that her plans were complete and adequate, Sylvia turned away from the window and drifted off to sleep.

John, lying in his berth, found it harder to collect his thoughts. He'd always respected Alex and he knew that this would be a very hard thing to tell him. Divorce was such an ugly word, carrying with it so many unpleasant ideas of wronged women and adulterous men. Not that it's really that way with us, he thought. After all, we both want this divorce. He considered the possible reactions from Alex, anger, hurt, perhaps outrage at the very idea of a divorce in his family. Although, John acknowledged to himself, given the story Syl had told him about her mother and the changes he knew Alex had made to the will it seemed as if Alex had expected something like this to happen. He might know more about his darling daughter then he'd ever been willing to admit to the world. In fact it was likely that at least some of Sylvia's escapades must have reached his ears.

John lit a cigarette and watched the silent land slip past the window. He remembered those days when he'd thought Sylvia daring and full of fun. He wondered when the fun had stopped and where they'd gone wrong. Why one marriage worked and another didn't. Look at Sam and Helen, he thought, they're as happy with one another as they were ten years ago. And then there's Michael. He's a good enough kid, but he's not mine. He swung his long legs over the side of the berth and stood up carefully in the small space. He pulled on his jacket and went to the club car for a drink, sure that he needed something to stop his thoughts if he wanted to get any sleep.

Early the next morning the train entered Charleston. John joined Sylvia, Michael and Annie moments before it jolted to its final stop. If Annie noticed anything strange or unusual about the Mr. and Mrs. emerging from separate compartments, she wisely held her tongue and kept busy with the child. The glorious autumn morning touched their cheeks with a remembered hint of summer warmth. A breeze rustled the leaves that were only beginning to turn red and gold here in the south. The porter handed John down. He turned and helped Sylvia and then Annie with the child held in her arms. They looked the perfect picture of a happy prosperous family.

Aware of the watching eyes, Sylvia daintily tucked her hand through John's crooked arm and smiled up at him. "I'm sure Daddy sent a car for us. He knew we were coming in today." She searched the platform for the familiar face of her father's driver. A tug of anxiety pulled her mouth into a pout. "Do you suppose he forgot?"

"I'm sure they remembered, Syl." John disentangled his arm from her touch. "Perhaps the train was early or Rufus is late."

"Rufus is never late." She glanced up at the town hall clock, high on the tower across the street from the platform. "And the train is exactly on time. Something's wrong. I can feel it."

Annie crossed herself at the fearful words. Sylvia glared at her. "Now don't start that. You'll make something bad happen."

John laughed. "Sylvia, calm down. Rufus will be here in a minute and if he's not we'll take a cab."

"Don't you dare laugh at me, John. Something's wrong and I know it." Her voice rose sharply.

"Find a cab and let's go. I can't stand to wait another moment."

John started to respond with anger to her demanding tone, but noting the way she clasped her hands in tight fists at her sides he swallowed the bitter words and tried to smile reassuringly. "Good idea." He glanced around the rapidly emptying platform and signaled to a red cap. "Take this luggage and get us a cab, please," he ordered.

The black man, splendid in his uniform, touched his cap and quickly loaded the leather luggage onto his pushcart. "Right this way, sir." He stepped out smartly and the small entourage followed, John and Sylvia walking apart, Annie trailing with the child.

Once they were settled in the cab, Sylvia sat tense and visibly trembling. Her obvious fear affected Annie who appeared ready to cry. Michael began to fuss and squirm. John, unsure of what to do or say, turned to the window and silently watched as the streets of Charleston went past. They rounded the last curve. Sylvia sat up straighter and directed the driver to make the sharp turn between the high stone gateposts. The drive continued across sweeping green lawns and beneath old magnolia trees, Annie breathed in with a small gasp as she realized the splendor of the Alexander mansion.

A full three stories high the house sat like a high, wide, heavily trimmed, wedding cake glistening in the sun. Tall pillars graced the wide verandah and supported the slopping roofs. Late blooming flowers were massed in planters and repeated in the gardens. Everything had a quiet air of expensive elegance. The cab slowed to a stop. Sylvia clamored out and ran up the elegant stairs and across the verandah. She flung open the door, heedless of its' beveled glass inset. "Daddy!" she called. "I'm home, Daddy."

John thrust money into the cabbie's hand and hurried after. He entered the house as Sylvia started up the graceful front stairway. She stopped in mid stride as Mammy appeared at the top of the stairs, her face sober and tear streaked. Sylvia's hands rose to cover her face. She sobbed once and collapsed in a dead faint. John struggled to catch her, holding her in his arms he faced Mammy, the unspoken question loud in the room.

"He's gone, sir." Mammy began to cry again. "Not more than five minutes ago he just looked at me, said, 'Tell Sylvia I love her' and he died. Died just like that." Sobs racked the poor old woman's body.

John struggled to find words to say that could bring her comfort and found the only possible combination, "Miss Sylvia needs you, Mammy."

She pulled herself together. "Oh, my poor little girl," she said through her tears. "Bring her up here to her room, Mr. John. I'll get a cloth for her head. She'll be coming to in a moment." Mammy bustled ahead and pulled back the pale blue silk coverlet. "You just slip off her shoes, Mr. John, and I'll be right back."

John did as he was told. In this house Mammy's orders were never ignored. She'd been with Sylvia since her birth and John knew how deep and strong her love for Sylvia ran. He sat quietly as Mammy bathed Sylvia's face and crooned soft words of comfort. Sylvia stirred slowly. Her eyes opened and she looked about in confusion. She started up but laid back at Mammy's murmuring, "There, there, I's here, Baby."

"Mammy?"

Yes, Lovey?"

"Daddy's ..." Sylvia was unable to continue.

"He's gone, Baby. Gone to heaven with the angels now." Mammy's gentle hand stroked Sylvia's forehead in a tender caress. Tears gathered in Sylvia's eyes and softly overflowed. She cried silently, without sobbing. Her misery was so acute that John could feel her pain. He moved to the bed and laid his hand against her cheek.

"I'm sorry, Syl, so sorry."

Her green eyes, clouded with sorrow, searched his face. "We were too late, John, too late."

"It's all right, Syl." John tried to comfort her. "Your father knew you loved him."

Sylvia shook her head, "Too late," she whispered and turned her face into the pillow.

A child's cry reminded John of Annie and the boy still waiting in the entry hall. Mammy, too, realized that they were waiting. She looked at John, torn by her desire to do what was right and by her desire to stay with her beloved child.

"I'll go, Mammy. You stay with Miss Sylvia."

"Thank you." Mammy smiled her old lined face lighting with gratitude at his understanding. "I made up the beds in the nursery for young Michael and his nurse and I's sure that cook will be in the kitchen if'n they hungry."

"I'll take care of it, Mammy." He squeezed her shoulder gently.

"Did you call the doctor?"

"Rufus did. He should be along directly." Sylvia stirred and Mammy turned back to her charge. "There, there, everythin' is goin' to all right, Baby."

John slipped out of the room and closed the door gently behind him but not before he heard Sylvia say, tearfully, "Nothing's ever going to all right again, Mammy."

The crying in the lower hall turned to wails of despair. John hurried down the wide stairway unsure exactly how to handle what must be done but knowing that he'd have to take care of things at least for the time being.

Annie stood rocking the wailing child, looking scarcely more than a child herself. Her wide trusting eyes were filled with tears as she asked, "What should I do now, sir?"

"What's wrong with the boy?"

"Nothing's wrong." Annie spoke defensively, tucking Michael's head more securely into her shoulder. "I think he's just hungry and a little afraid in this strange house."

"Well, let's get him some food and see that he's settled." John smiled warmly at Annie. "I imagine you'd like to get settled yourself."

He led the way across the foyer and into the dining room. The bright sun sparkled through the cut glass of the high chandelier and tossed bright rainbow hued reflections on the highly polished table and over the beautiful place settings. The table had been laid with the best china, ready to welcome the travelers after their trip.

Annie half sobbed and John paused to examine her. "It's just so sad," she said, her voice breaking. "The house is ready for a party and now it's a death that we have instead."

"He was an old man who'd lived a full and very good life," John said carefully, aware that the words were trite at best and might even sound cold to the young girl. "He'd been very ill, you know."

"I know, sir, but it's so sad."

John nodded. "Come on. The kitchen's right through here. The boy needs his breakfast."

The doorbell chimed as John reached to open the door. "That'll be the doctor." He hesitated.

"You go, sir," Annie said. "We'll be all right."

"Someone else will get it."

As if in response to his words the door swung open and a young black maid hurried through. She jumped, surprised to see them in the dining room. Looking back over her shoulder, she called, "Mrs. Murphy. Mr. John and Miss Sylvia are here."

Mrs. Murphy bustled out, her broad Irish face smiling at the sight of the child. "You get the door, Drusilla. Welcome back, Mr. John." She reached for Michael. "Give me the wee thing, miss. You look ready to drop."

Recognizing a woman who knew what to do, Annie relinquished the child and followed Mrs. Murphy into the kitchen. Mrs. Murphy called back over her shoulder, "Go on, girl. Answer the door. It'll be the doctor, I'm sure."

"I'll go, Drusilla." John smiled at the frightened young girl. "Is Mr. Alexander's body in his room?"

"Yes, sir. Thank you, sir." Her brown eyes flashed her relief at being removed from the task of escorting the doctor to the dead man's body.

"Mammy is with Miss Sylvia in her room. Perhaps you could go up and see if they need anything." John suggested as he hurried to the door.

The day passed as John made the decisions about the funeral and burial. Sylvia stayed in her room with Mammy hovering close. He was able to forget about Annie and Michael secure in the knowledge that Mrs. Murphy had taken them under her wing and would keep them out of the way.

Late that evening John looked in on Sylvia and found her alone. She smiled wanly and motioned for him to enter. "Hello, John," her voice sounded thin and strained, stretched by her tears.

He sat down on a pale yellow velvet slipper chair and stretched out his long legs. "How are you doing?" he asked kindly.

"We were too late," she said not answering his question.

"He knew you loved him, Syl. And he knew we were coming. Mammy said his last words were for you."

Sylvia waved her hand impatiently. "That's not what I meant." She sat up and adjusted a pillow behind her head. Her fair hair was tousled and her eyes questioned him as she spoke. "I know he loved me, John. I've always known that. In fact," her fingers played nervously with the edge of the silken coverlet, "I was counting on that remember?"

His initial surprise was quickly replaced by understanding, "You mean we were too late to talk to him about the will, don't you?"

"Exactly." She smiled, allowing her lips to turn up only the slightest amount. "Don't think me evil, John. I loved him but I needed him to change that will and now it's too late."

"Perhaps it's not as bad as we've imagined."

"Do you think so?" Renewed interest brightened her face. She slid down the pillow and cuddled the thick quilted silk under her chin. "I'll bet it'll be okay. Daddy wouldn't do anything to make me unhappy."

John's face flushed as he realized the selfishness of her words. She wasn't thinking of Alex's death at all, only of her own inheritance. Somehow Sylvia always managed to astound him.

"When will they read the will, John?"

He stood and paced the floor. Pausing at the mantel, he pretended to admire a Dresden figure of a girl in a hoop skirt. When he had regained control of his annoyance, he set the figure down and replied, "The funeral will be day after tomorrow and the will can be read any time after that. Sam will arrive on the morning train and he'll take care of those arrangements."

"Try to get him to do it as soon as he can, Darling." She smiled brightly. "I don't want to sound crass, but the sooner we can end this farce the happier I'll be."

John's contempt rose in his throat like bile. A light tap sounded at the door.

"Come in," Sylvia called, once again sounding wane and bereaved. Mammy pushed the door open with one ample hip and balanced a tray on the other. "I's brought you a bite to eat, Baby." She placed the tray on a small table and helped Sylvia to a sitting position. "Just some biscuits and ham and a little of this and that from the kitchen. You sit up now and eat some of this. You goin' to need to keep your strength up."

"Yes, Syl," John agreed, his voice heavy with sarcasm. "You need to keep your strength up. I'll drop in later."

Alone in his room John faced the unpleasant facts. Alex was dead, the will had most likely not been changed and if it hadn't how could they go ahead with a divorce. I'll talk to Sam and my mother tomorrow, he decided, they are the two most sensible people I know. He stretched out on the bed and fell at once into a deep sleep.

John went with Rufus to meet the early train. He was relieved to see the friendly faces of not only

Minette and Sam but that of Walter, too. He hugged his mother and shook hands with the men. "Thanks for coming down."

"Somehow I always thought I'd go first," Walter mused in the car. "Alex was still a young man, not more than sixty-five, was he?"

"Sixty-seven, Grandfather," John smiled gently at Walter "and not as young, in most ways, as you."

"Flattery," Walter scoffed.

"It's true." Minette reached for Walter's hand. "You are not old."

"Well, death makes me feel old, especially death of a man almost twenty years younger." His face sobered. "How's Sylvia holding up?"

"She's fine," John answered coldly.

"Fine?" Walter's keen eyes probed his face.

"Of course, she's upset but she's bearing up well," John tried to cover his lapse.

"Good," Walter nodded as if his impressions were confirmed.

John searched for a way to change the subject. He looked helplessly at this mother and she caught his unspoken plea. "He'd been ill for several months," she said calmly as though they were continuing a conversation. "Sylvia mentioned how worried she was just the other night, the night you came home from Europe, and while even an expected death is unpleasant, I'm sure it must be easier than if she'd had no warning."

"Sylvia was very close to her father," Walter said, sternly. "I sincerely hope you are giving her the support she needs."

"I'm giving her all the support she'll accept, Walter. She's not been neglected."

"Neglect isn't what I was speaking of there are always enough people to give Sylvia attention. I want to know if you are able to let the past be forgotten and stand beside her as a husband should?"

"That is none of your business." Anger turned his words to chips of ice.

"He's right, Walter," Sam interrupted, attempting to make peace. "Let's drop this topic."

"Sorry, John," Walter shrugged slightly as he accepted the reprimand. "Forgive an old man for interfering."

John nodded, curtly.

"What can I do to help?" Sam stepped into the silence with his question.

"All the arrangements have been made. The funeral is tomorrow." John kept his eyes on Sam refusing to look at this grandfather. "I'm sure there are some legal details you'll need to work out. Sylvia is quite anxious to talk to you about the reading of the will."

"I'll speak to Alex's attorney here in Charleston and get the ball rolling. The business won't be affected at all. We had everything drawn up very clearly when we set up AmCo."

"I think Sylvia is more interested in the personal details."

"I'm sure she is," Sam agreed.

"I'd like to be busy, too." Minette chimed in. "What is there for me to attend to?"

"There'll be a million people in and out of the house in the next two days and I'm sure you'll be kept busy attending to the visitors, Mother. Mrs. Murphy is a good cook and a great housekeeper but I'm sure she'll need your organizational skills."

"Won't Sylvia want to attend to those things?" Minette asked, puzzled at the request.

"I doubt it very much. She'll want to take the credit, but she'd much rather someone else handle the details."

Walter grunted, a disapproving sound, but kept his counsel and didn't join in the conversation. The big car swept on and soon they were delivered to the Alexander house. Drusilla appeared in the entry, ready to show them to their rooms.

"I'd like to talk to you a moment, Mother," John requested.

"Certainly, come with me to me room and we'll have a chat right now." She held out her hand and John took her warm fingers into his own. They went up the stairs hand in hand, their friendship as apparent as their kinship. Drusilla offered to unpack but Minette told her to leave everything and come back later.

Minette's gentle smile soothed John as he said, "I feel better already, just knowing you're here." He sighed and took a deep breath. "You look terrific, Mother." He examined her well cut navy suit and realized that his mother was still a beautiful woman. "If I didn't know you were my mother, I'd swear you weren't a day over thirty-five."

Minette laughed, the delighted sound ran up the scale and John laughed with her. "Thank you, John." Minette tilted her head and kissed his cheek. "Now that's enough small talk, sit down and tell me what's on your mind."

Minette seated herself on a small damask covered love seat, one shapely leg curled under her body. She waited patiently as John found a comfortable place on the wide window seat. He fiddled with the drape and then with the plump pillows, piled on the window seat. Finally he plunged in, "I need your advice, well maybe not your advice, but I need to tell you some things." Minette nodded, smiling her encouragement. "Sylvia and I came down here to talk to Alex about his will."

"His will?" Minette straightened her legs and folded her hands in her lap.

"Yes, I know that sounds cold hearted but that's why we rushed down. Before I went to England, Alex told me he was changing his will so that Syl wouldn't inherit unless we stayed married but now that I've been gone a year and come back we know that we want to end this marriage." John watched the emotions chase rapidly across his mother's face but she stayed silent, waiting for him to go on. "We got here too late. Syl is beside herself with anger. She was sure she could get Alex to rewrite the will."

"I'm not sure I understand what this will has to do with getting a divorce."

"Everything," John stood and began to pace back and forth across the beautiful Persian carpet "absolutely everything. Sure, I could afford to support Syl but if I insist on a divorce she'll lose out on her inheritance."

"What about Michael?"

"Oh, I suppose I'm obligated to support him, too." John waved his hand indifferently. "After all my name is on his birth certificate."

"John." The command in Minette's tone stopped John's pacing. "Sit down somewhere and look at me." Obediently, John returned to the window seat and faced his mother. "Are you trying to tell me that Michael isn't your son?" He nodded. "Are you sure?" Minette scarcely paused as she continued, "Excuse that question. Of course, you're certain or you'd never have said such a thing."

Minette sat perfectly still, her head cocked in a gesture that John recognized from childhood. "I'm not really surprised, in fact I should have realized what was going on, but I think that this is definitely a skeleton that the family should keep in the closet. Michael is a child, a dear, bright, friendly child and the sins of his family shouldn't rest on his shoulders."

"I know that, Mother. And I agree. I've promised to acknowledge him. To the world he'll always be my son. I'll do everything I can to assure that he has a good childhood, that he attends the right schools and is always acknowledged as an Augustus."

"Oh, John," sadly Minette shook her head. "None of that will matter if the child doesn't have love."

"Don't be melodramatic, Mother. He'll have plenty of love."

"I hope so."

"I'm concerned now about how to handle the next couple of days." John resumed pacing the floor. "Syl is fine. I'm sure she'll do all the right things at the funeral but after the will is read I've got to be ready for her."

"Ready for her?" Minette questioned his strange choice of words.

"Well, she's not going to like it if the money and power of the Alexander fortune by passes her somehow."

"No, I suppose not." Minette considered the thought. "I'm sure she'll be upset but..."

"Not upset, Mother, she's going to be furious. She'll want to fight the will. She'll try to break it and she'll blame me for all of the problems."

"Now, look who's being melodramatic. You can't be held responsible for her father's will."

"In the seven years we've been married I've been personally responsible for everything from the sunrise to the breaking of a heel on her favorite shoes. I can be equally as responsible for good as I can for bad but I'm held accountable much more frequently for bad. It's been my experience that I get credit for good things only when Syl wants something."

Minette shook her head, sadly. "How bitter you sound."

"Bitter?" Irony tinged his voice. "I guess I do sound that way and I suppose I am." He crossed to his mother and sat beside her on the elegant settee. She extended her hand and he gave her his. "I guess I'm feeling sorry for myself. I can see all my hopes and plans disappearing before my eyes and I feel guilty because I'm feeling sorry for myself when I should be thinking of Alex."

"My poor boy," Minette brushed his hair back from his forehead with her free hand. "You're only human, of course, you think of yourself first. Don't waste your time brooding about things that may not happen." She squeezed his hand. "I'll go and talk to Sylvia. It sounds to me like she may need to talk to another woman."

Minette stood up and smoothed her skirt and adjusted her jacket. "Come," she commanded. "Show me her room."

"Thanks, Mother." John hugged her close. "I can always count on you to calm me down and to be absolutely sensible."

"That's the French in me," Minette grinned.

John laughed. Suddenly he thought of Lillian Rathborne. "I met a woman on the plane," he said. Minette raised an eyebrow. "Not that kind of woman," he smiled. "A very warm and wise old woman, you reminded me of her."

"I'll assume you mean the warm and wise part not the old."

They laughed together, bringing thoughts of his childhood to John. Minette had always been ready to laugh at him and with him. She'd never been the kind of mother who mistook boyhood pranks for serious business, that wasn't to say she hadn't been strict but somehow she'd always recognized the times when understanding was needed not punishment. John smiled down at her his eyes alight with love. "I'm glad you're my mother," he said.

"Thank you, John," she answered, her eyes as serious as his tone. "I've always enjoyed being your mother. I'm proud of you and of everything you are." She stood on her tiptoes and kissed his cheek. Tears sparkled in her violet eyes and she blinked them away. "The French are also too emotional," she said.

Minette reached for John's hand and swung it gently as they walked down the wide hall. Their feet made no sound on the thick Oriental runner. Sunlight danced in motes of dust and somewhere an open window emitted the smell of burning leaves. They reached Sylvia's open door and looked at each other in amazement, surprised by the sight that greeted them. Dresses were draped over chairs and the bed, they hung from the curtain rods and floated from the lamps. Sylvia sat cross legged on the floor examining boxes of shoes. A small hat with a long black veil was perched backward on her tousled hair. Minette laughed aloud. Sylvia dropped the shoe and sprang to her feet.

"Minette," she cried "you're exactly the person I need."

"It looks to me that what you need is a dress shop in which to hang these garments." Minette stepped over a pile of discarded garments and looked around. "Whatever are you doing?"

"Choosing clothes, of course," she gave Minette a quick hug and waved her hand in a wide sweep. "I woke up this morning and realized that I didn't have a single suitable thing to wear." She picked up a slim gray dress and held it against her body, checking the effect in the mirror. "Do you think I'll have to wear black long, Minette?" She dropped the gray carelessly on the carpet and picked another garment to examine. "Black just isn't my best color."

Minette stooped and retrieved the discarded dress carefully she smoothed it and hung it on a hanger. "I'm sure no one will think ill of you if you choose to wear something other than black."

Sylvia laughed. "If you really think that, you don't know the south. Why the little old ladies in this town would never forgive me for such a thing. They'd hold it against me for years and pass it on from one generation to the next. No sir! I need to wear black for the funeral and probably for a year at least."

"It'll give you a chance to do some serious shopping," John said sarcastically.

"Yes," Sylvia answered, missing his contempt. "I'll have to buy practically everything. Why I don't think I even own a decent black slip."

John caught Minette's eye and shrugged. She raised one eyebrow and he caught the glint of mischief in her glance. "I'm sure you have plenty to do, John." Minette suggested. "Why don't you go ahead and I'll help Sylvia with all this."

Relieved, John closed the door as Minette asked, "How in the world did you get such a large selection of clothes sent in such a short time?"

Sylvia surveyed the room. "I just called the best stores and told them that I needed to see everything they had in stock that was my size and suitable for mourning and this," she waved her hand "is what they sent."

Minette laughed. "I suppose it helps that they all knew your father, but I do find it to be incredible that you have assembled this collection of clothing without leaving the room and by nine-thirty in the morning."

"Well, I needed a few things to wear during these next days and seemed like a practical way to get things. After all it wouldn't be right for me to be seen out shopping until Daddy is buried."

"I'm sure you're right." Minette struggled to keep the laughter out of her voice. It might be selfish for Sylvia to be so preoccupied with clothes but it certainly was practical.

Minette busied herself straightening and folding the rejects as they were dropped casually here and there. She watch Sylvia hold up first one dress and then another. She managed to comment on each, but her mind was busy trying to think of some way to approach the matter of the will and the divorce. Sylvia settled on a plain black suit with a gray silk blouse with a chic hat and veil to wear to the funeral, a soft black wool jersey that lightly skimmed her curves to wear to the viewing, two black dinner dresses, one silk and the other organza, three simple afternoon dresses each black but each different and cut to accentuated her femaleness. "Do you think this will be enough?" she asked seriously. "I'm not impressed with the blouses they sent but perhaps I should choose at least a couple more to wear with this suit." Minette remained quiet. She knew the questions were merely rhetorical as Sylvia thought aloud. "Yes," Sylvia agreed with herself, "I'll take these blouses and this sweater."

She sank down on the edge of the bed and smiled up at Minette. "There," she sighed "that's done. Thanks for your help. I hate to shop alone."

"Should we box the rest of these things?" Minette asked.

"Oh, don't bother. Mammy will take care of it." Sylvia jumped up. "Let's go downstairs and get some breakfast, I just realized that I'm starving."

"I'd like to see Michael," Minette requested tentatively.

"Sure. He's with Annie in the old nursery, I think." Sylvia leaned into the mirror as she brushed her hair with an ivory backed brush. She examined her makeup and adjusted the seams in silk stockings. "We'll eat and then you can go see him." She giggled. "I haven't seen him myself since we arrived."

Minette followed Sylvia from the room. She was reminded of the months when John had been a baby and of her own obsession with never letting him out of her sight. I suppose I'm old fashioned, she thought, but it seems strange that a mother would stay away from her child when the poor little thing is in a strange place surrounded by unfamiliar people and things. But, she reminded herself, Sylvia has just lost her father and perhaps she's not thinking as clearly as she appears to be, perhaps she's unable to cope with her child right now. Aloud she asked, "Is Annie good with Michael?"

"Good?" Astonishment sharpened Sylvia's voice. "I'd say wonderful, excellent, and marvelous! She's much better than merely good."

"You're really lucky to have found someone so perfect. Many people complain about the help they are able to get."

"Yes, Annie is a jewel. She keeps Michael so busy I sometimes forget that he's in the house."

Minette stopped in mid stride. Sylvia realized that her words had shocked Minette and she laughed shrilly. "I didn't mean that the way it sounded. I only meant that she is able to keep him so content that we seldom hear him cry."

"Of course," Minette murmured. They continued down to the dining room, Sylvia chattering about the dresses she had chosen and Minette not hearing a word as she ruminated on the words Sylvia had let slip. Poor child, she mused, a father that doesn't claim you and a mother that can forget you are in the house. What kind of an existence is that for a child? Something will have to be done to bring John to his senses. Having resolved her thoughts, Minette entered the dining room with Sylvia.

Walter and Sam were seated at the large oval table, a country breakfast spread out before them. Walter rose gallantly. He crossed to Sylvia and held out his arms. "I'm so sorry, my dear," he said. "Your father was a good man and I shall miss him greatly as I know you shall."

Sylvia stepped into his hug and laid her head on Walter's shoulder. Her eyes filled with tears and Minette heard her breath catch in a sob. Walter heard, also. He patted her back, "There, there, child. Everything will be all right. You've a fine husband and a beautiful child of your own."

"I know," Sylvia agreed as she stepped back and dabbed at her eyes with a lace trimmed hanky she produced from her pocket. "It's just that I miss him so. I can't imagine life without Daddy."

What an actress, Minette thought. Only a minute ago she was chattering away about food and clothes. She caught Sam's eye and realized that he hadn't been taken in by Sylvia's act either. But it was obvious Walter was captivated and at the moment it was Walter for whom Sylvia was performing.

Gallantly, he held her chair accepted her teary thanks. Minette noticed that despite the pale, droopy appearance Sylvia was presenting she helped herself to eggs, grits, sausage and a large country biscuit.

Between bites, Sylvia turned to Sam and asked, "When do you think the reading of Daddy's will can take place?"

"I imagine your father's attorney will decide the details but I'm sure you won't have to wait long," Sam spoke carefully, keeping the irritation from his voice.

"Good." Sylvia sipped at her coffee. "Perhaps I should call Mr. Patterson and tell him we'd like to clear up the details as quickly as possible so that we can get back to the city."

"There's no rush, Sylvia," Walter reassured her. "John is free to stay here with you as long as is necessary."

"Thank you, Walter," Sylvia beamed at him. "But I know he'll be anxious to get back to the city and to the office. And," she sighed, "this house just isn't the same without Daddy. I'm afraid I'd miss him more here in the midst of my memories."

Walter reached across the table and patted her hand. "I understand." He looked at Sam. "Why don't you call this Patterson fellow right after breakfast and see if you can hurry things up a bit. Some of these southerners move rather slowly."

"Sure," Sam agreed. "I'd planned to call him anyway but I don't think he'll be willing to see me until after the funeral. He's a very formal old gentleman."

"After the funeral, naturally, but perhaps the day after instead of the week after."

Sam took a bite of his biscuit swallowing his annoyance along with the butter and honey. Minette caught his eye and cocked her eyebrow as she, too, took a bite of biscuit.

"The funeral is tomorrow morning and as soon after as you can arrange it would be fine, Sam." Sylvia turned her tearful gaze on him. "I'd really appreciate it if you can hurry things along so we can get it over with." She shuttered slightly. "It's all so morbid. The sooner done the better, I think."

Greedy little monster, Sam thought. I wonder how she'll feel when she finds out the terms of the will. Poor John.

"Is something wrong?" Walter asked catching Sam's expression.

"No, just thinking."

"Good." Walter laughed. "Attorneys are supposed to be thinking all the time."

Sam scarcely smiled at the joke. He swallowed the last of his coffee and pushed back his chair. "If you'll excuse me, I'll go make that phone call now."

"Let me know what he says, Sam," Sylvia instructed him. "I'd like to be able to make some plans."

I bet you would, Sam thought, but he kept his face blank as he nodded his agreement. Sam entered the library and closed the door behind him. He didn't want to take the chance that someone might overhear his conversation with Mr. Patterson. Postponing the moment that he dreaded, Sam crossed to the wide windows and looked out across the rolling lawn. Rufus was pruning a hedge, a large black dog frolicking around his legs. Sam could hear Rufus laugh as he shooed the dog away. The peaceful scene helped him collect his thoughts and reminded him that it was true that it took all kinds to make up the world. Sylvia wouldn't be pleased but he'd get the reading of this will over with as quickly as he could. Let her know the truth, and John, too, for that matter, and then they could make up their minds about divorce. He picked up the phone and asked the operator to connect him.

John stood in the corner of the viewing room and watched Sylvia. She wore the black jersey gown she'd chosen that morning. Her hair was pulled back in a severe style that somehow gave her a vulnerable look. He admired the picture of a bereaved maiden that she was able to present.
"She should be an actress." John jumped, startled by the words that echoed his own thoughts. He looked down into sparkling blue eyes that flashed at him from beneath pure white hair. "I'm Abigail Hoffman." She extended a callused, tan hand. "I know you probably don't know the name, but I wanted to tell someone in the family what a fine man Alex was and how sorry I am to see him go. It's a loss not only to me but to the entire community."
"Thank you, Mrs. Hoffman. I'll tell Sylvia you expressed your condolences."
"It's Miss not Mrs., and don't bother." The woman eyes darkened as she glanced across the room at Sylvia. "Good luck, young man. You'll need it married to that one."

Before John could think of an appropriate answer the woman spun on her heel and strode out of the viewing room. He watched surprised by the agile, youthful movement. What a strange woman, he thought.

All evening people came and went in rapid succession. It seemed as though the entire city of Charleston had turned out to pay their respects to Alex. Sylvia smiled gracefully and accepted condolences. John stayed by her side and gave the impression of being a supportive husband. During a brief lull he brought her a cup of coffee and commented, "I'm amazed at the way you can call all of these people by name, Syl."

She flashed her smile, "In the south, John, children are taught manners above and beyond anything else. Besides most of these old biddies haven't changed in twenty years they still wear the same dresses they wore when I first learned to curtsey to them."

"I know this is hard, but you really are handling it extremely well."

Sylvia let her guard down for a moment and John caught a glimpse of her sadness. "Thank you, John," she said gratefully. "I'll be glad when tomorrow is over."

"I know you will." He pulled her close to his side in a friendly half hug. "Hang in there, old girl. It's only a couple more hours and we can go home and have a very large glass of brandy."

Another elderly couple approached them and John dropped his arm. Sylvia moved away with them and Sam appeared at John's side. "Do you want to step outside and talk for a second, Cuz?"

"Sure."

They walked out and leaned against the brick wall of the funeral parlor. "Lot of people here tonight,"

John commented. "Alex was a real leader in this city." Sam drew out a pack of cigarettes. They lit up and inhaled deeply and exhaled slowly.

"I finally talked to Mr. Patterson this afternoon." John waited. "It's all set. He didn't want to do it but he agreed to come out to the house tomorrow at seven to read the will."

"Seven," John agreed. "Sylvia will be glad. She was just saying how happy she'd be when tomorrow was over."

"I'm not so sure she'd going to be glad at all. In fact I'd bet on the fact that she'll be very displeased."

John studied his cousin's face. "What's in this will anyway?"

"I'm not positive." John looked unconvinced. "I mean it, John," Sam protested. "I haven't been privy to the full facts. I didn't write the final will only that one small statement that Alex asked for just before you went to Europe. But I can guess what the statement meant and what other provisions would need to be included in order to bind the money as securely as he appeared to want it bound."

John finished his cigarette and ground it out beneath his heel. "That bad, huh?" He shook his head, sadly. "Well, we'll just have to wait and see tomorrow, won't we? I'd better get back inside or as I keep being reminded, people will begin to talk."

"Right, Cuz." Sam slapped him lightly on the back. "I'll do anything I can to help. You know that don't you?"

"I know Sam."

The City Chronicle
November 12, 1938
Tattletales by Sharon Chatsworth

It is with great sorrow that this reporter shares with you news of the death of Stanley "Alex" Alexander. Mr. Alexander died quietly in his sleep on November 9th. He was the sole owner of the Alexander Shipbuilding Corporation which merged last year with Augustus Industries, of this city, to become Amalgamated Manufacturing. Mr. Alexander was known for his many philanthropic donations to the arts both in our city and in his native Charleston, South Carolina. Funeral services were held November 11 at Christ Episcopal Church of Charleston. Internment followed immediately at Church Cemetery. He is succeeded by his daughter Sylvia Alexander Augustus and by his grandson, Michael Augustus. Our sympathy reaches out to the Augustus family in this time of great sorrow.

Chapter 7

Sylvia sat on the sofa and listened intently to the opening lines of her father's will. The words sounded onerous in the quiet room. Alex really is dead, she thought, dead and buried. Tears gathered in her eyes and threatened to overcome her composure. She fought against them and concentrated on the room.

Nothing had changed in her entire lifetime. The beautiful Persian rug with its soft blues and reds seemed no more faded then it had ever been. This sofa was newly redone but once again it had been upholstered in thick, deep blue damask. Her glance swept the room. The same paintings hung in the same places, a portrait of her mother over the mantel, her own bridal portrait, in an ornate gold frame, on the piano. Absent-mindedly she compared the two pictures. Her father had been right, the resemblance was very strong. The girl in the portrait was merely a shadow of the woman but the face she saw in the mirror each morning looked much the way her mother did in the painting. It's because I'm getting older, she realized. Her lips tilted in a cynical half smile and she turned her attention back to Mr. Patterson.

His voice droned on through the many small bequests. Her thoughts wondered away again as she waited for the important bequests to begin. I'll miss him, she thought. Daddy was always so good to me. I hardly noticed that I didn't have a mother. In fact, she decided, not having a mother was kind of romantic and fun. A change in Mr. Patterson's tone captured her attention.

"To my faithful man, Rufus Lincoln Jones, I leave the sum of five thousand dollars and an income for the rest of his life of five thousand dollars per year and the 1937 Lincoln."

"Thank you, sir." Rufus drew out the sir in a heartfelt rolling of the r.

"To Mattie Matthews, my grateful thanks for the devotion she has shown while raising my daughter and my appreciation for the love she has showered on this family for thirty years. I leave to her the sum of five thousand dollars and an income for the rest of her life of five thousand dollars per year. In addition, I request that the executor of this will buy for her the most beautiful fur coat they can find."

Mammy burst into tears and sobbed loudly. "Bless you, Mr. Alex," she cried, raising her eyes heavenward. Sylvia went to her and hugged her close patting her back and hushing her, the way Mammy had quieted her tears so many times.

When a sense of order had been restored, Mr. Patterson resumed. Ahem," he cleared his throat "the next is a rather long list of charities. I'll pass over them at this time if no one has an objection." He looked over the top of his gold rimmed glasses and waited. Sylvia nodded and he continued, "To my dearest friend and companion, Abigail Hoffman, I leave the sum of one million dollars, my collection of impressionistic paintings, the DaVinci sketch from my bedroom and the letter which has been entrusted to the law firm of Patterson, Patterson and McQuire."

Sylvia gasped her face pale. John watched her surprise and wondered to himself who Abigail Hoffman was and what she meant to Alex. He started to move to his wife's side but checked his movement and watched instead as Walter leaned forward and patted her knee. Abigail Hoffman, he reminded himself, that strange woman at the funeral, of course.

Mr. Patterson continued his calm reading of the will, "To my darling daughter, Sylvia Anne Alexander Augustus, I leave the remainder of my estate with the following provisions." Mr. Patterson cleared his throat. "Might I have a drink of water, please?"

Drusilla hurried from the room to comply with his request. Everyone shifted nervously as they waited. John noted that his own concern over what was coming was reflected in Sam's worried expression. Drusilla returned with a crystal pitcher filled with tinkling ice and sparkling water. She set the pitcher on the polished desk and stepped back.

Deliberately, Mr. Patterson poured himself a glass and drank deeply. "Perhaps," he said, looking up at the expectant group, "it would be best if all but the immediate family were to leave the room."

"That seems most unusual, sir," Walter protested.

"Unusual perhaps, sir, but not unheard of, the provisions of Mr. Alexander's will are extremely private and I feel it is wise to share these provisions, first, with only the family."

"Certainly, Mr. Patterson, if you think that it's best." Sylvia smiled at the gathered help, using all of her well learned southern charm. "You all don't mind, do you?" Despite the question, it was obvious that she was giving an order and they left the room quickly.

"Now then, Mr. Patterson," Sylvia crossed her legs with a flash of silk stocking and spoke crisply, "is it as shocking as all that? Go ahead and read the rest."

"First let me say that I tried to dissuade your father from the course of action that is set forth by these provisions. However, he was not to be persuaded and further let me assure you that, at the time this will was drawn, your father was of sound mind. There is no legal way to change this will. No court will over rule his stated wishes."

"This all sounds quite dreadful." Sylvia kept her voice and face calm with effort. "For heaven's sake, please, just read it and we can discuss it afterward."

Mr. Patterson nodded. "The sum of five thousand dollars is to be paid directly to my daughter, Sylvia Anne Alexander Augustus, on the first day of each calendar year. All other moneys will be held in trust for her until she reaches the age of sixty years, at which time, she will become the sole owner of all moneys and properties remaining. She may, in addition, withdraw from the estate any amount which does not exceed the interest earned by the trust in any calendar year upon approval of the withdrawal by the executor and providing that she is married at the time of the withdrawal to John Weston Augustus.

In the event that the marriage between Sylvia Anne Alexander Augustus and John Weston Augustus is dissolved by other than the death of either person the entire estate will be held in trust until the youngest progeny of John Weston Augustus and Sylvia Anne Alexander Augustus shall reach the age of majority. At that time the moneys in the trust will be divided equally between the progeny.

Sums equal to the educational expenses for each and all progeny shall be paid to the petitioning progeny only at such time as it has been proven to the executor that the petitioning progeny is enrolled at a qualifying educational institution and is pursuing an appropriate course of study and is obtaining an appropriate grade point average.

In the unlikely event of Sylvia Anne Alexander Augustus' early demise, the executor will administer the estate and will provide for the equal distribution of all moneys and property as follows; each child born of the union between John Weston Augustus and Sylvia Anne Alexander Augustus will receive on their eighteenth birthday the sum of one hundred thousand dollars, on their twenty fifth birthday the sum of one hundred thousand dollars and on their thirtieth birthday the remainder of their portion of the estate. Any issue of Sylvia Anne Alexander Augustus who is sired by other then John Weston Augustus will not share in this estate.

The real property of this estate is to be kept intact and available for use by Sylvia Anne Alexander Augustus and her progeny. Property expenses will be paid by and managed by the estate executor. No property may be sold to any other person or corporation. At such time as the estate is fully distributed all real property will be contributed to the State of Carolina. "

Stunned silence filled the room. Walter's cane crashed to the floor. Color drained from Sylvia's face and was replaced by a dull red flush. "Well," cold anger hardened her words, "Daddy left quite a surprise, didn't he?" She glared at Sam. "You might have told me."

"I didn't know," Sam protested.

Sylvia waved his words aside. "John, it seems you were right after all." Graciously she turned to Mr. Patterson and extended her slim white hand. The diamond she wore caught the light and flashed. "Thank you, Mr. Patterson. I know this has been an uncomfortable afternoon for you."

"Indeed, Miss Sylvia." The old man clasped her hand and held it. "Your father loved you very much." He looked deeply into her eyes and sighed. "I know you feel hurt and angry, but that will pass and you will come to understand how worried he was about your future." Sylvia twitched her hand and he allowed it to escape his hold. "When you've had a few days to think, we'll talk again, but for now I think you've heard enough." He nodded to the family. "I'll see myself out."

Left alone the family avoided looking at one another, embarrassed by the knowledge that they had been given to share. For a long moment no one moved, then Sam rose and headed for the bar, "I think we all need a drink." Mutely, John and Sam poured and served. Sylvia gulped down her drink in a quick swallow and held out the glass, to Sam, for a refill. Sam glanced at John, who nodded slightly. God knows, he thought, I can understand why she'd want to numb the reality.

Minette laid her arm across Sylvia's shoulders, "It's not so bad," she comforted, "after all what is really changed. You will receive a small income each year and you can buy anything at all that the executor approves."

"My life might as well be over," Sylvia's cold voice dripped with icicles. She stood abruptly; shook off Minette's touch, and strode across the room to take her refilled glass from Sam. She raised the glass to John and said mockingly, "Here's to us, Darling, and to happily ever after."

Minette stepped between John and Sylvia. Anger darkened her violet eyes as she addressed Sylvia, "Your father was a good man, a wise man. That will is his last message to you and I'd suggest that you think carefully about the reasons he had for leaving your inheritance so tied in knots." As always when she was upset Minette's accent grew stronger and she gave her sentences a French influence. "It is not the business of anyone else what goes on between you and your husband. Your anger is not a pretty thing."

With her eyes blazing and her head held high, Minette turned away and set her glass down, she extended her hand to Walter. "Come, Walter, Sam," she commanded, "let's leave these two alone."

Walter struggled to his feet. Sam picked up the cane and placed it in his gnarled hand. Walter regarded his grandson. He started to speak, shook his head sadly and left the room supported by Minette's arm.

John refilled his own glass. Sylvia sank down onto a chair. "This is a fine mess, isn't it?" she asked.

"Yes," John agreed. "I don't suppose there is much we can do about it either."

"Sam should have told us."

"I don't think he knew, Syl."

"Don't be silly. Of course, he knew." John watched the angry flush rise like a red tide across Sylvia's cheeks. "I wouldn't doubt but what you knew, too." The thought grew in Sylvia's mind and became a fact. "You did know, didn't you?"

"Don't be ridiculous." John said impatiently. "I wanted a divorce as much as you did, remember?"

"I still want a divorce!"

"For God's sake, so do I." John paused to take a drink. "You heard that will. We can divorce but you will have nothing from your father except a roof over your head if you choose to live in Charleston."

"Maybe we can fight it," Sylvia's hope was evident in her voice.

"Didn't you listen to Mr. Patterson?"

"I heard. But he's only a backwoods lawyer surely someone in the city could break the will."

"Syl," John cautioned.

"John, I'm sure of it. How could he leave a million dollars to that Abby Hoffman and nothing to his own daughter?"

"He didn't exactly leave you nothing."

"It's the same as nothing." Sylvia paced the floor. "If I can't touch the money until I'm an old lady, what good is it?"

"You can buy anything you want."

"Only if I'm married to you and only with some old fuddy-duddy's approval. That's worse than not having anything at all." She spun around. "What was it the will said about my children?"

"That our children would inherit."

"That part about the father?"

"It said quite plainly that during the time that I was alive only children born of the two of us could inherit."

"What about Michael?"

"Michael?"

"Yes, Michael. Do you think Daddy knew he isn't your child?" Anxiety caused Sylvia to stand trembling at the thought.

"Oh, Syl," compassion for this selfish woman moved John. He caught her in his arms and hugged her close. Tears started and turned to sobs. He held her and allowed her to cry, murmuring gently and stroking her hair. At last the storm subsided.

Sylvia raised her tear stained face. "I'm sorry, John."

"You needed to cry," he said. "Here's my handkerchief. Blow your nose and you'll feel better."

Sylvia did as he suggested and even managed a tiny smile. "I do feel better," she sighed. "But you didn't answer do you think Daddy knew about Michael?"

John considered his answer carefully. He remembered Alex's words and his explanation for inserting the clause in the will in the first place. He decided not to lie. "I suppose he had at least a suspicion. He wanted to assure the future for you and for your child and I think he did the only thing he could think of doing."

"It's so unfair," Sylvia declared. "I think we'll have to fight it."

"Syl," John admonished. "I don't like this marriage any more then you do but at least for now I think we are bound by the will."

"What about Michael?"

"The world believes he is my son. I don't intend to tell anyone any different and I don't see why you would want to."

"But what if someone finds out?"

"Every family has secrets, Syl." John sighed. "Only Sam knows for sure and he'll never tell."

"What about Minette?" John shook his head. A lie to protect his mother didn't seem wrong she was certainly not a match for Sylvia. "She's not even suspicious," he lied.

"I still want to talk to an attorney when I get back to the city."

"Do what you want," John gave in. "Alex is gone but with this will he'll certainly not be forgotten."

"It's not right that he can sit in judgment over my life and then leave all that money to his mistress." Sylvia's anger was rising again.

"Mistress?" shock colored John's question. "Abby?"

Sylvia laughed shrilly. "Why do you think he left her all that money and the painting from his bedroom?"

"Are you certain?"

Sylvia laughed again. "Don't act so surprised. All men need an outlet, don't they?" She pulled a cigarette from her silver case. John leaned forward and lit it. Slowly, she exhaled through her nostrils and explained. "It's been going on for years. Abby's an artist. Rather well known at that. When I was nine or ten, I wanted to paint more than anything else in the world so Daddy arranged for me to take lessons from her. I loved her and talked about her incessantly until finally Daddy invited her to the house for dinner. After that she was around a lot. We used to go places together, you know to the park, to the ocean. Daddy laughed and we all had such a good time. I thought she was my best friend but they must have been having an affair even then, although I didn't realize it until I went away to boarding school. One Sunday they drove up to see me and to tell me they wanted to get married." Sylvia blew a thoughtful smoke ring toward the ceiling. "I was devastated. It had never occurred to me that Daddy might want a wife." Savagely she stubbed out the cigarette. "Anyway, I reacted rather badly I yelled some things at the two of them and then ran out."

John could easily imagine the rage of a young Sylvia who felt her beloved Daddy was deserting her. He realized how hard it must have been for Alex to raise such a headstrong child alone, but then it was Alex who had spoiled her.

"As luck would have it," she continued. "It was pouring down rain and I got soaking wet. I caught a chill that turned to pneumonia and by the time I was well again Abby had disappeared from our lives." She took out another cigarette. "At least I thought she had, until today. They've probably been having a dirty little affair all these years."

John pictured the woman he'd met at the funeral home. "Perhaps," he said reasonably, "it isn't a shoddy affair at all, but a genuine love story."

"Don't be silly, John. My Daddy could never love someone like her," Sylvia sneered.

"He left her a sizable inheritance."

"Yes, he did. I think that I shall have to fight that, too. I see no reason why that woman should be entitled to any of my money."

The City Chronicle
Thanksgiving Day 1938
Tattletales by Sharon Chatsworth

Today is a time of special thanksgiving in many American homes as we gather together and praise the Lord for the peace that is still to be found within our country's borders despite the turmoil in the world. One thankful family celebrating together today is the entire Augustus clan who will spend the day at the lovely lakeside home of Samuel and Helen Augustus. Helen is well known for the magnificent table she sets and the casual charm of her parties where children are as welcome as any adult. And speaking of children is it true that another Augustus will be born into this clan come spring?

Chapter 8

Back in the city the days were cold and short. The icy wind whipped rain around corners and against windows, threatening to turn to snow at any time. John kept busy at the office and avoided Sylvia and her anger. Late in the afternoon Sam knocked at the door and came in. He dropped down on the sofa and casually propped his boot clad feet on a small table. John grinned at him. "You'd better sit up and look businesslike or Walter will shoot you."
Sam laughed. "Not to worry, Cuz. The old man's gone home for the weekend."
"Weekend? It's only Wednesday," John frowned. "Is he sick?"

"Good Lord, where's your head? Tomorrow's Thanksgiving."

"Are you sure?" John shook his head as if to remove the cobwebs. "I'd no idea."

"You must be working entirely too hard." Sam studied his cousin. "The whole family is coming out to our house for the day and to spend the weekend. Didn't Sylvia tell you?"

"She may have, but I don't think so." He shrugged. "If the truth be told, Sam, I haven't seen Sylvia in at least a week, maybe more."

"Aren't you living at home?"

"I sleep there, but that's all. I've been busy, working long hours, here at the office."

"Don't try to fool me, John. I work for this firm, too, and we aren't that busy. I still have time to see my wife and family."

"You want to see yours, I don't"

"I thought you and Sylvia were going to work this out." Sam's puzzled eyes caused John to look away. "Didn't you tell me that you'd stay married and raise Michael as your son?"

"I did and I will." John said solemnly. "It's not as easy as you might think."

"Are you feeling sorry for yourself, Cuz?"

"Sometimes," John admitted. "But usually I keep too busy to think about any of that. I make a point of seeing Michael every morning before I come to the office. He's a good kid. Doesn't cry much and Annie takes excellent care of him. He'll never know from me that I don't love him."

"What about Sylvia?"

"She contacted a couple of attorneys when we first got back, but they told her that she didn't have a case against Abby Hoffman or a chance to overturn any part of the will. I can tell she's still angry but

I'm staying out of her way and hoping it will pass."
John shifted in his chair and ran his fingers through
his already rumpled hair. "She goes out most
evenings, to clubs or to the theater with friends.
She tells them I'm busy and will join them later but
I never do."

"How long can you keep this up?" Sam's genuine
concern showed on his face.

John smiled bitterly, "Don't fret about it, Sam.
We're working things out. It takes a while to decide
how to be married when neither one of you wants to
be married."

"Well, Sylvia agreed that all three of you would be
up for the weekend. I'm surprised she didn't let you
know, but you are coming aren't you?"

"For a family gathering around Helen's well laden
table!" John chuckled. "You can count on it. When
are we expected?"

"Walter, Aunt Mary Elizabeth and Minette are
driving out tonight." Sam shifted his long frame
still further down in the chair and sighed
contentedly. "I don't know when Helen expects
you, she's the one that talked to Sylvia, but I'd say
that you could certainly come out tonight. There's
plenty of room and I know everything's ready.
Nothing Helen loves more than a full house."

"She's a real jewel, Sam." John felt a twinge of
jealousy. "I hope you realize how lucky you are."

"I do. Sometimes I take Helen for granted but
always I know how much I need her and how
fortunate I am that she chose me to be her husband."

A comfortable silence filled the room as each man
pursued his own line of thinking. Sam's eyes closed
and John grinned as he watched him drift off in a
quick cat nap. While Sam dozed John finished the
work and cleared his desk. He closed a drawer with

a slight bang and laughed as Sam jumped and was instantly awake.

"Still able to fall asleep anywhere and anytime, I see," John teased.

Sam stretched. "Every genius is able to do it. We don't need a full night's sleep like you mere mortals, just a nap now and then."

"Sure thing. Let's get out of here. It's so quiet everyone else must be gone for the holiday."

"Right," Sam paused with his hand on the door knob. "So you'll be up tonight?"

"I think in the morning."

"We'll be counting on it." Sam waved, "In the morning then."

John followed him out the door. The phone on his desk rang. He turned back to answer. "The heck with it," he said, aloud. "Whatever it is can wait until Monday." He closed the door firmly behind himself.

He sorted quickly through the mail Duncan had placed on the silver tray in the entry. Nothing important, he noted and returned the envelopes to the tray. He patted the carved lion and humming to himself he went up the stairs to the nursery. It was an unusual time of day for him to drop in, but he felt an urge to see the boy.

Annie sat with Michael in the center of a braided rug. They were both giggling as Michael tried to balance a block on his head. John laughed. Startled, Annie tried to scramble to her feet. Her heel caught in the hem of her dress and she fell against him. She blushed and took a sharp breath. "Good afternoon, sir," she managed to say ignoring her embarrassment. "Is something wrong?"

"No. Nothing wrong, Annie," he reassured her. "Sit down and go on with your game."

Michael scrambled to his feet and toddled across the rug to John's side. He smiled gravely, his eyes fixed on John's face. Looking down at the tiny boy grief ripped through his heart. If only this were really my child, he thought. Then he swept Michael up in a hug and tickled his neck. The child's somber expression gave way to delighted giggles.

"What were you doing?" John asked Annie.

"Building towers, sir."

"It happens that I'm the champion tower builder in this city." John dropped to the rug and drew Michael to his side. "Come on, Annie," he gestured toward the rug. "We'll need your help."

Annie shook her head and stood watching. John carefully built up a tall tower and then, holding Michael's small fist, showed him how to knock it down. Again John built a tower and Michael knocked it over. Their laughter mingled as John began a third tower, this one with Michael's help. "He's very bright, isn't he, Annie?" John asked, proudly.

"Yes indeed, sir." Annie bragged. "He's ever so much better with his hands then most babes."

Michael hit the blocks and chuckled as they tumbled across the rug. Annie and John smiled.

"What a happy little scene," Sylvia's coldness indicated that she was not amused. The laugher stopped and instead John felt guilt flush his face. "Annie, I've told you I won't have Michael playing rough games."

"Sorry, madam," Annie bobbed her head.

"I was building towers with your son, Sylvia." John's guilt had turned to anger at her unreasonable tone.

"Towers? It appeared to me that Michael was throwing blocks when I opened the door."

"Towers are built so that boys can knock them down." John tried to hide his irritation.

"My son is to be raised as a gentleman. I'll not allow him to be turned into some kind of hooligan."

"Syl, for heaven's sake," John lost his hold on patience and fought to control the urge to say something he knew he'd regret. Taking a deep breath he changed the subject. "Sam stopped by my office and informed me that we were expected at their house for Thanksgiving dinner and the weekend. If you mentioned it, I'd completely forgotten."

"I didn't mention it," Sylvia dropped her eyes defensively.

"Why not?"

"I was hoping we wouldn't have to go, but now that you are aware of the invitation I suppose we'll have to." Sylvia shrugged her shoulders and allowed the fur coat she was wearing to drop off. John reached forward automatically and helped her.

He stroked the soft brown fur. "Is this new?"

Sylvia brushed the fur sensually. "Yes, I picked it up this afternoon." She draped it casually over one arm. "Annie, find something quiet to do with the boy. Mr. Augustus and I will be in my room."

She swept out of the room and John followed. Behind the closing door, John could hear Michael's curiously sad voice asking, "Mama?" Sylvia didn't appear to notice.

"So what's up, Syl? Why don't you want to go out to Sam and Helen's?"

"If you must know I find it boring."

"Boring?" John lifted his eyebrows in surprise. "I always thought you enjoyed being out in the country, walking by the lake, and playing cards with Walter, all of those things."

"Well, I didn't!" Sylvia's green eyes flashed. "I always pretended to like them so that your family would think we had a happy marriage."

John accepted her words without comment. "Why did you tell Helen we'd come?"

"How do you say no to a tradition? She caught me off guard and I'd agreed before I even thought about what it would mean to spend the whole weekend trapped in that huge house with all those children."

"Don't you mean trapped with me?"

They'd reached the door to Sylvia's bedroom and she took advantage of entering the room to avoid answering his question. Instead she suggested that he sit down.

John looked around the room. It had been well over a year since he'd been alone with her in this room. With surprise he noted that everything was different. It was definitely a woman's room now, with no hint of a husband. The walls were covered in the palest possible yellow silk. Soft yellow drapes flowed at the sides of tall French doors that opened onto a small balcony. Through the glass he could see evergreens set in yellow pots. The bed was covered with a thick comforter of yellow, white and delicate blue flowers. Small, lacy pillows were piled high on the bed and on a blue velvet chaise lounge. The picture over the mantel had been changed from the portrait he remembered to a Chinese screen depicting soft bamboo and tiny birds. Next to the fireplace stood two small chairs covered in stripes that repeated the delicate colors of the room.

John chose one of these chairs and sat carefully, feeling like a bull in a china shop. Sylvia tossed the coat across the bed and stood in front of her dressing table. She examined her face and began to brush her hair. It was a long moment before either one spoke and then they began at the same time.

"You first," John conceded.

"I don't really feel trapped with you, John." Sylvia sat on the bench facing him. She turned the silver hairbrush back and forth in her hands. "I've hardly seen you since we came back from Charleston."

"I've tried to stay out of your way."

"And I've managed to stay out of yours, but up there for the weekend everyone will expect us to act like man and wife." John nodded, considering the problem. "I know we are but..."

"Syl," compassion softened his voice, "I understand. It's not easy to pretend."

"So what should we do?"

"Do you really want my opinion or do you want to fight?"

Sylvia lifted her chin. "I'm done fighting. What do we do?"

"We stay married, married in absolutely the most civilized way possible." He tried to reassure her. "It won't be so bad, Syl. I've my work and you've your friends. This house is plenty big enough for three."

"But..."

"No buts. To the world and that means to my family, too, we are married. So this weekend we go to Sam and Helen's and we act as happy as we can without being phony. We stay busy and out of trouble. I think this will be a good practice session for us. The holidays are coming and we'll be invited out a lot."

Sylvia considered his words. "You sound so reasonable. Aren't you angry?"

"I was but it seems to have passed. At first I felt sorry for myself and then I blamed everything on you and then on Walter. I even took a shot at blaming Alex, but I finally realized that I was the only one responsible for the way I was feeling and that if I was going to get on with my life I'd better face up to myself and get busy living the way I want to live."

"But I know you don't want to be married any more than I do," Sylvia questioned his apparent detachment.

"True," John acknowledged. "Marriage, the way we've known it, hasn't worked for either one of us."

Sylvia turned her back and avoided his eyes by brushing her hair. "I can't go back, John." She raised her head and allowed her eyes to meet his in the mirror. "I've tried to convince myself that we could make a marriage work. We can't." She turned to face him and bravely struggled with a smile. "I don't even want to try anymore and yet I know we're trapped."

"Do you have a plan, Syl?"

"I think so." She moved to the chaise lounge and fiddled with the pillows. Then, taking a deep breath, she plunged into a speech that John realized she'd been prepared to give. "I've thought a lot about how to stay married. I mean, I know we have to. At first I hoped that the money wouldn't matter, that you'd be willing to support me." John started to speak and she gestured to him not to interrupt. "But even if that were possible, I find that the money matters to me. I want the security of your name for myself and I want to be able to use Daddy's money for things like that coat." She pointed to the fur spread across the bed. "The will Daddy left has tied us more firmly together then marriage vows could.

I think we have to work out a marriage that will fool the world, the family and even my son as he grows older."

She leaned forward and folded her hands in her lap. Her green eyes were somber as she said, "I won't sleep with you again, John."

John fought for control of his expression and managed not to grin. Women, he thought, I haven't touched her in over a year and yet she's managing to make it sound like it's her idea.

"I'll go to Sam's with you this weekend and we'll have to share a room, but that's all."

"Of course," John agreed solemnly. "I wouldn't expect anything else, Syl."

"It'll be hard, awkward, I suppose but we are both adults," Sylvia continued, unaware of the irony in John's words. "With Michael and the rest of the children in and out of everywhere it shouldn't be hard to keep Walter and Minette from suspecting anything and Sam will go along with whatever you say or do. Helen will simply follow Sam's lead."

John nodded, waiting for Sylvia to reach the point, knowing that there was more to this lecture.

"I'll feign a headache or something Thursday night and insist on returning to the city Friday morning to see a doctor. You and Michael can stay with Annie and come back as scheduled Sunday night."

So that's it, John thought. She's up to something. "No need for you to do that, Syl," he said sympathetically. "I'll say that I have business I have to attend to and then you can stay and enjoy the entire weekend in the country."

Sylvia's face fell in dismay. John watched wondering how she'd get out of his trap.

Sylvia shook her head, "No, John, that wouldn't be fair. They're your family and you've been gone a long time. I'm sure they'd rather spend the time with you."

John chuckled. "You're a quick thinker, Syl." Sylvia managed to look indignant. "Let's not lie to each other." A protest rose to Sylvia's lips but John stopped it with a look. "I think that if we are going pretend to be married we'd better stick to the truth. I realize that you have something you'd like to do here in the city and that you'd like to be alone, or at least not with me."

He gave her time to answer, but when she gave none he continued, "It's not important to me who you see, what you do, or if you do it with a lover, but it is important that you are discrete."

"How about you?"

"I shouldn't think that it would matter in the least to you how I handle my life or if I have lover. I would, however, take the utmost care not to allow the gossips in this city to get wind of anything they could rub in our noses or the boy's." John crossed his legs and expounded on his thought. "I don't imagine we'll be able to totally avoid gossip but I think if we present a united front we can keep it to a minimum."

"What about Walter?" Sylvia asked nervously. "You know how angry he is when any questions are asked about the family."

"You're right. But this time I'm prepared to tell him that we will do things our way, not his. It's time he realized that I'm capable of making my own decisions."

"He'll be very angry when he hears the gossip."

"If he hears the gossip," John corrected. "I'm sure that we will both refrain from telling others how we manage our marriage."

"Are you saying that you don't mind what I do?" Sylvia's puzzled eyes considered this possibility.

"That's exactly what I'm saying," John declared firmly. "You are free and so am I. We are married only in the eyes of the world. As long as we appear in public as Mr. and Mrs. John Augustus no one will dare to question us."

Sylvia weighed his words and then nodded. "I can see that it just might work." She nodded again. "Yes," a note of hope entered her voice, "I think it will work."

"So, are you ready to go to the country with me?"

"I will be in the morning, and" Sylvia smiled shyly, "you're right I want to see someone else over the weekend."

He'd asked for honesty but his stomach twisted at her casual words. Unaware Sylvia went on blithely, "No one you know and I'll be very discrete, in fact we'll go out of the city and hide somewhere."

Thanksgiving Day dawned crisp and clear. Wednesday's rain had scrubbed the sky and clouds until they shone. John was up early and walked briskly through the park. He was surprised to find that the discomfort he'd felt the night before over Sylvia's easy acquiescence had disappeared with the sunrise. A load had lifted from his shoulders and he found himself whistling as he returned to the brownstone.

Going to the nursery, he asked Annie to rouse Sylvia while he stayed with Michael. "If your mother isn't up soon, we'll get a late start," he told the wide eyed little boy as they played peek-a-boo together. Annie returned and reluctantly he left the nursery and went off to ready himself for the day.

They gathered in the front hall with the luggage and waited for Sylvia to arrive. When at last she ambled down the stairs a small bag in her hand, a cynical smile lifted her lips, she surveyed the mound of luggage, "Goodness, are we going for a month?"

"It takes a lot for the babe," Annie explained defensively.

"Oh yes, I suppose it does." Sylvia checked her reflection in the mirror and straightened her bright red hat to a more becoming angle. "I'm ready if you are, John. Why don't you and I take the roadster and Annie can follow in the big car with Michael and all that luggage."

"I thought we'd all go together so that Andrew can have the day with his family."

"That'll never work. I don't want Michael climbing all over me all the way up there."

"It's only an hour's drive," John objected.

"An hour with all four of us in one car is a very long time." Sylvia patted Michael's hair. "He's a nice little boy, but he can't sit still for more than a moment."

"She's right, sir," Annie agreed. "The babe will be able to move about more in the big car."

"Okay," John decided it wasn't worth a fight. "I'll get the roadster and tell Andrew we'll need him after all."

Skillfully John steered the shiny red roadster through the city and onto the open highway. Most of the trees were bare but here and there a few bright leaves clung to the branches making brilliant drifts of color among the evergreens. Neither spoke, but both were busy with their own thoughts. John found himself whistling under his breath.

"It's going to be all right, Syl." He reached across and covered her hand with his. "I can feel it in my bones."

Sylvia laughed at him, "You sound like Walter."

Catching sight of the lake, John slowed to make the sharp turn into the private drive. Ahead of them stood the huge Tudor house set among tall pine trees with a long sloping yard that ended at the shores of the sparkling lake. They sped up the drive and slid to a stop. The tires spit gravel into the air.

"Uncle John," Chris yelled, jumping off the stair rail where he'd been awaiting their arrival, "I wish Daddy could drive like that."

Sam stepped out the front door in time to hear his son's opinion. "I drive a car full of children and dogs, not a snappy roadster."

"We could buy one and then you could make it go fast like Uncle John."

"I think not, sport." Sam grinned. "Run in and tell your mother that John and Sylvia are here." He opened the roadster's door and gave Sylvia his hand. Casually he kissed her cheek and extended a hand to John as he came around the rear of the car. "Look at the trouble you've caused now, Cuz. My own son thinks I'm a sissy."

They laughed together. For a few minutes in the bright, cold sunshine everything seemed right with the world. The lake lapped gently at the shore, the honking of geese somewhere far away drifted to them along with the rich scent of the pine trees. John took a deep breath. "I think I can understand why you live clear out here in the wilderness."

"It's the only place to raise children. Come on in. The family is gathered here and there. Walter has been teaching Chris to play chess and Minette is in the kitchen with Helen doing something to the turkey." He glanced around as if looking for something. "I'm not sure where the rest of the kids are, I thinking Aunt Mary Elizabeth took them for a walk, but they'll show up." He stopped. "Speaking of kids, where's Michael?"

"He and Annie are coming up in the big car." Sylvia explained quickly. "There's so much stuff to bring along for a child and John and I thought it would be nice to be alone." Sylvia tucked her hand through John's arm. "Let's go in."

John avoided Sam's glance and allowed himself to be propelled up the stairs and into the house. Minette met them in the entry with a kiss for each and again they explained Michael's absence. John sniffed the air and exclaimed over the rich odor of the turkey.

"Helen has out done herself this year," Minette said. "There's enough food for an army."

They laughed together and the day settled into the predictable holiday routine creating a peaceful space in the busy war torn world. Andrew arrived with Michael and Annie and was sent back to the city to spend the day in the comfort of his own home. Sam's children were delighted with Michael's company and played with him as if he were a new toy. John relaxed as he watched even Sylvia enjoy the camaraderie of the family.

Dinner was served as the setting sun cast a soft pink glow across the heavily laden table. Following that great American tradition they all ate too much of the food which was as delicious as the drifting scents had promised. Even Walter took a second slice of pumpkin pie. He raised his glass in a toast, "I'm proud to be the oldest member of this fine family. If your father and mother could be with us today, Sam, our family would be complete." He tilted his glass in a toast, "To all of you and to all of yours."

"Hear. Hear." Sam raised his glass in return. "I spoke to my parents this morning, Grandfather, and as much as they would like to share this holiday, with Dad's asthma they are better off in Arizona. And," he winked at Helen, "since you've mentioned family and the good feelings that being with them produces, this seems like an appropriate time to tell you that Helen and I have decided to take the kids out to see my parents and then on to California to spend Christmas with Helen's family."

"Whoopee!" Peter's happy shout caused the grown-ups to chuckle. "When are we going, Dad?"

"Will we see cowboys?" Jennifer asked.

"For sure?" Christopher added his question.

"Calm down, all of you," Sam ordered jovially. "Yes we are going "for sure", Chris. I can't promise cowboys, Jen, and we'll leave as soon as school is out for the Christmas holiday and come back after the New Year," he answered each question.

"Wow!" Peter's excitement was explosive. He wiggled in his chair so hard that John reached over and steadied the chair.

"Take it easy, Peter." Sam smiled indulgently. "You've another month to wait."

Helen also smiled at her children. All four had her fair haired, blue eyed, delicate look but each had a personality all their own. Christopher at eleven was a real scholar, interested in anything with a motor and in airplanes in particular. Peter fairly burst with excess energy. He was like quicksilver and despite being a year younger than his brother could out play him at any sport. Jennifer would be eight in just a few days and already she showed an interest in the opposite sex that Helen found appalling. She seemed to know exactly how to bat her long lashes to get her way. Beth, the youngest at four, was paying no attention to the conversation but was busy feeding Michael as Annie watched carefully.

"We'll miss you at Christmas," Minette said, "but I'm sure your parents are counting the days until you arrive."

Helen eyes glowed at the thought of seeing her parents. "This will be the first time my parents have seen Beth and it's been almost two years since we've seen Sam's folks." She busied herself to hide her emotion. "Finish up now, children and you may be excused."

Released from the adults, the children hurried from the dining room. The boys talking loudly to each other about the trip and Jen still asking persistently if they thought there would be cowboys and Indians. Beth waited for Annie and they left the room together. Beth's voice carried back to the family as she asked to help give Michael his bath.

"Beth certainly enjoys having a baby in the house," Minette commented.

"I hope she like it as well next spring," Sam said casually.

"By next spring, you'll hardly be able to call Michael a baby," Sylvia said.

"I didn't mean Michael." Sam grinned widely. "I meant I hope she likes having a new baby in the house."

"Helen!" Minette jumped to her feet. "You mean?" Helen nodded. Minette rushed to her and hugged her tight. "Oh, how wonderful," she exclaimed. "When will the child be born?"

"Congratulations." John shook Sam's hand and kissed Helen's cheek.

"Wonderful news," Sylvia murmured half to herself.

"Wonderful news for sure," Walter beamed at Helen and turned to Sylvia, "I suppose you and John will be announcing some good news of your own one of these days."

Sylvia managed a smile but John recognized the angry glint in her eye as she answered, "Not for a while, Walter. Michael isn't even out of the nursery."

Sam attempted to ease the tension, "Everyone isn't as anxious to fill their house with a bunch of noisy kids as Helen and I seem to be."

Diplomatically, Mary Elizabeth picked up the conversation and began to question Helen about her health and her ability to make the long trip over Christmas. John flashed a sympathetic look at Sylvia and helped keep the conversation away from their future children. He felt no surprise when, only a few minutes later, Sylvia pleaded to be excused giving a headache as her excuse.

A crackling fire cast warm shadows over the comfortable living room where the three men relaxed. Walter dozed next to the hearth. Sam smoked quietly watching both the flames and the tension in John's face. Occasionally the shouts of the children could be heard from some distant corner of the house. "I should go and help Helen," Sam said, "but I'm too full and contented."

"After a big meal a man should take a nap," Walter said from the depths of his chair. "Your grandmother always said that and I believe she was right."

Sam chuckled. "Sounds like a fine idea to me but I can hear those children of mine rising the roof and I know Helen is still busy." He put out his cigarette and reluctantly pulled himself to his feet.

Neither Walter nor John moved, they sat silent as the shadows deepened and the fire became the only light in the room. Walter drifted back to sleep and John could hear his gentle snore. As the peace of the room settled around him, John's thoughts drifted to Valerie, as they always did when he relaxed. He stared into the flames but saw first her face and then scenes from their brief time together. He watched her beautiful face with its' wide generous mouth turned up in her ever ready smile, he heard her laughter and the sound of her voice. His heart ached as he had never believed possible. If only I could see her again, he thought. Just once to see her and know that she is all right, that she is happy.

Something crashed in the hall and startled him back to the present. He reached up and switched on a light as Minette entered the room. "What are you doing in here in the dark?" she asked.

John looked guilty but found an acceptable excuse. "We were just dozing in front of the fire." He smiled at his mother. "I think I may have eaten more than I needed."

"We all did, I'm sure. I'm going for a walk. Would you like to join me?"

John hesitated, afraid that Minette would want to talk about Sylvia.

"Come along." Minette urged. "I'd like your company."

"Okay." John stood and stretched. "I'll run up and get a coat."

He knocked on the door of the room he and Sylvia were sharing and waited for her soft answer. Sylvia was curled up in a large chair leafing through a magazine. She didn't move as he crossed the thick carpet and took his coat from the closet. "I'm going for a walk with Mother," he explained, slipping into the coat. Sylvia nodded. "Can I get you anything before we go?"

"You could ask someone to bring me a cup of tea." She pressed the back of her hand to her forehead in a theatrical gesture. "I seem to have developed a terrible headache."

John realized the import of her words. "You've decided to go back to the city tonight then?"

"Of course I have. I told you I would." There was defiance in her words as well as a subtle challenge.

"When are you leaving?" John refused to show his annoyance with her plan.

Oh," Sylvia flipped her hair and cocked her head to one side as she smiled slightly. "Not for an hour or so. First I'll have the tea and let the word spread that I'm not feeling well and then I'll take the roadster and scoot back into the city."

"All right," John agreed. "If that's what you want to do. Annie and I will bring Michael home Sunday afternoon. Will you be home by then?"

"I'll plan on it."

John hesitated with his hand on the door knob. "If I'm not back from our walk when you leave," he said without turning, "drive carefully."

Minette watched him as he came down the graceful curving staircase. When he was close she asked quietly, "What's wrong?"

"Nothing." John shook his head as if to clear it. "Syl doesn't feel well. I'll just be a minute, I'm going to step into the kitchen and ask someone to take her a cup of tea."

With his chore accomplished, John rejoined his mother and together they stepped out into the night. The air had turned wintry cold and the night sky was filled with bright stars. The moon, high in the sky, made the path easy to follow. Their breath hung in white clouds. Only the sound of their footsteps on the path broke the silence. At the edge of the water, Minette paused and raised her face to the moon. John was surprised by how young she looked.

"Why didn't you ever remarry?" he asked.

Minette hid the surprise she felt by dropping her face and looking away. "What in the world made you ask that?" she asked a hint of amusement in her voice.

"I was thinking how young you look and how beautiful," John stumbled over his words as he tried to explain, "and marriage is on my mind a lot these days."

Minette nodded. "Let's walk and I'll try to think of an answer." They strolled the path that ran along the shore, alone for the moment in a silent world. It took several minutes before Minette began to speak. She started slowly, "I was very young when I met your father. Two days before my sixteenth birthday. I was walking home from school with my friends. We were laughing and being very silly. At a cafe two handsome Americans sat watching us. They spoke. We answered. It was almost summer and our spirits were high. We flirted a bit and went on to our homes." Minette's face glowed at the memory. "The next day they were sitting at the cafe again. And the next. And the next. Such devotion is very flattering. The fourth day, we not only stopped to talk but agreed to have a cup of coffee. It was all very exciting, if any one of us had been seen by someone who knew our families we would have been in terrible trouble."

John laughed. "I can imagine you in your school uniform, so pretty and so young."

"And so naughty," Minette added. "In France a nice girl doesn't talk to strangers and never to men that are not properly introduced by someone in the family. Your father was handsome and so sure of himself. His clothes were beautiful and it was obvious that he had plenty of money. I was enchanted." Her footsteps slowed as she gathered her memories. "After that they were there every day and soon Michael and I began to separate ourselves from the others. While they drank coffee, we would take a short walk and he would tell me about America and about his family, where they lived, how they lived, all of that. It was like listening to fairy tales. My friend, Suzanne, cautioned me and told me it was dangerous to fall in love with an American but..." She shrugged, "when one is sixteen cautious words are wasted words."

They walked on. The moon created a path across the water and John watched the memories shadow his mother's eyes.

Again she spoke, "School ended and I made a million excuses to be free during the days. It was very easy. My mother trusted me and I took advantage of her trust. If she wondered why I'd suddenly become so interested in visiting museums she never said a word. Michael and I went everywhere. He had a car and we could go out in the country and still I could be home in time for dinner." She stopped and faced John. "I became pregnant."

John caught her hands. "With me?"

"Of course," she smiled up at him. "I loved your father in the crazy, excited way that only the very young can love but he wasn't ready for marriage and when I told him I was pregnant he offered to help me arrange an abortion." Tears filled her eyes and threatened to over flow. "I couldn't do that. I went home crying and when my mother held me and asked me what was wrong, I told her." The tears flowed freely down her cheeks. John brushed them away with his gloved hand. "My mother understood. She was a wise woman. But even so she had to tell my father. He was very angry. At first I almost feared for my life and then I realized that it was Michael he wanted to hurt."

John pulled his mother close in a warm hug. "How awful for you," he said, remembering the story Walter had told him about his father's death and knowing what must come next.

Minette pulled back a step. "Let me finish, John. There is only a bit more to tell. My father and my oldest brother went to the hotel where Michael was staying and confronted him. I followed them and stood hidden in the hall while they shouted at one another. Michael laughed and said I wasn't his responsibility that he wasn't sure he was the father of my child. It was more than I could stand. I ran away."

Minette shivered and started walking. "All I could think of was leaving. I went to my father's office and I stole money that I knew he had and I caught the boat to London. The next day it was in the Paris newspapers, how my brother had shot and killed Michael and that my father had suffered a heart attack and was dying. The French press was very civilized, in those days, and Michael's name was not mentioned, only mine and my family's. I couldn't go home so I went to a steamship company and got a job as a maid on a vessel coming to America."

Sadly, Minette shook her head. "It was all so senseless, so much hurt."

"It wasn't your fault, Mother," John excused her. "You were so young."

"Senseless," Minette said emphatically. "I've kept this secret for thirty four years and that was foolish, too. I've never been able to go home and I've never been able to remarry because I was never married in the first place. It feels wonderful to finally tell you."

"I'm glad." John squeezed her hand. "Please finish."

"There isn't much else to tell. When the ship arrived in America we docked here, in the city Michael had told me about. I was frightened and alone but I'd made one friend on the ship. She was an older Irish girl and she forced me to call on Walter and tell him the whole story. He was surprised to see me but understanding. He didn't even hesitate or check my story. He simply took me home and introduced me to Edith and they accepted me as if Michael and I had really been married. After a while, I could almost believe the story myself."

"Walter told me part of the family history about two years ago." He hesitated unwilling to hurt his mother, "Did you know that my father was born to Walter and a mistress?"

Minette nodded, "Edith told me not long before she died. She thought it was a kind of family curse that the best loved child was born out of wedlock."

John shook his head, amused and saddened, "I love you, Mother."

"Thank you, John." Minette stopped and pulled his face down so that she could kiss his cheek. "I've loved you from the first moment I knew I was carrying you. I've never regretted your birth, not for an instant."

"It must have been hard for you." They reached the end of Sam's property and turned back toward the house.

"Having a child was never hard." Minette responded. "Walter protected me from everyone with his love." Sadness darkened her voice. "Losing my family all in one afternoon was very hard."

Busy with their separate thoughts they walked in silence. The wind off the lake quickened and the cold began to penetrate. John turned up his collar and Minette wrapped her head in the long wool scarf she wore around her neck. "We'd better get inside," John said lifting his face into the wind. "It smells like snow."

The curve of the lake brought them even with the house. They started across the lawn as the front door opened. Sylvia stood silhouetted in the bright glow of the entry light. She glanced back as if she were talking to someone. They heard her harsh tone and the sound of the slamming door but they were too far from the house to catch her words. The roadster's engine roared and was flung into gear. The little car leapt forward spraying gravel in every direction as it hurled down the drive and around the curve.

"Gracious!" Minette exclaimed. "What in the world is the matter with Sylvia?"

"Not much, I'd imagine," John answered sarcastically. "She wanted to return to the city tonight and I expect she has done just that."

"It isn't going well between you is it, darling?"

"No, Mother. It isn't." The finality of his tone told Minette clearer than any words just how bad things really were and how determined her son was not to discuss anything. Without questioning him, she took his arm and held it close as they climbed the stairs.

The warm air rushed out to greet them as they entered the house. Minette laughed, delighted at the sensation. "I had no idea how cold it was until I came in."

"The radio is forecasting snow for tonight." Sam joined them in the entry hall.

"It feels like it," Minette allowed a graceful shiver to run down her spine.

"You just missed Sylvia."

"We saw her going out as we came up from the lake," John responded.

"We tried to talk her out of leaving. She said she didn't feel well and she wanted to sleep in her own bed tonight."

"Don't worry about it. I knew she wanted to go back to the city tonight."

"But if she's ill..." Sam started to protest.

"She's not ill, Sam."

"Oh," Sam stopped. "I see. Well then let's go in by the fire and play a few rudders of bridge."

"Great," John's relief at Sam's easy acceptance showed in his sad eyes. "You'll have to be my partner, Mother."

"Give me a minute to run upstairs."

John lowered his voice, "She planned it Sam. There was someone else she wanted to spend the holiday weekend with. Coming here with Michael and me was a cover, just for appearances sake."

"Then your marriage is truly over."

"Not over." John said bitterly. "Unfortunately, it will never be over." John turned his back and hung his coat, struggling to regain his composure. "We've reached an understanding as to how we can continue to appear married, and at least semi-happy, to the world. We realize that the family will know how things are but, as you well know, the "Fabulous Augustus Clan" will cover for their own and not a single word will ever be mentioned in polite society about the newest skeleton hanging in our collective closet."

"You sound very bitter, Cuz."

"Bitter, mad, hurt, angry, stupid, you name it, I probably feel it."

"Sam," Helen called from the living room. "Are you coming?"

"Just a sec. Minette went upstairs for something." He searched John's face. "I'm here to help you, Cuz, Helen and I both. We'd do anything at all for you."

"I know, Sam and I appreciate it. It'll get better. I'm just not used to it yet."

"What about Michael?"

"Poor kid," John sighed. "He's got one heck of a life ahead of him, doesn't he?"

"What's wrong with Michael?" Minette caught only the last of their conversation as she descended the stairs.

"Nothing's wrong. Sam and I were just talking, Mother."

"He's a fine child." Minette declared, catching on at once to all the unspoken nuances. "This family owes him the best possible life and all the love we can muster between us."

"You sound positively fierce, Minette." Sam tried to soothe her.

"I am fierce." Minette drew herself up to her full height. "It doesn't matter what happens between John and Sylvia that child was born in innocence and he deserves to be raised in love."

"Every child deserves to be raised in love." Helen stuck her head into the entry. "Are the three of you going to stand out here discussing childrearing or are we going to play bridge?"

Early the next morning, John came awake to the gleeful shouts of children. For a moment he lay still, confused by the sounds and by the unfamiliar room, until Sam's voice loudly admonished the children to hush before they woke their Uncle John. The bedroom was full of bright light, John thought he'd overslept and then realized that the brilliance was caused by the sun reflecting on new snow. He flung back the bedclothes and dressed quickly, as eager as the youngsters to be out in the clean, fresh world.

The dining room was a bustle of activity as all four children struggled to dress themselves in their winter gear. Walter was offering advice as he ate his breakfast and Annie tried to coax an excited Michael to eat. Helen helped Beth into her bright red snowsuit and tied her cap securely over her curls. She straightened Jennifer's coat and wrapped a muffler around her throat. When she pronounced them ready and they ran off shouting and pushing to be the first to make tracks in the new fallen snow.

John drank his coffee and quickly finished his own breakfast, "Come on, Sam. I think we should help those kids build a real old fashioned snowman."

Sam jumped to his feet, delighted at the opportunity to be out in the snow. The cold snow had softened in the bright sun and was perfect for packing. A snowball fight quickly developed between the boys and their father. Laughter rang across the lake interspersed with teasing voices. John helped the girls start a snowman and soon they were joined by

Sam and the boys. Helen and Minette waved encouragement from the window as they filled the yard with a whole group of snow people.

Annie brought Michael out, dressed in an old pink snowsuit that had belonged to Beth. They all laughed as he tried to walk on the slippery snow and then as he tasted the strange new stuff. John scooped him up onto his shoulders and gave him a tour of their snow people, introducing each with a name and a story, much to the delight of his nieces and nephews. Helen came to the door and gave Beth a loaf of bread. Annie reclaimed Michael and walked with him to the edge of the lake. She and Beth tore the bread into small pieces and helped Michael throw it to the ducks. The older three played a game of Angels in the snow.

"I haven't had this much fun in ages," John said leaning against the porch pillar and lighting a cigarette.

"It's a beautiful day," Sam agreed.

Helen knocked on the window and motioned for them to come in. They rounded up the children and helped Annie brush away the snow. Everyone's cheeks were rosy and they all had cold fingers and toes but Helen had hot chocolate and cinnamon toast waiting for them by the fire.

The rest of the weekend flew past. John was able to forget that Sylvia was in the city with someone else. He relaxed in the bosom of his family and let his problems drift away as he played with Michael and with Sam's children. He took a long walk with Christopher and was astounded by his knowledge of airplanes.

At night he slept soundly with nary a bad dream to interrupt his rest. When Sunday arrived he helped Andrew pack the luggage, helped Annie and

Michael into the big car and reluctantly returned to the city.

Back in his office on Monday morning, John immersed himself in work. Annie hadn't mentioned Sylvia on the drive back to the city, but he knew that she must have wondered about Syl's abrupt departure and had most likely drawn her own conclusions. John could only hope that she would be discrete enough not to gossip.

At eleven a knock on the door interrupted his concentration. His secretary entered and explained, "I know you didn't want to take calls, but there is someone on the line with a really confusing message."

"That's all right, Susan." He stretched his long arms above his head and yawned. "I needed a break. What's the message?"

"The caller is a woman who says she works at Central City Hospital and that she has to talk to you in person."

"What about?"

"I'm not certain. She sort of hinted that someone you know needs help but she wouldn't say who it was or what they needed."

"I can't think of anyone I know that's in the hospital but I'm intrigued." He thought for a moment. "Go ahead and put her through, if it's a pitch for money, I'll be mad at myself but at least it's a new approach."

Susan disappeared and the phoned buzzed. John answered it quickly prepared to brush off the caller and get back to work. Instead he found himself listening carefully to the soft, uneducated voice of the caller.

"Thank you for speaking to me, Mr. Augustus," the voice said politely. "I know you're a busy man and I'll only take a minute of your time."

John spun is chair around to face the window and propped his feet on the wide ledge, a position Walter despised. "Who are you and what is it you'd like to tell me?"

"My name isn't important but I'll tell you. I'm Mrs. John Kline and I work at City Hospital as a maid."

John could hear the nervous quiver in her voice and decided this was no ordinary phone call. "Yes," he said softening this voice to encourage her.

"It probably doesn't mean anything and now that I've reached you I feel foolish."

"Well, now that you've got me you might as well tell me what's on your mind."

"Yes, of course." The woman took a deep breath and started talking in a rush. "Last Wednesday afternoon the emergency room admitted an old woman. She's very ill and no one has come to visit her."

"What in the world does that have to do with me?" John asked, totally confused.

"I thought perhaps you could come and see her."

"Why in the world did you think that?" John's astonishment at this turn of events was evident in his tone.

"Because she needs you," Mrs. Kline said firmly.

"I'm sorry, but I don't believe there's anything I can do. Why don't you try to reach her family?"

"I'm sure the hospital has done that, sir. But she's from England and there isn't anyone here."

"England, huh? That's interesting but hardly my affair."

"I suppose not, sir, but," the patient voice continued insistently, "your business card was the only thing with a local name and address that we found."

"And where did you find that?" John asked suspiciously.

"In her hand, sir. The hospital felt it wasn't important but I figured if she had it in her hand when she collapsed it must mean something."

John dropped his feet from the window ledge and sat up straight in his chair. "Who is this mystery woman?"

"Her name is Lillian Rathbourne and..."

"Lily!" John leapt to his feet. "Why didn't you say so? City Central Hospital? I'll be right there." He hung up on the startled sputtering coming from the receiver, grabbed his coat and rushed out of the office. Susan jumped to her feet at his sudden appearance.

"Is everything all right, Mr. Augustus?"

"No, it's not. I'm going to City Central Hospital. I don't know when I'll be back." He started for the elevator.

"Can I do anything?" Susan called toward his retreating back.

"Take care of things here for me. I'll call you later." The elevator doors slid shut and he disappeared from sight.

Lily, he thought, I should have found out what's wrong with her. He saw again her remarkable eyes and remembered the enjoyment of their flight together, their easy talk and laughter. She can't be very ill, he decided, it was only a couple of weeks ago that we met and she was certainly fine then.

He grabbed a cab and instructed the driver to hurry. The cabby rocketed the car through the traffic and pulled to a stop in front of the hospital in record time. John thrust a twenty dollar bill toward the cabby and ran up the steps and into the lobby.

The receptionist stood as he rushed pell-mell through the door, determined to stop his rush if needed. "May I help you, sir?"

"Mrs. Rathbourne, what room is she in?" He demanded.

"Is she a patient here?"

"Of course," John's impatience at even this slight delay was evident in his tone. "I'd like to see her, please."

"One moment," the receptionist resumed her seat and slowly looked through her listing of patients. She kept one red lacquered fingernail carefully on the list as she looked up at John and said, "She is a patient here but I'm afraid I can't let you up to see her."

"Why not?" John struggled to keep his anger under control.

"She's not allowed visitors, sir." The red nail tapped the page. "Only the immediate family."

John didn't hesitate a moment before he lied, "I am family. I'm her grandson."

The nail tapped more briskly. "It says here that she has no family."

"Well it's a mistake. She's my grandmother and I want to see her." John scowled.

"I'll check, sir." The receptionist picked up the phone. "Please take a seat over there, sir. I'll be right with you."

John turned his back and started to walk obediently toward the waiting area, changing his mind he swung back to face the woman. He watched as she placed the call on the switchboard and tried to catch her words when she talked into the mouthpiece. It was apparent from her glare in his direction that whoever she was talking to did not confirm his story. The woman disconnected and looked up at John. She managed to keep her voice polite as she said firmly, "The patient has no family in this country."

"Who's her doctor?" he demanded. "I'll talk to him."

"I'm sorry, sir. I can't release that information."

"Who can?" John's voice was rising along with his pulse rate. "Let me talk to someone in charge."

"Just a moment, sir," an angry edge became apparent in the receptionist's voice as she struggled to remain professional.

John drummed impatiently on the edge of the desk with his fingertips and waited impatiently for the woman to find someone to help him. I'm coming, Lily, he sent a silent message. He drummed harder and the receptionist glared at him.

"Take a chair, sir," she ordered. "I'm trying to reach Dr. Morgan."

John realized that he'd been acting like a bore. He smiled at the woman. "I'm sorry," he apologized. "It's just that I'm so worried about Lily. I had no idea she was ill until someone called me this morning. I'm the only person she knows in the states and I want to help her."

"I understand, sir." The combination of his smile and his obvious distress softened the woman's impatience with him. "I'll let you know as soon as I reach Dr. Morgan. He'll be able to help you."

"Thank you." John took a chair and lit a cigarette. He smoked in quick motions, keeping one eye on the switchboard. He flicked the ashes into an ashtray and jumped when a hand clasped his shoulder.

"John, what are you doing here? Is someone ill?"

"Dennis. I am so glad to see you." He stood and shook hands with Dr. Dennis Fairchild. "That woman at the desk won't let me upstairs to visit a patient."

Dr. Fairchild looked puzzled. "Why not?" he asked.

"Some silly rule." John shook his head. "Come over and vouch for me, Dennis."

"Sure, but who is it you want to visit?"

"It's a long story and I'd be glad to explain it all to you some other time but right now I need to get upstairs and check on Lily." Hesitation marked the doctor's face. "It's nothing sinister, Dennis. She's just an old woman I met on the plane when I flew back from the continent. I'm the only person she knows in the states and that woman won't let me see her because I'm not family."

"Okay. Calm down and I'll see what I can do." Dennis strode confidently over to the desk and John watched as he engaged the receptionist in earnest conversation. He saw the woman shake her head and then laugh at something that was said. John tapped his foot and ground out his cigarette. Dennis returned. "Come and have a cup of coffee with me, John."

John started to protest and then caught Dennis' wink. He walked with him through the reception area and toward the elevators.

"The receptionist is right. Mrs. Rathbourne has a no visitors order," Dennis explained as soon as they were out of ear shot of the desk, "but I figured you must have a good reason for your lie about being her grandson so tell me what's up and I'll try to help."

Rapidly, John ran through the story of his meeting with Lily and the phone call he received. Dennis listened closely and nodded, "Okay," he said. "I'm going to break a rule for you." He laughed. "Not a very important rule or I wouldn't do it. Come on I'll take you up to Mrs. Rathbourne's room."

"Do you know what's wrong with her?" John asked relieved that one problem was solved but worried again about Lily's health.

"No," Dennis admitted, "but I know her doctor and I'll find him for you and you can get the details from him."

"Thanks, Dennis." John sighed empathically. "I don't know what I'd have done if you hadn't come along."

"You'd have waited in the waiting room until the hospital administrator had time to see you and sooner or later you would have gotten through the red tape. This is just easier." The elevator doors opened and the two men entered. The receptionist looked after them. She knew it was wrong, but, she shrugged and decided that it wasn't any of her business if Dr. Fairchild wanted to break a rule.

The nurse at the floor desk looked up at their approach, "Can I help you, Doctor," she inquired politely.

"I'd like to see Mrs. Lily Rathbourne's chart."

"Certainly, Doctor." She found the chart and efficiently handed it across the desk. "Room 516, will you require assistance, Doctor?"

"No, thank you. I'll just be talking to the patient, Nurse. Come, John." He turned smartly on his heel and John followed. They rounded a corner and Dennis stopped. He flipped open the chart. "Let me check this. I don't want to take you in to see someone who is really too ill to have visitors," he explained.

John nodded and watched as Dennis scanned the entries. His relief was apparent when his friend looked up and smiled. "Nothing serious," Dennis closed the chart. "Looks like she caught a cold that she didn't take care of and now she has a slight case of pneumonia. But it's under control and she's doing fine. Her doctor is Charles Schmidt. He's young but he's good. Your friend was fortunate he was in the emergency room when they brought her in."

"Thanks, again, Dennis." John extended his hand. "I owe you one. A friend in need is a friend indeed, as my Grandma used to say."

Dennis laughed. "Let's go see your new "Grandma". I want to meet this lady."

John tapped on the half closed door to room 516 and pushed it open. Lily sat on the bed resting against a pile of pillows. She looked up at their entrance and her wide mouth turned up in the smile John remembered from the plane. He crossed the room quickly and embraced her frail shoulders gently. "Lily," he said.

"Hello, John." Lily kissed his cheek. "Thank you for coming."

"I'd have come sooner if you'd called me."

Dennis cleared his throat. John was reminded of his manners. He introduced Dr. Fairchild and explained his part in John's appearance at Lily's bedside. Lily's delighted chuckle filled the room and erased John's fears that she might be seriously ill. "I'm pleased to have you as my grandson," she admitted. "And thank you, Dr. Fairchild, for delivering him to me."

"You're welcome, Mrs. Rathbourne. It's been a pleasure taking part in this escapade but now I'd better make a note on this chart for Dr. Schmidt and then go and attend to my own patients."

When they'd thanked him again and he was gone, John demanded, "Why didn't you call me?"

"I thought it was just a cold and then when I realized I was really ill it was Wednesday afternoon and there wasn't an answer at your office."

With a pang, John remembered the phone call that he hadn't answered. He covered Lily's hand with his own. "I'm sorry, Lily. I was in a rush to leave the office and I didn't answer the phone when it rang."

"Don't be silly, John. You don't know if that was my call or not. What matters is that you are here right now and I'm delighted to see you."

"And I'm delighted to see you, Lily." They laughed together. A nurse peeked in to see what was going on and Lily introduced John as her grandson. The nurse was visibly flustered at meeting a member of the Augustus family. She blushed, prettily, and withdrew to spread the word that Lily not only had family in the states but that she was related to the Walter Augustus family.

"I'm afraid I've done it now," Lily admitted. "That nurse was so thrilled with the idea that I was related to you that everyone in this hospital is going to know in a matter of minutes."

John laughed, his joy at her sense of humor lighting his eyes. "I can't think of anyone I'd rather be connected to. The rest of the family will just have to get used to the idea that we have a new and absolutely terrific member." He held her hand between his own. "Tell me about your treasure hunt. Did you find the person you were looking for?"

Lily sobered at once and again she looked tired. She sank back against the pillows and shook her head. "You were right, John. This is a very large city."

"Nothing, at all?" John asked searching her face for clues.

"Not a hint. Perhaps I'm too late after all."

"Tell me about the treasure, Lily. Maybe I can help."

"I'd like that, John. I'm tired and I'm going to need help if I'm ever to find my daughter again."

"Your daughter?" John asked surprised by the thought that anyone who knew this woman would chose to disappear from her life. "Tell me the whole story, Lily." He sat back in his chair but continued to hold Lily's hand as she began, her eyes soft at the memories.

"It all happened a long time ago, before you were born. I was married and had two children, a son and a daughter. We lived in Paris. My husband was a harsh man but not a bad person. He was stubborn and rather rigid, but most men are, you know." She wiped away a tear and continued, her melodious voice breaking under the emotion. "My daughter became pregnant by an American and in one afternoon my entire world was destroyed. My son was accused of murder, my husband suffered a heart attack and my daughter disappeared."

John sat up straighter so excited he could hardly breathe. His heart pounded as he asked the necessary question, "Tell me your daughter's name." Lily's eyes widened, surprised by the intensity of his tone. "I'm not certain what name she would have used in the states, John. Her given name was Minette Louise de'Roth."

"I knew it, Lily!" John jumped to his feet unable to contain his excitement. "The minute you spoke to me on the plane, I knew there was something special about you."

"Thank you, John." Lily laughed, caught by his excitement. "I think you are special, too."

"Lily, I know the answer to your treasure hunt."

"You do?" Lily's skepticism was more apparent than surprise.

"I do." John declared.

"All right," Lily laughed again. "If you know so much, tell me the answer."

John sat on the edge of the bed and took Lily's hands in his own. He smiled into her eyes and spoke carefully. "You really are my grandmother. My mother is Minette de'Roth." He waited for her to understand. Her eyes filled with tears and her hand trembled beneath his. She shook her head. "It's true, Lily." John reassured her. "You really are my grandmother."

Tears rolled silently down Lily's cheeks and John wiped them away gently. At last she managed to speak, "After all this time." She shook her head again. "I just can't believe that it's over after all this time."

Lily asked excited questions and John explained what he knew of his mother's story and of her life. He talked about his childhood and about his mother. When a nurse interrupted to say that the visiting hours were at an end he glanced at his watch in surprise. He stood up and kissed Lily's soft cheek, "Are you ready to meet your daughter?" he asked.

"Oh, yes!" Excitement flushed her cheeks and caused her eyes to sparkle. "Do you think she'll be ready to meet me?"

"I'm sure she'll be delighted," John reassured her. "You eat your dinner like a good patient and take a little nap and I'll bring mother over for visiting hours this evening."

John walked from the hospital toward Minette's townhouse trying to decide how to break the news. Despite his confident words to Lily he had no idea how his mother would respond to his surprise. What if she didn't want to see her mother? She'd told him the tragic story of their separation but she hadn't mentioned a desire to return to France or a desire to see her mother again. It was quite possible, he supposed, that there was more to this story. John shook off the bad thoughts. It was inconceivable that anyone could know Lily and not want to see her again and hadn't Minette mentioned how understanding her mother had been about her pregnancy. He reached his mother's building and hurried up the steps.

The doorman tilted his hat and held the door for him. "Your mother just came in, sir."

"Thank you," John's pleasure at the news he carried caused him to grin at the man.

He rang his mother's bell and waited impatiently for her to answer. "John," Minette raised her cheek for his kiss. "What a lovely surprise. Come in." She drew him into the living room and helped him remove his coat. "Sit down. I've just this moment come in from shopping. Excuse me a minute and I'll put these bags away." She swept up her purchases and left the room.

John took a deep breath and made himself comfortable on the soft beige sofa. He loved this room, it was so different from the house he shared with Sylvia and very different from the house he and his mother had shared with his grandparents when he was growing up. Everything was done in shades of gray and beige, a scheme that should have been dull and drab but with Minette's skillful use of beautiful fabric and accessories the rooms offered a warm and inviting backdrop that set off every art object to perfection.

Minette returned to the living room and curled up in her favorite chair with her feet tucked feet under herself. John smiled warmly, "Whenever I picture you I see you just that way. Curled up like a child in that chair."

Minette laughed. "I do sit this way often, I suppose. It's probably not ladylike but it is comfortable. I remember my mother complaining about what it would do to my posture but I've never noticed any problem."

"I like it, but you're the only mother I know that sits that way."

"Did you drop by this afternoon to discuss my sitting habits or was there something else on your mind?"

John shifted nervously, trying to think of some way to tell her his news.

"When you look like that I know you've something terribly important on your mind. What have you been up to today?"

"You're right that I have something to tell you but I'm not sure how to begin," he confessed.

"Why not start at the beginning and go on from there?"

"That's easier said than done, Mother. Some things seem to have neither a logical place to begin nor any logical way to proceed."

Minette swung her feet down and stood up. "This sounds serious. Why don't I make us some coffee?"

John nodded. "Come out in the kitchen with me perhaps it will be easier for you to talk."

John waited while Minette prepared the coffee and placed it on the stove to perk. When she was seated across from him he cleared his throat and began hesitantly, "Did you ever want to go back to France? Did you want to see your family again?"

"What in the world makes you ask that?" The surprise on Minette's face so exactly matched the surprise John had seen earlier on Lily's face that he was surprised he hadn't recognized their resemblance to one another when he first met Lily on the flight from Europe. He watched Minette carefully waiting for her answer. "Of course, I wanted to see my family again. I wasn't angry with them. I knew that my father was hurt and that he'd gone with my brother that night in order to do what he felt was right. That my brother had killed Michael was a crime that I felt responsible for but one that I knew the French government would prosecute him for. I was very ashamed of myself. I felt that I'd done a terrible wrong to my family, one that I was sure they could never forgive."

The coffee began to perk and she reached over and turned down the flame. "In France an illegitimate child is a terrible disgrace. With Michael dead there was no hope that I could be married in time to give you his name. My father had suffered a severe heart attack that was entirely my fault my brother would most likely go to jail for a long time for trying to protect my honor. I saw nothing to do but disappear and that's what I did. But, of course, I've always dreamed of seeing them all again. Until that terrible afternoon we'd been a close, happy family."

"Why didn't you ever go back to France?"

"In the beginning, I didn't believe I could and then as the years slipped by." Minette shrugged. "Who knows? It never seemed like the right thing to do." She poured them each a cup of coffee and sat with her chin in her hand, her eyes clouded with memories. "Are you considering trying to find your family roots?"

John shook his head. "I've never felt rootless, Mother. You and Walter and Edith gave me a wonderful childhood in the bosom of a loving family. But something has happened that I need to tell you."

Minette gazed at him, calmly waiting for him to continue. "When I was flying back from Europe, I met a charming older woman. She was wise and funny and we talked so easily. It seemed as if I knew her. She told me she was coming to the city to hunt for a treasure that she'd lost many years ago. I offered to help her if I could and I gave her my card so she could reach me." Minette sat motionless her eyes wide and blank. "This morning," John continued, "I received a call from a cleaning woman at the hospital. The woman had been admitted last Wednesday and they hadn't been able to locate any relatives. This cleaning woman took it on herself to call me and tell me that the woman was ill. I rushed to the hospital and found that she has pneumonia but she's recovering and will be fine. We renewed our friendship and I asked her about her treasure hunt." John kept his blue eyes fixed on his mother's face as he quickly continued. "She hadn't had any luck at all and was very discouraged. When I asked Lily to tell me the whole story so that perhaps I could help," Minette set her cup down with a thump and met his gaze squarely "The story she told me was very familiar."

"My mother's name was Lily." Tears welled from Minette's eyes and ran down her cheeks.

"I know." John almost whispered the words. "She's looking for you."

Minette groped for John's hand and he grasped it. Gently he stroked her fingers as she sobbed and digested his news. "After all this time," she murmured.

"She's waiting to see you, Mother."

Minette dashed away her tears and jumped to her feet she hugged John and fairly danced around the room. "Oh, Darling!" she exclaimed. "It's so wonderful. I never would have thought that this day would come. Will you come with me to the hospital?"

John laughed, delighted by her happiness. "Of course, we have to wait until visiting hours though."

"I'll get ready. When can we go?"

"At seven."

Minette glanced at the kitchen clock. "We'll go at six-thirty," she said decisively. "I want to be there as soon as I can. We've wasted enough time. She started to leave the kitchen but turned back to hug him again. "I'm so excited. Do you think she'll be glad to see me?"

"Mother," John squeezed her, "Lily came all the way across the ocean without a clue as to where you were, determined to find you. Naturally she'll be glad to see you."

"I know," Minette agreed, "but I'm a bit afraid. It's been a very long time."

At the hospital John escorted Minette to Lily's room and watched as the two women greeted each other. Almost at once the constraints fell away and they began to chatter together in French. John withdrew to the waiting area and picked up a magazine. An hour passed before Minette appeared. "Mother wants to see you John."

Lily took his hand, her eyes filled with unshed tears as she said, "I want to thank you, John. This is the happiest day of my life."

John kissed her soft cheek. "Welcome to the family, Grandmother."

The City Chronicle
January 23, 1939
Tattletales by Sharon Chatsworth

The city lies blanketed under a carpet of snow and all the socialites seem to have fled to the south for a taste of warmer weather. Mrs. John Augustus (Sylvia) and her son Michael are spending a quiet month in Charleston while Mr. Augustus stays on in the city attending to the family business. Mr. and Mrs. Samuel Augustus haven't been seen in the city since their return from California but the beautiful Mrs. Minette Augustus has been seen everywhere, and I do mean everywhere, showing our fair city to her mother, Mrs. Lily Rathbourne of London, England. It does this reporters heart good to see two such lovely women enjoying themselves together.

Chapter 9

John joined his mother and grandmother at their luncheon table. He apologized for keeping them waiting, gave them each a kiss and seated himself. "I see you two made the paper this morning," he commented.
Lily arched her brows in a silent question.
"In the Chatsworth column," John explained.
"She must be desperate for news if she doesn't have anything better to report then our activities," Minette snorted.
"What column is this?" Lily asked.

"The local gossip, she writes only on the doings of the people she considers to be interesting to the general public and not always in the best of taste."

"Actually, Grandma," John teased, "she usually finds something scandalous to write about. Fortunately, you and Mother have been behaving yourselves and there was nothing she could say except that you'd been seen shopping together."

"Since she likes to report on the comings and goings and what everyone was wearing as they came and went, your grandmother and I will most likely make the column again." Minette injected. "Lily is ready to go back to Europe and I've decided to accompany her."

John sobered at once. "Are you sure?" he asked. "Things are rather unsettled over there."

"We're sure," Minette said empathically. "I want to see France again and this is the right time to go."

"Minette's brother is ill," Lily expounded on their reasons. "He'd like to see her again."

"And I need to see him. He went to jail for three long years for his part in the protection of my virtue." Minette sighed. "I really must go, John."

John smiled at the two women. In their time together, they'd grown more alike each day. The resemblance between them was so strong that John was surprised anew that he hadn't recognized Lily immediately. They both had the same wide mouth and beautiful eyes, although Minette's were blue and Lily's appeared almost violet. They were built alike, slender and delicate but with a core of steel. He saluted them with his wine glass. "I understand. When are you leaving?"

"We've made reservations to sail a week from Tuesday. An ocean voyage will be fun for us."

"I'm offended that you're not flying, Mother." John teased. "I know you hate the idea."

Minette blushed. "I know it's silly, John. After all, if you trust those things, I'm sure they're safe but..." her voice dwindled off.

I want to see your Michael again before we leave." Lily said. "Will they be back from Charleston?"

"I think so. I'm not certain of Sylvia's plans."

Lily shook her head sadly. "If you'll take an old lady's advice John, you should reconsider this marriage of yours. It is possible to do what's right and still be happy."

"I wish I could, Lily." John played with his knife and avoided looking at her. "I don't know how to change things and I don't know if I want to." He shifted his gaze to the other occupants of the restaurant.

"It's not really my business but," Lily spoke softly, "in France many marriages are arranged and they are not always happy. However, they are always filled with respect and common goals. You and Sylvia need to achieve that type of arrangement or you'll both be miserable."

"We are miserable," John admitted.

The waiter brought their lunch and John was spared from further discussion of his marriage but he knew that Lily was right, without respect for one another; he and Sylvia were living in an armed camp. They avoided each other and when they did meet any conversation escalated rapidly into a defensive confrontation. It couldn't be good for Michael to have parents that were always at each other's throats. Thank heaven for Annie; she was an absolute angel with the boy. He decided to call Charleston as soon as he got back to the office and make sure that Michael would have one more visit with his grandmother and great grandmother before their departure.

The family gathered at John and Sylvia's to bid farewell to Lily and Minette. After the children were settled with Annie the adults gathered together in the living room. Duncan served drinks and withdrew. Walter spoke first, "It has been a real joy meeting you after all these years, Lily. Minette has been like a daughter to me since the first moment I laid eyes on her. She is a fine woman, a wonderful mother and a credit to her upbringing."

"Hear, hear." Sam raised his glass.

Lily laughed, "I'm not sure I can take any credit, Walter. I doubt that I have had much to do with the charming woman she is today. I am very proud of my daughter and of her son. I've been most relieved to discover that she is a member of such a fine family." She smiled warmly at Minette. "During the long years of our separation I have worried about her and about the circumstances of her life but if I could have chosen a family for her, I could not have done better than to choose this family."

"It's been quite an experience meeting my other grandmother for the first time and falling so madly in love with her," John teased. "I think my heart may break with both you and my mother gone."

"You must bring your family to visit me in France." Lily answered. "This will be my last trip across the ocean."

"We'll do that, Lily, but I think it will have to wait until Michael is older and the political situation has calmed down."

"Speaking of politics," Sam changed the subject, "I don't like the sounds of what's going on. You two need to stay informed and aware of the situation so that you can return to the states at a moment's notice if it becomes necessary."

"Don't be such a sour puss, Sam," Helen admonished her husband.

"Sam's, right, ladies," Walter said soberly. "You need to pay attention and if it looks as though France is going to be caught up in the war you should get home as fast as possible. You too, Lily, you always have a home here with us."

"Thank you, Walter," Lily acknowledged his offer, "but France is my home and I want to be there."

"I don't think there is really any need to worry yet," Walter admitted. "I'd guess that war is coming but I think it's at least a year away. Before then you should both get back on this side of the ocean. The United States is going to be the only safe place in the world."

The tension caused by the war talk eased as the family chattered and laughed. Minette and Lily spent time in the nursery saying good bye to each of the children and especially to Michael. There was a flurry of hugging and kissing and then only John was left with the two most important women in his life.

"I should go up and put the last few things in to my bag," Lily said excusing herself.

"I'll be up in a few minutes if you need help, Mother." Minette offered. "I want to talk to John for a moment." She drew John down beside her on the sofa. "I try not to interfere in your life, John," she started.

"You never interfere, Mother."

"This time, I am." Minette took a deep breath and plunged into what she needed to say. "I'm going away, John, and I may not be back for a long time." John tried to protest. "I'll stay with my mother as long as she needs me. I owe her that and I want to do it. She's suffered enough over the years because of my childish mistake and I need to do what I can to make it up to her, if I can." John nodded his understanding. "I want to see you happy, John. Every mother wants her children to be happy and I'm no different. You've set up a terrible situation in your life and it must be straightened out. I know you don't feel love for Sylvia but it's obvious to me that you have learned to care for Michael during these last few months. For his sake, let the past go and begin to build a decent future."

"I do like Michael but he's not my son."

"It doesn't matter whose child he is by blood. A child becomes yours by love and Michael deserves your love."

"That sounds good, Mother, but it doesn't work that way. Sylvia and I fight every time we see each other. How in the world could we possibly build a future together?"

"You could start by treating each other with respect. Didn't you listen to your grandmother at lunch?"

"I heard what she said but this isn't France," John tried to contain his annoyance, knowing that Minette meant well.

"No, but it is life. You've made a commitment that you are only half honoring. A man who doesn't give his all is not a whole man." Minette looked at him sadly. "You are too good to let Sylvia's mistake destroy your life and Michael's. Shake off those bad feelings and get on with making your life all it can be."

John wanted to argue with her calm logic but he couldn't think of anything to say that didn't sound like self pity. The silence stretched for a long minute and then Minette sighed. "Please try, John.

I love you very much and I want you to live a life free from guilt."

"I'll try, Mother," John promised.

"Good night then. I'll see you in the morning." She kissed his cheek and left him alone with his tortured thoughts.

With Minette and Lily off to France life settled back into usual routines. John went to the office each morning and put in a long day. He played with Michael for a few minutes whenever he arrived home early enough. Sylvia kept busy with her friends and a round of shopping, lunches and parties. They seldom saw one another. It was easy for John to forget Minette's words and allow his marriage to drift along.

Gradually winter lifted from the city and the hint of warm days to come floated on the wind. In Europe the unrest escalated. The aggressive Nazis policy toward Czechoslovakia allowed then to take the nation without invasion and then the Spanish Civil War ended. With help from the Nazis the Spanish Republican government was replaced with a dictatorship led by General Francisco Franco.

John saw Sam at the office and kept his promise to Christopher to show him around the airport. Chris' enthusiasm was infectious and he found himself laughing freely and enjoying every minute of the boy's company. Their conversation roamed over many topics and finally Chris said, "My mother's going to have a baby soon."

"Yes, I know." John answered cautiously, unsure of where this might lead.

"She has to stay in bed a lot."

"Does she?" John asked, startled by this news and surprised that Sam hadn't mentioned it. He wondered if something might be wrong.

"I think she got sick when we went to California for Christmas," Chris shared his meager knowledge.

"I don't think she's really sick," John tried to reassure the boy. "Sometimes when woman are pregnant they just need more rest."

"I don't think so." Chris scuffed his toe along the ground. "She looks funny and she cries a lot."

John hid his worry and kept his voice unconcerned as he said, "Let's go into the control tower. You can watch how they help land the planes."

"Okay!" Chris' excitement chased away his worry but John was unable to push his aside.

He took Chris back to the house and asked to see Helen but was told she was resting. He hurried back to the office determined to ask Sam what was going on but Sam was tied up in a meeting and the opportunity to talk alone didn't present itself.

Days slipped by until one morning he was reminded of the conversation when he saw Sam rushing down the hall and into the elevator. He called his secretary, "Get hold of Sam for me, please. Tell him I need a few minutes of his time."

Susan reported back that Sam had been called home. "Okay. I'll be over in Walter's office if you need me."

Walter's door was open so John walked right in. Walter put down the report he was reading and took off his glasses when John closed the door. "What's wrong?" he asked.

"That's what I want to ask you." John sat in a chair and leaned forward over the desk. "I took Christopher out to the airport the other day and he seemed to think that there might be something wrong with his mother. I haven't been able to catch up with Sam and I wondered if you'd heard anything."

Walter polished his glasses in his familiar manner. "No," he answered slowly, "I haven't seen much of Helen since they got back from their trip but I figured she was probably staying close to home now that the pregnancy is showing." He laid his glasses, folded neatly, in the center of the blotter. "What did young Christopher say that worried you?"

"That his mother had to stay in bed a lot. What really surprised me is that Sam just went rushing out of here and his secretary said that he'd been called home."

Walter reached at once for the phone on his desk. "I'll call and see if everything is okay." He started to place the call and then set the receiver back on the cradle. "I don't want to stick my nose into his business. Why don't you call?"

John swallowed a chuckle, amused that Walter would refrain from interfering in anything that even remotely resembled family affairs. Checking on Helen's health didn't seem like interference. He stood and said, "All right. I'll call." He started toward the door.

Walter stopped him. "You might as well call from here." John nodded, keeping his face straight with an effort. Walter might not want to make the phone call but he wanted to know if anything was happening.

Christopher's agitated voice answered on the first ring. "Chris," John said calmly "this is your Uncle John. Could I speak to your mother, please?"

"She's not here. An ambulance came and picked her up and took her to the hospital."

"When?" John struggled to control his voice so as not to frighten the already worried boy.

"Just a few minutes ago."

"Who's at home with you kids?"

"Mattie's here." The quiver in his voice was more apparent as he tried to answer John's questions.

"Everything will be all right, Chris," John reassured him. "Let me speak to Mattie for a minute."

He covered the receiver with one hand and started to tell Walter what had happened but the rich southern voice of the housekeeper came on the line almost immediately. "Mr. John?"

"Yes, Mattie. What's going on?" The worry in John's tone was now obvious. Walter picked up his glasses and began to polish them again keeping his eyes on John's face as if he could read the answers there.

John could hear Mattie as she said, "Christopher you take Beth and go in the kitchen. There are some fresh cookies on the table. I'll be there in a moment." She waited a second and then spoke into the receiver. "Miss Helen hasn't been feeling well at all these last couple of months but this morning she started bleeding real bad. I called the doctor and he wanted her in the hospital. They sent an ambulance to pick her up. I called Mr. Sam and he's meeting her at the hospital."

"Is the baby coming?"

"I expect so. But it's awful early for the wee thing."

"I'll go to the hospital. Do you need any help with the children?" Walter put on his glasses and stood up ready to go with John. John quickly concluded the conversation and hung up. "The baby's coming early," he explained although no explanation was really necessary.

They hurried from the office and caught a cab to the hospital. John was reminded of his last trip to the hospital and said a silent prayer that this would be another happy occasion.

The maternity waiting room was located across from the main entrance and it was easy to spot Sam pacing the floor. His haggard face brightened slightly as they entered. John clasped his hand, "How's Helen?"

Sam shook his head. "I've no idea. They won't let me see her."

"What happened?" Walter questioned.

"Helen's been having quite a time. She never complains so at first I didn't realize that anything was wrong but then the doctor told her to stay in bed more. We didn't think that was so unusual after all this is the fifth child and she is thirty-four." Sam's face paled and anguish touched his eyes. "I couldn't stand it if anything happens to Helen," he confessed softly.

"She'll be fine," Walter said firmly. "She's a strong woman."

"It's awfully early for the baby to be born," Sam said. "Almost two months too early."

Their worry hung like a thick cloud as the minutes passed. It was impossible to think of words that would be reassuring to Sam. Each time a nurse or doctor passed the room the three men looked up expectantly. John got coffee and he and Sam smoked a constant stream of cigarettes. Occasionally they spoke but for the most part they sat in silent worry each praying in their own way that everything would be all right.

At last, Dennis Fairchild entered the waiting area and collapsed wearily onto a chair. He sipped from the cup of coffee he carried. Sam stopped his pacing and demanded, "Is Helen okay?"

Dennis nodded. "She's stable, Sam. We've stopped the bleeding but we have to take the baby and she doesn't want us to do it."

"What do you mean?" Walter asked.

Dennis kept his eyes on Sam as he answered, "Helen can't carry this child to full term. Her body just refuses to do it. I need to perform a cesarean."

"Well, do it then," Sam said impatiently.

"It's not that simple. Helen is determined to wait. She knows that the baby would have a very slim chance for survival."

"What if you don't operate?" John asked the question all three were thinking.

"Helen's life is in danger. She's had a rough pregnancy. Her strength is low and now she's lost a lot of blood."

"I won't allow anything to happen to Helen." Sam's voice shook. "Save her life, Dennis."

"I need her permission to operate, Sam."

"I'll talk to her. She doesn't understand." Sam started for the door. "Show me her room, Dennis."

Left alone in the waiting room, Walter dashed unshed tears from his eyes. "It'll be fine," he said, "I know it'll be fine."

John didn't answer. He could imagine what Sam was feeling. The anguish he still felt over the loss of Valerie was a constant ache in his heart. He thought of the many times he'd seen Sam and Helen holding hands or smiling across a room at one another and the joy they shared over their children. She has to recover, he thought. Sam and the kids need her so much.

That was exactly the argument Sam was preparing to use. He sat beside the hospital bed waiting for

Helen to wake from her exhausted sleep. Her beautiful face was very pale. He watched her quiet breathing and whispered a silent prayer that she would listen to him. Her fingers stirred in his hand, her eyes opened and a faint smile touched her lips. "Hi, Sam."

"Hi, Beautiful Lady." Sam brushed his lips over hers. "How do you feel?"

"Okay," Helen tried to smile. "They want to take the baby."

"I know." Sam struggled with the tears he felt.

"She's too little."

Sam pressed his finger to her lips. "I love you, Helen. I need you and so do the other kids." Helen tried to speak but Sam continued. "Dennis thinks he can save the baby if he operates tonight."

Helen shook her head. "Sam, it's too early. She's only a tiny little child. She needs to grow before she enters the world."

Sam smiled gently at the way Helen insisted on using the female pronoun to describe the baby. "I know how you feel, Honey. I want to protect this child, too, but I need you. I can't endanger your life." He took both her hands in his and kissed the fingers one by one. "Helen, I couldn't go on if something happened to you. Dennis feels that there is a chance that he can deliver a healthy child tonight but that he can't make any promises if we wait."

"I'll be all right, Sam." Helen insisted. "I can carry this child long enough to give her a chance to survive. I know I can."

Color rose in her cheeks and Sam was afraid she was becoming more upset. He kissed her eyelids. "Rest, Love," he said. "I'll stay right here."

Helen lay back on the pillows and drifted off to sleep. Sam touched her face gently. She looked so fragile, so pale. A nurse came in and took her pulse and blood pressure. Helen stirred but did not waken. Dr. Fairchild looked in and, seeing that Helen slept peacefully, he beckoned for Sam to come out in the hall.

"Helen wants to carry the child," Sam said.

"I know," The doctor sighed, "but it's impossible. She was bleeding very heavily when they brought her in. If the child hasn't been damaged there is a large chance that it will be. I've only managed to stop the bleeding temporarily. Helen is very ill, Sam. Her life is in danger as well as the child's."

The solemn words felt like a fist to Sam's stomach. He'd been able to ignore the significance of the doctor's desire to operate at once. "Are you sure?" he asked, hoping for a reprieve from the harsh truth. Dennis nodded sadly. "Her blood pressure is low and if she starts to bleed again, we'll stand a chance of losing them both."

"When do you want to operate?" Sam gave up the argument he'd been having with himself.

"As soon as possible," he glanced at his watch. "Within the hour would be best."

Sam squared his shoulders. "Okay," he said firmly. "I'll explain it to Helen." He returned to her bedside and stroked her familiar hand, rousing her gently from her sleep. He smiled at her as her eyes fluttered awake. "I've been talking to Dennis, Honey. He's going to operate."

She opened her lips to protest but Sam stopped her with a gentle kiss. "It's the only chance the baby has. I love you, Helen. I promise that everything will be all right." He cupped her face with his hand and tried to smile. He kissed her mouth and wiped the tears from her eyes unaware that his own eyes were full of unshed tears.

Now there was nothing to do but wait. Sam paced the floor in one direction and John paced in the other. Walter polished his glasses and sat quiet and withdrawn. They scarcely spoke to one another. An attendant brought them coffee that grew cold in the untouched cups.

At last Dennis appeared. "It's over," he said. "Helen is fine. She lost a lot of blood but she'll be okay. The baby is a girl. She's very small, only three pounds one ounce and she's having trouble breathing. We'll do everything we know how."

"Thanks, Dennis." Sam extended his hand, "I know you will."

"I've called in a specialist for the baby but at this time I can't tell you what her chances are."

"Can I see her?" Sam asked. Dennis nodded too weary to discuss it further. He escorted Sam to the nursery window. Sam gazed in amazement at the tiny creature that was his new daughter. All the children had seemed small to him when they were born but this child was incredible. If she survived these first days he knew it would be a miracle. Silently he willed his strength into her tiny limbs.

Dennis took his arm and turned him from the window. "Helen will be awake in a few minutes."

The City Chronicle
May 1st, 1939
Tattletales by Sharon Chatsworth

Last night a glittering party welcomed Sarah Lynn Augustus home to her waiting family. Sarah was born to Mr. and Mrs. Samuel Augustus on March 23rd of this year. She is the smallest baby to be born and survive at City Central Hospital. The story of her first six weeks is a heartwarming message to the world of the incredible will to live that even the smallest human being is capable of displaying. Present at the gala event were all of Sarah's proud siblings, parents, aunts, uncles, cousins and grandparents with the notable exception of Mrs. John Augustus.

Chapter 10

"That Bitch!" Sylvia threw the paper down on the table in disgust.

"Did you need something, Mrs. Augustus?" Mrs. Peters inquired, poking her head into the breakfast room.

"What?" Sylvia jumped at the intrusion. "Oh no, nothing, I was just talking to myself." She took a drink of coffee to steady her nerves and picked up the paper again. The words of the Chatsworth column jumped out at her. How does that woman know everything that goes on in this town, she wondered. No one was at that party but family last night and here it is reported in the morning paper that I was absent. She's got some nerve insinuating that there was some dark secret about what I why I wasn't there.

Sylvia stretched and smiled a catlike, secretive smile. What a juicy column it would make if she knew the truth. Last night with Mark had been wonderful. He was always so exciting, so full of fun and adventure. It was really too bad they couldn't be open about their affair. The way it was some of her friends were beginning to suspect that there might be something going on between them. Perhaps they should be more careful about being seen only as part of a group. She'd been putting out the story that Mark was merely escorting her at the request of her husband but it had been several months since she and John had been seen together while she'd been out with Mark almost every night. I suppose I should have gone to that thing last night. She brushed away the thought with another, but who wants to look at another one of Helen and Sam's little blond babies.

She finished her breakfast and went upstairs to get ready for her day. Glancing in at the open door to the nursery she noted that Annie and Michael were occupied with a book and she went on without pausing. Having a child had turned out to be a lot easier then she'd expected. There certainly wasn't any reason to make a big production out of it the way some people did. How in the world Helen could stand to have all those children, one right after another, and let them cling to her all the time was beyond Sylvia. Give me a nursemaid any day, she thought. It's so boring and messy to have a small child.

Sylvia congratulated herself on how well she'd managed to arrange her life since John's return. Annie had full charge of Michael, but she did try to see him at least for a few minutes each day although lately she had to admit to herself that she sometimes missed a day here and there. Michael didn't seem to mind though and Annie really was very conscientious about his walk in the park and all that other stuff that children were supposed to need.

She felt that everything was under control and that appearances were being kept up. She slept late and after dressing went out to lunch with friends and then shopping or to keep an appointment with her hairdresser or a beautician. Around five she tried to return to the house and fit in a quick visit to the nursery. Then she was free to bathe and dress for the evening.

John came home between six and seven and it was easy to avoid meeting him since he always went straight to the nursery and then to his room to change. While he was occupied, Sylvia slipped out of the house and took one of the cars. It would have been more convenient if Mark could have called for her but then she'd never be able to make excuses about why John couldn't join the group. As long as he stayed out of sight it was easy to say he was working too much. Mark knew the truth, of course, but he was glad to play along with her fantasy.

Sylvia shrugged off her thoughts of family and began to think about which shoes to wear with her new suit. Dressing for the evening, Sylvia continued to muse about this last year. Things were much better for her now that she didn't have to worry about John and what he thought about her lifestyle. Being married in name only had a lot of advantages, if only people like that Sharon Chatsworth would mind their own business. I suppose I'll have to be more discrete, at least for a little while since Chatsworth is watching, she decided. Carefully she outlined her eyes with kohl in the dramatic new style she'd learned only yesterday. She tilted her head and examined the effect. It would take a little getting used to but she certainly looked different. Mark will like it, she thought. He likes variety and spice in fact, she chuckled, being forced to be more discrete would be good for him. A little intrigue and not quite so much availability on my part will pique his interest.

She smiled to herself as she continued with her makeup. Meeting Mark Phillips had certainly added interest to her life. He was so different from John, so ready to enjoy life. Sylvia laughed aloud at the memory of last night's party. The party had been marvelous, unlike any party she'd ever attended. Everyone had been a little drunker, a little crazier than usual. The band had played longer and louder, the men had flirted with the women in open, extravagant ways. And darling Mark had courted her outrageously. At midnight the Jordan's had made a public announcement of their intent to divorce and, immediately, Mark started singing, "For He's A Jolly Good Fellow". The band and all of the guests had joined him. It had been so funny.

She knew that Mark was the kind of man she should have married. He was as blond as a Norse god and as good looking. His clothes were always the latest rage and sometimes just a shade flamboyant. They made a spectacular couple. He was only an inch or two taller but somehow that added to their look. On the dance floor they moved as one and, she grinned at herself in the mirror, in bed their moves had turned out to be spectacular. Yes, she acknowledged to herself, Mark had certainly added a new and very enjoyable dimension to her life. He'd introduced her to a whole new crowd that spent their time enjoying their money instead of worrying about it the way John and his friends did.

She realized that the people she ran with were the ones that John would call fast. But "fast" was why she liked them. I can't inherit Daddy's money, she thought, but I can certainly spend it. She slid into a new Worth gown and admired her silhouette in the pier glass. The black taffeta fit like a second skin. The dagger slim heels accentuated her legs. Glancing over her shoulder, she checked that the seams of her silk stockings ran up her slim calves in perfectly straight lines. She gathered her tiny leather bag with its jeweled clasp and hurried downstairs. The crowd was meeting at a brand new nightclub tonight and she was sure she'd be able to make a grand impression. But first, she planned, I'll drive over to Mark's apartment and we can have a quiet drink together. I'll tell him right away that we need to be more careful. Starting tomorrow I'll have Andrew drive me for a while. That should throw off the gossips. After all a woman that arrives alone and leaves alone, in her husband's car, can't be up to anything too terrible.

John read the Chatsworth column while he ate a sandwich at his desk. He felt a slight twinge of anger at the woman's obvious attempt to cast a cloud over his marriage and a greater annoyance at Sylvia for not being more careful. He realized that she was going out a great deal and he'd known that she had a boyfriend since Thanksgiving but it was going to cause a problem if the whole city started talking about it. He supposed he should mention it to Sylvia but things had been going so well these past months he hated to rock the boat. He pushed it aside.

His days were full of work. The world was coming closer to war every day and they were changing things in the company as rapidly as possible so that AmCO would be able to fill the supply orders that were expected to come. By the time he reached the house at night he wanted peace and quiet, not a fight with Sylvia. Most evenings he spent an hour or so with Michael, ate his meal, and read for a bit before falling into bed exhausted. The only place he went was to Sam and Helen's. Helen was recovering from Sarah's birth but it was apparent that the strain had been very hard on her and they, too, were keeping close to home. Every time he went out to the big house on the lake he was overwhelmed by the peace and happiness that seemed to penetrate every corner. Last night the joy had been especially intense as the four older children welcomed their baby sister. Her survival still seemed like a miracle. Yes, he decided, I'd better talk to Syl before that gossip stirs up a stink that will cause problems for the rest of the family. How Sylvia and I live needs to be kept inside our own walls, Syl will just have to be more careful and pay more attention to being seen at the right places at the right times, with the right friends.

By the time he reached home, Sylvia had gone out for the evening and the words of caution he'd meant to use were forgotten. Stopping at the nursery he found Michael in his nightclothes carrying a book and his teddy bear. John hugged him close and carried him to the rocking chair. Michael's warm body relaxed against him as they rocked gently and read the storybook. The room was warm and peaceful, an island of calm in John's hectic life. The book finished John continued to rock. Michael relaxed and fell asleep in his arms. Annie returned to the nursery and smiled at the picture they made. She offered to carry Michael to his bed but John shook his head and carried the boy himself. He tucked him under the covers and kissed his warm cheek. He was overwhelmed by a rush of emotion. I love this child, he thought. The realization surprised him and he watched as Michael slept, trying to understand how it could have happened that another man's son had become so important to him. Minette was right, he decided. A child does become yours through love not by birth. He tucked the covers more securely around the small sturdy body and went to eat his solitary dinner.

Spring raced into summer and the Augustus men watched in dismay, with the rest of the world, as Germany became more aggressive and the stories travelers brought back to the states became more frightening. On a Thursday afternoon late in June they gathered in Walter's office for a family conference.

"What do you hear from your Mother?" Walter began.

"She and Lily are settled in Paris. They are experiencing some shortages but nothing extreme. Lily's health has slowly started to deteriorate, but Mother assures me that they are safe."

"I don't think they are really safe. Those Germans are up to no good. I think they need to return to the United States as quickly as possible," Sam declared.

"I agree," John responded. "I've tried to convince them in every letter that I've written but so far they ignore my advice." He sighed. "Women can be very stubborn, you know."

Walter chuckled. "That's certainly true. Whoever that was that said women are the weaker sex had no idea what he was talking about." John and Sam laughed. "But seriously," Walter continued, "the situation in Europe is steadily going downhill. We are going to see them at war with one another before the year is out. I think it's time you went back to England, John."

John nodded his agreement. He'd been expecting this request and the answer was ready on his tongue. "I think you're right. Walter. I'll leave immediately. I can get the company over there organized and ready to meet the war effort and I can go over to France and make Mother and Lily board a ship headed for the states."

"Perhaps you should go directly to France," Sam suggested seriously.

"Do you think that the war is that imminent?"

"I'm afraid I do."

The men made their plans and it was decided that John would leave immediately after the Fourth of July. That would give them time to arrange the work at the home office so that his presence wouldn't be missed. "You may be gone a long time, John," Walter said as the meeting drew to a close. "If this war is the kind I think it will be, you'll need to stay in England until it's over. The Allies will need all the planes and equipment the states will be able to produce. We'll need you there to keep things running."

"I don't mind, Grandfather," John smiled to reassure him.

"What about Sylvia?

"She'll understand." John avoided Walter's eyes and kept his real thoughts on the subject to himself. He knew that not only would Sylvia not mind, she'd be thrilled at his departure. I'll miss Michael though, he admitted to himself in surprise.

Telling Sylvia about his plans proved to be harder then he'd expected. Three days went by and he still hadn't seen her at home. Finally he wrote a note and propped it up on her bed pillow. Late the next morning Susan announced a call from his wife and her breezy, social voice bubbled out of the phone, "Hi, Stranger."

"Good Morning, Syl. Thanks for calling. I need to talk with you."

"That sounds ominous," Sylvia teased.

"Not at all, we don't see much of each other and I'm making plans that will affect you. I think we'd better get together and talk, that's all."

"Plans?" Sylvia asked, hope coloring her voice. John knew she was thinking about divorce.

"Yes, plans." He kept his voice calm with an effort. "I'll be going back to Europe. Can you meet me for lunch and we'll talk about it?"

"A date! What fun!" Sylvia's brittle tone irritated John and he struggled to refrain from making a comment that would set off her anger.

"Call it a date if you like but meet me at Luigi's in an hour, okay?"

Sylvia promised reluctantly. Sam came in as John hung up and glared angrily at the phone. "What did the phone do Cuz? You look mad enough to strangle the poor thing," he joked as he slumped down in a chair and propped his feet up.

"I'm not mad."

"Well, you could have fooled me."

"I was talking to Sylvia."

Sam nodded wisely, "Things are still the same between you, huh?"

"Things will never be the same again. Living anywhere in the same vicinity as that woman keeps life in an uproar." John sighed and rubbed his eyes. "I haven't been able to catch up with her since we decided I should go back to England, so I've arranged a lunch "date". I felt she should know my plans." He grinned sheepishly at his understatement.

Sam chuckled at his cousin's embarrassment and nodded, "Least you could do, tell the lady before you disappear." He put his feet back on the floor and sat up. "Anything I can do to help?"

"As a matter of fact there is," John hesitated, unsure of how to broach the problem he'd been trying to resolve.

"Spit it out, Cuz. There's nothing you can ask that I won't do, if I can."

"Thanks, Sam. I'm grateful for all the support you've given me and I know that you have plenty of problems of your own without taking on mine."

"I'm a busybody at heart," Sam replied. "Why do you think I became a lawyer? Give me someone else's business to poke my nose into and I'm at my best."

"It's not really a problem," John tried to explain, "but I'm afraid it's going to be."

Sam waited. He'd learned from experience that silence often drew out the most complete answers.

"I'm worried about Michael. I don't know how aware you are of what's going on with Syl and me." Sam shrugged and offered no comment. "She's out a great deal. Not that I can blame her. I'm not sure who her friends are or exactly where they spend so much time but I do know that she doesn't have much time to spend with Michael."

Sam though of his own wife and the devotion she showed to is children and his home and the amount of time she managed to save for him. He watched John pace the floor and continued to wait.

"I'd like you to stop by and see Michael anytime that you can squeeze it in." John continued, dropping back into his chair. "Annie is wonderful and she adores the boy but it's not the same thing as having his mother with him."

Sam considered his answer carefully. "Are you saying that you're afraid that Sylvia will neglect Michael?" he asked.

"I don't suppose you can really call it neglect, after all the housekeeper is there. The nursemaid is always with him and Duncan is certainly able to take charge in any situation." He sighed deeply. "It's just that Sylvia is very busy with her life and right now Michael doesn't have much of a place in that life. Maybe when I'm gone she'll spend more time at home."

"Perhaps, it must be as difficult for her as it is for you. After all I'm sure she wanted a child."

"Never!" John spoke so emphatically that Sam drew back. "Michael was an accident in every sense of the word. Walter wanted us to have a child. I wanted us to have a child and Sylvia was caught by a pregnancy that she didn't believe possible until it was too late to have an abortion."

"Surely you exaggerate. She'd never have had an abortion." Sam was shocked at the thought.

"Yes she would. I'm sure that if her doctor would have been willing she'd have done it without blinking an eye."

"Poor Michael," Sam natural sympathy shifted to the child. "You don't have to worry, John. I'll keep an eye on things while you're away and if Sylvia will allow it I'll treat Michael like one of my own."

"It may not be easy. If Sylvia thinks you're checking up on her she'll get nasty."

Sam nodded, accepting the judgment. "Yes, I can see that. Well, I'll just have to be very careful. Helen will help me figure a way. She's very good with people you know."

"I know. And speaking of Helen how is she?"

"Better." A shadow crossed Sam's face. "Sarah's birth was very difficult for her. And now she still requires a great deal more time and energy then most newborns. The doctors think there may be something wrong with her heart but they say it's too early to be sure."

"I didn't realize," John said, shaking his head sadly.

"We just found out ourselves and we're not talking about it yet. There's no need to get the family upset if it all turns out to be nothing."

"Are you sure you want to take on the added responsibility of Michael while I'm gone?"

"John, I'd feel responsible for Michael and Sylvia with you in Europe even if you hadn't asked. We are family you know."

"Right," John grinned. "I appreciate it, Sam."

Telling Sam about his concerns proved to be much easier then telling Sylvia that he was leaving for Europe. He'd scarcely gotten the words out of his mouth when her green eyes flashed with anger and her long, slim fingers began to tap on the table.

"Again?" she demanded. "Why are you going?"

"I'm the logical one to go, Syl. The European offices are familiar with me and I'm familiar with them," he explained trying to keep his irritation from showing. "Sam and Helen have a new baby that isn't very well and Walter is much too old."

"I think the company could find some nice young man that would jump at the chance to go abroad."

"I'm sure we could but I'm going and I don't intend to argue with you about it, I simply wanted you to hear it from me and not from someone else. I'll be gone several months and if a war starts I may be gone a very long time."

"What about me?" Sylvia's mouth turned down in a petulant pout.

"Sylvia, don't be ridiculous. You'll be relieved to have me out of the city and you know it."

"I'd like to go abroad, too."

"This isn't a pleasure trip, Syl. The world is on the verge of war and I'm going over on business. This is not a time for people to be traveling."

"Minette is "over there"," she argued.

"Minette is one of the reasons I'm going. She needs to get back here before the war begins. I'm going to insist that she and Lily catch the first available boat."

"You talk as though the war was a reality."

"Don't you ever read the papers?" John was exasperated by her inability to realize the seriousness of what he was saying.

"I read the papers but I haven't seen anything that makes it sound as if a war were right around the corner, the way you make it sound."

"Syl, I only called you today so that I could tell you my plans. Let's not argue. I'll be leaving on Sunday night. I'm going to London and I'll be staying at the Savoy until I can find a flat. I've made all the necessary arrangements with the bank so that you'll have funds to meet the household expenses. I've left Sam all the information he'll need if something were to happen to me."

"John!" Dismay caused Sylvia to speak loudly and several interested patrons turned to hear what they were saying. She lowered her voice, "Don't you dare talk like that. Nothing is going to happen."

"It's better to be ready. I want you to know that I've asked Sam to visit Michael."

"I don't think that's a very good idea, John. I don't like him exposed to that noisy bunch of ruffians that Helen is raising."

"Those kids are his cousins and even if they weren't you couldn't find a better bunch. Anyway they're all part of the same family."

"Oh, Yes," Sylvia sneered. "The mighty Augustus Clan."

"Like it or not, Syl, you are part of that clan, too. I think it would be wise if you tried to remember that once in a while. It seems to me that I've seen your name in the paper a few too many times lately."

"That old busy body Chatsworth doesn't have anything better to do then pick on me."

"Don't give her anything to write about and I'm sure she'll find someone else to write about."

"I'm not going to stay home and wither away while you're gone."

"I didn't expect you to." John smiled at her. "Syl, go and have a good time but please be careful and don't forget about Michael. He needs a mother."

"He has a mother. I'm more of a mother to him than my mother ever was to me," Sylvia responded defensively.

Sadly, John realized that it was true. Sylvia had never experienced a mother's love and perhaps that was why she seemed incapable of giving love to her son. He'd believed that she would change but Michael was almost two and she still hadn't shown a desire to spend time with him. In fact, she seemed to spend less and less time at home.

"What are you doing to keep yourself busy these days?" he asked.

Sylvia's sharp laugh cut across the dining room. "Oh, Darling," she said, her voice flirting but her eyes cold, "you know, just the usual. I go to dinner and the theater, a bit of shopping and a party now and then, nothing unusual."

"Who do you see?"

"Are you questioning me?" She cocked an eyebrow at him, a note of anger creeping into her voice.

"No, I'm just curious. I don't see much of you."

"I thought that was how you wanted it."

"And how you wanted it," he reminded her.

She raised her wine glass, "Peace. Let's not fight."

"Peace," he agreed.

With all his personal arrangements completed, John concentrated on business and managed to get things together for his departure. Saturday arrived. He packed his final bag and went to the nursery. He tapped on the door and entered.

Michael scrambled to his feet and ran to him. John tossed him in the air and laughed at his delighted chuckle. "Annie, I'd like to take Michael over to the park today. I'll be leaving for England in the morning."

"Certainly, sir," Annie jumped up from the rocker, where she'd been darning a long black stocking. "I'll just be putting on his hat and he'll be ready to go. It's just up from his nap, he is, and raring to run."

"Would you like to go to the park with me, Sport?" John asked.

Michael ran to his coat hook and grabbed his hat. "Go," he said, happily.

Annie helped him put on the jacket and admonished him to be good with his Daddy. Michael nodded soberly as he listened. John took him by the hand and together they went down the stairs and out the door.

The park in full summer bloom was glorious; trees were brightly green and flowers blossomed in all the corners. The air was a soft caress and birds sang and flitted through the trees. Bees hummed and darted from bloom to bloom, butterflies floated on the breeze. They strolled down the sidewalk hand in hand. John shortened his long stride so that Michael could keep up. Michael grasped John's finger in his warm, pudgy hand and John felt his heart soar at the trust this child placed in him. They came to the playground. A number of other children were busy digging in the sand and swinging on the swings. Michael stood silent, watching. He didn't drop John's finger nor did he make a sound. "Do you want to play?" John asked. Wide eyed, Michael shook his head. "Okay, Sport." John lifted him in his arms. "Let's go down to the lake and watch the boats."

"Boats," Michael agreed.

John pointed out the birds and trees and flowers as they walked. Each time he named an object Michael agreeably repeated it. John laughed and Michael joined in, delighted that he was making his father happy. In this pleasant way they crossed the park and arrived at the lake shore. John sat on a bench and put Michael beside him. "You're turning into quite a big boy," he commented.

"Big boy," Michael parroted.

Other children ran and yelled along the walk but Michael seemed content to sit on the bench beside his father and listen as John explained that he was going away for a long time but that he would be back. He told him about going to England in an airplane and that his Uncle Sam would come to visit him and perhaps take him out to his house to play with his cousins. Michael kept his eyes fastened on his father's face and listened carefully to every word. John felt as if he were able to understand everything. It was like talking to an adult instead of a two year old. "So, Michael," he finished, "what do you say?"

"Me go, too," Michael answered, emphatically.

"Not this time, Sport." John hugged the little boy. "You need to stay home and take care of your mother."

"Mother?" Michael questioned.

John knew that the child couldn't reason well enough to mean things the way they sounded but for an instant his heart twisted at the questioning tone. "Mother and Annie will stay with you and I'll be back soon."

"Annie," Michael said happily.

The City Chronicle
September 4, 1939
Tattletales by Sharon Chatsworth

Throughout the free world today, families
scrambled to try to make contact with relatives in
England and France. Among those from our fair
city who have been caught abroad by the
declaration of war are several very important
people.
John Augustus of AmCO is in England and will
remain there to conduct the business of his family
owned company. Mr. Augustus' mother, Minette
Augustus is in France with her mother Lily
Rathbone. Also in England is Valerie Smithson,
daughter of Gregory and Marie Smithson. She has
been working abroad for the past nine months as a
correspondent to Woman's Wear Daily. Miss
Smithson is expected to continue at her post in
London according to our contact at that fine
publication.

Chapter 11

John tried again to place a call to Paris and again he
failed. He seen Lily and Minette in August and had
tried to persuade them to return to the states.
Minette had refused due to Lily's failing health and
Lily had maintained that she had no intention of
leaving her homeland in a time of crisis. John
hoped to reach them now and convince them that it
was not only foolish but very dangerous to remain
in a country that had declared war when there was a

very safe and secure place waiting for them both in the states. He decided that when he reached them he would use Michael and his need for loving care as an enticement to convince them they should pack immediately.

He knew that Minette was concerned about Michael's care and he figured that Lily would listen to Minette. However, he hadn't bargained with their sense of patriotism. It was late when he finally got a call through and the connection was terrible. Through the static he could just make out Lily's voice and her refusal to leave. "I am determined to do whatever I can to help my country, John. Take care of yourself and stay in touch," she said.

When Minette came on the line she too refused to consider leaving. "We'll be fine, John. This is my homeland. I want to do what I can. Tell Michael that I love him when you see him and remember that I love you, too."

John tried to argue with her but the line went dead and he was left in his flat holding the phone unable to do anything to make the two women reconsider. He placed a call to Walter and explained the situation the best he could.

"Darn fool women," Walter complained. "They never can do what's best without an argument. You'll have to take the time to go across to France and bring them back."

"I can't do that, Walter," John explained. "My mother and I have an agreement that she can live her life and I can live mine, without interference from each other."

"That's the dumbest thing you've ever said," Walter growled across the transatlantic line. "She's your mother. You can't leave her in a country that is at war!"

"It's her choice, Walter," John said stubbornly. "She'll do what's best and I know she won't do anything foolish."

"Staying in France at a time like this is foolish. I'd demand that you come home yourself if it were possible. The company needs you there for now but the first chance you get I want you out of there."

"Don't worry, Grandfather. I'll take care of myself," John soothed the old man. His grandfather's demands were still hard to live with but he found that having an ocean between them made it easier to refuse to do things his way. They rang off with nothing settled.

His job took his full attention and he worked from early morning until late into the night. The military needed everything and AmCO was ready to supply them. He arranged for manufacturing and shipping and helped to create new ways to meet the new demands. The weeks flew by. The war escalated and casualties were announced daily in the news. Somehow it all seemed unrelated to his life. He knew that there was a war going on, after all that was why he was in England, yet the reports of death and destruction had no reality for him. Each day was simply a repeat of the day before as he hurried from one meeting to another and worked longer and longer hours.

Minette wrote to reassure him that she and Lily were fine that they were keeping busy and still had no intention of leaving their home. A letter arrived from Sam in late September saying that he'd had no luck convincing Sylvia that Michael should be allowed to spend time with his cousins. He related that Sylvia was seldom seen by himself or by Helen but that all seemed well with Michael. John found the letter unsettling but since he didn't have the time or inclination to return to the states, he put it out of his mind and stayed busy.

He'd found a flat close to his office in a very old building with high, wide leaded glass windows and intricate carved doors. The landlady was a charming redheaded woman full of bubbling laughter and mother to all her tenants. She and her husband tried to draw John into their lives but he remained standoffish and alone. The evenings should have been lonely but instead John kept himself too busy to think or feel.

The weather changed and turned cold and damp as winter descended on the London. The news from the war zones continued to worsen. John's worry about his mother and grandmother could not be ignored any longer. He scheduled himself for a long weekend and headed across the channel to see them.

Minette was delighted at his unexpected presence. She hugged him fiercely and took him to Lily's room. Lily, too, was pleased by his arrival but John realized at once that her health wasn't good and as soon as he and his mother were alone he asked, "What's wrong with Lily? She seemed so young and alive last year."

"I know," Minette said sadly. "She put on a very good act when she was in the states but even then she was quite ill. I didn't know until we were in France but she has cancer. It is very important that I stay with her, John." Tears threatened to overflow from her eyes and she brushed them away impatiently. "She came all the way to find me after thirty-five years and now she has only a few months left. She wants to die here, in her own bed, and I'll see that she can."

John hugged his mother. "You're a wonderful daughter," he said. "Can I do anything to help?"

"Actually, you can." Minette's practical French nature reasserted itself. "Some things are becoming hard to find. I need to have good food and warm blankets. Can you send them?"

John looked around the comfortable room, surprised by the request. Minette watched him defiantly. Her fierce look dared him to question her need. John wondered what it was that she was hiding but he didn't ask. Instead he nodded and answered, "Of course. I'll see that you receive everything I can get my hands on. England is beginning to ration also but I'm sure that I'll be able to supply most of your needs."

"Thank you, John. There is a great need." She smoothed her hair back with the palms of her hands. John noticed that the touch of gray had increased and that there were new lines etched around her mouth and eyes.

"Are you taking care of yourself?" he asked. "You won't be able to help Lily or France if you make yourself ill."

"I'm fine, John." She kissed his cheek. "This is my home and I'm happy to do whatever I can to help."

At the boat train, they hugged one another and Minette reminded him to tell Michael that she loved him and that she would be back in the city as soon as the war was over. "If you need me, Mother, I'll be here as quick as I can," John said looking deep into her eyes.

"I know," Minette brushed away the tears and smiled bravely. "Have a good life, Darling. I love you."

He watched her slender figure recede as the train pulled out of the station. Her parting words repeated in his mind and he wondered at their meaning. Did she mean that she didn't expect to ever see him again was she afraid of the war and what it might mean to herself and to her family? John considered turning back toward Paris and insisting that she go back to the states at once. But, he argued with himself, she wants to be right where she is. Surely, Minette would leave Paris if there were a real threat to her life, John reassured himself. He left for England, his task unaccomplished but convinced that Minette was happy and would be careful. She was doing what she felt was right. On the crossing, he listened to the conversation of his fellow passengers and his uneasiness returned. He decided to call Walter the following day and request that he try to convince the two women to leave their home.

Walter tried but he had no more luck then John. He called to report his failure and suggested that the two must know what they were doing. After all he declared, "Minette had always shown herself to be sensible woman." John agreed and allowed his worry to drift away.

The unrest in the world, however, could not be ignored. War accelerated daily and the news from the front grew more frightening. Walter and Sam both called frequently to check on the safety of their manufacturing plants and of the shipping lanes.

Orders increased and the AmCO corporation began its' recovery from the lean depression years.

In early December, John received an angry letter from Sylvia. She was furious with his continuing stay in England and demanded that he return to the city at least for the holiday season. "I'll not be able to attend a single party without a husband to serve as my escort," she wrote. John immediately fired back a reply that he was sure she'd have no trouble finding someone to escort her, and that he didn't intend to return to the city for a long time. His letter scarcely had time to clear the Atlantic before the phone rang and Walter's voice demanded to know what he'd done now to get Sylvia so upset.

"Not much, Walter," John said coldly. "It takes very little to get Syl mad."

"Well, she's got a point when she says you haven't been home in a long time and that she'd like you to spend Christmas with her and Michael."

"I don't think that's what she has in mind at all, Walter," John replied, picking his words with care. "She wants an escort to some party and for some reason she's got it in her head that I'm the only man that can serve the purpose."

"Maybe she's right. Some parties are for married couples only and even through the two of you are married she's the odd woman out around here."

"Sylvia has plenty of friends."

"I know that, John," Walter said dryly. "I read about Sylvia and her friends most every day in the Chatsworth column. If she wants you home enough to call me there must be a mighty good reason. Why not come home for Christmas? It would give you a chance to see your son and a break from business. All work and no play makes John a dull boy," Walter chuckled at his joke.

"I'll think about it." John paused. "How is Michael, Grandfather?" He asked.

"I don't see much of the boy," Walter said sadly. "Sylvia keeps him pretty much to herself."

"How about Sam and Helen, does she let them see him?"

"It's not that she doesn't let us see him, John. They're just very busy with their lives and our paths don't cross often."

"I don't understand," John admitted. "We used to see Sam and Helen almost every day. I can't believe that Sylvia is too busy to let Michael see his relatives."

"Michael's still too young to make any requests as to who he'd like to see or not see." Walter's sigh came over the long distance wires and he sounded old and weary. "Sylvia doesn't care much for our family these days. I suppose Alex's death was harder for her then we know."

John realized Walter was making excuses for Sylvia's behavior over the past months and he wondered, but didn't ask, what had really been going on during his absence. "Perhaps I'll come home at least for a week or so." John considered the idea. "I'll call you in a day or two and let your know what kind of arrangements I've made."

"Good, John. I'd like to see you and I know that Sam and Helen would, too. Your Aunt Mary Elizabeth was speaking of you just the other day and I know she's anxious to hear what you have to say about conditions in Europe. She's become very active in the Spanish War Orphan League."

"Okay, Grandfather. I'm convinced. The family needs me home for Christmas. I'll be there."

John hung up the phone, tilted back in his chair and propped his feet on an open drawer. His assistant came in and was delighted to find him in such a pleasant mood. Business had been booming but John seldom found things to smile about. The entire English staff had decided that he was very hard to work for, fair but moody and not very friendly.

"Good afternoon, sir."

"Come on in, Henry." John swung his feet off the drawer and straightened up. "What can I do for you?"

"Some of us are getting together tonight to celebrate and we thought you might like to join us."

John started to shake his head no, than he reconsidered. "What are you celebrating?" he asked instead.

"This is St. Nicolas Day. We're going down to the pub and throw darts and drink a few pints," Henry explained. "You'd enjoy the group, sir."

John grinned. "You're right, Henry. My grandfather was just saying that all work and no play would make me dull. I could use a break. But if I come you'll have to stop calling me sir. I can't down a pint with someone who doesn't use my name."

"Certainly, sir... I mean, John," Henry said shyly. "We go to the Bull's Head. It's just around the corner. I'll be proud to walk around with you."

"Right," John agreed. "See you at six then, Henry."

During the afternoon John found himself looking forward to the evening. It had been months since he'd spent any time relaxing and enjoying himself. The last time he could think of was over a year ago, on Thanksgiving, at Sam and Helen's. No wonder I'm such a grouch, he thought. Quickly he plowed through the pile of work on his desk and at six sharp he walked into Henry's office, eager to be on their way.

Working in England hadn't changed John's American style. He wore a business suit and a top coat but as always his head was bare. Next to Henry's very proper three piece suit, wool topper, and derby hat he looked positively casual. They walked together around the corner and entered the pub. It was very dark and for a moment John had trouble seeing into the gloom. Then Henry was greeted by a babble of voices and he drew John forward for introductions. Some of the group were people John recognized from the office but most were other friends of Henry. A wave of homesickness washed over him as he realized how much he missed his own family and friends. He shook it off and plunged into the conversation. Everyone was full of talk of the war and speculation as to the acceleration that they all expected to occur during the next year. Henry suggested that they talk of something less gloomy and turned their conversation to the approaching holiday season.

"Tell us about Christmas in the United States?" someone requested.

The others chimed in, urging John to talk. He took a long drink from his ale and began, "It's colder there and the snow is very deep, at least it is where I live. The stores are all decorated with lights and ribbons and so are most of the houses and businesses. There is a Santa on every corner, ringing a bell and collecting for the poor. People are friendlier at Christmas." His eyes took on a faraway look as his words caused him to picture the holidays he'd spent in the city, surrounded by love. "There are a lot of parties where everyone dresses in their best and eats and drinks entirely too much."

"We do that, too," Henry commented and they all laughed together.

"Tell us about Christmas Eve," one of the young women coaxed.

"In the States, Christmas Eve is time for family in most homes. The men rush around and do their last minute shopping and then hurry home when the stores close at noon. Some people open their presents but in our family we always wait for Christmas morning." John finished his ale and set the glass carefully on the table. "Enough," he said. "I'm buying this round." He stood and walked to the bar to place their order. He heard Henry call for a game of darts and turned back to say he wanted to be included.

The door burst open and a laughing group was swept in on the chill wind. He barely glanced in their direction but his eye was caught by the bright red coat that one of the women wore. It drew his attention to the face. He felt his body go rigid and he caught his breath in a sharp gasp.

"Valerie!" The word was torn from him a strangled cry. It was barely loud enough to be heard but the woman sensed it and looked toward him.

"John!" She started forward and stopped, unsure of what her response should be.

John didn't hesitate an instant. He crossed the room and swept her into his arms in a massive hug. For several long seconds they stood like that. Arms wrapped tightly around one another, unable to speak. Gradually Valerie regained her poise and tilted her head up to look at him.

"John," she said again. "I can't believe it's really you. What are you doing in London?"

He wanted to say, "looking for you" the first thought that entered his head. But he restrained the impulse and said instead, "I'm working here. I've been here about two months. What are you doing here?"

"Working."

They realized together that they were still standing wrapped in an embrace. They stepped apart and grinned sheepishly. "Hey, Val," one of the men she'd come in with said, "aren't you going to introduce us to your friend."

Introductions were made all around and Valerie's group joined with John's. Drinks appeared for everyone and the conversation grew noisy as the American newspaper people became acquainted with the English workers. John's heart was pounding and he realized anew how much he loved this woman and how much he wanted to be alone with her.

He leaned close and whispered in Valerie's ear, "Let's get out of here." She nodded. He took her hand and they moved away from the party and found their coats. They departed without looking back or saying good bye.

Out in the cold John again took Valerie's hand and held it carefully between both of his. He looked down into her eyes. All of the stars in the sky were repeated there. His love overwhelmed him and he drew her close in a tender embrace. "God, Valerie," he breathed into her soft dark hair. "I've missed you so much. More than I can ever tell you."

"I know, Love," she whispered back and lifted her lips for his kiss.

They joined together in a long minute of absolute bliss. John's knees trembled and he could feel Valerie's breath quicken as she trembled in his arms. "Let's walk," he suggested.

She kissed him lightly once again and took his hand.

They moved in perfect step their bodies lightly touching. The wind whistled and grabbed at them as they turned the corner but neither noticed. Their voices lifted and stumbled over one another as they hurried to tell each other everything that had happened since their last meeting, two long years before.

Finally John asked the one question that was burning in his mind. "Is there anyone else, Valerie?"

She stopped and faced him, her eyes wide in her small face as she looked at him. "I love you, John," she said carefully. "I think I've loved you from that first moment when I woke and found you in the room watching me. When you stopped calling me I tried to keep busy. I looked for someone to love. I knew that you hadn't wanted to stay with Sylvia but I was angry and I thought that if you'd truly loved me you would have found a way."

John started to protest but she laid a gloved finger on his lips to silence him and continued, "I understand more now. Not everything but at least more. I didn't find anyone else. You are my one true love and you will be until the day I die. Now that I've found you again I never intend to let you go. These two years have been agony for me."

"And for me, Darling," John kissed her gently and tucked her arm through his. "I live just a few blocks from here. Will you come home with me?"

Valerie's answer shown in her eyes and was repeated by her silent nod. Together they turned into the wind and John hurried her toward his warm flat.

Hours later they curled together in blissful fulfillment. Valerie's dark head rested on John's chest. His arm curved protectively around her and kept her close. She absentmindedly stroked his chest in slow circles as they talked.

"I love you so much," John declared. "Being with you has completed my life. I've never felt anything like this before." He kissed the top of her shining hair. "Do I sound corny?"

"You sound like my one true love," Val said kissing his chest. She propped herself up on one elbow and looked at him." "I understand what you mean. Coming together with you in love is perfect there are no words to tell you how wonderful." She bent over him and her thick dark hair formed a curtain around his face as she kissed him deeply. He pulled her closer and his tongue explored her mouth. They drew apart and smiled at one another.

"We were meant to be," he said.

"Yes," she agreed and settled contentedly into his embrace.

They lay together for a few minutes each happy in the mutual enjoyment of their love. The warmth of their bodies created a cozy cocoon under the blankets. John felt his heart expand, filled with a greater happiness then he'd ever known or imagined. He squeezed Valerie's shoulders and pulled her on top of him. He kissed her with passion running his hands down her smooth back and over her firm buttocks.

Valerie whispered to him, "Would it be rude to say I'm starving?"

John laughed, "Me, too." He grinned at her. "I'm sure that even the world's greatest lovers need to eat." He picked up his watch from the night stand and held it to the light. "Good Lord, it's after eleven. Did you have any dinner?"

"No, but I could eat a horse now."

"I didn't either. What would you like?" He laid the watch back on the table and put his arms around her again, reluctant to let her go for even a moment.

"We'd have to get dressed if we go out."

"True," John teased. "I don't think there's a single place in London that caters to the nude no matter how much in love they are."

"Can't we eat here?" Valerie ignored his comment and stuck to the problem of her growling stomach.

"We could if you don't mind what we eat."

"Come on." Valerie threw the quilt aside and stood up.

"You're so beautiful," he said as he watched her move.

Valerie blushed, embarrassed by his frank admiration. She picked up his discarded shirt and pulled it on. "Do you mind if I wear this?"

"Everything I have is yours, fair maiden." John sat up and faked a courtly bow.

Laughing they went to the small kitchen. John opened a cupboard and surveyed the contents. Two cracked tea cups, a box of loose tea and a battered teapot. "Nothing in here," he closed the door and opened another.

"John," Valerie giggled. "Do you have any food?"

"I don't know," he confessed. "I try not to be here very often."

Valerie looked in the old fashioned ice box.

"I know there's nothing in there," John admitted. "I wasn't sure how it worked."

"Men!" Valerie shook her head in mock dismay. She opened another cupboard and found plates and glasses but no food. "That does it, my love. We'll have to get dressed and go to my place. At least I have food and a refrigerator that works."

"We could eat out somewhere and then come back here." John was reluctant to let her out of his sight for even a moment now that he'd claimed her to be his own true love.

As if Valerie could read his thoughts, she answered, "I live alone, John. We can spend the night there and then tomorrow we can make our plans."

"But won't people notice?"

"Thank you for protecting my reputation." Valerie stood on tiptoe and lightly kissed his lips. "I don't think anyone will notice one night and if they do I really don't care." A cloud crossed her face as she remembered his marriage, "Do you?"

"I only care for you, my darling." John pulled her close in a tight hug. "My marriage is over and even if we were closer to home I'd never let you go tonight. Let the gossips say what they like. I want you by my side forever."

"Then we'd better eat before I perish." Valerie changed the mood with her gentle teasing. "Do you want to pack a bag?"

"My but you're practical. Here I am overcome with love and you're thinking of clean shirts." They laughed together, delighted at their silliness as lovers often are.

Valerie dressed as John packed a small duffel bag and gathered his shaving gear. They went out into the cold night air and hailed a cab. Valerie gave her address and quietly they sped through the night. The cab deposited them in front of her building and suddenly, standing together in front of the dark doorway, Valerie grew shy and frightened. John sensed her hesitation and asked, "Are you sure you want me to come in?"

"Oh, yes." Her radiant smile lit her face and reassured him. "I've dreamed about this moment a thousand times. I just feel a little bashful now that the time is here."

"I love you, Valerie." John set his bag on the stone step and took both her hands in his. "I want you to be my wife. Will you marry me?"

Valerie's eyes filled with tears and she raised her face for his kiss. "You are my love, John Augustus." The tears spilled over and gently he wiped them away.

"Why are you crying?"

"I'm just so happy, John." He held her in his tender embrace and stroked her hair. He didn't seem to notice that she hadn't answered his proposal.

They tiptoed up the creaky old staircase until, on the third floor; Valerie stopped and unlocked an old fashioned, heavy door. She pushed it open so that John could enter. He surveyed the room. "I'd know this was your home anywhere," he declared.

The walls were washed in a soft rose tint with sparkling white woodwork and high white ceilings. Fresh flowers glowed from every corner and books were piled on every surface. The overstuffed furniture was upholstered in soft printed chintz and the wide, high windows were draped in a cascading flow of thin white fabric that hung loosely, tied back with ribbons to frame the city in the many tiny window panes. The table had been painted a glossy black and where ever there was a spare space snap shots framed in brass had been place with care. John sighed happily. "It's perfect, Valerie, the most beautiful room for the most beautiful woman."

She blushed at his extravagant praise. "Thank you," she said simply. "Most everything is something I found at a bargain price and brought home to clean up. It was fun and it kept me busy."

Valerie fixed a simple meal for them in her spotless, tiny kitchen. John sat and watched as she moved about mixing biscuits and preparing an omelet. He was fascinated by the way she moved and with her obvious skill and knowledge in the kitchen he realized that he'd never seen Sylvia fix even a simple snack. They talked as she worked and Valerie told him the details of her job and how happy she was to be working as a reporter for Woman's Wear Daily.

"Don't you miss the states?" he asked.

"No. I missed you and this job has been my salvation." She said, pausing in her work to kiss him. "Now that I've discovered how much I like the work I can't imagine not working. It's exciting to know what's happening in the fashion world before anyone else. I meet so many interesting people and I learn so much about them. You'd be surprised to learn what secrets the famous reveal to reporters. I only wish I could print everything I've learned."

John laughed. "I know one reporter who writes everything she hears whether she should or not."

"Sharon Chatsworth. Right?"

John nodded.

"She's not really a reporter. She's a gossip." Valerie dismissed her with a wave of her hand.

"Well, there's certainly a few times I wished she'd stayed out of my business."

Valerie laughed. "You and all the other rich and famous people in the city." She placed the filled plates on the table and poured them each a cup of coffee. Gracefully she seated herself and smiled across the small table. Happiness radiated between them. A clock struck the hour.

"Midnight," Valerie said. "I feel like Cinderella."

"Are you going to disappear?"

"Never," she promised reaching across to squeeze his hand. "I've found my Prince Charming and I'm never going to let you go."

The City Chronicle
December 21, 1939
Tattletales by Sharon Chatsworth

The rich and famous of our fair city turned out in all
their finest last night to celebrate the holiday season
at the home of Mr. and Mrs. Henry Newcastle. It
was a delightful to see not only Walter Augustus
and his charming daughter Mary Elizabeth but also
in attendance were both of his grandsons and their
wives. John Augustus had returned to the city only
hours before the gala event and the surprise of his
presence was the highlight of the glittering
occasion. Sylvia Augustus made a startling
entrance on her husband's arm wearing a shocking
pink gown created by that flamboyant designer,
Elsa Schiaparelli. The sheath of pink velvet
wrapped the glamorous Mrs. Augustus in a most
devastating manner. The gowns slender line was
accentuated by the deep plunge of the neckline; the
padded shoulders and the closely cut long sleeves.
This couple was observed carefully by your reporter
last night and perhaps the old saying that absence
makes the heart grow fonder is true but, I think, not
so in this case.

Chapter 12

Sam met John at the airport and suggested that they
stop somewhere before going home.
"Sure," John agreed, not anxious to see Sylvia he
was relieved by the request. "It's good to see you,
Sam"

"Good to see me but not to be back in the states, huh?" Sam was quick to catch the innuendo of John's words.

"I can't say I'm looking forward to a visit with Sylvia," John admitted.

"That's part of what I need to talk to you about. Let's get inside where it's warm and we'll catch up on what's happening around here."

They hurried across the frozen airfield. John noticed the dirty snow piled along the edges and shivered as he closed his coat more firmly against the wind.

Sam laughed. "It's been cold and they're predicting snow again for tonight. The kids are delighted, nothing like a lot of snow to keep a gang of kids happy."

John nodded. "How are the kids and Helen?"

Sam sobered, "The baby's not well. The doctors don't hold out much hope for her survival."

John struggled to find words to express his grief at Sam's news. He shook his head sadly. "How's Helen taking it?"

"Better than I am," Sam admitted. "She's a marvelous woman and she'd fight like a lioness for any one of our kids." Sam rubbed his hand over his face as if he could erase the worry.

They pushed open the door to the diner and the warm air filled with the smell of baking assaulted their senses. John sniffed the air appreciatively. "Smells good in here. I haven't smelled real coffee and apple pie since I can't remember when."

Settled with mugs of hot coffee in from of them, John leaned back in the booth and asked, "So, Sam, what's on your mind?"

"You are," Sam answered bluntly.

John waited, not sure how to answer.

"When Walter told me you'd be here for Christmas I was really surprised. Things are.... different, John."

"Different?"

"I don't know how to tell you." Sam hesitated again.

"Just start at the beginning and go on to the end, like Grandmother always said." John encouraged him with a smile. "If it's about Sylvia, I'm ready."

"It's sort of about Sylvia and ... and everything else, too." Sam took a drink from his mug and set it down firmly. "Sylvia is very busy these days. The gossip columns are filled with her activities and with the details of her wardrobe." John nodded. "And Walter's health is failing rapidly."

John sat up straighter. "Is he ill?"

"Not ill exactly, just aging. Something seems to be bothering him. He's not been himself since you went back to England, but when you said you'd be here for Christmas he seemed to perk up. The business is going great guns so that's not where his worry lies. I'm not sure what it is but something is eating at him."

"He's getting older, Sam."

"Yes, of course. But it's more than that. You'll see." He took another drink of coffee and plunged into what was really on his mind. "I want to tell you something, John. I need to be the one you hear it from because ... well, just because."

John took a deep drink of his own coffee and braced himself for what he was sure was coming. He decided to make it easier on his cousin. "If it is about, Sylvia, I think I can guess what I'm about to hear. She has a lover that the whole town knows about, right?"

Sam nodded in relief. "Right, how did you know?"

"It wasn't hard to guess, Sam. Our marriage is over in all but name and we agreed before I left that we could both do as we pleased as long as we were discrete about it."

"I don't think you could call Sylvia discrete." Sam said. "Her picture is in all the papers and usually with the same man."

"Do I know him?"

"I don't think so. He's from the west coast somewhere. Mark Phillips."

John grimaced. "The name is familiar but I don't know him. He's been a friend of Sylvia's for some time," he explained carefully. "I'm surprised that she hasn't been more careful but I'm not upset."

He wanted to confide in Sam about his own relationship with Valerie but somehow this didn't seem like the right time and he swallowed the words. "Is that what's troubling Walter?"

"I'm sure that it's at least part of the problem. I think he feels responsible since he was so instrumental in your having a son and staying married."

"No more than Alex and his damn will."

Sam winced at the bitter tone.

"Isn't there some way I can get a divorce, Sam?" John pleaded.

"Sure, you can get a divorce. The problem is all the strings that Alex attached to his will. Don't forget that they affect not just you but also your son."

"I know. But I want out of this marriage. I...," He hesitated and changed the subject. "How is Michael?"

Sam wondered what he'd been about to say but didn't ask. "I haven't seen him more than a time or two since you left. Walter tells me he's fine."

"Does Sylvia encourage Walter to visit?" John asked in surprise.

Sam smiled grimly, "Of course not. Annie brings Michael to see Walter at the office as often as she can. I don't think Sylvia even knows about the visits. But I suppose she'll find out. Kids aren't very good at keeping secrets."

John blanched, hoping that Sam couldn't read him well enough to know that he was keeping a secret. Quickly he started talking. "I only came for Christmas because Walter seemed to feel it was so important. I really didn't want to come at all but Sylvia needs an escort to some party."

"Yes, to the Newcastle party, tonight. Helen and I are going, too."

"Well at least at a Newcastle bash there'll be plenty of people around. I won't have to spend much time alone with her."

Sam didn't need to ask who he meant by "her". It was obvious that John felt a certain duty toward Sylvia and the Augustus family but that he wasn't expecting to enjoy the evening."

"Tell me about England," Sam suggested.

John laughed. "Trying to change the subject?"

Sam grinned, "Yep. I can't stand any more depressing talk. How's the business and what have you been up to for fun?"

"I'm sure you know everything there is to know about the business and what makes you think I've been having fun?"

Sam studied his cousin carefully. John had to control an urge to squirm under his close scrutiny. "I didn't really think you were up to anything, Cuz, but now that you mention it you do have a certain look that tells me I wasn't paying attention. What's new with you?"

John took advantage of his empty cup and called the waitress over for a refill. He joked with her about the weather and effectively turned the conversation away from himself and back to general topics. Sam glanced at his watch and gulped the last of his coffee. "We'd better get out of here. Helen will shoot me if I'm late again tonight. We're staying in the city at Walter's and I'm sure I was expected at least half an hour ago."

"Does that mean I'm in trouble, too?" John asked, raising from his seat and pulling on his top coat. "What time is this shindig?"

"Not until eight, but Helen and I are taking Walter and picking up Aunt Mary Elizabeth and you know Helen, she can't stand to be late."

"I certainly don't want to be held responsible for your behavior. We'd better get going. I expect Sylvia is waiting."

Sam drove the car swiftly through the crowded city streets and they arrived at the door of the brownstone more quickly than John had imagined possible. He hesitated, his hand on the door handle. "Thanks for meeting me, Sam. I'm really glad to see you."

"It's good to have you here, John, even though it's only for a few days. Welcome home."

John put his key into the lock and pushed open the heavy front door. He entered the house slowly, looking around, feeling more a stranger then a man returning to his home. The highly polished floor reflected the lights from the chandelier just the way it had his entire life. The hall tree was draped in a festive garland of greens and the smell of pine drifted on the warm air. He patted the carved lion and hung his coat over a chair. He glanced at the mail, piled on a silver tray, but didn't read through the stack. This is ridiculous, he silently lectured himself. I've lived here over 30 years, it's my house! Why should I be uncomfortable?

The door from the dining room opened and John turned in relief. Duncan stopped in midstride. "Good evening, sir." He recovered his composure quickly. "I didn't hear you come in. Did you have a pleasant trip?"

"Quite. Where is everyone, Duncan?"

Duncan looked around as though he expected to see others in the room. "Miss Sylvia hasn't come in yet, sir, and Annie is in the kitchen with Master Michael."

John heard the "Master" applied to the two and half year old and registered it with surprise. He didn't feel it was appropriate but it certainly sounded like something Sylvia would like. He started trough the dining room, headed toward the kitchen.

Duncan's commanding tone stopped him, "I've laid out your evening wear, sir. You've time to bathe if you wish. Miss Sylvia said to tell you that you needn't be ready until 7:30."

John glanced at his watch. "I've plenty of time. I'll say hello to Michael and Annie and then go up. Do I have the same room?"

Duncan nodded. "As you wish, sir. The child may be a bit messy."

John smiled ruefully at the butler's obvious surprise over his desire to see Michael, and without commenting pushed open the swinging kitchen door. He was delighted to hear happy laughter and he felt the tension of his homecoming begin to ebb as he entered the room.

Mrs. Peters and Annie looked up at his entrance. Mrs. Peters smiled her broad, happy grin and said, "Well, look who's here. Welcome home, Mr. John." Annie scrambled to her feet and bobbed in a curtsy. "Welcome back, sir," she managed to say as she brushed her skirt and straightened her hair.

"It's a pleasure to see both of you." John smiled at them. "Where's Michael?"

Annie giggled. An answering giggle sounded from under the table. John knelt down and lifted the edge of the cloth. The small boy's face broke into a wide grin and laughed aloud as he shouted, "Boo!"

"Goodness," John sat back on his heels and pretended to be frightened. "You gave me quite a start. Have you seen a little boy named Michael?" he asked solemnly.

"I'm Michael."

"Are you sure? I was looking for a very little boy. You look much too big."

"Annie," Michael called, sticking his head out and looking up, "I'm Michael?"

"Of course you are, love." Annie scooped him out and into her hug. "This is your Daddy. He's come all the way from England just to see you."

"Daddy?"

"Yes, Michael." John held out his arms. "I'm your Daddy." His heart pounded as the realization struck him that he was indeed this boy's father. It didn't matter if he had been born of his loins or not he wanted to be Michael's father. "Can I have a hug?"

Michael shook his head and buried his face in Annie's neck. "I'm sorry, sir," Annie said, embarrassed by her small charge's obvious reluctance to go to his father.

The rebuff hurt but John realized that the child had no idea who he was, no memory of having seen him before. "It's all right, Annie. There's no reason why the boy should come to me. I'm a stranger to him." He reached out and gently touched Michael's hair. "How has he been?"

"Oh, he's wonderful, sir." Annie beamed proudly. "He's as good as gold and as smart as they come. It's joy to be his nanny."

"I can see that you've taken fine care of him." He smiled at the girl. "Thank you, Annie and you too Mrs. Peters." He pulled out a chair and seated himself at the table. "Tell me about him," he requested.

The two women exchanged a swift glance; they weren't used to the master of the house nor to his casual presence in their kitchen. Mrs. Peters spoke first, "I'm sure, Mrs. Augustus has told you all there is to know about the child."

John shook his head. "Not as much as she might," he said. "Sylvia isn't much of a letter writer."

Annie read between the quiet words. She'd watched the unhappy couple together and was well aware of how little time Sylvia found to spend with her son. She sat Michael on the floor and provided a train to push. "He's very bright," she began. "He knows all of the colors and can count a bit. He loves to have someone read aloud to him and he's able to say some nursery rhymes without any help at all."

Michael listened to the talk and judged this person harmless. He rose and offered the train to John. "Play?" he asked.

John took the toy and knelt on the floor. He made train noises as he pushed it across the floor. Michael laughed, delighted by the attention. John smiled and pushed the train faster as he continued to chug and toot.

Sylvia swept in to the kitchen looking for the dress she'd expected to find pressed and ready in her dressing room. Her angry tone quickly turned to a soft flirtatious drawl when she found John on the floor. "Darling, I didn't expect to find you on your hands and knees in the kitchen." She held out her hands to him in a gracious, well-rehearsed gesture. John ignored her hand as he stood and carefully brushed his trouser legs.

"Hello, Sylvia." He surveyed her freshly cropped hair and skillfully made up face. "You're looking very well."

"Why thank you." She managed a slight blush. "You look rather splendid yourself. Did you have a pleasant flight?"

"As good as could be expected." They eyed each other, as wary as fighters in the ring, unsure of when and how the other would attack. Michael broke the tension by clutching Sylvia's skirt.

"Mama, up?" he asked.

"Not now, Michael. I'm in a hurry." Sylvia scarcely glanced down as she withdrew her skirt from his hand. "Annie, is that dress ready?"

"Yes, Mum." Annie picked up Michael and hugged him as she answered. "I was just about to take it up."

"Do it then. John, you'd better get changed. We'll need to leave at 7:45 and I'd like to have a drink with you in the drawing room before we go." She swept out of the room, leaving the door swinging to and fro.

"Yes, Mum," John muttered half under his breath. He caught Mrs. Peters grim expression and grinned. "The lady has spoken," he said. "We'd best hop to it, I suppose."

"Indeed, sir." Mrs. Peters grinned back at him, relieved by his humor. "May I get you anything?"

"No, I've everything I need." He rumpled Michael's hair. "See you tomorrow, Sport."

John whistled as he approached the drawing room. He felt refreshed by his shower and ready to face anything that Sylvia had to say. Thoughts of Valerie made him smile to himself. He wondered what she was doing and glanced at his watch to try to figure the time difference. Sylvia wasn't down yet so John made himself a drink and sat stretching his long legs out toward the fire. He sipped the drink and waited patiently. At last he heard the staccato tap of heels on the parquet floor and turning toward the door he watched Sylvia's entrance.

She wore a long, shocking pink gown that wrapped her splendid figure in a tight flow of glowing color, the neckline plunged almost to her waist and a tantalizing glimpse of her breasts could be seen. John set his drink on the table next to his chair but he didn't rise to his feet. "That's quite a dress," he said cautiously.

"Do you like it?" Sylvia turned in a slow circle and John noted that the back was cut even lower than the front, he marveled to himself at the feat of engineering that kept the gown from slipping down to reveal more than it had been designed to reveal.

He walked to the bar. "May I mix you a drink?" he asked without answering her question.

"Scotch, please."

"Soda or water?" he asked politely, a stranger to his wife and her habits.

"On the rocks." He poured and turned back to see that seated the dress was even more amazing. A long slit allowed all but the uppermost part of Sylvia's thigh to show.

He bit his lip to refrain from commenting and took a hasty sip of his own drink.

"I wasn't sure you'd come," Sylvia started. "Walter said he'd call but I'm never sure I can trust him these days." John remained silent, waiting for her to reveal what was really on her mind. "I don't think Walter likes me much. In fact," she looked squarely at him, defiance blazing in her eyes, "none of your family likes me anymore."

"What makes you say that?" John tried to figure how he was expected to respond. "Sam picked me up at the airport this afternoon and he said they'd hardly seen anything of you."

"I'm sure that's not all your beloved cousin had to say." She finished her drink in a gulp, drew in a deep breath and squared her shoulders. "It's true that I never see them if I can avoid them." John nodded. "I have a lot of friends now, John. Most of them are people you don't know."

"I'm sure you do, Sylvia. I'd expected that you would. After all we agreed that our marriage would be one of convenience only. I'm not concerned about who your friends are. Only that you are discrete and that you don't do anything that will hurt Michael and his position in the city as he grows older."

Sylvia looked embarrassed and struggled to regain her composure. She tried to drink again from her glass and looked at it in dismay when she realized that it was empty. She laughed nervously, "I'm afraid I've made a tiny little mistake, John."

"What kind of a mistake, Syl?" John held his breath, afraid that she was going to tell him she was pregnant again.

"I really did try to be discrete." She pouted prettily. "But you were gone and I needed to have some fun."

"What have you done?" John's knuckles turn white as he clenched his glass.

"My name has been in the paper a lot." John nodded and remained quiet. "I go out often and you know how that old Sharon Chatsworth likes to snoop in other people's business."

John remembered his conversation with Valerie and decided to help her off the hook. "I know that your name is being linked to only one man Sylvia."

She sprang to her feet and crossed to the bar. John couldn't help but watch the way she moved in the dress. It's strange, he thought, I should feel something more than a touch of lust but I don't want her, not really, in fact I feel sorry for her. Swiftly she poured her glass full of scotch and drank a large swallow. "It's all right, Syl. I'm not surprised or angry that you've found someone else."

"It's worse than just the gossip."

"How much worse?"

"Much. I lent Mark a great deal of money and now he can't pay it back."

John laughed, relieved. I should have known she was too smart to be pregnant, he thought.

"It's not funny, John. Mr. Patterson says I can't draw any more money out of Daddy's estate without your agreement."

"How much money did you lend this fellow?"

"A lot," she hedged.

"You don't have to tell me, Syl, but I'm not going to help you draw more money from the estate either. Your father left you an adequate income and I've been paying all of the expenses for this house plus a very generous allowance."

"John, you have to help me. It costs a lot to live the way I like."

John chuckled. "I'm sure it does, Syl, but I'm still not going to help you draw out money."

"Why not?" Sylvia smiled a sly, foxlike grin. "It's not your money. What would it matter to you?"

"I don't suppose it would matter to me," he said, choosing his words with care. "Your father left that money tied up the way he did for a reason. I'm not exactly sure what he had in mind but I think he was trying to guard against something for you."

"Oh, John, don't be foolish." Sylvia tapped her fingers on the side of her glass. "How can a dead man guard a live woman?"

"I was speaking figuratively, Sylvia. Perhaps this kind of foolishness is exactly what he wanted to discourage."

"What foolishness?" Sylvia's voice took on a shrill note as her displeasure rose. "You've lent money a dozen times to help someone start a business venture."

"True," he agreed, "but I always know who I'm giving it to and exactly what they intend to do with it."

"I know Mark and I know what he wanted to do with the money. He used it to back a play." She tossed her head and stamped her foot defiantly.

"A play!" John was truly astounded. "You mean a Broadway play?"

"Well, it didn't make it to Broadway," she admitted. "It didn't exactly get produced yet." She saw the protest on his face and continued quickly. "But it will. It's a very good play. They just need a bit more time and money."

"Sylvia, I can't believe I'm hearing you say this. What in the world possessed you to back a play?"

"I didn't." She pouted prettily, looking up at him through her long lashes. "Mark knows the playwright and I lent him the money so that he could back the play."

"I understand that, Syl." He took a deep breath and continued, trying to make his next question sound pleasant. "Is this why you were so anxious for me to come back to the states?"

"I wanted to see you."

"Don't play games." John waved away her words with an inpatient gesture. "I know you aren't that anxious to spend time with me."

"Or you with me," she reminded him.

"True, so tell me the real reason behind your demands."

"It's simple. I went down to Charleston to talk to Mr. Patterson and withdraw some money and he told me that I couldn't have any more for months." Sylvia held out her glass. "Pour me another, Darlin'." John took the glass without comment and carried it to the bar while she continued. "He wanted to know why I needed so much money and I had to think of something fast so I told him that you needed the money."

"You what?"

"Well, I had to say something, didn't I?" Sylvia crossed the room and removed the filled glass from his fingers. "Anyway he wanted to call you and I wouldn't let him. I made some silly excuse about your being on the continent and impossible to reach. I don't think he believed me because the next day he called Walter and asked if he'd be willing to sign some papers that would allow me to have next year's money now."

"Sylvia!" John slammed his glass on the bar.

"Now don't get mad, Darlin', as soon as Walter called me I told him that the money wasn't for you."

"What excuse did you give Walter?" John asked, afraid of what he might hear but needing to know the answer.

"I told him the truth."

"Which truth is that?"

"That I needed the money for my expenses."

"And," John encouraged, "what did Walter say?"

"Oh, you know Walter," Sylvia hedged. She took a long drink and smiled at him across the rim of the glass.

"Yes, I do know Walter. What did he say?"

"He suggested that I should talk to you, that perhaps you could see your way clear to give me a bigger allowance for this house."

Suddenly John realized what she was hinting at, "Sylvia," he demanded, "did you tell Walter that I wasn't providing enough money for you and the boy to live on?"

Rage darkened his face and Sylvia dropped her eyes before she answered. "I didn't say that, John. I just said that I needed more money then you were willing to give me." She heard his sharp intake of breath and glared at him. "Well, it's true. I do need more money then you provide."

For a long moment John glared back at her his anger soared and he realized how much he disliked this petty, deceitful woman. She stood silent, defiant and convinced that she had done no wrong. "Sylvia," he started and then stopped not sure what he intended to say. He shook his head sadly and swallowed the last of his drink. Suddenly he chuckled. Sylvia looked at him in surprise. His chuckle turned to a guffaw and then to a roar of laughter.

Sylvia watched him in amazement, unsure how she should react to this unexpected show. "Aren't you angry?"

He nodded through his laughter and managed to choke out, "Furious." He struggled to control himself and slowly the laughter died away.

"I don't think it's very funny." Sylvia frowned at him.

"The whole situation is so ridiculous. I can just imagine Walter's face when he heard that one of the clan wasn't providing for his wife. He must have been livid."

Sylvia managed a timid giggle. "I thought he was going to have a stroke."

"You're damn lucky he didn't. I would have killed you." His renewed fury stopped Sylvia's rising relief and she shrank back. "My grandfather is a good man, too good to be bothered by the likes of you." He stepped close to his wife and said carefully and distinctly, "I won't help you get money to support your playmate and I'll see to it that no one else in this town does either. Do you understand?"

Sylvia nodded, frightened by the look in his eye and the intensity of his voice. She opened her mouth to protest. John stopped her words with his look. "I don't want to hear any more about it. Get up and we'll go to this party you dragged me back to attend. I'll straighten things out with Walter but you'll have to face yourself."

He turned on his heel and strode out of the room. Sylvia gulped the last of her drink and, almost running, she followed him to the car.

The ride across the city to the Newcastle's was accomplished in frozen silence. Each was busy with their thoughts and the driver knew better then to interfere in what was obviously a family fight of some kind. He handed Sylvia out at the brightly lighted door and John offered his arm. There was no affection in the gesture, only the well-bred politeness that he'd been taught all his life.

The door swung open and they were thrust into the swirl of a high society gala. One well powdered and sweetly scented lady after another raised her cheek for a kiss and John obliged as he shook hands with the men and calmly answered questions about the situation in Europe. All the while his eyes swept the room hoping to catch a glimpse of Walter and Aunt Mary Elizabeth. Sylvia clung to his arm as they entered the crowd, he longed to shake her off, but even a wife in name only deserved to enter the room on her husband's arm, he supposed.

At last he saw Sam standing, with an arm around Helen, talking to a group by the far wall. "Excuse me," he said to Sylvia and shrugged her hand away. "I see Sam over there with Helen. I imagine Walter is somewhere near. I'll pick you up when it's time for dinner."

"John," Sylvia started to protest but one glance from his angry eyes and she was silent.

He made his way through the party goers. Several people stopped him and tried to engage him in conversation but each time he moved away quickly and headed again toward the far corner of the room. He still hadn't seen Walter but he was sure that he would be here holding court from an armchair the way he always did at a party and sure enough the crowd parted for a moment revealing Walter. His lined face was lit with a polite social smile his gnarled hands were folded over the golden knob of his cane. He was engrossed in something that was being said.   John stepped closer and waited for Walter to acknowledge his presence.

He felt an arm drop down over his shoulders and heard Sam's jovial voice, "Well, look who's here!"

Walter looked up, and for a second John was stunned by the grief he saw in Walter's eyes, but the moment passed as Walter stretched out his hand in greeting.   "John."

"Hello, Grandfather."   John clasped the extended hand and shook it firmly.

"How are you, boy?"

For once the insult of the greeting didn't bother John. He only felt happy to be back in the bosom of his family.   "I'm fine, sir. How are you?"

"Older." Walter shook his head sadly and repeated, "Older."

"But ornery as ever." Mary Elizabeth turned from her conversation and hugged her nephew. "Welcome home, John."

He kissed her cheek and commented on how well she looked.   Helen appeared and more kisses were exchanged. John was caught in the whirl of family, the happy babble of folks he loved who were glad to see him back in their midst. Others at the party looked toward the group and commented on the Augustus clan, on what a close knit family they were and how good it was to see them all together. If anyone noticed that John's wife was missing from the group they accepted the fact without comment. After all the entire city had been reading about her antics in the Chatsworth column and they weren't surprised to see her standing apart talking to her own friends. Finally John found himself alone with Walter.

He drew a chair close to his grandfather's and seated himself. "Walter," he began, "I think we need to talk."

Walter nodded. "Is this the time or place?" he asked.

"You always said that when there was an unpleasant task to do the sooner it was begun the sooner done."

"True. Go ahead, boy."

Again, John let the "boy" slip past without comment. "I had a brief conversation with Sylvia before coming to this party. She explained to me why you were so anxious to have me home for the holidays. She doesn't need money, Walter." John paused, unsure that he knew exactly how to continue but one look at Walter's incredulous face convinced him that he should. "She wants more but she doesn't need it. I'm paying all of the expenses for the house and giving her several thousand more each month that she spends anyway she wants to; buying things and going places. She has drawn against her father's estate until they won't let her take out any more."

Walter nodded, relief erasing some of the tension lines from around his eyes. "I knew it couldn't be true but she seemed so distraught, so sincere."

"Syl is a fine actress. I'm not surprised that you believed her. Lord knows, I've been taken in often enough myself."

"She told me that you'd left angry and had refused to give her any money at all for her personal use, that that was why she'd needed to draw so heavily against the estate."

"Not true, Grandfather." John touched the old man's knee. "When I left we were both glad to see me go. Our marriage is over." Walter shook his head in disbelief. "Over," John said again with emphasis. "We agreed to stay married since Alex tied the money so securely to our marriage but we have no interest in being man and wife." John heard his own words and though with dismay of his promise to Valerie that they would be married someday soon. He shook off the feeling and excused himself with the thought that this was not the time or place to discuss the details of his plans for the future. "After all," he told himself, "I have to talk to Syl about it first."

"I know that things are unpleasant between you, John, but can't you work it out."

"I don't think we want to," John answered sadly. "We each have our own lives."

"What about Michael?"

"Good question," John thought but aloud he said, "I'll see that he is taken care of no matter what happens between us."

"There's more to raising children than that." Walter closed his eyes for an instant as if he were in pain, then he concluded, "I hope you realize before it's too late."

"My goodness," Sylvia slurred southern drawl interrupted, "you two look so serious. Don't you know this is a party?"

The two men looked up at her, thinking how beautiful but deceitful this woman had proven herself to be. They looked at each other and the thought seemed to pass between them in a silent moment of communication and then without saying a word to his wife, John stood up and walked away. He joined a conversation about the war threat in Europe and managed to ignore Sylvia.

Sylvia smarted under his rebuke but she wasn't about to let anyone see that anything was wrong.

She worked the room carefully staying just close enough to John so that the other party goers would think they were together. John could hear her voice and an occasional snatch of conversation. One time he was amazed to hear her bragging about Michael like any other mother and then a second later he heard her tell someone how much she hated his long absences and how lonely she was when he had to be away. He wanted to make a caustic remark but just in time he remembered that he had agreed to this farce and that it was as much his job as hers to let the world think that they were a happy couple so instead of the remark he turned and took her arm. "Can I get you anything, Syl?" he asked, creating the perfect picture of the solicitous husband.

She smiled up at him and in her eyes he saw a flash of gratitude, "I'd love another drink."

Later when dinner was announced, John and Sylvia went in to the dining room together. He seated Sylvia and was relieved to see that his own place card was on the opposite side of the table and down several places. A dark haired woman was seated to his left and for a moment she reminded him of Valerie. His voice caught in his throat and he found it difficult to introduce himself. He was rescued by the arrival of Dennis Fairchild who slumped into the chair on his right and began a discourse on the inconsiderate behavior of pregnant women and their need to deliver offspring only at times when the doctor had other plans.

John laughed at his complaints and reminded him of how much he loved his work.

"True, true," Dennis agreed. "How's that charming grandmother of yours? I was hoping to see her tonight. Although in this mob I'd never have found her."

"My charming grandmother and my equally charming mother are still in France."

"France" Dennis sat up straight. Several people looked in their direction and he lowered his voice as he continued, "Is that safe? France is at war."

"I spoke to Mother on the phone only yesterday and I was across the channel to visit a few weeks ago. It's still safe enough, although it's getting harder and harder for them to buy the things they need. Lily is determined to stay and Mother won't leave her there alone."

Dennis nodded. "Mrs. Rathbone talked about returning to France when she was in the hospital." He smiled gently. "I'm glad it was possible."

"You knew she was ill, didn't you?" John asked. He didn't wait for answer. "You doctors are amazing. You always know everything but you never tell a thing."

"We take an oath, dear boy." Dennis tilted his glass and attempted to lighten the mood. "Tell me about life in England. Amy and I were over on our honeymoon but that seems like centuries ago."

"How is Amy?" John took the opportunity to turn the conversation back to light party talk.

The dinner hour drifted on with small talk and the sound of silver striking china. The food was delicious and John couldn't help but compare it to the somber meals he knew were being served in many parts of Europe. It was possible here in the beautiful room surrounded by these beautiful people to forget the turmoil in the rest of the world.

He made conversation with the people around him and watched Sylvia as she flirted with her dinner partner. His thoughts strayed to Valerie and he wished with all his heart that he could share this bright gathering with her. She was more beautiful than any woman in the room and he longed to be with her. Finally, using his long flight as an excuse, he plucked Sylvia from the group and made their farewells.

Sylvia climbed into the car awkwardly and slumped in the corner pouting slightly. "I wanted another drink," she said.

John looked at her closely. Her hair was slightly mussed but other than that she appeared to be perfectly groomed and yet there was something not quite right about her looks. He realized she was drunk. "I think you've had enough for tonight, Syl."

"What'd you mean?" She drew herself up indignantly into a straight, prim figure. "Do you think I'm drunk?"

John recognized the antagonistic tone in her voice and decided instantly that it wasn't worth a fight. "Of course not," he pacified her, "I'm tired and I thought it was time to go home."

"Oh." Sylvia relaxed back into her not quite drunken slump. John watched her out of the corner of his eye and wondered just how much she had had to drink. He shook his head. It's really none of my business, he decided.

"That was rather a nice party, don't you think?" Sylvia asked, carefully pronouncing each word.

John murmured a sound of agreement but didn't pursue the conversation. They lapsed into silence and the ride home was accomplished without further contact.

The entire city was dressed in its holiday best. Store windows sparkled with lights and fancy merchandise. A Santa stood on every corner shaking his bell and calling out a greeting to passersby. Nowhere was there evidence of the shortages seen in England. John strolled slowly up the broad avenue. He looked into each window and considered the display. His mind was on Valerie and he whistled to himself as he deliberated over a Christmas present to take back to her. Everything looked attractive and yet somehow nothing seemed exactly right. Unable to decide he entered a toy store instead and delighted the clerk by buying everything she suggested as being appropriate for "an almost three year old boy". He ordered the packages to be wrapped and sent and then purchased still more for Sam's tribe. Feeling like Santa Claus himself, he left the toy store and continued on his search for the perfect present.

A large jewelry store caught his eye and he paused to examine the contents of the window. He moved on. He'd always purchased jewelry for Sylvia and the memory was connected to too many unpleasant times when he'd used the gift as a bribe to calm the troubled waters of their relationship. Clothing wasn't right either, he decided. Valerie was always beautifully dressed but he had no idea what size would be right or what she might need or want. Flowers, he thought, flowers are perfect but not enough to show Valerie how much I need her. And yet flowers were the only thing that appealed to him, the only gift that seemed to whisper her name. He surrendered to the thought and entered a flower shop. The sweet smell of hothouse roses brought with it the memory of the soft floral scent that Valerie always wore. "I'd like to send some roses to a friend," he told the clerk.

"Certainly, sir. What did you have in mind?"

"They must be beautiful, absolutely perfect long stemmed, deep red roses."

"Of course." The clerk rubbed his palms together. "I'll see that our very best are delivered."

"No, no." John realized that he'd neglected the most important instruction. "My friend lives in England. Can you arrange to have them delivered there?"

"Yes, sir. We offer the new Floral Telegraph Delivery. It's rather expensive, I'm afraid."

John waved away the remark. "If you can guarantee the best I'll be delighted to pay. I want three dozen roses to be delivered as quickly as possible to a very special lady."

"She must be special indeed." The clerk drew out his order book and prepared to write up the order.

"More than just special," John smiled broadly. "Much more, I'd say she's the most special lady in the world."

"And a very lucky one if I may say so. Three dozen roses will make a most spectacular display."

"Perfect! Valerie deserves the finest."

They concluded the transaction and John left the shop reassured that the delivery would be made in record time and that the roses would be of the finest quality. Whistling happily he continued on his way. He found himself imagining the delight on Valerie's face when the flowers were delivered. He still wanted to buy a present to give her but the for now the flowers would let her know that even though an ocean separated them she was in his thoughts and in his heart.

A few more blocks and he'd arrived at the AmCo building. The doorman recognized him and called him by name as he tilted his hat in greeting. John hurried in and stepped into a waiting elevator. He was anxious to talk to Walter away from the party crowd. And Walter was anxious to talk to him. As John entered the office, Walter rose stiffly from his chair. John found himself again thinking how much Walter had aged in the months they'd been apart. He clasped his grandfather in a warm hug and then seated himself. The two men smiled warmly in a moment of familiar communication, glad to be together again. "It's good to see you there, in that chair, John. I've missed you."

John was surprised by the sentimental words and hesitated before he answered, "I've missed you, too, Grandfather." He knew that Walter expected more but each thing that he "should" say he cast aside as not being true and he didn't want to lie. He couldn't say he missed his family when he felt as if his family was Valerie and she was in England. He couldn't say he missed the city when he'd not given it a thought. He chose to say no more and waited for Walter to continue.

"How's Michael?"

John's face lit up and Walter smiled at his reaction. "He's terrific. He's growing like a weed and smart as a whip."

Walter nodded. "Annie brings him by the office to see me whenever she can. He's a good looking boy, takes after Sylvia that way."

The innocent comment caused a twinge of hurt. John was certain that Walter had meant no harm with his remark and yet the fact that the boy had no family resemblance to the Augustus clan hurt. Quickly he changed the subject. "I'm only going to be here a short time so I wanted to spend some time in the office with you and Sam. We need to make sure that the plans for the expansion we need for the manufacturing of uniforms is well on its way. Unless I miss my guess the USA will be joining this war." He hurried on before Walter could speak. "And I want to reassure you again that Sylvia is well taken care of despite her complaints."

Walter waved away the words. "I believe what you told me last night. I'm sorry that I didn't realize the truth without you having to tell me."

"It's easy to be taken in by Sylvia." John smiled ruefully. "Lord knows, it's happened to me a few dozen times."

"Perhaps, John, but I know you and I should never have given her words a second thought, much less believed her. We need to do something to keep her from spreading such vicious rumors."

John noted his grandfather's use of the word we and he felt the need to protest. "It's not your problem. She's my wife and I'll talk to her."

Walter straightened in his chair and regained the image of the strong leader he'd always been to the entire family and to the company. "This is a family problem. I'll not allow Sylvia to besmirch the Augustus name."

"I've made it perfectly clear that she'll not get another penny of my money or the use of my name if she even breaths another word against the family."

Walter inclined his head sadly. "Such a pretty woman," he shook his head. "I suppose it's her bad blood showing. Her mother ran away with a drummer, you know."

John supposed he should defend his wife but after all "bad blood" seemed as likely an excuse for her behavior as any other and the moment passed as Walter continued. "There's no need to talk business until after the holidays. Why don't you spend some time relaxing and seeing friends?"

"I won't be staying for the holidays. I intend to return to England tomorrow."

"Tomorrow!" Walter thundered the old strength apparent in his voice. "Surely you'll stay until after Christmas."

"No, Walter." John carefully pitched his voice very low with an effort. "I want to be back in England on Christmas Eve."

"Whatever for? Your family is here. No man should spend Christmas alone."

"I won't be alone. Valerie is in London and I'll be spending the day with her." John glanced at Walter's face afraid of what he would see there. He hurried on before Walter could speak. "I'm sure you don't approve but I love her and now that I've found her again I don't intend to give her up."

Walter sighed deeply. He removed his glasses and began to polish them carefully on his large linen handkerchief. John took a breath and plunged on. "My marriage to Sylvia is over. I told you so last night at the party and I'm telling you again now."

"You told me it was over but that there would be no divorce," Walter reminded him.

"So it appears but there must be something we can do, some way we can break that damn will."

"Have you spoken to Sam?"

"Of course, he wasn't able to do anything before but now he must! I have to be free."

"And what if he can't?" Walter hooked his glasses back over his ears and regarded John seriously. "What then? Will your Valerie be willing to be a back street wife? Or are you willing to throw over all your obligations to Sylvia and to your son?" John started to interrupt but Walter waved him to silence and continued. "I know he's Sylvia's son and not yours. But blood isn't the only thing that makes a family. There are many other ties that bind. There is honor and right and obligation and..... there is money. That child did not ask to be born into your loveless marriage. I know you may feel I was at fault to force you to stay with Sylvia but, be that as it may, the child is now an accomplished fact. The world believes him to be your son and for you to smear Sylvia's name in the mud would bring dishonor on not only Sylvia and the child but on all of us."

"Honor! Dishonor! I've heard enough about honor to last me the rest of my life. I don't care about the damn Augustus clan. I don't care who it hurts. I want to be happy." John stood and paced the floor. "Can't you understand, Walter? I love Valerie. I know that more than ever before. The few days we've had together have been the best in my life and I'm willing to sacrifice whatever is necessary to whatever god demands it. But I'm not going to give her up and I'm not going to stay married to Sylvia one single day longer then I have to!"

"I hear you, John. There's no need to shout."

"Sorry." John returned to his chair and composed himself. "I have to make a life for myself. It isn't fair that I should spend the rest of my days in a loveless marriage just for the sake of the family fortune."

"Fair has very little to do with life." John waved away the words but Walter continued, "I know that you're thinking I don't understand the depth of your feelings, that I'm much too old to have such passions and much too old to remember them if, in fact, I ever had them. Believe me, boy, I've felt passion many times in my life for many different things and many different ways. True, passion has changed as I've gotten older but the feelings are no less strong, no less compelling. The difference lies in my ability to weather the storm of passion and then think long enough and clearly enough to choose the action that's right."

"It's not right for me to remain Sylvia's husband."

Walter nodded slowly. "Perhaps, that is true. These last few years have certainly been hard on both of you. It doesn't take a wise man to have seen that. But is this urge you feel to rush out and dissolve one marriage just so that you can start another any better?" Walter held up his hand. "No. Don't answer. I know that you think you've thought everything through, that you know exactly what you want and how to achieve it. I'm asking you to slow down, to take the time to really get to know Valerie. Go back to England. Live with her if you must. Try it; find out if everyday life with her is better than your life with Sylvia."

"I love Valerie. I want her to be my wife. I want to love, honor and protect her. I want to build a life with her, to grow old with her."

"And didn't you once think those same thoughts about Sylvia?" Walter asked reasonably.

"I was young then. I didn't know what it meant to be married to someone."

"True enough. First love is often based on sexual attraction and not much else. I'm not suggesting that you give up this young woman. I'm merely offering the idea that it would be wise to take your time and be sure that this is what you really want for the rest of your life before you give up everything that you already have."

John sat silent and Walter waited calmly for his response. Something in Walter's words made sense to John but he didn't want to admit that his grandfather might be right. At last he looked at

Walter and shrugged. "I can't do anything about it now anyway. I'm leaving soon and it will be months before I'm back in the city." He sighed and smiled grimly. "That sounds like I'm agreeing to take my time, doesn't it?"

Walter nodded. "Agreeing to do the only possible thing is not an evasion of your responsibility only an acceptance." Placing both hands flat on the desktop, he pushed himself up from the chair. "I'd like to show you some things over in the plant and then you'd better get home to your son. If you're leaving tomorrow you'll want to spend some time with him."

John lifted Michael from the car and set him down carefully. The small boy's sturdy legs staggered slightly and then held him firmly. John held out his hand and Michael took it without hesitation. They walked together up the steps to Sam's front door. John was overwhelmed by a wave of emotion and he looked down and grinned. Michael grinned back, excited by the unexpected pleasure of having this new adult all to himself. "Want to visit your cousins, Sport?"

Michael was unsure of the word but the tone of the question was evident. He smiled broadly and nodded. "What's a cousin?"

"You'll see." John assured him. "Cousins are just kids like you. You can play with them and see their Christmas tree."

"Christmas tree," Michael repeated sure of what that meant."

John lifted the knocker and let it fall against the door with a sharp rapping sound. The door swung open almost at once. "Uncle John!" Christopher shouted. "Hey, Mom. Dad. Uncle John's here."

"Well, let him in, son." Sam hurried into the entry. "John, it's good to see you. Helen will be delighted." Michael stepped back, overcome by the exuberance of their greeting. "And Michael," Sam was surprised. "Great! Come on in."

"I hope we aren't interrupting anything." John entered the house with Michael's small hand still firmly clasping his own.

"No, no," Sam reassured him. "Helen's with the baby but she'll be down in a minute and the kids will be thrilled to see Michael. Take your coats off. Christopher, run and tell your mother that John is here and then come back and you can take Michael upstairs to play."

Christopher hurried off. John removed his overcoat and helped Michael with his snowsuit. His liking for the child was evident in his manner and Sam beamed as he asked, "How did you get Michael over to visit?"

"I don't need permission," John said defensively. "And Sylvia's gone out for the afternoon. She has no idea where we are."

Sam clapped him on the back. "Well, come on in and get comfortable. The boy's grown like a weed since we saw him last."

Michael continued to cling to John's hand as they moved into the comfortable living room. A fire danced on the hearth and was reflected in the shiny tree ornaments. Michael gaped in wonder at the magnificent splendor of the twelve foot fir. John too, stopped in amazement. "That's some tree," he managed to say.

"Yup." Sam was delighted by their surprise. "The kids and I picked it out. Helen said we could get any tree we liked as long as she didn't have to go out in the cold."

"And you can be sure it's the last time I'll ever say anything so foolish again." Helen joined the two men giving John a hug and slipping her hand beneath Sam's arm. "That thing takes up the whole room."

"But it's beautiful," John said.

"Beautiful," Michael repeated.

The three adults laughed. Helen knelt down and hugged Michael. "You are such a sweet thing," she said, kissing his cheek. "It's so good to see both of you."

Christopher, Peter, Jennifer and Beth arrived with a noisy burst of energy and for a few minutes the room was a hubbub of laughter and voices as the kids tried to tell their favorite uncle all the news in the shortest possible time.

Finally Sam raised his voice, "Hush now. Why don't you take Michael and go play upstairs. We'd like a little peace and quiet."

The four trooped out of the room after extracting a promise from John that he would come upstairs to see their prized possessions before leaving. As peace settled over the living room John sighed happily. "You are surely blessed to have such a happy family, such a good life." A shadow passed over Helen's features and John realized his mistake. She looked older and more tired than he'd ever seen her look before. "How is the baby?" he asked gently.

"Not good." Tears gathered in Helen's eyes and she fought to control them as she answered carefully. "She's such a good baby so pretty and so bright. We've tried everything and yet she grows weaker every day."

"Can the doctors help?"

"It's her heart." Helen dashed the tears away.

A log broke and fell in a shower of sparks. Helen jumped to her feet. "I'll check on the kids." She hurried from the room. Sam watched her sadly and John struggled to find something to say.

Sam poked the fire back into place and turned with a shrug. "So tell me, Cuz, what's new with you."

"Not much." He stretched out his long legs and crossed his arms behind his head. "I need to talk with you about Sylvia but it certainly isn't new and right this second it doesn't seem nearly as important as the baby's health."

"If you want to talk divorce again, there isn't anything I can tell you that you don't already know."

John sighed. "I need to do something about the situation, Sam." He stared into the fire, composing his thoughts. Sam waited, watching his face and saying nothing. "I understand that we are tied together, but I've got to make some kind of arrangement."

Sam raised his eyebrows in an unspoken question.

"I'm seeing Valerie again," John blurted out.

"Here?"

"No, of course not, she's living in London. I ran into her at a pub just a few days ago."

"A few days doesn't exactly mean you're seeing her."

"In this case it does. I love her, Sam. I've never stopped loving her, never stopped missing her, and now that I've found her I won't let her go."

"How does she feel?"

"We love each other. We want to be together."

Sam was determined to play the devil's advocate. "Does she know you can't get a divorce?"

"I have to get a divorce." John dodged the question.

But Sam was persistent. Again he asked and John was forced to admit that Valerie thought he'd be taking care of the arrangements while he was in the states.

"And what do you intend to tell her when you get back to London?"

"I'm going back tomorrow and I'll tell her the truth. There just wasn't time to do anything this trip but that I'll get things started somehow."

Sam studied John without speaking. John felt like squirming under his quiet gaze. "It's not a lie, Sam. I will do something."

Sam nodded and watched the fire. John wished he'd never started this conversation. "I'm tired of being judged by this damn family," he thought.

As if Sam had heard John's thought, he said, "I can guess how you feel, John. Being in love is an overwhelming rush of emotions and I know you'd like to be free of Sylvia and Michael so that you could live your life the way you'd like. It must seem as if the Augustus family is still running your life."

John tried to protest but Sam waved him to silence. "I'm not judging you or your actions. I'd like to see you happy but how can I possibly encourage a divorce when I feel it's wrong? Sylvia and Michael need you."

"Michael, maybe, but certainly not Sylvia! She's found a life of her own and I'd say she's quite happy."

"Then you're either blind or a fool. She wasn't acting the part of a happy woman last night."

"Last night she was with me instead of her lover and I'd just ruined her plan to weasel money out of Alex's estate. I shouldn't think she would have been happy."

"And why does she need more money?" Sam asked and then answered without a pause. "She's running around with a fast crowd, they party too much and drink too much and seem to live a rootless life. Sylvia is like a little girl trying to find acceptance. She hasn't been a success at anything much and she's unable to face herself."

John realized that Sam's evaluation of Sylvia was all too true. "So what am I supposed to do? She's a grown woman. I can't tell her how to act."

"She is still your wife, Cuz."

John grinned bitterly. "So I've been reminded. What do I do? She was drinking entirely too much last night; in fact, she was actually very drunk although she seemed to handle it very well. I get the impression from Annie and Mrs. Peters that she's seldom home and that she spends very little time with Michael."

"I have heard that she is drinking a great deal," Sam said softly.

"You've heard? Does that mean it's common gossip?"

"I'm afraid so. I wish there was an easy way to tell you but perhaps it's better to hear it from me them from someone outside the family."

John straightened his shoulders and looked grim. "I'll handle this before I leave tomorrow. She won't like it but she'll have to listen."

"That's enough of this dreary talk." Sam jumped to his feet. "If you're leaving tomorrow you've only a few hours and then, God only knows when we'll see you again. Let's go find Helen and the kids and start celebrating Christmas the way a family should."

Sam hurried out into the hall calling for Helen and the kids as he went. Michael came running down

- 255 -

the stairs with the rest of children and John caught him up in a giant bear hug. Helen appeared carrying Sarah. Gently John traced the baby's delicate features with one finger and was rewarded with a toothless smile. "She's a real beauty," he said, keeping to himself his observation of her blue lips and listless movements.

Hours later Michael and John returned to the brownstone. John carried the sleepy child into the house and reluctantly relinquished him to Annie. "Did you have a good day, sir?" she asked.

"We had an extremely good day!" John grinned as he flipped his hat onto the hook of the hall tree. "Is my wife in?"

"She just came in. I think she's gone to her room."

"When you take Michael up ask her to come down, please. I'll be in the living room."

John patted the carved lion's head for luck and prepared himself for the talk he needed to have with Sylvia. He thought about the affection he'd felt at Sam's house that afternoon and realized again that he'd give most anything to be able to have that kind of a relationship with his wife. But, he reminded himself, it's not Sylvia I want to have, it's Valerie. And with Valerie I know I could build a fine and happy life. We'll have beautiful children and she'll make a splendid mother.

But daydreams accomplished nothing and right now was the time he needed to accomplish a great deal. If only there were some way to get a divorce; some way that wouldn't destroy Michael or Sylvia, in fact, he admitted to himself, some way that won't damage the Augustus name or hurt Walter. His thoughts chased round and round as he explored again every possible avenue and once more he returned to the conclusion that there was no way out of this marriage that would leave Sylvia's money intact.

"Well, John, you certainly look contented." Sylvia swept into the room; her long blue velvet robe swirled around her slender body and brightened the highlights in her loose hair.

"And you look lovely, as usual."

"Goodness! Compliments! I am impressed." Sylvia's voice held just the slightest touch of sarcasm. "Annie said you summoned me."

John recognized the tone as one that signaled Sylvia's desire to start a fight. He decided not to rise to the bait and instead smiled as he said, "I need to talk to you, Syl. I'll be leaving for London again in just a few hours and there are several things we need to get straight before I go."

"Leaving?" Sylvia's voice climbed several decibels. "What do you mean? You just got here."

"True." He kept his voice quiet and reasonable despite his annoyance. "And now I'm leaving."

"What about Christmas?"

"Christmas? I'd rather not be here for Christmas, Sylvia. I came home because Walter insisted. I found out what he wanted and now I'm leaving again."

"What about what I want?"

"What you want is of no concern to me. However what you do is of great concern and that's why I asked you to come down." John's level gaze stopped her protest. "Sit down, Syl. I've a lot to tell you."

She moved to the gold brocade sofa and sat down gracefully, carefully arranging the soft folds of her robe. She folded her hands and gazed back at him. "Go ahead, dear," she said softly.

"This isn't a game, Syl. I'm dead serious about everything I'm going to say."

"My goodness," the southern drawl crept into her words, "you sound positively formidable."

"Michael and I spent the afternoon at Sam and Helen's"

"John! I don't like Michael going over there. Those children are so rough." She shuttered.

"They are warm, delightful kids who are being raised in a warm loving family, something Michael doesn't have. I want him to spend time with them. I know you don't like to see Helen so you don't need to take him but Annie is to arrange time for Michael to see his cousins on a regular basis. I'll talk to her before I leave."

"You can't tell me how to raise my son!" Anger flashed in Sylvia's eyes.

"I can and I will. You seem to forget that legally he's my son just as much as he's yours. Which brings me to the next topic, Sam says there is absolutely no way that we can get a divorce but I'm not willing to accept his decision. I want you to see another attorney. I'll give you a list of names and I'll pay the bills. Just have them sent to the bank."

"Do you think someone else can help us?" Sylvia's anger died away as hope flared.

"I don't know but there has to be a way to break that will. People get divorced every day and wills are broken every day. You'll have to take care of it because there is very little I can do from England and besides I think it would look better for you and Michael if the divorce, when it comes, is initiated by you."

Sylvia clapped her hands together, like a child. "I knew you'd think of something, John."

"It's not accomplished yet," he cautioned.

"But it will be. I can feel it in my bones. Let's have a drink to celebrate." She sprang to her feet and the full robe parted to reveal her slim legs.

"Sit down, Syl. Drinking is the next thing I want to talk about."

"Drinking?"

"Yes, drinking. Don't play innocent with me. I saw you with my own eyes last night and I've been told today that the whole town is talking about your habits."

"Oh, pooh. That's just your old, stuck in the mud, cousin talking. Just because his wife doesn't drink more than one glass of wine, he doesn't think anyone else should either."

"No, Sylvia," John spoke carefully, making an effort to keep his tone patient and reasonable. "It's not just Sam. I've heard from others that your behavior is the talk of the town. I don't expect you to become a nun or even change your habits but you've got to be more careful." An angry flush stained her cheeks red and she started to protest but John continued, "Personally, I don't care what you do, who you do it with, or how much you drink but you need to know that talk about your behavior can't be tolerated. It will affect Michael and it will affect the family."

"Stop preaching, John." Sylvia tossed her shinning hair back and prepared to do battle. "Anyone who's talking about me must have a very boring life. I've scarcely done a thing since you've been away and I'm certainly not drinking too much. Last night I was too nervous to eat dinner and the drinks went straight to my head. Why, I doubt that I had more than two glasses all evening and I'm sure I didn't finish that."

The memory of their conversation before the party flashed through John's mind. He was sure that she'd had at least two and maybe three drinks before they left the house and now that he was thinking about it, she'd seemed to be a bit tipsy when she came in from lunch. Sylvia cocked her head and smiled flirtatiously, "You know I'm not a drinker, John. Why I can barely stand the smell of the stuff, much less the taste."

For a moment John considered arguing with her. He knew that quite contrary to her words she'd always been able to keep up in any group of drinkers. In fact before they'd married there had been gossip about her habits, but at that time he'd ignored them and defended her as being high spirited. He decided to ignore it again. "I don't want to fight, Syl. I'm leaving for London tomorrow morning and all I want is to get some things straight tonight."

"I'll see to it that Annie takes Michael to see his cousins occasionally."

"Thank you." John was aware that her acquiescence meant that she wanted to drop the subject but he decided to say just enough more so that she would realize how serious he was when he warned her about her behavior. "I've sent a letter to the bank authorizing them to take control of my stateside expenses. All the bills will be paid by the bank and I've set certain limits as to what and how much you can charge. I can assure you that they will not pay for liquor or for parties. If you want to do those things you'll have to find someone to pay for you or use the money Alex left you."

"How dare you!" Sylvia leapt to her feet, fire in her eyes. "What gives you the right to try to control me like this?"

"I've every right in the world. I'm your husband!"

"This isn't the middle ages!" Sylvia spit out the loud words. "I can do whatever I want whenever I want and you can't do anything to stop me."

"I control the money, Syl." John managed to speak calmly despite his anger. He knew she was become more infuriated by the second but this time he was determined that she would understand. "Our agreement was to stay married and to live our lives separately. You've chosen to embarrass me and to make a public display of yourself. I don't choose to pay for that kind of behavior. I want a divorce as much as you do but I want it to be polite and quiet. Do you think you can manage that?"

"I can manage to get a divorce."

"But can you act like a lady while you do it?"

The coldness in John's tone was frightening and suddenly Sylvia realized just how angry he really was. She sat down and folded her hands. "I can manage quite well, John." She tilted her head and the light danced across her high cheekbones. John was aware of her beauty and felt a momentary regret as he realized the loss of this beautiful woman. "I was raised to be a Southern lady and I can handle anything."

"I hope you can, Syl." John spoke softly. "I really hope you can."

John watched out the window as the plane slipped down out of the fog and gilded to a stop at Heathrow Airport. It seemed he'd spent an inordinate amount of time on planes lately. He pulled on his camel hair topcoat and wrapped his muffler around his throat to keep out the cold damp wind. Crossing the tarmac quickly he glanced up but was unable to see a single star. Sounds came through the fog first muffled and then very clear in the strange distorted way that such nights have. He collected his duffle bag and hailed a cabby. Somehow it didn't feel right to be here in a foreign country when his family was gathering around the table ready for the Christmas Eve feast. He wondered what Michael would think of the turkey and if he'd like his presents. It would have been fun to see him open them, he thought, remembering the joy of Christmas mornings when he was a child. Minette crossed his mind and he smiled and decided to call France first thing in the morning.

"Here you are, Governor." The cabbie's rough voice broke into his reverie.

He paid, added a generous tip and stepped out into the night looking up at the dark windows of Valerie's flat. The cold wind whistled around the corner and whipped his coat away from his body. He pulled it close and picked up his bag. For once in his life he felt unsure and a bit afraid. What if she's not home, he worried.. Maybe she's gone out with her friends. He felt foolish standing there and decided he should at least knock after all he'd come all this way to spend Christmas Day with his love. He braced his shoulders. It certainly wouldn't make any sense at all if he didn't at least find out if she was home.

Quietly he climbed the stairs his heart thumping like a school boy's. He tapped gently on the door and waited. There was no answer. "Damn," he swore aloud as he dropped his bag. "Now what?"

The door swung open. Valerie's surprise was evident in her eyes. "John?" she questioned, in amazement and held out her arms. He stepped into her embrace. Home at last.

"You'd better come in." Valerie laughed as she tilted her head back and smiled broadly. "The neighbors will think we're crazy standing out here in the hall like this."

"I don't care what the neighbors think," John declared. "I'm so glad to see you. I feel as though we'd been apart a million years."

They entered the flat, hand in hand, unwilling to stop touching for even a brief second. "God, I missed you." John stroked her silky, dark hair and searched her face.

"And I you," she answered. "The roses were delivered yesterday. Look how beautiful they are."

"Not as beautiful as you. Tell me I never have to leave you again."

Valerie cupped his face in her small hands and met his eyes squarely. Solemnly she vowed, "You never have to leave me again. I love you."

John wrapped her close in a hug and held her. He felt every curve and swell of her small, sweet body. He breathed in the warm fragrance of her hair. "I love you, too, my darling. I love you more than words can say." He tipped her face toward himself and kissed her gently. Then his tongue was probing and reaching for the welcome he found in her mouth. His hands gilded down over her back and lifted her firm sweet bottom. He felt his manhood rise as he felt her response. Lifting her in his arms, he carried her to the bedroom.

The room spun and twisted beneath their passion. Her mouth welcomed his in a way that he'd never known existed before. It was as if they'd been made for one another. They fit together. Her hands touched him in just the right way and his answer created music in their hearts, the climax left them trembling in each other's naked arms.

John stroked the tangled hair away from Valerie's damp forehead and kissed each eyelid. "You belong to me."

Her somber grey eyes met his and she gazed deep into his soul. He trembled at the look, afraid that she would know that he hadn't managed to free himself from Sylvia. With one finger she traced the line of his cheek and across his mouth. "I do belong to you, John. Forever! Don't forget."

"I'll never, my darling, never!" He buried his face in her hair and kissed her soft shoulder. "I'll never forget."

They lay entwined in the warm aftermath of their love making. Smiling and talking about the small things. John wanted to tell her about his inability to divorce Sylvia but the time didn't seem right, the moment passed and they drifted into sleep.

Christmas morning dawned. The sound of church bells rang through the clean, clear air. John stirred and stretched. Still half asleep he felt the soft, warm skin of Valerie's naked back pressed against him. Carefully he rolled onto his side and gazed down at her precious face. She looked more like a child then a woman. The full curve of her cheek and the slight pout of her lips caused his heart to swell with a tenderness he'd never felt before. She opened her eyes and was instantly awake. "Merry Christmas, Darling," she said with a smile.

"I love you."

"I love you, too."

It was the perfect way to start a perfect day. He lowered his heart and kissed her mouth. She returned the kiss with a passion matching his own her hands gilded over his back and then pulled him tight against her. They fit together in the most magical way, touching from head to toe, the warmth of their skin exciting them both. His hands stroked her breast and his fingers brushed the nipple. He couldn't wait a second longer and thrust himself into her moist eager body. Her response was immediate and their mutual delight drove them quickly to the peak and over. He collapsed on her and she laughed in delight. He rolled to his side taking her with him, still safe inside. "Merry Christmas," he managed to say.

Their need for one another was a constant, obvious thing. John followed her with his eyes when Valerie went out of the room and welcomed her back with a kiss and a hug. They touched and laughed and talked in the silliest manner. They bathed together and then fixed breakfast getting in each other's way and kissing whenever they touched.

"I feel sixteen years old," John declared.

Valerie tilted her head back and examined him carefully. "You have a very heavy beard for such a callow youth," she said rubbing her hand across his chin.

John went to shave and Valerie followed him, she perched on the edge of the tub and watched. Their eyes met in the mirror and they laughed at themselves. Valerie sobered. "If I'd known you'd be back for Christmas, I would have trimmed a tree."

"This is the best Christmas I've ever had." John laid his razor on the sink and took her in his arms. "I've everything I've ever dreamed about right here in my arms."

They spent the day together listening to Christmas music on the radio and ignoring the news casts. John wished he'd found a Christmas present while he was in the states but Valerie declared that she didn't mind and he promised to take her shopping for anything she wanted.

The City Chronicle
February 15, 1940
Tattle Tales by Sharon Chatsworth

Cupid was seen last night hovering over the beautiful Sylvia Augustus. Despite the fact that hubby, John, is still in England attending to the increase of the family fortune, the Mrs. was dancing until dawn in the arms of a handsome movie star. Her brilliant red dress with the sparkling starburst of pailettes on each shoulder caught the eye of every guest at the Valentine Ball given by the Rodney Van Dorfmann's. ....

Chapter 13

Sylvia pushed her pale pink satin sleep mask up and squinted in the sudden glare. She stretched carefully, her head ached and her mouth appeared to be full of cotton, even the careful stretch caused the room to spin. Cautiously she turned her head and looked at the jewel encrusted bedside clock; it read 10:45. She groaned aloud and sat up slowly hanging tight to her pillow as the room spun again.

Holding her pounding head, Sylvia stumbled across the room and into the bath. She groaned again as she gulped down a handful of aspirin tablets and several glasses of cold water. The water brought momentary relief and she examined her face in the mirror. Last night's makeup was smeared into a clown face; her eyes were puffy and quite red. "Ugh," she groaned aloud and splashed water on her face then patted it dry, leaving makeup smudges on the towel. Slowly and carefully she made her way back into the bedroom clinging to furniture to avoid stumbling. She pulled the bell cord that would summon someone from the kitchen and lay back across the bed, praying that the aspirin would take effect and sooth the pounding in her head.

A discrete knock announced the arrival of Mrs. Peters. Sylvia didn't move the arm she flung over her eyes nor did she acknowledge the polite, "Good morning, madam." that was murmured.

"I need tomato juice and coffee and send Annie in to clean up this mess while I bathe. I'm going to be late for the Art Museum luncheon."

"Annie has taken Michael to the park, madam. I'll get your juice and clean up."

"That girl is never here when I need her" Sylvia complained. The door clicked shut and Sylvia groaned again, but forced herself to sit up and then managed to get into a hot shower. She stood, leaning against the tile and letting the hot water and steam cleanse her body and ease away the effects of last night's party. Emerging from the shower, she smiled at her reflection, "Much better," she said nodding to her reflection.

A tall glass of cold juice had been placed on the vanity, the bed was neatly made and her rumbled gown and scattered undergarments had disappeared. A silver pot of coffee with a delicate cup and spoon along with a plate of toast was arranged in the bay window.

Sylvia nibbled on the toast, aware that her stomach needed something to settle it. Glancing at the clock again she realized that she'd have to hurry or she'd miss the entire luncheon and that would certainly start that Chatsworth woman talking again.

Her head continued to pound despite the aspirin, food and shower. "I've got to get rid of this headache," she told herself. Picking up the crystal goblet of juice she dumped half of it in the sink, opened a vanity drawer, withdrew a silver flask and refilled the glass. Taking a long drink she toasted herself in the mirror and began to do her makeup and hair.

A scant ninety minutes later she swept into the private dining room at the Art Museum and circulated quickly, kissing her acquaintances and making half stated apologies about "how children always seem to need something just when you are in a hurry to get somewhere".

The younger women laughed with her and smiled in sympathy. The older women exchanged glances but kept their opinions to themselves, after all Sylvia was still Mrs. John Augustus.

As the speaker droned on about the impressionistic movement, Sylvia allowed her thoughts to drift. Last night's party had been a stunning success. From the moment she entered the Van Dorfmann mansion in her brilliant red Worth gown she'd been aware of every man's attention. Parties in this dreary city were so much more fun now that a new group of men were being invited. Mark had been furious with the amount of attention she'd paid to the glamorous movie star, Rex Rockford. Sylvia almost laughed aloud as she thought of his jealous rage. He needs to remember that I don't belong to him, she thought. I'm a free woman and I can do as I please. Well, she acknowledged to herself, maybe not free but there are certainly advantages to having a husband "in name only". I can always fall back on the "I'm a married woman" excuse or simply ignore it, whichever fits the circumstances.

Perhaps it was a good thing that none of the attorneys that John had suggested were able to find a way around her father's will.

The polite spattering of applause brought her thoughts back to the luncheon table. Mary Beth Cartwright grinned at Sylvia as she lit her cigarette. "Why, darling, you've barely touched your lunch. Is something wrong?"

"No just watching my figure." Sylvia lit a cigarette of her own and sipped her glass of wine. "There was entirely too much good food at Rodney and Cynthia's party last night. I'm afraid I made pig of myself."

"I'm surprised you had time to eat. It looked to me that you were entirely too busy." Mary Beth took a deep drag and slowly exhaled allowing the smoke to drift toward the ceiling in lazy rings.

"Bitch!" Sylvia thought, returning Mary Beth's appraising stare. She managed to smile sweetly, "It was a lovely party wasn't it. I did so enjoy meeting Mr. Rexford. Did you get a chance to talk with him? He tells such delightful stories about Hollywood."

"Actually, Syl, it reminded me of college," Allison Howell declared. "The way that man was fawning over you not another woman had a chance. Why, Mark was stomping around looking positively livid!" Sylvia and Allison giggled and Mary Beth exchanged disgusted glances with the other young matrons at their table.

"I'd love to stay and chat," Sylvia said, crushing out her cigarette and pushing back her chair, "but I really must run. Can I drop you somewhere, Allie?"

"No thanks. Mother is here somewhere and I'll need to see her home."

Sylvia waggled her fingers in the acceptable gesture that passed for farewell and strolled out of the room. A moment of silence followed her departure from the table and then Mary Beth turned to Allison. "Well, Allie, what is going on? Are they separated or what?" Allison shrugged. "Don't play innocent with us, Allison Howell. I've known you your entire life and I can tell that you know something."

"No I don't, honest. I mean I know that John is in London and has been for months and I know that Mark Phillips has a terrific crush on Sylvia but then most every man that ever met her has had a crush on her for at least a while."

"Is it true that she is out every night dancing and drinking?" Mary Beth persisted.

"Well, a group of us goes out together and, of course, she goes with us. It's lonely for her in that great big house."

"What about Mark?"

"Sometimes he goes along sometimes he doesn't. What is this, Mary Beth? Are you collecting information for the Chatsworth column?"

Mary Beth blushed slightly and looked embarrassed. "No, of course not, I just worry about my friends and I'd hate to see anything bad happen to Sylvia. She's had enough unhappiness in her life already. Who wants to go over to Barneys and shop a bit this afternoon?"

Gratefully accepting the change in topics the conversation returned to children, homes, and clothing. But as the group broke up each woman carried with her the seeds that had been planted and each woman vowed to watch more closely to be certain that their husband didn't fall prey to Sylvia's charms.

Sylvia had managed to keep the smiled pasted on her face until she was out of museum and back in her car but then fury at her "friends" caused her hands to shake and her face to distort in anger. "Rotten bitches," she muttered.

"Did you say something, mam?" the driver asked politely.

Sylvia glared at him, causing him to close the door as quietly as possible and head for the house by the shortest route. Sylvia sat in silence, stewing over the conversation she was sure had taken place the moment she left the room. The car swung left and she glanced out the window. She shrugged and forced herself to relax. "What difference does it make?" she thought. "I can do anything I want to do. And right now I want to go home take a nap and then meet Mark at the club." She smiled to herself at the thought his jealousy and decide to wear her sea green chiffon, a dress she knew would make her eyes glow like a vixen's and whose daring cut would cause everyone to look twice when she entered the room.

John and Valerie walked along the river bank holding hands and enjoying the warmth of the February sun as it ducked in and out of the clouds. Their pleasure in each other's company was so apparent that persons passing smiled and felt better.

"Want to stop for a bite, Love?" he asked using the English endearment that they had made their own.

"You really are beginning to sound like a Brit, John," Valerie teased. "When we go back to the city no one will be able to understand you."

"Then we'll just have to stay here," he declared. Wouldn't that be the easy way out," he thought. We could just stay here, people assume we are married;

no one cares if we aren't and no one knows about Sylvia. Perfect. He frowned. Valerie felt his mood swing and squeezed his hand.

"Come on," she said. "Let's go down to the market and see if we can find some fresh fish for dinner. I actually have some almost fresh vegetables and we'll have a feast."

John smiled again and swung her hand. "Yes, Miss Four Food Groups. I don't suppose you mean fish and chips and lots of grease, do you?"

She slapped his shoulder and grinned back. The joy of her secret bubbled up in her heart and she almost told but she wanted to be sure before sharing her news. "It won't kill you to eat a healthy meal and drink a glass of milk."

"Milk! Who said anything about milk?"

The shopping accomplished they returned to the flat that had become home to them both since Christmas day. Due to the rationing there had been no fish to be found but eggs and a wedge of cheese would allow Valerie to create one of her special omelets. John carried the string bag up the stairs and placed it on the table.

"I feel so domestic." He grinned happily. "I don't believe I've ever been shopping for groceries in my whole life."

"What?" Valerie starred at him. "Never, how did you get food?"

"I don't know," John admitted. "It was just there."

"Just there! Did you think food appeared in the kitchen and cooked itself?" She giggled. "You really are a spoiled child, John Augustus!"

"Of course not," he defended himself. "I knew it came from somewhere and that someone had to cook it. I just never thought about it."

"Stop." Valerie laughed holding up her hand. "You're just making it worse. I think it is time you learned a few facts of live."

"I know the facts of life." John leered in her direction.

"Not those facts! Tie on that apron you're going to learn to take care of yourself."

As the news in Europe worsened so did the news from home. John kept a close watch on the political situation and worried more each day about the safety of those he loved; Lily and Minette in France and Valerie in England. The war with Germany was escalating and with the Scapa Flow bombing near Scotland it seemed possible that bombs might drop in England or France. And so he spoke with Minette and he tried to convince her to go back to the states but she was determined to stay with her mother and Valerie only laughed at his concerns and told him she'd rather be with him than anywhere else in the world.

At the close of each business communication Walter asked what John had heard from Sylvia and when John's answer was always vague and uninformative he suggested that she was missing her husband and that John should make an effort. John attempted to ignore these messages but in early March Sam called and his concern could not be ignored.

John listened carefully as Sam told him that Sylvia's drinking had become the talk of the city. "What do you think I can do?" John asked.

"I'm not certain but something has to be done before something bad happens." Sam hesitated. "She's very angry."

"I know that, I'm angry, too. We're stuck together and we both hate it."

"I saw Michael yesterday." Sam paused. "He had a terrible bruise on his arm."

"What? What are saying? Sylvia may drink too much but she wouldn't hurt a child!"

"I'm not accusing her of anything. But someone grabbed his arm hard enough to leave a hand print and when I asked Sylvia what happened she claimed that he'd fallen."

"Maybe he did, he's only a baby."

"It was a hand print, John. I'm a father and I know what a bruise looks like when a child falls."

John sat staring out the window and considered Sam's message. Sadly he reached for the phone and dialed his house; he couldn't think of it as his home despite the fact that he'd lived there most of his life. When Duncan answered he asked for Sylvia and waited impatiently. He considered his words carefully and took a deep breath as her chipper, familiar voice filled his ear.

"John darling, what a pleasant surprise, to what do I owe this pleasure?"

"I just thought it was time for me to check in. Is everything all right?"

"Of course not!" she sated emphatically. "What a silly question, we are still married and nothing has changed, nothing is all right."

"What about Michael?" he probed carefully.

"Michael? Michael is fine. Why?" John thought she sounded defensive but it might have just been that he expected her to be careful.

"I've heard a few rumors that worry me, Sylvia."

He heard what sounded like ice rattling and asked angrily, "Good God, are you drinking?"

"What's it to you if I am?" Sylvia was too surprised to ignore his question but she recovered quickly. "It's breakfast time here, John. I have a glass of juice."

"Juice or a Bloody Mary?" John demanded. "I know you are drinking too much, Sylvia. I've heard about the exploits of you and your friends at the St. Regis." John tried to steady himself, he knew that he wouldn't get anywhere by putting Sylvia on the defensive. "I just called to check on you and Michael. Have you allowed him to visit his cousins?"

"In fact Sam was here yesterday when I came home from lunch and I told him I didn't want Michael visiting his house any more. Those children are much too uncouth. He gets in plenty of trouble without their influence."

"He needs to play with other children and Sam's kids are family, he needs them."

"He has Annie. That's enough. He needs to learn to behave and to respect others. He doesn't need to learn any more bad behaviors."

"I didn't see any bad behavior at Christmas."

"Oh for heaven's sake, John, you stayed a couple of days. You don't have any idea what a spoiled little brat he can be. Just yesterday morning I caught him sneaking into my room. Lord only knows what he planned to do."

"What did you do when you caught him?" John tried to stay calm. He could hear the ice in Sylvia's glass clink as she took a drink and then she gave a nervous little laugh.

"I sent him on his way, of course. What did you think?" She quickly covered her defensive tone with a flirtatious laugh. "Is there some reason for this call, John? I really must get ready for my day."

"I'm concerned about your drinking and I'm worried about Michael."

"Well stop worrying. Everything here is fine. I don't drink too much. I simply have fun with my friends and whatever you've heard and whoever you heard it from it just isn't true."

John sighed. "Okay, I'll call again in a few days."

"Don't bother. I really don't like talking to you."

Sylvia waited for the click to signify that John had disconnected and then she slammed the phone down. "Damn gossips!" She took a deep drink of her Bloody Mary finishing the drink and heading for the bar to mix another.

The City Chronicle
March 25, 1940
Tattletales by Sharon Chatsworth

The Easter Parade will be a wondrous event this afternoon if the rumors are correct as I'm sure they are. The word on the Avenue is that beautiful socialite; Mrs. John Augustus will be wearing a suit and hat designed by Schiaparelli. Perhaps famous hubby, John Augustus, purchased the outfit for her during his recent trip to Paris.

Chapter 14

"Lord," Sylvia muttered aloud as she read the Chatsworth column. "Hell will freeze over before John sends me a present from Paris."

"Excuse me, Mam? Did you need something?" Mrs. Peters paused in her work and looked at Sylvia.

"No, nothing, I was just wondering when John was in Paris." She realized that she was sharing thoughts with the help and quickly changed the subject. "Is my suit pressed and ready? I need to get dressed soon."

"Yes, Mam. Will you be taking Michael to the parade?"

"Michael?" Sylvia looked confused. Mrs. Peters realized her error and held her breath but Sylvia reached for her glass and sipped her drink absorbed by her reflection in the mirror. "Perhaps I'll wear my hair up," she murmured. "No down would be better with my new hat."

Mrs. Peters left the bedroom and hurried to the nursery where she encouraged Annie to take Michael out to the park to participate in the Egg Hunt and, if she were asked she would have had to admit, to get him out of his mother's path.

Sylvia hummed to herself as Andrew drove her to the Avenue. She was pleased with her smart wide shouldered, tailored suit. The large shoulders accentuated her tiny waist and slim hips and the bright turquoise color highlighted her coloring. Her "new look" beret made of dyed to match felt tilted dramatically forward and was accented by lovely green peacock feathers. She smiled at her refection in her compact mirror as she refreshed her bright red lipstick. Andrew swung to the curb and she stepped out to embrace her friends.

Allison squealed in delight. "Sylvia! What a divine color. Where did you find that suit and that perfectly wonderful hat?"

"It's the latest thing from Paris." Sylvia smiled and spun around. Let them think that John had sent it, no harm in allowing people to believe that her husband was attentive.

The group of friends linked arms and began to stroll down the avenue greeting friends and admiring each other. "Have you seen Mark?" Sylvia asked. Several heads shook in answer. "Hmm, I thought he was meeting us here but perhaps I misunderstood, or maybe he's been delayed." Sylvia forced herself to look unconcerned and smiled happily.

After strolling a few blocks they reached the St. Regis Hotel and the group left the Easter Parade and turned in for a refreshing cocktail and brunch. Sylvia tried not to watch the door as she ordered and sipped her cocktail. Allison whispered, "Don't worry he'll be here soon."

Sylvia glared at her. How dare Allison think she needed reassurance? Mark adored her and whatever was keeping him was no one's business. She ordered another cocktail and began to pick at her food as she turned to the others at the table and joined the chatter.

Sylvia kept a bright smile pasted on her face and managed to avoid watching the door but she couldn't keep her thoughts away from Mark. She ordered still another cocktail and felt the familiar feeling of wellbeing. The alcohol lifted her mood. Her laughter brightened and she urged her friends to dance the day away.

The sun was setting in a spectacular display of red and purple as Sylvia was driven home. Andrew watched her dozing in the rear seat, mouth open, and snoring lightly. He shook his head sadly and thought what a waste it was to see someone who had so much be so unhappy. As he pulled to the curb he jerked the car lightly in order to wake her in a way that would maintain what dignity she had left. He held the door and reached in to help her out of the car keeping a tight grip on her arm while she steadied herself and pulled her suit jacket down over her slim hips.

"Thank you, Andrew," Sylvia over articulated her words in the universal way of drunks.

"Just let me get your hat, Madam and I'll help you with the stairs." Andrew kept one hand on her arm and reached in for the crushed hat that had been so expensive and so beautiful only a few hours before. Sylvia tried to push him away but stumbled in her high heels. Andrew said nothing but guided her up the stairs and into the foyer where he was relieved to find Annie and Michael. "Perhaps you could assist Mrs. Augustus. She is a bit tired."

Annie raised her eyebrows at Andrew but merely nodded. Michael, surprised at seeing his mother, flew toward Sylvia and flung his arms around her knees shouting, "Mommy, I saw the Easter Bunny." Sylvia grabbed Michael by the shoulders and pushed him away. He fell and began to cry. "Stop that this instant," Sylvia shouted. "Get your filthy hands off me."

Michael continued to wail frightened by the loud, angry words. Annie swept him up from the floor, glared at Sylvia and hurried away. Andrew wasn't sure what to do next but Sylvia solved his dilemma by slumping into a chair and appearing to pass out. Summoned by the noise Duncan entered the foyer and dismissed Andrew, covering for Sylvia's behavior was becoming a regular part of his job.

In England John gave up his apartment and moved in with Valerie. If the landlady was suspicious of their marital status she chose to look the other way in the light of their obvious happiness. They worked hard and hurried home each night to be together. The war brought shortages but they found it fun to "make do" and laughed at the strange meals they were able to put together.

Then on April 9th the Nazis invaded Denmark. German planes dropped leaflets over Copenhagen calling for the Danes to accept the German occupation peacefully, and claiming that Germany had occupied Denmark in order to protect it against Great Britain and France. In John's position he was aware of the likelihood of an invasion of England or France by Germany and began to make plans to get

Valerie, Minette and Lily out of harm's way and back in the states.

He arrived home with a bottle of good wine and a plan. After dinner they settled in front of the small gas fire and John poured the wine. He raised his glass to Valerie, "You are the love of my life." She smiled and touched her glass to his and raised it to her lips. John continued, "I'm worried about Minette and Lily. They need to leave France now before it is too late and I want you to go with them." Valerie started to protest. "No wait, my love. They will need you to help them both on the ship and when they arrive home."

Valerie considered his words. "Have you talked to them recently?"

"No," John conceded, "but I intend to go over this weekend and bring them back with me."

Valerie took a deep breath and spoke carefully. "If I'm about to meet your family, I think I need to tell you something." John looked at her quizzically. "I was hoping to be able to say we were married or at least about to be married before I met them but," she paused and then rushed on, "I'm pregnant."

John was stunned. Somehow he hadn't considered this possibility but he recovered quickly and hugged Valerie close as he whispered his love and delight at her news. "We'll go back to the states, too. Sylvia will have to give me divorce now." He grinned happily. "Do you think it's a boy?"

Valerie laughed. "I've no idea if we will have a son or a daughter but I'd like to be married before the baby is born."

"We will be I promise, when will he arrive?"

"Late October or early November."

"Then I'd better get busy. I'll need to fly home and talk to Sylvia in person. But you know she wants a divorce as much as I do."

Valerie laid her head on his shoulder and snuggled into his warmth, happy that he was happy but she couldn't help thinking, I hope that is still true.

John made his travel arrangements to the states and then made a hurried trip to France. He'd promised Valerie not to mention the baby until the divorce was arranged so he kept his happiness to himself as he tried to persuade Minette to return to the states. Lily's health was deteriorating rapidly. The cancer had spread and the doctors felt she had only a few weeks left. Minette reminded him that she had promised her mother that she could be buried in France and she meant to make her mother's last days as pleasant as possible and she meant to keep her promise

Finally Minette told John, "I'll consider returning to the states when Mother is gone, but I can't promise anything. I was born here and France will always be my heart's home."

As John flew from Paris to the states he considered how to approach Sylvia. He wanted to settle this divorce business once and for all. He would give her all the facts and surely she would file and receive a fault-based divorce after all a baby on the way certainly proved adultery.

The City Chronicle
May 1, 1940
Tattletales by Sharon Chatsworth

Happy May Day, dear readers. I hope you all found a lovely basket of flowers, from someone who loves you, hanging on your door knob. I know that one lucky lady was surprised by the appearance of her husband at the front door this morning. John Augustus is home from England for a quick visit with his family.

Chapter 15

Duncan cleared his throat and asked, "May I speak to you, sir?" John looked up from the paper he was skimming; it was amazing how that Chatsworth woman seemed to know things almost before they happened. He was surprised by the look he saw in Duncan's eyes. The butler had never seemed to consider him an important part of the family and now he was asking for a moment of his time.

"Certainly, Duncan, since Mrs. Augustus is out this would be a good time. Please sit down."

Duncan sat, obviously uncomfortable. John waited.

"It's good to have you home, sir." John nodded sure this wasn't the reason for Duncan's request. He watched as Duncan took a deep breath and managed to continue. "I don't mean to interfere or talk about family matters but I am concerned." John waved at him to go on. "Mrs. Augustus is out a good deal." John nodded again. "She seems to be under a strain and is often anxious."

John decided to help the man out. "Do you mean drunk?"

Duncan tilted his head in acknowledgment. "She finds it difficult to deal with Master Michael."

This caught John's full attention. "What do you mean deal with? I thought she left things up to Annie."

"She does and Annie does the best she can to keep Master Michael away from his mother but like any boy he loves his mother and looks for her attention."

"And when Michael does encounter Sylvia.......?"

Duncan took a deep breath and dropped his eyes. "There are bruises, sir."

"Bruises!" John almost shouted. He managed to gain control. "Thank you, Duncan. I'll take care of it. Please ask Annie to bring Michael down as soon as possible."

The butler stood. He nodded to John and left quickly.

Annie arrived with Michael so quickly the John was sure she and Duncan had planned this horrible meeting. Michael walked to him carefully and held out his chubby hand. John swept him up and hugged him tight. "Hi, Michael, I'd rather have a hug than a handshake."

"Me, too", Michael giggled.

"Let's sit here at my desk and you can tell me all about Annie and your Mommy. Have they been being good?"

"Annie's always good," the little boy declared emphatically, "and I'm pretty good some times."

"What about Mommy? Is she good, too?"

Michael looked away. "She's pretty and she smells good."

John smiled surprised that this 3 year old seemed to be trying to protect his Mother. "She is pretty," he agreed. "Why don't you run down to the kitchen and get a cookie while Annie and I talk?" Michael looked at Annie to be sure it was okay and at her nod he ran off happily.

"Okay, Annie, how serious is the problem? I didn't see any bruising."

Annie gulped. "Mostly I don't think Mrs. Augustus means to hurt him. It's just that he is so small and she doesn't like him to touch her." John frowned. "I mean Mrs. Augustus wears beautiful clothes and little boys can be grubby."

"Don't make excuses. I need to know the truth?"

"Well, sir. It only happens when Mrs. Augustus is ill she just holds his wrist too tightly or pushes him away too hard."

"Ill? Do you mean drunk?" Annie nodded. "How often, how many bruises?"

"Not often. Usually Mrs. Augustus is busy but," she hesitated and then finished in a rush, "but too often. I try to keep him quiet and out of sight."

"I'm sure you do a fine job, Annie. Thank you. I'll take care of this."

God Almighty, John thought. Now what do I do. He's not my kid but I love him and he needs to be protected. No child should need to be kept quiet and out of sight in their own house.

"John, Darling!" Sylvia's voice interrupted his pondering. "Where in the world did you come from? If I hadn't read it in the Chatsworth column I'd never have known you were home." She swooped down and tried to plant a kiss on his cheek. John stood to avoid the contact and waved her to a chair.

"Sylvia. You're looking very smart. How are you?"

"Lovely, Darling, and how are you? What brings you home?"

"Valerie is pregnant and I want a divorce."

"Well, welcome home. It's lovely to see you, too." Sylvia managed to stay calm despite the blunt message. "And exactly when did you and the lovely Valerie get together?"

"Not that it matters, but I've loved her a long time and we want to marry."

"Have you forgotten our little problem?"

"Of course not but no court in the land will uphold that ridiculous clause now that you have grounds for a fault-based divorce. You know you want it, too."

"I did, that's true. But not anymore, my life is full and happy and I like being married to an Augustus and having Daddy's money to spend." She smiled serenely. "I don't want to file for a divorce."

"What about your boyfriend? Don't you want to make a life with him?"

"Not that it is any of your business but I have no boyfriend."

"Mark Phillips?"

Sylvia waved her hand, "Mark was just a friend."

"Was? I thought you planned to finance his Broadway venture?"

"You put a stop to that, remember?" John stopped himself from retorting. "And now we are just friends. And I don't want a divorce." She smiled sweetly. "Sorry, darling. I like things the way they are. And, if your little friend is having a baby, that is no concern of mine. But I would appreciate it if you managed to keep it quiet so that my son and I don't have to suffer any embarrassment from your outrageous behavior."

John stared at Sylvia, he couldn't think of anything to say. Of all the responses he'd imagined this was one he'd never considered.

"Cat got your tongue?" Sylvia smiled again. "You can't always get what you want even if you are the great John Augustus. Pour me a drink and tell me about your little playmate."

"I have no intention of telling you anything about Valerie or about my life with her. You and I decided a long time ago that our marriage was a marriage in name only and now I want to put an end to that charade and build a new life."

"Not possible, darling. I am yours and you are mine until death do us part. Our marriage is a permanent bond and since I'm the innocent party and I don't want to file for divorce there will be no divorce."

"Innocent! You don't even know who is the father of your child."

Sylvia froze. Her green eyes hardened and her mouth drew into a tight line. "You, dear John, are the father of my child and in the eyes of the law I am the innocent party." She glared at him and turned to leave the room, her back stiff and very straight. Before John could protest she continued, "And don't you forget it."

"Is that a threat?"

"Call it anything you like, darling. Just don't forget we are married now and forever."

"Wait! We need to talk." John's thoughts raced as he tried to wrap his mind around this new attitude.

"There is nothing to discuss, John."

"Actually there is something else," John took a deep breath and Sylvia cocked her and watched him warily. "We agreed that we would live separate lives and that we would live in ways that did not embarrass the family."

"Well, I have to agree that with a pregnant girlfriend you haven't kept up your end of the deal. Does Walter know yet?"

John flinched. "I intend to tell him in the morning. I'd hoped that I would be able to tell him that we were divorcing but now ...."

"Yes, now it will be a bit more complicated won't it? Perhaps Sam could help you with your story. I'm going up to change and then I'll be out for the rest of the evening." Sylvia started for the door again. "Will you be in town long?"

"Sylvia," John began and then stopped as she waved casually and slipped out into the hall.

As confused as John was by this change in Sylvia he realized that he hadn't even mentioned the staff's concerns about Michael and he had no idea how to do so. He was worried about Michael but found it hard to believe that such a thing could be happening in his own home. As always, when in need of a sounding board, he reached for the phone and arranged dinner with Sam.

After the normal greetings and small talk, John told Sam about Valerie's pregnancy and Sylvia's refusal to even consider divorce.

Sam nodded in sympathy. "I'm not surprised. I'd heard that Mark Phillips has moved on to a very rich widow and that Sylvia is seen about town with a different escort every night. I imagine that even the thought of losing access to her father's millions would cause alarm. Walter mentioned her extensive wardrobe just the other day and if Walter is talking about women's clothing you know everyone has noticed." He smiled sadly. "Not sure what I can say, Cuz. You've got yourself in a pickle this time."

"I do. And now there seems to be more problems in the house. Duncan mentioned that Sylvia is short tempered." He hesitated to tell even his favorite cousin about the hints of abuse. "Not surprising, I know, she is living alone with a young child."

"Alone? She has a full staff and if rumor are correct is seldom home."

"Yes, but I'm sure it isn't easy raising a child. Don't you sometimes find it difficult to cope with children and their demands?"

Sam laughed. "Sure. Sometimes I'd like them all to be calm and quiet but I can't imagine living without them. You just don't understand how much fun it is to have a loving wife and a house full of children."

John smiled ruefully. "I'd like to find out. But I want it to be with Valerie and our children."

"What about Michael? Don't you consider him your child?"

"He's a great kid but," he shook his head, "I want children of my own." He took a deep breath and plunged in, "Have you noticed anything strange?"

"Strange?" Sam looked puzzled.

"Yes, does Michael seem .... okay?'

Sam looked carefully at John, "Are you trying to ask if I've seen any more bruises? Are you worried about his safety?"

"Well, not exactly. But Duncan seems to think there may be a problem."

"We are rarely allowed to see Michael. But if anyone thinks there is a problem there is something."

"He seemed fine to me. No bruises. Happy. Talkative. Unafraid. And he has Annie who obviously loves him."

"And Sylvia?"

John shrugged, "Well, you know Sylvia, it's hard to guess." He considered, "Honestly. I don't know. We can't talk without getting into an argument and now she's completely flipped around and is proclaiming that we are "married forever and ever." He sighed. "I don't know what to do. If I tell Grandfather about Valerie and the baby he'll be very upset so I'd rather wait until I have a solution to this mess." He rubbed his hand over his face. "I need time to figure this out."

Sam stayed silent, as John continued. "I need to go back to London and talk to Valerie. We need to decide together how to handle this."

"What about Michael?"

"I'll talk to Annie and be sure she knows how to reach me but for now I think he'll be fine." Sam frowned and John went on. "I know that sounds selfish but he looks fine and I really don't know what I can do. He'll be fine."

Sam wasn't comfortable but he hoped John was right. "Be sure to let Annie and Duncan know that they can call me anytime for any reason."

John nodded grateful for the seemingly simple solution. "So, I'll see Grandfather tomorrow and then leave as soon as possible for London. I need to find a way to get Sylvia to agree to a divorce. Got any ideas?"

"Not about divorce. I don't have any experience in that arena." Sam kept his opinions about John's focus on his marriage instead of his son to himself. He'd never considered John to be selfish but now he wasn't sure.

Four days later John was back in London. He picked up a bouquet of flowers on the way from

Heathrow to the flat and hugged Valerie close as he gave her the news. "I'm so sorry, darling. I was sure Sylvia would agree to a divorce."

Valerie trembled in his arms and laid her head on his shoulder. Tears gathered in her eyes but she brushed them away and lifted her eyes to search his face. "I love you, John. Somehow this will be alright. Our baby will have a happy life."

John gathered her close and vowed to himself that he'd protect and care for his family, this family, no matter what happened personally or to the world.

On May 8th he received a telegraph from Minette informing him that Lily had passed away in her sleep. He hurried across the channel to support and comfort his mother and to convince her that she must leave France at once. But again, Minette refused his help and urged him to return to England. He considered telling his mother about the new baby but it didn't seem to be the right time and May 10th he returned to London alone only to learn the next morning that Germany had invaded France, entering through the Ardennes forest and via the Low Countries.

The German forces easily bypassed the Maginot Line and quickly conquered the countryside as the marched toward Paris. John tried frantically to reach Minette but all communication ceased and she seemed to have disappeared. He hurried across the channel again and was dismayed to find that everyone who knew his mother and Lily were simply gone.

No one could tell him anything and then one afternoon an old man approached him on the street and spoke quietly as they passed. "Ne cherchez pas, il n'est pas sûr pour votre mère. John stared after the man as he translated the message – "Do not search, it is not safe for your Mother - Chilled by the words, he realized that it was quite likely that Minette had joined the resistance. Fear gripped him and his heart raced. He knew she felt an obligation to help her birth country but it had never occurred to him that she would go this far. He longed to run after the old man and force him to tell him where he could find Minette. He wanted to tell her about the baby and to seek her advice and most of all he wanted to get her out of the war zone to protect her and keep her safe. But he knew that he had to heed the warning and he turned back to his hotel and the next morning he caught the boat train and returned across the channel to London and to Valerie. If he couldn't protect his mother he was more determined than ever to protect Valerie and their unborn child.

The world darkened. Holland surrendered. The Allied troops were evacuated from Dunkirk. Belgium surrendered and then Germany bombed Paris. But within their flat John and Valerie ignored the world and lived together in bliss. They talked of names for the baby, planned the future and ignored the fact that they could not marry. They allowed the landlady and their few friends to believe that they were man and wife.

Then in the middle of June, Sam sent an urgent cable –"Walter very ill. Can you come? Other family needs attention." John held the cable in his hand and stared out his office window. His first thought was that he would need to hurry back to the states but leaving Valerie didn't seem like a possibility. Italy had declared war on Britain and France, Norway had surrendered and the Germans were in Paris. How could he leave the woman he was sworn to protect? If Sam meant that Sylvia needed attention John didn't even want to think about that. He cabled back – "Situation tense. Must delay travel. Keep me informed about all." He knew this wasn't the response Sam expected but it was all he could bring himself to say.

He shook off his concern for Walter, ignored the possibility that Sylvia was causing a problem and didn't mention anything to Valerie. But only a few days later another cable arrived from Sam – "Sylvia hospitalized. Michael safe. Situation dire. Need your attention now."

This time John knew he had no choice and that evening he held Valerie close and told her that Walter was ill and he needed to travel to the states as quickly as possible. Valerie lifted her eyes to him and he saw her unspoken questions but he told himself Valerie understood. And, despite her better judgment, Valerie held her tongue and did not make any demands.

Going directly from the airport to the house he was surprised to find his aunt in charge of his household. And Mary Elizabeth was not happy about the situation. She gave him time to say a quick hello to Michael and then led him to his office where she took the chair behind the desk. This was so unlike her that John said nothing and sat down across from her to hear her explanation.

Instead Mary Elizabeth spoke sternly, "John, what is the matter with you? Your family needed you weeks ago and I know Sam let you know so don't pretend to me that this deterioration is a surprise to you." She stormed on, "Your grandfather is dying, your wife is a drunk and your son is injured and you've done nothing about it. You don't even call home, much less call Walter. Your mother would be so ashamed."

John didn't think he'd ever seen his aunt this angry, not even when he and Sam were young and had caused trouble. He tried to say something in his defense but every thought made him seem weak and selfish. Instead he blurted out, "Michael injured? I just saw him he looks fine."

Mary Elizabeth shook her head, "Of course he does. It's been over 2 weeks since Sylvia pushed him down the stairs and a child heals quickly – on the outside."

"Pushed him down the stairs?"

"Oh I'm sure she didn't intend to do him real harm, but she was drunk and he was in the way. If Annie hadn't been coming up the stairs behind him it would have been much worse, as it is Annie has a broken arm and Michael will never forget this."

John dropped his head into his hands and rubbed his eyes. Without looking at his Grandmother he managed to say, "Tell me what happened."

"I just did. Sylvia was drunk and ready to go out for the evening. She was already angry because Duncan had insisted that she use your driver rather than drive herself, so when Michael ran up the stairs toward her she lashed out and pushed him away. He lost his balance and fell into Annie. She was able to protect him but by doing so she suffered a compound fracture of her arm and cracked ribs. Sylvia stormed out without stopping to check on either of them. Duncan had the good sense to call Sam, who came at once and took Annie to the hospital and Michael to his home. The next day Walter and I confronted Sylvia and insisted that she get treatment." Mary Elizabeth took a deep breath.

"It was not easy. Walter is very ill and he should not have had to deal with this."

"Where is she now?" John asked. "

"We convinced Sylvia to see Dr. Fairchild and she was committed to Glenwood Sanatorium in Trenton for treatment."

"And what does that mean, exactly? How long will she be there?"

"You need to speak to the doctor yourself. All I can tell you is that none of us have seen her since she was hospitalized. It is your responsibility to take care of your family."

"I know. I'm sorry that I wasn't here. I'll call Dennis in the morning and find out what I can do."

"Pretty words, John, but you must take control of this situation. You have neglected your family........." John tried to interrupt but Mary Elizabeth held up her hand and continued. "I know you think you are unhappy with Sylvia but there is a child. I expect you to see your Grandfather tomorrow and discuss this with him. Decisions must be made."

The following morning, John called Dennis Fairchild's office and after explaining who he was and that he would only be in the city for a few days, the receptionist checked with the doctor and he was told that if he could come in at once the doctor would see him between patients. John hurried downtown and was relieved when he only had to wait a few minutes before being escorted into Dennis's office.

"John," Dennis extended his hand, "I'd say it was a pleasure to see you but this is not exactly a social visit and I have only a few minutes. Sit, please." He waved toward a chair and John dropped into it but before he could speak Dennis continued, "I'm not really Sylvia's doctor at this point. When I saw her it was obvious that she was out of control and I called Glenwood and referred her to Dr. Madison. There was an open bed and she was admitted immediately. I can tell you that Walter signed the admission documents but other than that you'll need to contact Dr. Madison."

"How long will she need to be hospitalized?"

"I can't even speculate, John. You need to talk to Dr. Madison and I suggest that you do it in person. Now I need to get back to work." He stood and started toward the door, "I did treat both Annie and Michael. Annie arm will heal but it was a bad break and she may never have full use of it again. Michael was only bruised but he was very frightened and Mary Elizabeth has consulted me because he is having nightmares most nights. See my nurse on the way out and she'll provide contact information for Dr. Madison."

John remained seated for a minute after Dennis's abrupt departure. It certainly seemed that Dennis was angry with him but how could that be, it wasn't his fault Sylvia was a drunk. He wasn't even in the country, for heaven's sake. He shook his head, collected Dr. Madison's contact information and left the office.

After calling Glenwood and getting an appointment to see Sylvia's doctor at the end of the day, John called the office to check that Walter would have time to see him. Instead he was connected to Sam. "Hey, Sam," he said cheerfully. "Where's Walter? I thought I'd come in and meet with him this morning."

"Walter? He's at home of course." Sam said surprised by the question.

"Home, isn't this a work day?"

"John, what is wrong with you?" Sam's irritation was apparent. "Walter is dying. I've been begging you to come home for months. Haven't you been paying any attention to anyone but yourself?"

"Whoa. You know I've been working, working hard."

"Perhaps that's true but you've also been ignoring your responsibilities to your family, your whole family."

"Got it, Sam, you don't need to preach to me. You know I love Walter, I've been busy and you know that I've had to go over to France several times for Mother and Lily. I just didn't realize that Walter was so ill." He could almost see Sam's shrug and was glad that they were on the phone and not face to face. "I'll head over to grandfather's house now and then I have an appointment with Sylvia's doctor at Glenwood but, if you have time, I'd like to talk to you tonight." Sam didn't say anything and John continued, "Could we meet for dinner?"

"No. I want to have dinner with Helen and the kids and you should spend time with Michael."

John didn't like the judgment he heard in Sam's voice but he held back the harsh words that he wanted to say and instead suggested, "How about breakfast then? I can meet you at the diner early and we can talk before going into the office."

"I really don't have time. Why don't you talk to Walter and Dr. Madison today and then come to the office in the morning and we can talk there. I'm sure that the management staff would appreciate an update on the European situation. I'll set up a meeting at 9 AM, if you can be there."

"I'll be there." Only after the phone had gone dead in his hand did John notice that Sam hadn't called him "Cuz" even once and that he'd hung up without his usual cheery farewell. It seemed that Sam was mad at him, too.

So it was no surprise that Walter also seemed less than pleased to see him but John ignored his chilly greeting and inquired about Walter's health. Walter shook his head, "I don't have time for small talk, John. What do you plan to do?" Walter watched John's face and didn't give him a chance to respond. "You need to grow up and take responsibility. I don't want to hear any more excuses from you. Your family must come first."

"I have an appointment with Dr. Madison this afternoon and after I know more I'll be able to make plans," John responded defensively.

Walter nodded sadly. "Family, John. Always remember family. I'm tired now. Come and see me when you have a plan. We will all support you if we can but you need to take control of this and you need to make it right."

"But Grandfather......." John started to protest. Walter shook his head sadly and waved his hand in dismissal.

The high, wide elaborate iron gates of Glenwood stood wide open between solid stone pillars. The rolling green lawns, bright flowers beds, and well-dressed persons strolling about created the illusion that the elegant Georgian house at the top of the long drive was a private home or perhaps a small exclusive resort. John felt himself relax, how bad could things be? Sylvia would love this place. It looked like one of the fine old homes in Charleston She'd feel right at home here. He strolled into the spacious front hall and gave his name to a beautiful young woman seated at a fine, English regency desk. He refused her offer of refreshments and settled himself in a comfortable wing-backed chair, crossing his knee and picking up a magazine.

John flipped through the pages but his thoughts were busy with possible scenarios, there had to be a way to make this come out the way he wanted. It simply wouldn't be fair if he and Valerie couldn't marry. After only a short wait the receptionist escorted him to Dr. Madison's office, where John was relieved to be greeted by a well-dressed man, of about his own age.

"Thank you for seeing me on such short notice," John said as he shook hands. "I've been out of the country and I just learned that Sylvia was ill yesterday."

Dr. Madison considered him carefully and then spoke, "I hardly think that can be true Mr. Augustus." John flinched. "Your wife is an alcoholic. An out of control alcoholic and I'm sure you have known it for some time. She has been admitted here for treatment and while we can help we cannot keep her from drinking in the future. She will need to do that herself."

"What does that mean?" John asked defensively. How was it possible that everyone seemed to think it was his fault?

"It means that she has been committed to this hospital for 30 days during which time we can help your wife dry out, we can even give her medication that will make it impossible for her to drink without suffering terrible consequences but we cannot wave a magic wand and guarantee that Mrs. Augustus will stop drinking. Compared with men, women are more sensitive to alcohol's harmful physical, cerebral, and mental effects and your wife will need to want to stop drinking before any change can take place and if she makes that decision she will need the support of her family. A great deal of support."

John knew he was expected to say something supportive, something loving, but he couldn't lie, not about this. Instead he nodded and asked if he could see Sylvia.

Sylvia glided into the reception area where John waited. Her grooming was impeccable, not a shiny hair escaped her low chignon, and a beautiful green silk dress swirled gracefully around her legs. John rose to greet her, "You're looking well."

"Thank you, darling, nothing like a rest to bring out the best in a girl." Her smile didn't reach her eyes and the hand she placed on John's arm trembled slightly. "Would you like to see the garden?"

Without waiting for his answer she turned toward the French doors and keeping her hand lightly on his arm guided him out and away from the house. When there were out of the hearing range of any visible staff member Sylvia turned and glared up at John. The anger in her eyes flashed so brightly that John started to step back but her grip tightened and he remained close. "You need to get me out of here. Now!" she hissed at him. "This is intolerable and I will not allow your family to treat me like this."

"You've been out of control again, Sylvia. You need help."

"Exactly how would you know that, John? My husband has been gone for months while I put on a performance for everyone in this city pretending to be your loving wife."

"That is your choice, Sylvia. You know I want a divorce. But since you refused we made an agreement that you would not embarrass my family, that you would control your drinking."

"I don't drink any more than any of our friends do. Sam is just a meddlesome know-it-all and he convinced Walter to embarrass me by having me sent here.'

"Have you forgotten that both Michael and Annie were injured?"

"That was just a freak accident. I didn't push anyone. You know I wouldn't do that." Her green eyes filled with tears and she gracefully brushed them away.

"I don't think you would do anything like that on purpose but I have to believe the report that your drinking is out of control. If you want to get out of here you need to promise to take the medication Dr. Madison has prescribed and see a therapist."

"I don't need medication or a therapist. I just need your family to stay out of my life"

"If you're willing to divorce me now I will sign you out of here today and you can live anyway you want. And I'll make sure my family stays out of your business."

"That's not going to happen, John. I won't give up my inheritance just to be free of you and your family."

"As your husband I can sign commitment papers and you will be here for a long time."

This time Sylvia's tears were real. "You can't do that!"

"I can and I will." John turned away.

"Wait!" Sylvia reached for his arm and John shrugged it away. "Give me another chance. I'll be more careful."

"What about the divorce?"

"Sign me out of here and as soon as I'm home I'll contact Mr. Patterson and start the process. Maybe he can figure out a way to allow me access to my inheritance."

"And you're drinking and partying?"

"I'll be careful."

"Careful isn't enough, you need to take the Antabuse." Sylvia reluctantly nodded. "You can't just agree. You really have to stop drinking until the divorce is final and the medication will insure that you don't drink. I don't care if you see the therapist. Walter will be upset by the divorce but he will just have to live with it." John considered the situation for a moment and then said, "Let's walk together and talk awhile. Then we can go back in and I'll explain to Dr. Madison that I believe you will be best treated if you continue your treatment from home."

Sylvia beamed up at him, tucked her arm through his and pulled him close as they resumed strolling through the garden.

An hour later, Sylvia stepped gracefully into John's car and giggled. "Poor Dr. Madison. He was beside himself with rage when you insisted that I be checked out."

"I don't think it was rage. I think he is genuinely worried about you. I'm sure that as long as you take the medication and don't drink you'll be alright but if you have even one drink the side effects sound like they are very unpleasant – even dangerous."

"Don't be such a fussbudget. I'm a big girl. You drop me at home and then go tell your family to mind their own business. You'll see everything will be fine."

John rang the bell at his grandfather's brownstone and squared his shoulders, as if readying himself for a fight. A few moments later he entered the library to find Mary Elizabeth and Sam talking to Walter. He smiled pleasantly, determined to make his decision known and get away a quickly as possible.

"I've checked Sylvia out of Glenwood." All eyes looked at him in surprise and he hurried on. "She really doesn't belong in a locked facility. Dr. Madison prescribed medication that will keep her from drinking and she has agreed to see a therapist."

"And did Dr. Madison agree that she should leave?" Sam questioned.

"Not exactly, but I think I know what is best for my wife and family. I have work to do in Europe and Sylvia needs to be at home with Michael."

"She is not capable of caring for Michael," Mary Elizabeth protested.

"I think you are being rather harsh. But it really doesn't matter she has Annie and the rest of the household staff to help and she has given her promise not to drink. I'm sure it will be fine."

"And do you intend to help, too?" asked Sam.

"Not that it is any of your business but of course I'll help. I'll make sure that Duncan has a way to contact me at all times. Besides, Sylvia will be much happier when we are divorced."

"Divorced!." Walter growled. "Exactly how is that going to happen?"

"Sylvia will contact Mr. Patterson and this time I'm sure he'll figure out a way to break that stupid trust."

Walter shook his head slowly. He removed his glasses and polished them carefully. "I'm disappointed in you, John.

"It doesn't matter, Grandfather. This is my life and I want to be happy."

"Happiness isn't something you can demand from life. Happiness comes to you when you live a life that is good and true and unselfish."

"Perhaps, but I know that Sylvia and I are not happy together and I want a change."

Walter seemed to slump down in his chair and for a moment John was shocked at how old and feeble he looked. But Walter's word stopped his concern, "Go on then. Go back to Europe. Live your life. The family doesn't need you."

Sam stiffened and Mary Elizabeth sighed. Walter continued, "Go now there is no need for you to attend tomorrow's meeting. Sam will handle it." He waved John away and closed his eyes.

Sam grasped John's arm and steered him toward the door. "You'd better leave. I'll talk to him and call you in a few days."

The City Chronicle
June 25, 1940
Tattletales by Sharon Chatsworth

Goodness Gracious! John Augustus flies in and out of town more quickly than the birds fly south. It was rumored that he was here to attend to family matters but to the best of this reporter's knowledge he was only in the city for 2 nights and even the mighty Mr. Augustus can't accomplish much in that short time. Perhaps there is something or maybe someone in England that has need of his attention.

Chapter 16

Sylvia slammed the paper down on the breakfast table causing her coffee to splash across the tablecloth. "Damn!" she swore and then quickly looked around and was relieved to see that no one had overheard her or seen her action. She pushed the sleeves of her watered silk robe up to her elbows and rubbed her temples. Her head hurt, her stomach hurt and her hands shook. She wanted a drink and she felt like she deserved one. That damn Chatsworth woman and her gossip. She rang the bell for more coffee and tried to compose her thoughts.

"Duncan," she said as she watched him clear away the soiled tablecloth, "I think I'll go home today. Please arrange a train ticket for me?"

"Certainly, Mam, to Charleston? Do you have a return date?"

"Yes, to Charleston and no I don't know when I'll return. Just make it one way."

"Of course. Will Master Michael and Annie be traveling with you?"

Sylvia shot him a look that he managed to avoid. "No they will not," Sylvia said emphatically. "I'm going up to my room. Tell Mrs. Peters that I need someone to bring my coffee up and help me pack. And call, Mr. Patterson and get me an appointment. I need to speak to him immediately."

"Right away, Mam." Duncan turned smartly and left the room. He delivered the message and then turned to the phone to make the travel arrangements. He wasn't sure how Mr. Augustus would feel about Sylvia being on her own but he knew that the staff would all enjoy a few days without her.

Arriving in Charleston the following evening, Sylvia breathed in the hot, sweet air and smiled in relief. Everything would be alright now that she was home. Nothing bad could happen here. She looked around the station expecting to see Rufus and then she remembered that he was retired, living on the money her Father had given him the will. She frowned, annoyed that not only was there no one to meet her she wasn't sure what arrangements Duncan had made for the house to be ready for her arrival. A porter appeared at her side and she impatiently accepted his help and told him she would need a cab. "Damn!' she murmured, almost under her breath, but just loud enough for a tall man in an elegant suit to turn toward her and take a good look.

"Silly Alexander, I see that your time in the north has not improved your vocabulary. You better remember where you are and clean up that language before Mattie hears you."

Sylvia whirled around and grinned up at the handsome man, "Beau Campbell. As I live and breathe!" She extended her arms and he pulled her close for a big hug. "I am so glad to see you."

"Ah, a damsel in distress, how may I help you fair maiden?"

"I forgot that Rufus retired and there is no one here to meet me and I have all this luggage." She waved her hand toward the pile of matched luggage that the porter was loading onto a cart. "I could take a cab but...," she allowed her voice to trail off prettily. "You'll do no such thing." Beau responded gallantly, just as she had known he would. Men were so predictable and Southern men even more so since they had all been raised to always help a lady, no matter what. "Just let me find my bag and my driver and I'll not only give you a ride I'll escort you to your door."

Sylvia thanked him and smiled sweetly as she allowed him to take charge of everything. It really was nice to be home, she thought. Everything in the south was easier. Here people knew who she was and they loved her and respected her and here neither the Augustus family or that awful Chatsworth woman would be watching her every move. She tucked her hand under Beau's arm and allowed herself to be led to his limousine.

Sylvia found herself relaxing as they drove toward her Charleston home. She smiled at Beau and asked about his family. Beau shrugged. "I guess the word didn't reach you up north. Cheryl and I have called it quits."

"Oh, no I hadn't heard," Sylvia touched his arm. "Are you okay?"

"Better than okay, we both wanted out. And we are both happier now,"

"Are you actually divorced?" Sylvia found it hard to keep the excitement out of her question.

"Not yet but we will be soon."

"How did you do it?" she demanded.

"Do it? You mean divorce?"

"Yes, divorce, how did you manage? Did Cheryl go to Mexico?"

"Whoa, Silly. What's all this interest in divorce?"

Sylvia caught her breath and twinkled up at him, realizing that she had sounded desperate she changed her approach. "Sorry, darling, I was just surprised that you and Cheryl were splitting." The car pulled to a stop and she smiled warmly at him. "Come on in. I owe you drink for rescuing me and I'd really love to hear what you've been doing since I saw you last."

Fortunately, Mrs. Murphy was still in charge of the house. Sylvia didn't question why she simply swept in with Beau, assumed that her bags would be taken care of and settled into a swing on the veranda. "Sit, darlin," she patted the cushion next to herself. "What would you like to drink?"

Beau smiled ruefully. "Allow me to do the honors, Sil. Name your poison and I'll pour."

For a moment Sylvia wondered if he was making fun of her but she tossed her hair and crossed her legs and smiled up at him, glad that she'd had the forethought to stop taking that dreadful medication, "Gin and tonic would be lovely."

Beau crossed the veranda and entered the drawing room. He noticed Mrs. Murphy in the hall and said, "Hello, Mrs. Murphy. It's a pleasure to be in this house again." She nodded stiffly and turned away. Rebuffed, he mixed two cocktails and returned to the veranda. They clicked their glasses and Beau murmured, "To old friends and good times."

Sylvia purred as she took a deep drink. "Beau, it is so lovely to see you." She smiled warmly and patted the cushion next to herself again. "Come sit with me and we'll catch up. Tell me everything."

This time Beau surrendered to her invitation and settled in. Sylvia sighed deeply. "It's so lovely here. I think I may move back."

"What about John? Surely he doesn't want to leave the city."

"Can you keep a secret?"

"You know I can, Silly." He grinned at her. "Remember high school? If I couldn't keep a secret we'd still be detention."

Sylvia giggled. "Sure enough, if Daddy had known one half the stuff we did he would have had a fit. Stir up another cocktail and we'll trade secrets just like old times."

Sipping her third cocktail in less than an hour Sylvia couldn't contain her curiosity any longer. She laid her hand on Beau's arm and said, "Ready for my secret?" At Beau's nod she continued. "John and I want to divorce," she paused dramatically and continued, "so tell me how you and Cheryl arranged everything."

"Well, Sil, it was actually quite easy. Our attorney, referred us to an attorney in Nevada and Cheryl went out to Las Vegas about a month ago and has rented a house and is establishing residence there. As soon as she has met the Nevada requirement to be a resident for 6 weeks the attorney out there will file the paperwork and we'll be divorced."

"Lord, that sounds perfect."

"But, Silly, don't you have a child with John?"

Sylvia hesitated and then smiled sweetly, "I do but John will give me custody."

"Well, then," Beau clinked his glass against hers, "here's to a happy divorce. Bottoms up, Sil. I need to get home and see my dog. What do you say to allowing me to take you out to dinner tomorrow night?"

"I'd be delighted, Beau. It'll be just like old times."

The next morning Sylvia dressed carefully for her appointment with Mr. Patterson. She chose a conservative dark gray suit and applied only the simplest touch of makeup. Her hands trembled and her stomach clenched. She thought about having a drink, just to calm her nerves. She shook her head and addressed her image in the mirror; "It's only Mr. Patterson, you've known him your whole life and he likes you. Daddy has been gone long enough that he'll realize that that ridiculous will must be overcome." She squared her shoulders and left the room.

The breakfast room was empty and nothing was laid out on the buffet for her breakfast, not even coffee. "Good Lord," she muttered and pushed open the door connecting the breakfast room to the kitchen where she found Mrs. Murphy enjoying a cup of coffee and reading the newspaper.

"Good Morning," Sylvia said icily.

"Good Morning, Sylvia," Mrs. Murphy's tone was civil but held no warmth.

"I'd like some toast and coffee."

"Help yourself," Mrs. Murphy turned a page and didn't look up.

Sylvia froze, unsure of what to do or say, and then Mrs. Murphy came to her rescue. "Mr. Patterson asked me to stay on here until you decide what to do with the house. But I don't work here anymore. I do oversee the cleaning staff and make sure that the house is maintained but there is no cook, no maid, and no chauffer. You'll need to take care of yourself while you are here." She turned a page and seemed to be absorbed in what she was reading.

"How do I get downtown?' Sylvia asked.

"I'd suggest you call a cab or," Mrs. Murphy smiled, "I suppose you could take a bus."

Sylvia was furious, she hadn't expected this. Biting her tongue, she turned away and reached for the coffee pot on the stove. Carefully she poured a cup and said, "But I have an appointment this morning with Mr. Patterson."

"Then I suggest you call now. The number is posted on the board by the phone." She turned another page and sipped her coffee.

Sylvia tapped her foot impatiently as she faced Mr. Patterson across his gleaming oak desk. "Surely Daddy didn't mean for this to happen," she fumed. "It's as if I don't have a home."

"Actually, Mrs. Augustus, you have a lovely home in the city."

"Oh for heaven's sake, you've known me my whole life, call me Sylvia. And I know I have a house in the city but this is my home, it always has been and it always will be."

"I believe that your father felt strongly that your home should and would be with your husband. His will was quite explicit. The house In Charleston was yours to enjoy during your lifetime and then it will pass to your son."

"I can't enjoy it when there is no staff."

"This past year I've tried to reach you both by phone and by mail to inquire what you want to do with the house."

Sylvia started to protest but an image of unopened letters from the law firm appeared in her mind and she quickly put on her most charming smile, "Oh dear, Michael keeps me so busy I don't know which end is up. But I'm here now and I really need to have the house staffed."

"Perhaps Mrs. Murphy could help you. I'm afraid that staffing and running a home is beyond me." He chortled slightly. "My wife takes care of all that."

"I don't think Mrs. Murphy likes me," Sylvia pouted prettily. "She didn't seem happy to see me."

"Well, my dear, she is retired now and is only living at the house because of my request that she do so. I wanted the property protected until I knew your intentions"

Sylvia sat up straighter and crossed her legs at the ankles. "It is my intention to live here, in Charleston, in my house." She glanced down at her folded hands and continued, "As soon as John and I are divorced I'll make Charleston my primary residence, mine and Michael's," she quickly corrected herself.

"Sylvia," Mr. Patterson said sadly, "we've discussed this. The terms of your father's will were very clear. If you divorce John you will receive nothing from your Father's estate until you are 60 years old. Not the $5,000.00 a year you receive now, nor will you be able to draw from the estate for additional expenses the way you do now."

"But the house is mine and I can live in it."

"The house belongs to the estate and while I might be able to allow you to live in the house the estate cannot pay your expenses unless you remain married to John."

"But," Sylvia began.

"There are no buts, Sylvia. Your father's will is not contestable." He considered her carefully and then spoke, "Your father was concerned about your welfare Sylvia. He was aware of your strengths and weaknesses and he had his will written to assure that you would always be protected."

"Protected? Protected from what?"

"From yourself."

Sylvia leaped to her feet, her face flushed with anger. "How dare you speak to me in that tone?"

"I dare because I promised your father that when this meeting took place I would. Your father was one of the brightest and best men in Charleston and he truly loved you. We talked often about your propensity to act without considering the results of your actions." He held up his hand causing Sylvia to sink back into her chair. "His will was created to keep you safe, at least financially safe. He was fully aware that he could not stop your drinking or your appetite for risky behaviors. He was willing to overlook the paternity of your son but he was not willing to allow you to destroy that child's chance at a good live."

Sylvia stared aghast at his words. She was humiliated and anger flushed her cheeks. She stood abruptly and strode to the window. Mr. Patterson waited patiently for her to regain control. She turned and considered her words carefully, "Thank you for your time. I'll need a car while I'm in town, please arrange it." She walked to the door and pulled it open, "Now."

Sylvia checked her reflection in the mirror. The ivory silk hugged her curves and the short skirt accentuated her legs. She smiled at herself, poured another inch of gin in her glass and lifted the phone. Beau answered on the second ring, "Hey," she drawled, "it's me and I want to pick you up tonight for our dinner date."

"I was just on my way out the door, what gives?"

"That darling Mr. Patterson sent over a lovely new Jaguar for me this afternoon and I'm dying to drive it. Sit tight and I'll be at your house in 10."

"Perfect, I like a woman who takes charge. I'll be waiting."

The City Chronicle
June 30, 1940
Tattletales by Sharon Chatsworth

It is with regret that this writer gives you the sad news that the lovely Mrs. John (Sylvia) Augustus suffered injuries in an automobile accident on Friday evening while driving in her home town, Charlestown, South Carolina. Her companion in the new Jaguar, Beau Campbell of Charleston died in the accident.

Chapter 17

Sylvia moaned and opened her eyes. But the bright glare caused her to close them again and moan more deeply. "Time to wake up, sweetie." A voice she didn't recognize said and someone patted her leg. "Come on, princess. I know you're awake."
Sylvia risked a quick look. She saw white, white everywhere. She moved her head and pain pierced her temple. She moaned and forced herself to look around slowly. She was in bed and a woman, a nurse, sat next to her patting her leg. She tried to focus but the nurse blurred and became two nurses. She closed her eyes again.
"Take your time," the voice said, "you've had an accident. You'll be fine just a few bruises and a concussion."
"Hospital?"
"Yes. You're in Roper Hospital."
"Happened?"

"I'm not sure, Mrs. Augustus. I'm going to let the doctor know you are awake." The voice patted her leg again. "I'll be right back."

Sylvia opened her eyes again and looked around. She focused on the man in the corner. "Sam! What are you doing here?"

"Mr. Patterson called and Walter asked me to come down." Sam stood and walked to the bed. 'Do you remember what happened?"

Sylvia started to shake her head but a blinding pain stopped her movement. She closed her eyes and whispered, "I don't think so."

"It's important, Sylvia. What do you remember?"

"Mrs. Murphy was rude to me," she pouted, "then Mr. Patterson said horrible things but," she brightened, "he had them deliver a new Jaguar to my home."

"After your appointment with your attorney, where did you go and what did you do?"

"I was quite upset. He really was horrid. And since I was on King Street I thought I'd do a little shopping to relax."

"Did you have a cocktail?"

"Goodness, Sam. What is this about? It wasn't even noon when I left Mr. Patterson's office."

"But did you have anything to drink?'

"Who says I did? Mrs. Murphy? I knew she was watching me."

"Stop it, Sylvia. I need to know what you had to eat and drink."

Sylvia wrinkled her forehead in concentration. "I stopped in at the Francis Marion Hotel to watch the luncheon fashion show and I was still quite upset so I had a glass of wine."

"Did you order anything to eat?"

"Sam!" She glared at him. "No, I did not eat. I wasn't really hungry and I knew I'd be eating a big dinner."

"Alright, how long did you stay at the Francis Marion?"

"I have no idea."

"Mrs. Murphy told Walter that you returned to the house shortly before 5 PM."

"And I supposed she reported that I'd been drinking."

"Had you?"

"Only a couple of glasses of wine at lunch," she shrugged and lifted her eyes flirtatiously. "I had a dinner engagement with one of my oldest friends and I needed to rest and then dress for that engagement so I may have been a bit short with her but I certainly wasn't drunk just irritated."

"And when the car was delivered, what happened then?"

"Happened? I was dressing, Murphy knocked and when I invited her in she told me. I was delighted and called Beau to tell him I'd pick him up for our date.'

Sam noted that the dinner engagement was now a date. He didn't comment but asked, "And, what did you have to drink while you rested and dressed?"

"I was delighted to see the Jaguar and I may have had a gin and tonic to celebrate while I dressed for dinner. Is that a crime?"

Again Sam didn't answer. "You drove to the MacDonald house about 7:30 PM and picked up Beau. Did he serve you a cocktail?"

"No, he was waiting on the front porch. He admired the car and we decided that since it was such a beautiful evening and such a beautiful car we'd drive over to Mt. Pleasant for shrimp."

"Did Beau offer to drive?"

"Hmmm, I think he did but it is my new car and I love to drive so I said no."

"And then what happened?'

"We ate shrimp?" Sam shook his head no. Sylvia looked puzzled. "We didn't eat shrimp? Why not?"

"Sylvia, witnesses say you were driving very badly on Highway 16, going too fast, wobbling across lanes, and passing without enough clearance and that when you approached the bridge you didn't stop to pay the toll but instead you seemed to speed up."

"Well, that bridge is fun to drive and we were having such a good time. Most people speed a bit."

"Most people stop and pay the toll."

Sylvia lowered her eyes and then looked up at him, "Am I in trouble, Sam? I'm sorry about the toll and the speeding. We were just having fun."

"The way I understand it is that you had at least four or five glasses of wine and two or three gin and tonics before you drove to the MacDonald house."

Sylvia started to nod and the pain stopped her, "Perhaps," she said. "But what does it matter? I don't get drunk."

"You do get drunk. And it matters because this time the police are involved."

"Police? Why in the world would they care what I drink? It's not as if I killed anyone."

"Actually Sylvia, that's exactly what you did. Don't you remember the accident at all."

Sylvia stared at him and slowly Sam saw understanding darken her eyes. "I remember the lights they were coming straight at me. The driver must have been on the wrong side of the highway."

"No Sylvia," Sam said carefully. "You were on the wrong side. The car you hit was driven by the pastor of the Mt Pleasant Baptist church. He was driving five young people to a chorale performance in Charleston."

Sylvia didn't move but her eyes became frantic and her fingers clutched at the hem of the sheet. Sam continued, "The children are all dead and the pastor is badly hurt." Sylvia didn't make a sound. "Your car spun out of control and Beau was thrown clear."

"Is he alright?" she whispered.

"He's dead." Sam said bluntly. "You were driving drunk. You killed six people and one more life is hanging on the edge."

Sylvia twisted the sheet and slowly shook her head, "No, Sam," she moaned, "that can't be true."

Sam glared at her with contempt. "It's true," he said bluntly.

Sylvia closed her eyes and hugged herself tight. "Daddy will kill me, Sam. Please don't tell him. I didn't mean to hurt anyone. We were just having fun."

"Sylvia?" Sam questioned. She kept her eyes shut and began to hum softly to herself. Sam pushed the call button for a nurse.

John woke to strident ringing of the phone. Valerie sat up clenching the blanket around her shoulders. A call in the middle of the night was never good news. The overseas operator made the connection and John flinched when he heard Sam's voice.

"What's wrong, Sam? Is it Walter?"

"No, it's Sylvia. There's been an accident." Sam took a deep breath. "She was driving drunk."

"Christ!" John swore. "Is Michael all right?"

"Michael wasn't in the car. She was in Charleston. John, she killed six people."

"She what?" John dropped into the desk chair and clutched the phone.

Quickly Sam explained the circumstances surrounding the crash and then waited for John to say something. When there was nothing from John he continued, "Sylvia is fine, just a slight concussion but she doesn't remember anything about the accident and...." he paused again. Still John remained quiet so he continued, "and she's had what the doctors are calling a nervous breakdown. They feel she needs to be placed in a sanitarium. They need your permission."

"Damn, that woman! You're my attorney Sam. Just take care of it. I hope they lock her up and throw away the key."

"She may be in the hospital for months, John. What about Michael?"

"Annie will take care of him. I need to think about this. Do what needs to be done and I'll call you a few days."

Sam hung up and turned to Helen, "He's a selfish bastard," he said.

"He's just angry and confused," Helen said gently. "He's a good man caught in a terrible situation, he'll come around."

"A situation of his own making," Sam muttered to himself as he reached for the phone to begin the commitment process.

The City Chronicle
July 4, 1940
Tattletales by Sharon Chatsworth

Even as we celebrated our independence from
England with parades and fireworks, picnics and
family fun, the British Prime Minister Winston
Churchill delivered a speech before the House of
Commons designed to suggest that the United
States is sitting on the sidelines while Britain stands
alone to defend freedom against totalitarianism.
This reporter says shame on you Mr. Churchill.
This is not America's fight and we will not let you
dictate to our President or to us.

Chapter 18

Duncan put down the paper and sipped his cup of
coffee. "Goodness," he said to Mrs. Peters, "did
you read the Chatsworth column? She's downright
political this morning."

She nodded, "I did. When even the gossip column
is talking about a war do you think it is good idea
for Annie to be taking Michael to England?"

""I do think that Michael needs his father and I
think that Sam has made the correct decision."

"But what if Mrs. Augustus comes home from the
hospital and he's gone."

"I don't think that will be a problem. Sam has
made the travel arrangements and I think he knows
what is best for Sylvia and Michael."

Mrs. Peters nodded, "I'm sure you're right. A boy
needs his father. I'd better make sure they are ready.

Annie has never flown in an airplane before and she is rather concerned."

Sam turned away from the window as the plane lifted off and squared his shoulders. He hoped he hadn't made a mistake. Surely John would welcome the child into his home despite his careless, uncaring attitude toward Sylvia. Michael really wouldn't be a problem. He was a good kid and Annie was wonderful with him. He'd call John as soon as he got home and let him know they were on the way. The flight from New York to Gander to Shannon and finally to London would take long enough to allow him time to get used to the idea.

Helen stared aghast at Sam. "You did what?" she exclaimed. "John is living with a woman! A pregnant woman!

"She's not just any pregnant woman. He really wants to marry Valerie, it's just that he couldn't and now that Sylvia is in the sanitarium he can't."

"But, Sam, what will your grandfather think? Did you tell them you'd arranged the trip."

"Of course, Helen, in fact it was Mary Elizabeth who suggested that Michael should live with John."

"But, does she know about Valerie?"

"Perhaps, she didn't mention her. She simply said that she believed that Michael should be sent to London to be with his father and that Annie should go along so he'd have someone familiar in his life, and I agreed, and that's exactly what we did. And now I need to call, John."

John slammed the phone down and swore aloud. What the hell was he supposed to do with a kid? Valerie looked up from the book she was reading and seeing the expression on his face she closed the book and asked, "What's wrong, darling?"

"My damn family again, Sam thinks he know what's best for everyone and Grandfather seems to agree with him but this time they've gone too far." Valerie gazed at him calmly waiting for the explanation. "Sam has sent Michael and Annie to London to live with me."

Valerie smiled slightly, "And is that so terrible? Since no one knows how long Sylvia will be hospitalized this might be a very sensible solution,"

"Solution? Solution to what?

"A solution for Michael, he needs a parent and you're the only one available."

"But he's not ...." John started.

Valerie interrupted, "What's wrong with you, John? Of course, your son is welcome to live with us. We have plenty of room and while it may be a bit awkward to explain to Annie the rest of our friends think you are divorced and we are married. It's "normal" for a child to live with his "other" parent when the custodial parent is ill. I'm going to see what I can do to make our guest room more welcoming for a child. I think we should try to find a few toys in the shops, I don't imagine they were able to bring many with them. And perhaps some books, does he like books?"

Michael wasn't fazed by his new home or the move to a different continent. He was delighted to see John and chatted happily about the plane ride and novelty of the food trays. He eyed Valerie carefully but didn't seem afraid just wary. The first night he settled down in his new bed without a protest and fell asleep quickly clutching a stuffed rabbit that he explained to Valerie, "had no name because it was a toy". Valerie seemed entirely captivated and John had to admit that it had been fun to talk to Michael. Annie, however, was a different matter. She had noted Valerie's expanding waist line and turned away without comment.

Over the next couple of days Annie avoided talking or making eye contact with anyone but Michael. John didn't seem to notice but Valerie could feel the tension. As always determined to approach things head on she went to the kitchen as Annie prepared breakfast. "Annie," she spoke quietly "we need to talk. I'd like to join you and Michael at the park this morning."

Unsure of what else to do, Annie ducked her head and nodded mutely at Valerie.

They walked together to the park, Michael holding Annie's hand, and as soon as Michael was settled Valerie spoke carefully, "I know this is extremely uncomfortable for you Annie. I'm sure you've noticed that I'm pregnant and I know that you know that John and I cannot possibly be married." She paused and took a deep breath. "We love each other, Annie, and we would be married if we could." Annie wasn't sure how to respond. But Valerie continued, "I'm glad that you brought Michael to his father. Even though many children are being evacuated from London I think Michael needs his father and he certainly needs you. I know it can't be easy for you but we'd really like you to stay. From watching you with Michael these last 3 days I know that you are a wonderful nanny. Please say you will stay."

Annie wondered if she really had a choice but Valerie seemed so sincere and even so honest. She nodded slowly. "I'll continue to take care of Michael, Mam."

"Thank you, Annie. And please, you don't need to call me Mam, just Valerie will do. Michael is a lovely child and it will be a pleasure having you in our home."

And then on July 10th one hundred and twenty German bombers and fighters struck a British shipping convoy in the English Channel, while seventy more bombers attacked dockyard installations in South Wales. The Battle of Britain had begun. Within days it became "normal" to hear the sirens and hurry to the nearest shelter.

But it wasn't normal and John fought to control his worry as he tried to find a way to send Valerie and Michael back to the states. Valerie refused each idea and declared that she had no intention of leaving England or John and instead she stocked the Anderson Shelter the landlady had had built in the garden and encouraged Annie to keep a basket of toys and food ready to grab at a moment's notice. Michael didn't like the loud sirens but seemed to have no fear when he was grabbed and rushed toward the shelter. Valerie marveled at the resilience of children and determined not to panic or to fear for her unborn child.

With such conflicting emotions in play the days and nights flew past. July faded into August and August into September. Valerie's pregnancy progressed in a normal manner and she and John delighted in the thought of their child being born. Annie relaxed in the face of their obvious love for each other and forgot that John was stilled married to Sylvia. John couldn't forget but he did manage to ignore Sylvia's hospitalization. Communication with the United States was often difficult or delayed so when he spoke to Sam he was usually able to keep the conversation on business. John never asked but Sam managed to slip in a comment here and there so John knew that Sylvia had not improved and that Walter was aging. More than Walter or Sylvia John worried about Minette, it had been months since he'd seen her and they'd had no communication at all. In his heart, John began to believe that she was dead.

October 15th dawned clear and bright and when the first sirens sounded at 8:15 AM Valerie and Annie looked at each other and shrugged. John was gone, having left the flat at 7 for an early meeting and would already be in his office and would take shelter there. Valerie gathered the breakfast that was prepared but not served and Annie gathered up Michael, his toys and books and a bit of knitting. After thirty-seven consecutive days of bombing they knew exactly what to do and the move to the Anderson was accomplished as they heard the first bombs explode.

After breakfast Annie settled Michael down with a puzzle and picked up her knitting. Valerie tried to read but found it difficult to settle her back hurt and she couldn't seem to get comfortable. By 10 AM she was up pacing back and forth in the small space. The ache in her back increased and as she walked she pressed her hands into the small of her back.

"Are you alright?" Annie asked. Valerie nodded and continued to pace. Annie looked worried. "Just give me a moment to light the camp stove and I'll make you a cup of tea."

Valerie gasped and bent forward folding her arms around her stomach. Annie clasped Valerie's upper arms and held her firmly. "Is the baby coming?" she asked.

"I don't know," Valerie took a deep breath as the pain receded. ""The pain is in my back."

"That's how it starts sometimes, "Annie said solemnly. "The all clear will blow soon and we can get out of here."

Valerie managed a smile and began to pace again. Annie busied herself with tea for Valerie and toast with marmalade for Michael. But the all clear didn't blow. Michael grew restless and then fell asleep on his cot as Annie told stories and sang folk songs. Valerie had grown too tired to pace and lay on her cot, her pain betrayed only by her ragged breathing. Annie sat down beside her and pressed her hands firmly against Valerie's lower back. She rubbed in a slow firm circular motion and gradually Valerie relaxed and even seemed to doze a bit between waves of pain. And finally at 4:15 PM the all clear sounded. Michael awoke and grinned broadly at Annie, "Let's get out of here," he shouted.

"Yes, let's," Valerie managed a small laugh at his excitement. Annie helped her to her feet and they stumbled together across the garden, Michael jumping and bouncing like a puppy in front. "Annie, I think I need the midwife. Would you call for me, please?"

Annie settled Valerie in a chair with a blanket and reached for the phone but the line was dead. "I'll just run out and find her," Annie assured Valerie. Valerie nodded. Annie saw the tears she was fighting and reached out and drew Valerie close in a warm hug. "It'll be alright. I'll just be a minute." She picked up Michael and hurried through the door.

Only a half hour later Annie returned without the midwife but with John, who hurried to Valerie and knelt in front of her chair. He picked up her hands and kissed her fingers. "Oh darling," he said "what can I do. Is the baby coming?"

"I think something is wrong. Where is the midwife?"

"She'll be here as soon as she can, darling. What can I do?"

"Rub her back, sir. Like this." Annie stepped forward and began to press on Valerie's lower back. "I think she's having back labor. It happened to my sister Jane. The labor was long but the baby was fine." She guided John's hand into place and he began to press and circle. "She should walk a bit if she can. It will help. I'm going to make Michael his tea now but I'll just be in the kitchen if you need me."

Annie was able to prepare Michael's tea, get him to eat, bathe him and dress him in his pajamas before the bombing began again. She kept an eye on Valerie and knew that the pain in her back was becoming more intense. As the warning sirens began to blare she asked, "Should I try to find the midwife again."

Even as she asked, Valerie moaned and clutched at her stomach. Annie moved to her and laid her hands gently on the baby bump. She could feel the muscles contract and smiled at Valerie. "That's good, the real labor has begun. Your back will be better and the baby will come soon."

John grasped Valerie's hand, "Should we go to the hospital?"

The pain receded and Valerie was able to speak. "No, John. It will be hours yet and the midwife will come soon. Annie, you take Michael to the shelter.

John and I will stay here and wait." John started to protest but Valerie took his hand and said, "We have to wait for the midwife. She'll be here soon and then we can all go to the shelter."

Bombs exploded every few minutes as the Germans pounded London. Valerie paced the floor as her pain intensified and the waves came closer together. Nearby explosions caused the house to shake and plaster to fall but Valerie held John's hand tightly and concentrated on the baby.

About 1 AM, the midwife finally arrived. John suggested they move to the shelter. The midwife performed a quick exam and informed them that the labor was too far progressed to go anywhere. She ordered John to the kitchen and after a quick survey of the flat decided that the cot Michael had been using for a bed would make the best delivery bed.

The calm, firm manner of the midwife helped Valerie to relax and shortly after 2 AM she delivered a healthy baby girl. The midwife cleaned the baby and placed her in Valerie's arms. John was summoned and they beamed at each other and at the baby. "Hello, Elizabeth." Valerie said softly and stroked the tiny head with one finger.

"She's beautiful and strong," the midwife said, "but she also needs to be safe. Father you take the baby to the shelter and your wife and I will finish here and then, if the all clear hasn't sounded we'll move your wife to the shelter."

"But," John started.

Valerie interrupted, "No, John. The plaster dust in here isn't good for her lungs. Let me give her a kiss and after she's settled with Annie come back and help me to the shelter."

John cradled the baby carefully as he stooped to place a kiss on Valerie's forehead. "Alright, darling, I'll be right back."

He crossed the garden and opened the shelter. Annie hurried over to take a peek. John pulled the shelter door shut behind himself and a huge explosion tore the air. The shelter was hit by what sounded like giant rocks. Annie grabbed the baby and John frantically pushed at the door but it wouldn't open. The shelter rocked with another explosion and more debris banged down on the roof. Michael awoke and burst into loud sobs. Annie's arms were full with the baby but she managed to pull Michael close to her side and showed him the baby. He was instantly distracted from his fear and reached out to stroke Elizabeth's tiny cheek. "Is it mine?" he asked.
Another horrible explosion shook the shelter and John slammed against the door with his full body. It gave way, opening just enough that he could see the horrible scene in front of him. The house was gone and a fire burned in its place. John screamed, "Valerie!" and pushing the door with his full body he escaped the shelter and ran. Annie stared after him, unable to believe her eyes.
Fire fighters appeared and pulled John away from the wreckage. A burly warden held John back, 'There's nothing you can do mate. The place is a totally loss." John sank to the grass and sobbed. "His wife's in there." The warden explained to the others and they averted their eyes from his grief and concentrated on keeping the fire from spreading.
Annie and Michael crept out of the shelter and stood in shock unsure what to do but afraid to stay in the shelter. Bombs continued to rain down on the

city but they seemed unimportant against the devastation in front of them. The fire warden noticed them and came over to help. "Boy or girl?" he asked noting the bundle in Annie's arms.

"Don't know," she replied. "Babe was just born to the Mum in the house."

"Lord," the warden muttered and crossed himself. "Bloody Huns."

"Annie," Michael pulled at her skirt, "it's a girl named Elizabeth."

"How do you know that?"

"Because Valerie told me and she said it was mine so can I hold it?"

Annie's mouth dropped open. "When did she tell you that Michael?"

"Just now, before she went away."

The City Chronicle
October 16, 1940
Tattletales by Sharon Chatsworth

The Blitz in London has struck close to home. Last night, the German Luftwaffe continued their heavy bombing of London's Battersea area. For those of you who don't know this is the neighborhood where John Augustus of our fair city is currently residing. This reporter is pleased to assure you that both Mr. Augustus and his young son, Michael who is currently visiting his father, are alive and well, however, their home suffered a direct hit and was completely destroyed.

Chapter 19

Mary Elizabeth looked up from the paper and studied her brother. He looked weary and sad. She hated to see him age so quickly but was grateful for each day they could spend together. The doctor had told them that it might not be long now but Mary Elizabeth tried to ignore his dire predictions and clung instead to the memories of the good years. But this situation with John was impossible. Something needed to be done to reconcile him with his grandfather before it was too late. She sipped her coffee and asked, "Have you spoken to John this week?"

"I leave that for Sam," Walter said gruffly. "He handles that whole mess." He angrily refolded the paper to a new page and continued reading.

Mary Elizabeth sighed softly but didn't voice her concern as she continued to drink her coffee. Instead she forced herself to think of the day's tasks and vowed to find time to talk to Sam.

Across town, Helen poured Sam another cup of coffee and handed him the paper turned back to reveal the Chatsworth column. "You'd best read this."
Sam scanned the brief paragraph, "Good God" he exclaimed shoving back his chair. "It doesn't mention Annie or Valerie. I'd better place a call right now."
In London there was no longer a house with a phone and no one answered the office phone. The operator tried several times and then suggested, politely that Sam try the call at a later time.

In the London office, John stared at the ringing telephone but he didn't answer in fact he didn't hear it. A thick fog had slowed the bombing raids for the moment but he was unaware of anything but his grief. He had no idea where Annie and the children were and, in fact, he had no thoughts of them. Earlier today he'd identified Valerie's body and arranged for her burial in St. Mary's Cemetery. The beautiful Georgian church on the banks of the River Thames had been a favorite place for Val. She loved to walk in the churchyard and was especially fascinated by the fact that Benedict Arnold was buried there. The priest had actually been relieved to hear that there would be no service just a burial and had agreed to do the internment in the morning. John buried his head in his hands and allowed the images of Valerie and their time together to flood his soul.

Annie huddled in the subway with the two children. The bombing seemed to have slowed but the all clear hadn't yet sounded. Michael stayed close to her side, watching the baby closely and reaching out frequently to stroke her tiny cheek. Annie had spent all of her cash today finding bottles and formula and diapers for the baby. Mr. Augustus had disappeared and she had no idea what to do or where to go. The baby began to cry again and Annie lifted her to her shoulder and patted her gently. A huge burp caused Michael to giggle and the woman huddled next to them in the subway turned to Annie and grinned.

"She's a bonny, wee baby," the woman said, reaching out a finger to stroke the tiny head, "with a lovely big brother."

Annie burst into tears.

"There, there child," the stranger patted Annie.

"The house was bombed and everything is gone," Annie gulped.

"You've your life and your children, love. That's really all that matters."

"But ...." Annie started.

"No buts. Chin up and keep going. Mr. Churchill says it's the best thing we can do to help our boys win this war." She took the baby from Annie and cradled her expertly. "Where's your family?"

"Glamorgan, Mam."

"Gla what?

"Glamorgan, Wales."

"Ah, I thought you talked a bit funny. Wales is where they are sending the children. It's said to be safe there." She handed the calm baby back to Annie and gathered up her bags. "I'm off now. Bye, Baby."

"Her name is Elizabeth," Michael said solemnly. "I'm Michael and she's mine."

"Right," the woman grinned down at him. "I stand corrected. Good bye Elizabeth and Michael and good luck, love. Remember chin up."

Annie gulped back her tears and almost managed a smile. She looked at Michael's solemn face and for a moment she resolved to manage until they could find Mr. Augustus. Then she leaned back against the wall and allowed her fears to engulf her. Michael snuggled in next to her and she wrapped one arm around him and cradled the baby in her other as they drifted off to sleep.

It seemed only a moment before a warm hand shook her shoulder and a deep voice asked, "Mam are you alright?" She opened her eyes slowly and found an elderly gentleman watching her carefully. "You cried out and I thought you might be in pain," he explained.

Annie slowly shook her head, she glanced at the sleeping children and then back at the stranger. "Mr. Augustus disappeared in the Blitz and I need to get the children home to Wales," she blurted out. "I used all the money I had today and now I don't know what to do."

"Well, Mrs. Augustus," he started and she interrupted.

"Annie,"

"Well, Annie," he began again, "I believe I can help you if you'll allow it." Annie stared at him solemnly, unsure what to say. "I work with the LCC, the London County Council, and it's our task to evacuate the children and mothers. Do you have family in Wales?"

"Yes, Sir. My Ma and Da live on a farm outside Glamorgan. It's my home,"

"In that case, it's very simple. If you can get yourself and the children to the train station, we'll see that you have passage to Wales. Can you do that?"

Annie nodded, staring at this stranger, but happy to allow someone else to make decisions. "All right, then. Buck up." He pulled a watch from his pocket and checked the time. "There is a train in two hours. You head for the station and I'll make the arrangements and meet you there."

"But the children," Annie started to protest.

"No, no you don't need to thank me. You and the children will be safer with your mother and father. Mr. Augustus would want you to safe wouldn't he?"

Annie had to agree that that was true and she nodded.

"Right, then. Up you go," he extended his hand and helped her to her feet. He bent and lifted Michael easily, "I'll carry the boy and your bag and you take care of the baby." He led the way out of the shelter and into the foggy, smoke filled street. Michael stirred and woke.

"Who are you?" he demanded.

"My name's Mr. Robbins, mate. Are you ready to walk on your own now?"

"Yes, please." Mr. Robbins set him down.

"Just go on that way," he gestured to the left, "and you'll find the station. If you have trouble ask anyone. They'll know the way. I'm off to arrange the tickets. I'll find you under the clock." He waved and hurried off.

Annie stood still and watched him walk away. She was unsure of what to do next but this Mr. Robbins seemed sure and Annie had no idea of how to proceed on her own. Perhaps he really would get them to Ma's and then her Ma would know exactly what to do, she always did.

She swung the bag of supplies over her shoulder and settled Elizabeth on her arm. Confidently Michael took her hand and they started down the street to the left. "Where are we going now, Annie?" Michael asked.

"We are going to go for a train ride and then to a lovely farm with lots of animals. Do you think you can help me find the train station?'

It sounded like a grand adventure to Michael and since Annie was the one person who'd never failed him he trotted along at her side pointing out a shoe, a teapot and then a ladies hat in the rubble. "It's rather messy in this place," he told Annie. "Mama wouldn't like this but Valerie says everything will be fine."

Annie looked at him sharply and almost told him that Valerie wasn't there but then she decided not to cause a problem but just to get home with the children and then figure things out.

Mr. Robbins was as good as his word and only minutes after they found the clock in the station he appeared wearing a big smile. "It's all set, Mam. I've your tickets straight through to Glamorgan. The train will be quite crowded but I'm sure you'll manage. Do you have enough supplies for the babes?"

Tears flooded Annie's eyes at his kindness, "I've enough for the baby," she stammered but I don't have any money to buy food for Michael."

"There, there, don't fret. The kind ladies of the villages meet the train at every stop and they'll have refreshments and expect no money. It's the least they feel they can do to help people like yourselves who have been bombed out. The train is loading. Come along and I'll get you started and if you give me your father's name I'll send a message to let them know you should be there with the children sometime tomorrow."

Mr. Robbins was as good as his word. He'd actually found a seat for Annie in one of the crowded compartments and room for Michael to sit at her feet. Children by the dozens were crowded together standing in the corridors when they couldn't find a place in a compartment. A few children were accompanied by mothers or older women but the majority of them seemed to be alone. Annie had heard that children were being evacuated from London but she hadn't realized how many or what that evacuation meant.

As the car swayed along Michael played quietly with the other children and then fell asleep against her leg. Elizabeth woke and Annie managed to change her wet diaper on her lap. She had no way to warm the bottle of formula but the baby drank a bit and then dropped off to sleep. Annie gazed at her tiny face, she'd never held a child so young and wasn't really sure if she was doing what she should. As the thought crossed her mind she seemed to feel a warm hand touch hers and the tension eased. Annie smiled at her silliness. Michael stirred and murmured in his sleep. Perhaps, she thought, someone is watching over us.

As night began to darken the sky the porter came through pulling the blinds down and reminding everyone "to keep the blinds down and follow the blackout rules". A dim blue light shining in the corridor caused everyone and everything to look strange. The train stopped often but Michael slept soundly and Annie watched over the children and thought about home.

Annie searched the station platform holding tight to her bag, to Michael and to the baby. She couldn't see her Da anywhere but then a familiar voice shouted her named and she whirled around to see her Granddad. "Annie, me love. What are you doing here?"

"Didn't you get a wire from Mr. Robins?"

"We did girl. Said Mrs. Augustus and children would be on this train and I've come down to meet them."

Annie burst into tears. Michael stared up at her his lip beginning to tremble; even Elizabeth stirred and began to whimper.

"Now, girl. Nothing is that bad. Is Mrs. Augustus with you?" Annie shook her head. "Well, then come along and we'll let your Ma sort this out. Is this all you have?" he asked as he took the bag of diapers and formula from her hand. "So, young man, are you ready for a ride in a pony cart?"

Michael gazed up at this grizzled man, he seemed very nice and Annie knew him so Michael decided to trust him. "Is that like a hansom cab, sir?"

"Don't know about that, but we've gas rationing here and a pony and cart it is. Right this way."

The ride out to the farm delighted Michael. The welsh pony whose name was Arian, which the old man explained meant silver because his coat was so shiny and gray, trotted along smartly tossing his head so that the bells on his harness rang out. Michael snuggled close to Annie, keeping one hand on Elizabeth and watching the fields full of cattle and sheep roll past. Annie smiled at him.

The City Chronicle
January 1, 1941
Tattletales by Sharon Chatsworth

Happy New Year one and all, the party of the season took place last night at the Cartwright Mansion on West 5th. The cities most elite and glamorous sparkled in their holiday finery. The food was sublime and the decorations were delightful but your reporter must tell you that without the charming Sylvia Augustus a certain element of fun was missing and the evening fell a bit flat.

Chapter 20

"Good Grief," Helen muttered and shook her head.

"What is it?" Sam asked.

"Nothing, really, it's just that Chatsworth woman commenting on Sylvia's absence from the social scene."

"Better that, I suppose than speculating on John's behavior. I did expect we'd hear from him at Christmas."

"He's grieving, Sam. I'm sure he spent Christmas with Michael and his memories."

"True," Sam nodded. "I agreed he needed time off when Valerie was killed but it's been more than two months and we need for him to get back to work. I had expected that he would send Michael and Annie back to the states by now."

"Perhaps he needs his son."

Sam doubted that John had changed that much but he supposed it was possible. "He hasn't answered any messages since Christmas."

Helen shook her head and smiled gently, "Not everyone works every day. They may have gone somewhere for the holiday."

"I suppose but London is being bombed and you'd think he'd send his son to safety. I'll call again tomorrow."

Sam woke early and placed the call to John's office in London. This time there was no wait the operator returned immediately with the information that the number was no longer in service and asked if he's like to try another number. There was no other business number to try and with the house gone Sam needed to think of another way to reach John. From his office he placed calls to suppliers and customers in London but all he learned was that John had closed the London office and placed the staff on leave and now that it was January they needed the office open and working. Sam decided he had no choice but to tell Walter what was happening. The war was escalating every day and the Augustus Empire needed the London office up and running in order to fulfill their contracts.

Walter listened carefully and shook his head sadly, "Grief. It's a terrible thing. John has gone off the rails and we need to find him but we also must maintain the company's good name. Who can we sent to London that will handle this discretely? No one but the family knows that Valerie and the baby are dead and I'd like to keep it that way. My understanding is that she had no family of her own so that should make it easier."

Sam considered carefully, "I think it has to be me. How else can we keep the gossip to a minimum?"

Walter nodded slowly, "Yes, I think you're right go quickly. Get the office up and running and come back. I need you here."

"What about John and Michael?"

"He's an adult and if he doesn't want to be found that's his business. See what you can find out but don't waste a lot of time, wrap it up in only a few days. How about promoting Stephen Alistair to manage the London office, he's impressed me and he has no family so an assignment in London shouldn't disrupt his life."

Helen worried about his safety but Sam and Stephen headed for London the next day where they discovered that the devastation of the city was much greater than either man had imagined from the news reports. Stephen agreed to stay and while he reopened the office Sam carefully inquired about John and Valerie. The office staff gave no indication that they suspected that John was in a relationship and Sam managed to keep them in the dark. At the house the landlord and the neighbors all spoke highly of Valerie and of what a lovely couple they were and how sad it was that she and her unborn child had been killed in the bombing. Everyone seemed to feel that it was natural that John would be laid low by his grief and they weren't surprised that he'd gone away with his son and the nanny. No one could tell Sam where they might be, in fact, the general agreement seemed to be that John had returned to the states or, if not, that he would soon. Sam had to marvel at his cousin's ability to keep his work and home lives so separate.

With the office open and under control and his belief that John would soon be home Sam returned to the states. It was apparent that the war in Europe would continue and that they needed everything; guns, ammo, uniforms and support. The company ramped up to be ready when the government contracts would be released and while Sam worried about John, Walter was sure that they would have heard if there was anything wrong.

Finally at the end of January, a cable arrived stating only; "Joined British Air Corp. Michael with Annie. All well. Sorry."

"Well, that's that," Walter said when Sam presented him with the cable. "We won't hear from him again until he's come to his senses. "You can handle things, Sam. It won't be easy and I know it wasn't what you wanted but until this war is over the family needs you."

'What about Michael and Annie?" Sam asked. "Shouldn't we locate them?"

"John will take care of his son. We need to take care of business."

And so, the subject was closed. Sam and Helen often talked about John and worried about Michael but Sarah was a greater concern. She was such a smart, sweet child. Her heart still wasn't strong. and she was often confined to her bed. Christopher read to her for hours and seemed to understand the need for quiet play. They were the best of friends. Every afternoon when Chris returned from school he headed straight to Sarah. Helen worried that Chris was neglecting his own life but when she suggested that he should invite a friend over, Chris just shook his head and smiled and said, "Right, Mom. Next week, okay?"

On March 11th, President Roosevelt signed the Lend-Lease Act and the factories accelerated to a whole new level as they began to ship uniforms, arms, ammunition, boots and socks in large numbers to the British troops.

Each day Sam listened carefully to the war news and he knew that Walter did, too They had no idea what regiment John had joined and no idea where he might be. When they met they talked about their concern for Minette and wondered about John. If it seemed strange to either man, that they didn't know where Michael was they passed it off by speaking about what a great "girl" Annie was and assured themselves and each other that all was well.

The news from Europe was frightening but the profits were huge and while Sam sometimes worried about ethics, he was too busy to do anything but keep working. The factories were all producing at full capacity and still Walter was sure that America would enter the war and that it wouldn't be enough, he pushed for Sam to hire more workers and increase production.

March turned to April and in Europe first Yugoslavia and then, only ten days later, Greece surrendered to the Nazis. In May Rudolph Hess was captured and imprisoned in Scotland and once again the heavy bombing of London was reported but now the English responded by dropping bombs on Hamburg and the news reels reported that the morale of the English troops was bolstered by this success. England failed in its attempt to remove Rommel from Egypt and the Augustus family continued to supply the needs of the Allied troops.

June, July and August passed quickly as the war news continued to worsen. Walter and Sam began to manufacture and stockpile US military uniforms and supplies. There was no doubt in either man's mind that war was coming to America and they planned to be ready.

The Nazi army began the siege of Leningrad and then marched on Kiev. Word of the harassment of Jews in the occupied territories was touched upon in the daily news but the reports were sketchy and hard to believe.

Having heard of the shortages in England, Helen purchased winter clothing for Michael while she shopped for school uniforms for her own children. Unsure of his current size she had to guess. Along with the clothing she packed candy, tinned meat, a few books and toys and crayoned messages from all five children. And at the last minute she added a few things for Annie. Sam send the package off to the London office in care of Stephen Alistair and when word came back that Stephen had no idea how to locate Michael and Annie, Sam told him to donate the items in the package and didn't tell Helen.

And then, on December 7th, bombs dropped on Pearl Harbor and America entered the war.

####

Are you feeling left up in the air, do you want to know what happens next?
The Augustus Family saga continues in my next book FAMILY MATTERS due out in December 2014.

Thank you reading my book.
If you enjoyed it, please take a few minute to leave
a review at your favorite retailer.

ABOUT THE AUTHOR

Tamara Merrill is a true left brain/right brain woman. She excels at most anything "crafty" and is considered a talented teacher of both computer skills and painting. During her lifetime she has tried a bit of everything and now Tamara has stopped reading excessively (she admits to a book a day habit) and has begun writing again. During the 60's and 70's, she published multiple short stories in the popular women's magazines of that era. But then the need for cash intervened and Tamara got a "real job" and stopped writing fiction. FAMILY LIES is her first full length novel and is book one of the Augustus Family Saga. Tamara currently resides in Coronado, CA.

35540874R00202

Made in the USA
Lexington, KY
14 September 2014